EX LIBRIS

Also by Nancy Tucker

That Was When People Started to Worry:
Young Women and Mental Illness

The Time in Between: A Memoir of Hunger and Hope

THE
FIRST
DAY
OF
SPRING

NANCY TUCKER

HUTCHINSON
LONDON

1 3 5 7 9 10 8 6 4 2

Hutchinson
20 Vauxhall Bridge Road
London SW1V 2SA

Hutchinson is part of the Penguin Random House group of companies
whose addresses can be found at global.penguinrandomhouse.com

First published in the United Kingdom by Hutchinson in 2021
First published in the US by Riverhead in 2021

www.penguin.co.uk

A CIP catalogue record for this book is available from
the British Library.

ISBN 9781786332387 (hardback)
ISBN 9781786332394 (trade paperback)

Typeset in 11.75/17.25 pt Times New Roman
by Integra Software Services Pvt. Ltd, Pondicherry

Printed and bound in Great Britain by Clays Ltd, Elcograf S.p.A.

The authorised representative in the EEA is Penguin Random House Ireland,
Morrison Chambers, 32 Nassau Street, Dublin D02 YH68.

Penguin Random House is committed to a sustainable future for
our business, our readers and our planet. This book is made from
Forest Stewardship Council® certified paper.

For my mum

THE
FIRST
DAY
OF
SPRING

CHRISSIE

I killed a little boy today. Held my hands around his throat, felt his blood pump hard against my thumbs. He wriggled and kicked and one of his knees caught me in the belly, a sharp lasso of pain. I roared. I squeezed. Sweat made it slippy between our skins but I didn't let go, pressed and pressed until my nails were white. It was easier than I thought it would be. Didn't take long for him to stop kicking. When his face was the colour of milk jelly I sat back on my heels and shook my hands. They had seized up. I put them on my own neck, above the place where the twin doorknob bones stuck out. Blood pumped hard against my thumbs. *I am here, I am here, I am here.*

I went to knock for Linda afterwards, because it was hours before tea. We walked to the top of the hill and turned ourselves upside down against the handstand wall, gritting our palms with smoke ends and sparkles of glass. Our dresses fell over our faces. The wind blew cool on our legs. A woman ran past us, Donna's mammy, ran past with her fat breasts bumping up and down. Linda pushed herself off the wall to stand beside me, and we watched Donna's mammy run down the street together. She was making noises that sounded like cat howls. They ripped up the quiet of the afternoon.

'What's she crying for?' asked Linda.

'Don't know,' I said. I knew.

Donna's mammy disappeared round the corner at the end of the street and we heard faraway gasps. When she came back there was a lump of mammies around her, all of them hurrying, brown shoes slapping the road in a thrum-thrum-thrum beat. Michael was with them but he couldn't keep up. By the time they passed us he was hanging a long way behind, panting in a crackling shudder, and his mammy tugged his hand and he fell. We saw the raspberry-ripple splash of blood, heard the yowl slice through the air. His mammy hauled him up and clamped him on her hip. She kept on running, running, running.

When the mammies were just past us, so we were looking at a herd of cardigan backs and wide, jiggling bottoms, I pulled Linda's arm and we followed. At the end of the road we saw Richard coming out of the shop with a toffee chew in one hand and Paula in the other. He saw us running with the mammies and he followed. Paula didn't like Richard pulling her, started grizzling, so Linda picked her up and clutched her round the middle. Her legs were striped where her fat folded in on itself. They hung out of a swollen nappy that dropped lower and lower with every step.

The First Day of Spring

We heard the crowd before we saw it: a rumbling blanket of sighs and swears, wrinkled by women crying. Girls crying. Babies crying. Round the corner and there it was, a cloud of people standing around the blue house. Linda wasn't next to me any more because Paula's nappy had fallen off at the end of Copley Street and she had stopped to try to put it back on her. I didn't wait. I ran forward, away from the lump of twittering mammies, into the cloud. When I got to the middle I had to squat down small and wind between the hot bodies, and when there were no more bodies to wind through I saw it. The great big man standing in the doorway, the little dead boy in his arms.

A noise came from the back of the crowd and I looked on the ground for a fox, because it was the noise a fox makes when a thorn gets stuck in its paw, the noise of something's insides coming out through its mouth. Then the cloud was breaking, disintegrating, people falling into one another. I got pushed over, and I watched through legs as Steven's mammy went to the man at the door. Her insides were coming out of her mouth in a howl. She took Steven from him and the howl turned to words: 'My boy, my boy, my boy.' Then she sat down on the ground, not caring that her skirt was around her middle and everyone could see her underpants. Steven was clutched against her, and I thought how it was a good job he was dead already, because if he hadn't already been dead he would have got suffocated by her rolls of breast and belly. I couldn't see his face under

3

the rolls. Didn't matter. I already knew what it looked like – grey as gone-bad liver, eyes like staring marbles. He had stopped blinking. I had noticed that when I'd got done killing him. It had been strange to see someone not blink for so long. When I'd tried to do it my eyeballs had burnt. His mammy stroked his hair and howled, and Donna's mammy broke through the crowd to kneel beside her, and Richard's mammy and Michael's mammy and all the other mammies swarmed and cried. I didn't know what they were crying for. Their kids weren't dead.

It took Linda and Paula a long time to catch up with the rest of us. When they arrived in the blue-house alley Linda was holding Paula's wet nappy.

'Do you know how to get this back on her?' Linda asked, holding it out to me. I didn't answer, just leant round so I could carry on watching the heap of howling mammies. 'What's going on?' she asked.

'Steven's there,' I said.

'Was he in the blue house?' she asked.

'He was dead in the blue house,' I said. 'Now his mammy's got him, but he's still dead.'

'How did he die?' she asked.

'Don't know,' I said. I knew.

Paula sat down on the ground beside me, her bare bottom nestling into the dirt. She moved her chubby hands around until she found a little stone, which she ate carefully. Linda sat on my other side and watched the mammies. Paula ate three more stones. People muttered and whispered and cried and Steven's mammy stayed hidden under a shawl of breasts and pink cardigans. Susan was there. She was Steven's sister. She was standing away from the mammies, away from the crowd. No one seemed to see her except me. It was like she was a ghost.

When the sun started to go down Paula's mammy came over, picked her up, hooked a stone out of her mouth, and took her home. Linda had to go too, because she said her mammy would have tea on the table. She asked if I was coming but I said no. I stayed until a car purred up and two policemen got out, tall and smart with shiny buttons on their clothes. One of them crouched and talked to Steven's mammy in words I couldn't hear, even when I closed my eyes and clenched my teeth, which usually helped me hear things grown-ups wanted to keep secret. The other one went into the blue house. I watched him slink through the downstairs rooms, and I thought about shouting, 'I killed him *upstairs*. You need to look *upstairs*.' I bit my lips shut. I couldn't give the game away.

I wanted to stay watching, at least until the policeman got to looking in the right place, but Mr Higgs from number 35 told me to run along. When I stood I was patterned with lines and bumps from the ground. I could see Steven better from standing. His legs were flopped over his mammy's arm, and I could see that one of his shoes had come off, and that he had mud on his knees. Susan was the only other kid still there, because she didn't have anyone waiting for her at home any more. Her arms were crossed over her chest and she was holding on to her shoulders, like she was hugging herself, or holding her pieces together. She looked thin and glowy. When she flicked her hair out of her face she saw me, and I was about to wave, but Mr Higgs took me by the elbow.

'Come on, lass,' he said. 'Time to go now.' I wriggled away. I thought he would just shoo me off, but he walked me all the way back to the streets, close beside me the whole time. I could hear his breath: hard and panty. It felt like slugs leaving slime on my skin.

'Look at that sky,' he said, pointing above our heads. I looked. It was all blue.

'Yeah,' I said.

'First day of spring,' he said.

'Yeah,' I said.

'First day of spring and a little lad lying dead,' he said. He made a tutting sound with his tongue on the roof of his mouth.

'Yeah,' I said. 'Dead.'

'You're not scared are you, lass?' he asked. I climbed onto Mr Warren's front garden wall. 'The police'll sort this out, you know. There's nothing for you to be scared of.'

'There's nothing I *am* scared of,' I said.

When I got to the end of the wall I jumped down and ran all the way back to the house. I took the shortcut, the one where you had to squeeze through the gap in the car park fence. I couldn't take the shortcut when I was with Linda because she couldn't fit through the gap, but it was easy for me. People always said I was small for eight.

None of the lights were on in the house. I clicked the front door shut behind me and flicked the switch on the wall, but nothing happened. There was no more lectric. I hated when there was no more lectric. It meant the telly didn't work and the house was dark-dark-dark with no way of making it light, and I got scared of the things I couldn't see. For a while I stood still in the hallway, listening for Mam. I didn't think Da would be there, but I listened for him too, stretching my ears like I could magic up his noises just by listening hard enough. Everything was quiet. Mam's handbag was on the floor by the stairs and I found a packet of biscuits inside. They were my favourite kind – sand-coloured, dotted with dead-fly raisins – and I ate them lying on my bed, remembering to chew on the side of my mouth without the rotten tooth in it. When they were all gone I held my hands up above my face and stretched out my fingers in starfish spikes. I waited until all the blood had drained away, then brought them down and stroked them across my face. They were so numb it was like they were someone else's, and it was strange, the feeling of someone else stroking my face. When they came back to life I put my palms on my cheeks and peered through my fingers in a hide-and-seek squint.

Bet you can't see me, bet you can't find me, bet you can't catch me.

That night I woke up when everything else was asleep. I lay still on my back. I thought Mam must have slammed the front door, because that was usually what woke me up in the night, or sometimes I woke myself by peeing the bed, but my sheets were dry and I couldn't hear anyone downstairs. There were no growing pains in my legs. I touched my belly, my chest, my throat. I stopped at my throat. Remembering was butter hitting a hot pan. Foam and sizzle.

I killed a little boy today. I took him to the alleys and held my hands around his throat in the blue house. I kept on pressing even when our skins were slippy with sweat. He died underneath me and a hundred million people watched him be carried down to his mammy by a tall, strong man.

I had the belly-fizzing feeling I got whenever I remembered a delicious secret, like sherbet exploding in my guts. Underneath it there was something else, something tighter and more like metal. I ignored it. I concentrated on the fizzing. Whoosh and whirr.

Once I had remembered about killing Steven I was too excited to go back to sleep, so I tiptoed out of bed and onto the landing. Outside Mam's room I stopped and held my breath, but her door was shut and I couldn't hear anything through it. The floorboards were cold on the bottoms of my feet, and I felt hollow, pale-coloured. The biscuits seemed a long time ago. There was never any food in the kitchen, even though the whole point of a kitchen was to have food in it, but I looked anyway. I climbed onto the worktop and opened all the cupboards, and in the one by the cooker I found a paper bag of sugar. I tucked it under my arm.

When I turned the front door handle I had to be extra careful, because it made a loud clicking sound if you moved it too fast, and if Mam was asleep in her room I didn't want to wake her. I slid the mat over the front step and pulled the door tight against it, so it stuck but didn't close. That was what Mam did to stop me knocking when I came back from school. The outside air gave me goose bumps where I was bare under my nightie, wind whistling up inside me. I stood at the front gate for a long time, looking up and down the empty street, feeling like I was the only person in the world.

Before, outside the blue house, I had heard one of the mammies say the streets would never be the same again. She had had her head on another mammy's shoulder, and had been making a wet patch on her cardigan with tears. 'It'll never be the same again,' she had said. 'Not after this. Not after someone's gone and done something like this. How can we feel safe when we know there's evil like that in the streets? How can we ever trust the kids are safe when we've got the devil here? The devil among us?' Remembering it made me glow. The streets were never going to be the same again. They used to be safe and now they weren't, and all of it because of one person, one morning, one moment. All of it because of me.

The pavement was gritty and scrubbed at my feet, but I didn't care. I decided to walk to church, because church was at the top of the hill and from outside church you could see all the streets in the grid. I kept my eyes on the steeple as I walked: spiked in the sky like a winter tree. When I got to the top I climbed onto the wall next to the angel statue and looked back at the warren of matchbox houses. My belly squeezed and I licked my finger and stuck it into the bag of sugar and sucked it clean. I did that again and again, until my rotten tooth hummed, until prickly crystals sanded the insides of my lips. I felt like a ghost or an angel, standing on the wall in my white nightie, eating sugar from a paper bag. No one saw me but I was still there. I was basically God.

'So that was all it took,' I thought. 'That was all it took for me to feel like I had all the power in the world. One morning, one moment, one yellow-haired boy. It wasn't so much after all.'

The wind picked up my nightie, and I felt like it would have lifted me into the sky if there hadn't been something heavy holding me down.

'Soon I won't feel this way any more,' I thought. That was what was holding me on the ground. 'Soon everything will be back to normal. I'll forget how it felt to have hands strong enough to squeeze all the life out of someone. I'll forget how it felt to be God.'

The next thought came as a voice, dropped into my head. 'I need to feel it again. I need to do it again.'

The time between doing it once and doing it again was suddenly mapped onto a clockface, with hands that ticked the seconds away. I watched it tick, heard it tick, felt it tick. The clock was a special secret just for me. People would sit next to me in the classroom and walk past me in the street and play with me in the playground and they wouldn't know who I really was, but I would, because I would have my ticking to remind me. And when the clock had ticked all the way round, so the hands were twinned at twelve, it would happen. I would do it again.

My fingers and toes were cramping with cold, so I started to walk back to the house. I felt even lighter than I had when I set out, and I knew it wasn't just because I was going downhill instead of up. It was because I had a plan. The front door was still stuck with the mat, and I closed it behind me with a careful click. I put the sugar back in the kitchen and climbed back up the stairs. Everything was still quiet. Everything was still dark. In bed I tucked my knees up under my nightie and put my hands in my armpits. I was very cold but very real. Very living. Every tiny part of my body had its own heartbeat, its own clock beat.

Tick. Tick. Tick.

JULIA

'It's the first day of spring today,' said Molly, running her knuckles along the seawall.

'Don't do that,' I said.

She lifted her hand and began licking off the concrete dust. I pulled her sleeve.

'Don't,' I said. 'It's dirty.'

In front of us a woman took hold of a toddler around the middle and lifted him with a small grunt. He walked along the top of the wall, arms held out either side of his body, face tilted up to catch the salt in the air.

'Mummy!' he said. 'Look at me!'

'Amazing, darling,' she said, looking in her handbag. We looked at the boy. We looked at him as he reached the end of the wall, tensed, and jumped into the woman's arms. She kissed his cheek and put him down.

'He didn't fall,' said Molly.

'No,' I said. 'He didn't.'

I hadn't seen her climb onto the wall on Friday – I had been watching an other-mother and other-kid. They were walking with their fingers knotted, swinging their arms in a lazy swish, and I was wondering how it would feel to have Molly's fingers laced between mine. Molly's fingers were small and thin, like skin-covered matches. I was wondering how they would fit into my gaps.

'Look!' she had shouted. When I turned I saw her balanced on the top of the wall. 'Look!' she shouted again. She didn't mean 'Look'. She meant, 'React.'

'Come down,' I said. I went to the wall and held up my arms. 'You can't be up there. It's not safe. I told you.'

'I can do it,' she said.

'Get down, Molly,' I said.

She didn't answer, didn't fold herself onto my hands, so I tugged her arm. It wasn't a big tug. I meant to catch her. She yelped as she pitched forward, and I scrabbled at her coat, and the chunk of it grasped in my fist slipped out as she tipped to the ground. The sound was a crunch. She stared up at me, her mouth puckered in a small *o*, and I felt splashed with icy water. There was a scream of silence before she cried, and when it came it was a thin, bewildered moan. Her arm hung limp in her coat sleeve.

I felt someone behind me and turned to see the woman and girl with the laced fingers. The woman didn't ask what had happened or whether I wanted her help; she knelt beside Molly, put one hand on her wrist and the other on her back, and asked, 'Is this where it hurts, sweetie?' When I moved my tongue around my mouth it made a noise like footsteps on wet pavement. I tasted of carpet. I wanted to yank the woman up by her collar and demand to know where she had learnt what to do when a kid fell off a wall, but I couldn't speak. My throat was blocked by a mesh of pushed-down scream.

'I'll go to one of those houses to use the phone,' the woman said, pointing to the row of cottages along the seafront. She bustled away before I could ask whether she was going to call an ambulance or the police.

I knelt beside Molly, put one hand on her back and one on her arm. Her wrist was white and waxy, and I found myself wishing there was blood. Blood was frank – the oily sluice of it on skin, the smell of metal and butchers. Molly's arm was live on the outside but dead on the inside, and I pushed down her sleeve so I could pretend it was bleeding instead. When the woman had been kneeling she had murmured things, but I hadn't heard them, so I couldn't copy them, so I didn't know what to say. I listened to the seagulls crying overhead and tried not to listen to Molly crying beside me.

Eventually the woman bustled back, holding a bag of frozen peas wrapped in a tea towel. I could tell she was having the time of her life.

'Here,' she said, giving me a look that said, 'I'm back now. You can get out of the way.' I got out of the way. 'Lovely lady in that first house,' she said. 'The ambulance is coming. They said we could drive her ourselves but I've not got the car. Let's pop your poor wrist on here, sweetie.'

She held the peas like a cushion and lifted Molly's hand on top. I didn't ask why she had assumed I also didn't have a car with me, because getting cross with people for making assumptions only really works when the assumptions they have made aren't true.

When the ambulance whined to the end of the road the woman tucked Molly's hair behind her ear and said, 'Here we go, sweetie, here they are to help you.' I watched the white van stop and spit out two grinning paramedics, who walked over without obvious urgency. They were heavyset and exhaustingly upbeat. Once they had established that the woman wasn't Molly's mother, that I was Molly's mother, that I was her mother despite the fact I was standing like a scarecrow while another woman comforted her, they took us to the ambulance. The woman waved as we climbed the metal steps.

'Good luck!' she called. I didn't reply, because I couldn't say the only thing I was thinking: 'How much did you see?'

The paramedics sat me next to Molly and said, 'There we go, now Mum can hold your good hand while we get you to hospital to have a better look at the sore hand, eh?' It took fifteen minutes for us to drive to the hospital. It took fourteen minutes for me to push my hand towards Molly's and pat it, lightly, twice. She had stopped crying. Snot crusted her top lip in a sandy trail.

The hospital was a rush of cubicles and beds and men in blue pyjamas. One of them showed me the X-ray of

Molly's wrist, and I saw the snapped bone surrounded by empty black space. I wanted to ask, 'Is that normal? Would another kid's X-ray look like that? Surely that's not what all people are like – not full of empty space like that. Is it because she's my daughter?' I didn't ask anything. I didn't say anything. Static hissed in my ears, as though the waves from the beach were breaking against the sides of my skull. Once the doctor had explained about the fracture he left us alone in a cubicle for a long time. I fed Molly chocolate buttons from the purple packet I kept in my bag for emergencies. She seemed happy to lie on the bed and let me put them on her tongue one after another, and if I was feeding her it meant I could keep the sweets coming in an unbroken chain, without pauses we might have felt we should try to fill with words.

Just as I was starting to think we had been forgotten, or left to rot in the cubicle as punishment for what I had done, a different doctor swept in with a nurse. He sat opposite me with a clipboard while she wrapped Molly's wrist in plaster.

'So,' he said, 'could you tell me again exactly how this happened?'

'She was walking on the wall,' I said. 'She's not allowed. She knows she's not allowed. She just got up there when I wasn't looking. But I'm usually looking.'

'I see,' he said. He wrote something on the clipboard, but he had it angled upwards, so I couldn't see. 'Walking on the wall. And then what?'

16

'She tripped,' I said. 'I was telling her to get off, and she just tripped. I tried to catch her but I couldn't.'

'OK,' he said.

'I think she just put out her hand to catch herself,' I said.

'Right,' he said.

'She's not allowed on the wall,' I said. 'She knows she's not. She's never climbed up before. I think it's because she just started school, just a few months ago. Other kids do stuff she's not allowed to do and she copies. She's never been hurt before.'

'Sure,' he said, but he wasn't writing any more. He was giving me a strange, slit-eyed look. He kept his slit-eyes on me when he said, 'Molly? Is that right, what Mum's said? About how you hurt your wrist?'

'What?' said Molly. The nurse had given her something to play with – a watch in a ladybird case with wings that snapped open and shut – and she had been too busy snapping to hear what I had said. I was suddenly aware of the snot on her lip, and the way most of her hair had worked free from its plaits, and the stain on the neck of her school jumper.

'How did you hurt your wrist?' the doctor asked, wheeling his chair so he was closer to her.

'I just told you,' I said. Something steely bubbled up my throat. He turned to me as if his neck was very stiff and he was very angry with me for making him turn.

'I know,' he said. 'Just want to hear it from Molly as well. Just to be sure.'

'I was walking on the wall,' she said. 'Then I fell off.'

'What made you fall off?' he asked.

'Just did,' she said. 'Just tumbled off.'

He scribbled on the clipboard. He was disappointed. I could tell. I didn't know whether to be relieved that Molly had lied or horrified that she'd known she needed to. I looked at my hands, knotted in my lap, and pretended one of them was hers.

We stayed in the cubicle until her cast was set and harnessed to her chest with a sling. The nurse lectured me about keeping it dry and staying off sports and going to the GP if her fingers started to swell, and I nodded, zipping it inside her coat and pretending it wasn't there.

By the time they let us go it was nearly eight. The outside world was dark. I hadn't looked at my watch since I had collected Molly from school, which was probably the longest I had gone without looking at my watch since she was born. We hadn't got back to the flat at three forty-five, or had a snack at four, or read the reading book at four thirty, or watched *Blue Peter* at five, or had tea at five thirty. Our fragile, sugar-work schedule was fractured, and so was Molly. That was what happened when I stopped concentrating.

*

The First Day of Spring

'Do you know how I know it's the first day of spring?' asked Molly. 'Because Miss King told us. That's why we made them flower crowns.'

'Ah,' I said. 'Yes.' She had come out of school the day before wearing a gummy halo of sugar paper and cotton balls, which had slipped down her head as we walked until it hung round her neck like an ugly, ineffective scarf. I hadn't risked asking what it was. It had taken her a long time to forgive me for thinking her papier-mâché Christmas tree was a volcano. 'It was such a good flower crown,' I said.

'Miss King said it was the best in the class,' she said. 'She's so nice, isn't she?'

'Angelic,' I said.

It was difficult to imagine a flower crown worse than the one on Molly's bedroom shelf. I thought perhaps some kids had just stuck paper straight onto their faces.

'If it's the first day of spring does that mean it'll get warmer now?' she asked.

'I don't know,' I said. The wind coming off the sea was so biting I couldn't imagine it ever being warm again. Molly scuffed her shoes on the ground and sighed.

'I'll ask Miss King,' she said. 'She'll know. She knows everything. She's so clever, isn't she?'

'A genius,' I said.

I pressed my fingers to my eyelids. They felt like flower petals: soft, furred, slightly swollen. The pain had roiled up as we had watched the other-kid walk along the wall, pouring to the front of my face like heated engine oil, and it wasn't shifting. High-pitched, humming. I kneaded the tops of my cheekbones until all I could feel was pressure.

'Can we go arcade after school?' Molly asked. She was looking past me, past the row of burger vans and the shut-up funfair. Fruit-machine noise trickled down to meet us – the rattle of money being sucked away.

'Can we go *to the* arcade,' I said.

'I asked *you* that,' she said. 'Can we? I've got coins.' She took four pennies and a tiddlywink from her pocket and shook them at me.

'No,' I said. 'Hurry up. We're going to be late.'

We weren't going to be late. We were never late. We left the flat at eight o'clock every morning and got to school at eight fifteen, before most kids had finished breakfast. If we had left later we would have risked seeing other-mothers on the journey, bleating and tutting and letting their other-kids walk on walls. I couldn't protect us from everything, but I could protect us from that.

By eight twenty we were at the school entrance, huddling under the WELCOME plaque. As we waited, an unwelcoming receptionist clopped up to the side gate, unlocked it, and slipped through.

'We're very early this morning,' I said, loud enough to carry across to her. 'Much earlier than usual,' I nearly shouted. Molly looked at me with something like pity, then pushed herself against the fence, patterning her forehead with a grid of grooves.

'That's breakfast club,' she said. She pointed to the dining hall, which was oozing the clink and chatter of spoons and kids.

'You've had breakfast,' I said. The receptionist had disappeared into the building, but I still said it loudly. 'You had breakfast before we left.'

'I could have more breakfast.'

'Are you still hungry? Do you need something else to eat?'

'Not really.'

By the time the caretaker ambled up to unlock the gates, we had been joined by the army of other-mothers and other-kids, and I had been reminded of why the other-mother avoidance plan was in place. They grouped in huddles, talking at whiplash speed, breaking into laughter that made my ears ring. I always had the same feeling when they engulfed me: that I was in disguise as a member of another species. The way they circled and cooed reminded me of pigeons, so that was what they became – a gaggle of birds – and I was a person with feathers stuck to my clothes. They looked at me and looked away, embarrassed by my big, stark sticking-out. When Abigail arrived Molly ran to meet her, and I felt naked without my little shield. Abigail had brick-coloured hair and tiny gold studs in her ears. I watched the two girls together, coiling around each other, breathing in each other's air. I felt their closeness as an ache, but I didn't know what I ached for – to have Molly all to myself, or a friend to coil around.

By nine o'clock the playground was a sea of ankle socks and polyester. Around us, other-mothers began plastering other-kids in kisses and high-pitched exclamations.

'Have a *lovely day*, sweetie!'

'I can't *wait* to see you later, precious!'

'I love you *so much*, angel!'

When the bell rang the other-kids tottered into lines and the other-mothers tottered home to do the laundry. I waited until Miss King saw me, then called Molly over. I gave her the book bag, the PE kit, the plastic pot of peeled-and-cut-up apple, and she went to Miss King like an iron filing to a magnet. She didn't turn to smile or wave. Across the playground, an other-kid had attached himself to an other-mother's waist and was refusing to let go. I felt for him: it was what I wanted to do to Molly each morning, before she could go to Miss King. I wanted to cling to her, and when her teacher tried to peel us apart I wanted to say, 'But we are made of each other. We are parts of the same whole. Don't you know she grew inside me, like one of my organs?' It seemed extravagantly cruel that there was no biological system for keeping Molly with me always, no way of carrying her around in a pouch above my pelvis like a joey.

The phone in the flat started ringing as I fumbled with my keys outside. Behind me I could feel people bustling and buses passing, stuffed with hot breath and bored faces. None of them seemed to mind the noise, but it made me want to sink onto the ground. I wanted to crouch, then kneel, then rest my forehead on the concrete. Dry headache boiled in the space behind my eyes, and the pavement looked quenching.

I hadn't known what the flat phone sounded like until Saturday morning. The shrieking had split the air and I had looked at the hob, at the oven, at the radiators. I had sniffed for smoke. Molly got up from the couch without shifting her eyes from the telly and reached for where the phone was mounted on the wall. I connected the sight and the sound slowly, clunkily, and the connection went into me like a corkscrew biting the soft flesh of a cork.

'No,' I said, crossing the room. 'Don't,' I said, pushing her hand away. We stared at each other until the sound stopped.

'Why didn't you answer it?' she asked, stroking her cast.

'Didn't want to.'

'Why?'

'Finish your programmes. It's ten o'clock. We'll go to the park soon.'

When she wasn't looking I took the receiver out of the cradle and let it hang, disconnected. On Sunday it rang later, when she was in bed. I came out of her room and stood next to it.

'I'm not going to answer, so you might as well give up,' I thought. 'You can call and call but I'm never going to answer.'

I looked at myself in the mirror next to the coat hooks. My eyes were bucketed by bruise-coloured rings, the whites webbed with threads of scarlet vein. I dug my nails into my arm and felt sticky half-moons spring up where I broke the skin. When the ringing stopped, the silence was like cool water closing over my head. I made myself count my breaths the way they had taught me to count my breaths when I was teetering on the edge of a rage, but the noise started again before I got to ten. It seemed even louder, even more insistent. I pushed my belly with my fingers and felt the hard pouch of an organ, and I kept one hand there – on the liver or spleen or whatever else lived in the dark inside swamp – as I picked up the phone. The voice that spoke was tight, like a can peeling open.

'Hello?' they said. They were breathing heavily. I imagined I could smell them through the holes in the receiver, the mustard-coloured smell of unbrushed teeth.

'Chrissie?' they said.

I pushed the button to disengage with my fingernail. The dialling tone was a dull cry.

'Right,' I thought. 'So that's that.'

CHRISSIE

At school on Monday they made us sit in rows in the hall, like for Friday assembly, except it wasn't Friday, it was Monday. The hall smelt of mince and pencil sharpenings and the sun lit up the dust in the air, made it dance in sparkling columns. My class came in when Class Six was already sitting down, and I looked in the rows for Susan. You could always spot Susan because she had the longest hair of any girl in the school. It went all the way down to her bottom. In the summer she sat on a cushion in the front garden after her bath, and her mammy sat on a stool behind her and chatted to Karen's mammy in the garden next door while she combed her hair, and Steven toddled up and down the path and every time he came up to his mammy she kissed him. Sometimes I leant on the wall to watch. By the time the hair was all combed through, the sun had dried it to a yellow-white sheet, and Susan's mammy ran her fingers through it like warm sand. Then she put the comb in her pocket and patted the top of Susan's head. Susan didn't often join in when we were playing out, even when it was something really fun, like the game where we snuck into Mrs Rowley's house through her broken back door and pinched her things, or Sardines. She mainly sat in the playground with the other Class Six girls, letting them take turns stroking her hair.

I could only really remember Susan talking to me one time, when I was in Class Two and she was in Class Four. I had been in the playground by myself, trying to walk all the way round the edge with my feet on the bottom bar of the fence, and she had come down the street with a woman who wasn't her mammy.

'Chrissie!' she shouted when she saw me. I felt quite special, because kids in Class Four didn't usually talk to kids in Class Two. When she got to the fence she held it and bounced on her tiptoes. 'Guess what?' she said. The not-mammy woman came up behind her.

'Susie's got some exciting news,' she said. 'Go on. Tell your friend, duck.'

'I got a baby brother,' said Susan. She said it with her shoulders up to her ears and her eyes shining. I didn't actually think it was very exciting news at all. People got baby brothers and sisters all the time. I felt pretty cross with her, because she had made me think something actually exciting had happened. Like the vicar had died or something.

'He's a right little sweetie, isn't he, duck?' said the not-mammy woman.

'She's actually a girl,' I said. 'Not a duck.'

'He's called Steven,' said Susan. 'Mammy and Da had two names, Stewart and Steven, and they told them both to me and let me choose. I chose Steven.'

'Who's that woman?' I asked. The not-mammy woman laughed.

'I'm Susie's Auntie Joan,' she said. 'I've come to lend her mammy and da a hand while they get to know the little one. What's your name, pet?'

'Chrissie,' I said.

'That's a nice name,' she said. 'Well, we'd best be getting to the shop.'

'Bye, Chrissie!' called Susan as they walked away. 'We've got to get the things for Mammy and Da and Steven now!'

'Nice to meet you, duck!' called Auntie Joan.

'I'm a girl!' I called, but I didn't think they heard me. I watched them until all I could see were Susan's long white plaits, hanging down her back like two bits of rope. When they were gone I spent a lot of time thinking about how different things would be if I had hair like Susan's – like how I would be very rich, because I would make people pay me for letting them touch my hair, and how everyone would like me. Probably even Mam.

I met Steven two weeks later, on a Friday. When I came out of my classroom there was a crowd of mammies in the playground, flapping and twittering, soft bellies, soft cardigans. I ran over to see what they were fussing about.

'He's beautiful!'

'Making me want another . . .'

'You're looking so well!'

'How's he feeding?'

When I got to the middle of the crowd I saw Steven's mammy holding the handles of a pram. Her face seemed bigger and brighter than usual, like she had swallowed a bit of the sun, and she was smiling such a big smile it looked like her mouth was going to break. I peered inside the pram to see what was making her so happy. A baby poked out from a white blanket, screwed up and cross-looking. It was quite a disappointment. I had hoped it might be something really interesting, like a badger.

Susan pushed through the crowd to stand on the other side of the pram, put her hand in, and stroked her finger across the baby's cheek. 'Hello, little brother,' she said. 'Hello, little Steven. I missed you, I really missed you.' I wanted to see what his skin felt like, so I reached in and started stroking the other cheek. It just felt like skin, really, like my skin or Susan's skin or any old skin. Another disappointment. I really didn't understand why everyone was making such a fuss of him. Susan and her mammy were sicking up love all over him, covering him in fat globs of it. It was such a lot of fuss for someone so tiny, who wasn't a badger or any other interesting animal.

He wriggled and rubbed his fists across his face. I ran my hand over his head and found a funny spongy part. I was seeing how far down I could press it when his mammy pulled me back. 'Careful, Chrissie,' she said. 'He's very delicate. You don't want to hurt him.'

Susan wasn't in the Class Six row that Monday, which meant she wasn't at school at all. When all the classes were sitting in rows, Mr Michaels told us we might have heard that something sad had happened at the weekend, that a little boy who lived in the streets had had an accident while he was playing and got killed dead. I was sitting next to Donna, who I didn't like because she was a goody-goody and she was also fat. I counted the dimples in her puddingy knees while Mr Michaels talked, and I wanted to put my finger inside one, just to see how it would feel, but she shoved my hand away when I tried.

'Get off,' she whispered.

I cupped my hands around my mouth and pressed them against her ear. 'I was there,' I whispered. 'When they found him. I was there.'

She flicked her head round to look at me. Our mouths were very close together, close enough that I could have kissed her, except obviously I was never ever going to do that because she was a fat goody-goody. Her breath smelt of jam.

'What did he look like?' she whispered.

'There was loads of blood everywhere,' I whispered. 'It was spraying out all over everywhere. Some of it even got on me.' I showed her a reddish-brown circle on the hem of my dress. 'See? That's a bit of his blood,' I whispered. She touched the ketchup stain with one finger and said, 'Wow,' then Miss White tapped our shoulders and told us to listen to Mr Michaels. On the way back to the classroom Donna walked ahead, talking to Betty, and Betty said, 'Really?' and turned to look at me. It gave me a hot, humming feeling at the bottom of my belly.

Things were strange that week. Susan didn't come to school, not on Tuesday or Wednesday or any day. At home time the mammies waited in the playground, and when their kids came out they scooped them up and clutched them to soft chests. People weren't allowed out to play like normal. In the afternoons I walked through the streets with a long stick, dragging it across bricks and gates with a *scrape-scrape-clang*. Sometimes I stopped and watched telly through a lounge window. When I knocked on doors mammies said their kids weren't coming out, and told me I shouldn't be out either. 'But I *am* out,' I said. They sighed and shooed me away. Most days I ended up sitting with my back against Mrs Whitworth's front wall, watching mammies go in and out of Steven's house with loaf cakes and pots of stew. I thought having a kid die wasn't too bad, really. It got you a lot of cake and stew.

Whenever I looked at the upstairs window of the house I saw Susan. She was always there, always with her hands pressed against the glass. It wasn't like she was trying to get out, just like she wanted to feel the cold on her skin. I could never see her face properly, but I could see the white of her hair, hanging down past her bottom. I guessed Steven hadn't come back alive, because I watched and watched the house and I never saw him.

At school on Thursday we started making Easter bonnets and Easter baskets and learning Easter songs because it was nearly Easter. We were supposed to have brought in a cereal box but I hadn't.

'Where's your cereal box, Chrissie?' asked Miss White.

'Don't got one,' I said.

'You *haven't* got one,' she said.

'Yeah,' I said. 'I don't got one.'

She folded her arms. 'Why not?' she asked. 'I reminded you before you went home yesterday.'

'Don't got no cereal,' I said.

'Don't be ridiculous, Chrissie,' she said. 'Everyone has cereal.'

'I don't,' I said. She gave me a piece of corrugated cardboard, which was the wrong sort of cardboard for an Easter bonnet, and she should have known that except obviously she didn't because I was the only person in the whole school who really knew anything. My scissors didn't cut through it, just chewed it like a baby chewing toast. I gave up and cut the end off Donna's plait instead. She cried. Miss White sent me to Mr Michaels but I didn't care. The hair had made a lovely snicking sound when the scissors had gone through it, and I played that sound again and again in my head while I waited to be told off.

After school I went to Linda's. Her cousin had given her a new *Mirabelle* magazine at the weekend, and we lay side by side on her bed to read it. Most of the pages were called things like 'How to Live Through Love and Stay Smiling.' *Mirabelle* clearly wasn't a very good magazine, because Linda's cousin had been reading it since forever and I had never once seen her smile.

When I was so bored I thought my brain was going to slither out through my nose like snot, I got off the bed and pulled my dress out of my underpants.

'Linda,' I said. 'Enough is enough.'

'What's enough?'

'Enough is. Enough is enough.'

'That doesn't mean anything.'

'Yes it does. It means we're going to play out now.'

She rolled onto her back and stretched her legs up in the air like a fly. 'No we're not. It's not safe. We'll die like Steven.'

'No we won't.'

'We might.'

'Well if we don't play out we'll die from being bored. And I'd rather die from playing out than from being bored. So I'm going. You do what you want.'

'Shh. Mammy will hear you.'

The First Day of Spring

When I was at Linda's house I had to spend a lot of time making sure her mammy didn't hear me. Linda's mammy wasn't a very cuddly sort of mammy. She was the sort of mammy who smelt of church and ironing, and who sometimes went months without saying any words except 'Be careful' and 'Stop that' and 'It's time for tea'. If you fell over in front of Linda's mammy she plonked you straight back onto your feet and rubbed your knees like she was scrubbing away dirt, muttering, 'No harm done, no harm done.' Except if it was me who fell over. Then she didn't do any picking up or rub-scrubbing. I knew why she didn't like me: because when I was seven I told her she had more grey hair than any of the other mammies (which was true) and that that must mean she was older than any of the other mammies (which was also true). That was why whenever she opened the door and found me on the doorstep she folded her arms tight across her chest, like she had to stop me leaking onto her.

I went down the stairs and out of the front door, treading lightly so I hardly made a sound. I didn't need to look behind me to see if Linda was following. She always followed. That was the whole point of Linda. I said we should call for Donna, even though I didn't like her, because she was the only person I could think of who might be allowed out. She had so many brothers that her mammy never noticed if one kid was missing. There were lots of reasons I didn't like Donna, apart from her being fat and a goody-goody, but the main one was that in the Christmas holidays she bit me on the arm just because I said she had a face like a potato (which was also true). I had a purple tooth-mark bruise for a week. So she was fat, she was a goody-goody, *and* she looked like a potato, but beggars don't get to choose who's allowed out to play. When we first rang Donna's bell her mammy tried to send us away, but then one of her other kids was sick on the floor in the kitchen and she changed her mind. She said Donna could come but only if William came too, because he was twelve and a big strong boy and he could look after Donna if there was any bother. Really and truly, William was a weedy, skinny boy who would have been no use at all if there had been any bother, unless the thing doing the bothering was a very tiny baby or a very tiny baby mouse, and even then he would have been no use at all because he was scared of tails. I bit my mouth shut to stop myself saying that. Donna had a pink bike with blue handles. If she came out I could make her give me a turn on it.

'Where are we going?' William asked when we passed the playground.

'Alleys,' I said.

'Nuh-uh. Not allowed. Our mammy won't let us,' said Donna.

'Your mammy's not here,' I said.

'She wouldn't let us if she was here,' she said.

'Well she's not here.'

'Well I'm not coming.'

'Well I never wanted you to come.'

'*Fine.* I'll *come* then.'

The alleys used to be places for people to live, the same as our houses in the streets. The poorest families lived there, in slummy rooms with black mould on the walls. The alley kids got bad crackles in their chests from breathing dirty air, and scabs on their tummies from being eaten by bedbugs, and scaly rashes round their mouths from the cold drying up their spit. Now the alley houses were being pulled down, and the poor families had nowhere to go. When the houses were gone they were going to build tall, shiny buildings made of boxes stacked on top of each other, and different people were going to live in the different boxes, but the alley families weren't going to live there because they were going to be expensive. There was a meeting about it at the church hall. Grown-ups took it in turns to stand up and say things like, 'It is a tragedy that we live in a community that does nothing to protect those most in need.' Me and Linda hung around at the back and ate the biscuits off the trestle table until the vicar told us to scram.

People had started tying white ribbons around the slats of the alley-house fences, so everyone would remember it was where Steven had died. I pulled one off and tied it in my hair. The blue house had cones outside with police tape stretched between them, but there were no policemen and it was easy to duck under. William found a window that hadn't yet been broken and started throwing rocks at it so we could push out the glass and climb through. We could have used the doorway, but if you were going to be boring like that then you might as well not even go to the alleys in the first place. I got almost all the way through the window before I wobbled and held on to the frame to stop myself falling. There was a biting pain in my palm, and when I jumped down I felt warm run over my fingers. Oozy, oily red. I wiped it on my dress. I didn't cry. I never cried. It just gave me another stain to pretend was Steven's blood.

Everyone wanted to see where he had died, so I took them to the upstairs room. I noticed things about it that I hadn't noticed when I had been there with Steven, like the couch cushions stacked in a pile by the fireplace and the bits of rubbish at the edges. The paper on the walls was peeling, and where the walls met the floor there were bubbles of rot that foamed in a cream-soda collar. In their corners, the alley houses were mainly liquid.

'How do you know it was here?' asked Donna.

'She was there when the man brought him out of the house,' said Linda. 'She ran ahead when I was putting Paula's nappy back on. She watched through the window. She saw the man pick him up off the floor in this room and take him downstairs to his mammy.' That wasn't actually true, but I liked how important it made me sound. When Donna looked at me I knew she was having to pretend not to be jealous, and for a moment I wanted to tell her it was me who had done the killing, to make her really properly jealous. I had to bite my mouth again. I was having to bite my mouth a lot since Steven had died.

'Is that really true?' Donna asked.

'Yeah,' I said. 'I saw everything.'

I walked to the patch of floor underneath the hole in the roof, where the sun came in and licked yellow light across the boards.

'This is where he died,' I said. 'This is exactly where he died.' The others came and stood in a circle. There was enough space in the middle for a little-boy body.

'How did he?' asked William.

'Just did,' I said. I spat on my finger and rubbed it into my cut.

'That's not how it works,' said Donna. 'People don't just die for no reason.'

'Sometimes they do,' said Linda. 'My grandda, he was at our house for fish supper, when I was five, and he died for no reason. He was just sitting in his chair with a fish cake on his knee. Then he died.' She looked around like she thought one of us was going to scream or fall over.

'Your grandda was probably a hundred years old, though,' said Donna. 'Steven was just a baby. It's not the same.'

'It's quite same,' said Linda.

'No it's not,' said Donna. 'That's thick.'

Redness rushed up Linda's neck, into her face, and she took the corner of her bottom lip between her teeth so her mouth was lopsided. Really and truly, Linda *was* thick. That was why not many people wanted to be her friend. She was thick at reading and writing and telling the time and tying her shoelaces, and sometimes she said things that were so thick you were surprised that she was even walking around, because you wouldn't have thought you would know how to walk when you were that thick. Her being thick meant she believed everything you told her, and that was fun sometimes. When we were in Class Three she swallowed her tooth in a mouthful of biscuit at play-time and I told her she would grow an extra mouth in her belly, and the new mouth would eat all her food, and she would waste away thinner and thinner until she died, and now that she had swallowed the tooth there was nothing she could do to stop it. She cried hard, her tears mixing with the red worm of blood running down her chin, and Mrs Oakfield sent her to the medical room. Mrs Oakfield asked if I knew why she had been so upset but I didn't answer. I was busy finishing her biscuit.

Linda hated being called thick because she knew deep down it was true, and I hated people calling her thick because she hated it. I pushed Donna in the chest.

'Shut up, potato face,' I said. 'He just died. The same as her grandda. The exact same.'

'Bet it wasn't the *exact* same,' said William.

'Yeah. Bet it wasn't,' said Donna.

'Look, everybody,' said Linda. 'You have to listen to Chrissie. She's the cleverest. She knows everything.' Her cheeks went pink, because she didn't usually say things starting with 'Look, everybody', especially not to Donna. She moved closer to me and I held her hand.

'Yeah,' I said. 'You have to listen to me, and you have to not be mean to Linda, because she's my best friend and if you're mean to her I'll get you. But you mainly have to listen to me because I'm the cleverest and I know everything. And I *definitely* know what happened to Steven.'

It wasn't just special that I was the one who knew what had happened to Steven. It was special that I was the *only* one who knew what had happened to him, out of kids and grown-ups and even policemen. At school they told us he had an accident while he was playing in the alleys, fell through the floor when the rotten-soft boards gave way underneath him, got his life knocked out of him like water from a slammed-down cup. 'That's why you must never go and play in the alleys,' they said. 'Do you understand?' Even if I hadn't killed him, I would have known that wasn't true. They'd found his body in the upstairs room, so he couldn't have died from falling unless he had been playing on the roof, and no one played on the roofs of the alleys, not even me, and everyone knew I was the best climber. He couldn't have died from cutting himself on glass either, because there hadn't been any blood when they had found him, whatever I had told Donna. He died from me putting my hands on his throat and squeezing until there was nothing left to squeeze.

Since Steven had died there had been police cars purring through the streets most days. On Tuesday one of them parked outside the school gates and two policemen went and talked to the baby class. I asked to go to the toilet so I could creep down to the infants' room and try to hear what they were saying, but the door was shut and Mrs Goddard caught me trying to crack it open.

'Stop loitering, Chrissie,' she said. 'You know you shouldn't be here. Back to your classroom, please.'

'You mean listening,' I said.

'What?' she said.

'Listening,' I said. 'You mean, "Stop *listening*, Chrissie." "Loltering" isn't a word.'

'Go back to your classroom, Chrissie,' she said. She didn't like me being right.

The policemen didn't talk to any of the juniors that day, which was unfair because I wanted to see them up close and I didn't want to do my worksheet. After school I saw their car parked outside Steven's house again, and I sat on Mrs Whitworth's front wall, waiting for them to come out. When they got to the gate one of them saw me watching.

'You should get home, lass,' he said. 'Your mammy will be wondering where you are.'

'No she won't,' I said.

'Well, you go home and put the telly on, then,' he said.

'There's no lectric,' I said.

He opened his car door. 'Go on, get off with you,' he said. 'Not safe for kids to be out in the streets alone.' He folded his body into the seat and they drove away. I watched the car until it disappeared round the corner. The police were spending a lot of time trying to find out what had happened to Steven. Knowing that gave me the sherbet feeling in my fingertips, the same feeling I'd had on my tongue the time Betty had dared me to suck a battery for ten seconds.

When we ran out of things to do in the blue house we went back to the streets. While we had been in the alleys the mammies had hung out washing between the roofs of the matchbox houses, and sheets and shirtsleeves waved us a swoopy hello. I told Donna to give me a go on her bike but she wouldn't, so I hit her and she pedalled home to tell on me. William had coins in his pocket, and when Linda went home for dinner he went to the shop to buy a meat pie. We sat in the playground with our backs against the swing poles while he ate it.

'How long do you think Steven will be dead for?' I asked. His mouth was too full of pie to answer. A tear of gravy slid down his chin. I could smell it – brown-smelling, salty – and my insides sucked. He chewed for a long time, and then he took another bite and chewed some more. I kicked his leg to make him pay attention.

41

'How long do you think Steven will be dead for?' I asked.

'Don't kick me!' he said.

'Kick you if I want to,' I said.

He slammed his fist between my eyes and knocked my head against the pole. The clunking sound rang in my ears. I didn't cry. I never cried. I tried to kick him again but he pulled his leg out of the way.

'He'll be dead forever,' he said.

'Nah,' I said. I knew that wasn't right. He had been dead for a long time already, and forever was a very long time more. I thought he would probably be back alive by Easter. Easter was a good time for coming back alive. He definitely wouldn't be dead for actual ever.

'Yeah,' said William. 'He will.'

'He *won't*,' I said, and I put my hands over my ears so I couldn't hear him any more. The sucking on my insides grew until it felt like there were clawing fists in my belly. 'Give us a bit of your pie,' I said. He shook his head without looking up. His cheeks were so full they bulged. 'If you give us a bit of your pie I'll let you put your hand down my underpants,' I said.

He swallowed and sighed. 'All right then,' he said. 'But only one bite.'

We stood up. I lifted the front of my dress, took his hand, and slid it between my legs. His fingers were warm and limp against me, and he was standing close, close enough that I could count the freckles on his cheeks. His breath was hot and smelt of gravy. We stood that way for a little while. His fingers stayed limp. I dropped the hem of my dress and hung my arms by my sides. I pretended to be a puppet. It was pretty boring, really.

When he took his hand out he put it straight into his pocket, and he shoved the rest of the pie towards me so he could put the other hand in the other pocket. I ate it quickly. It tasted of salt and lard, with rubbery meat that squeaked between my teeth. I was so hungry I forgot about chewing on the side without the rotten tooth, and pain snaked all the way down my neck. When I'd finished we climbed the swing poles, but we couldn't get as high as usual because of the grease on our hands. William said he was going to go home, and I said if he left I'd run after him and give him the worst Chinese burn of his life, and he cried. I didn't know whether it was because of the Chinese burn or because he had put his hand in my underpants. I didn't think either was something to cry about.

JULIA

By the time I got up the stairs the phone had stopped ringing. I washed the speckled milk out of Molly's cereal bowl and went back to the door. I stopped before unlocking it. My thoughts were wrapped around the phone, and when my thoughts were elsewhere I still forgot I could unlock doors for myself. I thought perhaps by the time I was thirty I would have unlearnt the instinct to wait for a grown-up to come with a key. When I was thirty I would have lived outside Haverleigh's walls for longer than I had lived within them.

Haverleigh was a Home, but the sort with a capital letter at the beginning and a fence around the edge, a place for kids too bad for their small-letter homes. They had taken me there from prison, in a car with greyed-out windows. Before I left my cell I ate the plate of food the guard brought up from the canteen: sausages with split brown skins, a dark circle of black pudding like the soil at the bottom of a plant pot. I ate it quickly, using my fingers, swallowing lumps and feeling them land like pebbles in

44

my belly. I didn't know if I'd ever be fed again. When I finished they put me in the car with two policemen and we drove for hours, down winding, twisting roads that made my breakfast wind and twist around inside. A thin film of grease settled over my gums, across my tongue, crouched in my lost-tooth gaps. It tasted of meat and something bitter, like petrol, washing up from my guts.

'I feel a bit sick,' I said.

'Take deep breaths,' said the woman policeman.

'Can I roll down the window?' I asked.

'No,' she said. She opened the glove compartment and passed me a paper bag. 'Here you go. You can be sick in there.'

I spent the rest of the journey trying to get the sick to come up my throat, because I wanted to spit it all over the backseat. They'd have to let me roll down the window if I did that. It didn't come until the car pulled to a stop in the Haverleigh drive and the woman policeman came round to open my door. The rush of cool air hit me in the face. I leant out and threw up on her shoes.

'Oh, God,' she said.

'Told you I felt sick,' I said, wiping my mouth with my hand and wiping my hand on the seat. She pulled me out by the elbow and I saw a squat, square collection of buildings. It didn't look like a prison at all. I twinged with disappointment. I had imagined barbed wire and bars on windows. I knew that would have impressed Donna when she came to visit.

The people who patrolled the Haverleigh corridors were less parents than zookeepers. They woke me at the same time each morning, took me to the bathroom, watched me shower, took me back to my bedroom, watched me dress, took me to the dining room, watched me eat, took me to school, watched me rip up my exercise book and hide under my desk. Most of them were kind. They called me things like 'mate' and 'pal' and 'kid', and taught me ways to pull myself back from the brink of a rage – breathing, counting, listing the objects I saw around me. During the days, the keepers were with me all the time, making me think they were there because they liked me, but in the evenings they started looking at their watches and saying, 'Are night staff here yet?' Whatever we were doing together, when the night keepers arrived the day keepers got up and said, 'Bye, kid, see you tomorrow.' That was when I remembered they didn't really like me at all. They were just being paid to be with me. That was when I threw the game board across the room, or ripped up my homework book, or slammed another kid's head into the wall. When you did bad things like that the keepers descended, one for each limb, held you so tight you couldn't move. I did lots of bad things. It felt nice to be held. I liked going limp in their arms and hearing them say, 'There. Well done for calming down. Good girl, Chrissie. Good girl.' It was almost like I wasn't bad at all.

Haverleigh buzzed with rhythms and noises all its own – alarms that screamed down the corridors, kids who screamed in their rooms – but most of all its sound was the rattle of the keys the keepers wore in fat bunches on their belts. When I started the new life I stood at every closed door I came to, waiting for a keeper to unlock it and let me through. Every time I realised I could open it myself I felt an urgent need to scream. People said it wasn't fair that I had been let out when I was eighteen, said I should have been locked up forever. I agreed: it wasn't fair. The people in charge had hidden me away, then thrown me into a life I hadn't expected to have to live, in a world I hadn't expected to have to understand. I missed the clanks and clinks of Haverleigh's halls, the big metal locks on its doors.

'That was my home,' I wanted to say, 'my small-letter home. It wasn't fair to make me leave.'

The cold weather brought a gust of workmen into the shop, and I spent the day putting parcels of chips into plastic bags and ringing up prices on the till. At dinnertime I took a chicken and mushroom pie from the heated display and ate it in the corner of the kitchen. The filling was mealy, bound by salty grey glue. I licked stray crumbs of pastry from between the tines of the metal fork and felt a small loss when it was finished.

At three, Mrs G came out of the office and tapped me on the shoulder.

'I have a woman on the phone for you,' she said. 'Sasha someone. She says she tried your phone upstairs. She says she is from the children's services. She doesn't say what she wants. You will come and speak to her?'

My tongue turned to a hot hunk of raw meat in my mouth. I looked at Arun, and with my eyes I said, 'Please tell me I can't go. Tell me I need to mop the floor or fry some more fish or see to the customers.' There was one old woman at a table in the corner, peeling the batter off a piece of cod. Arun flapped his hand and said, 'Yes, yes, go, Julie,' and I followed Mrs G. I felt like a kid sent out of the classroom. In the office, she patted my shoulder, went to the couch, and picked up her knitting. I thought she would go back to the kitchen, but she chose two pink-wrapped sweets from the bowl on the coffee table and sat down.

'Don't take notice of me, dear,' she said. 'You get on with your phone-calling. I will be listening to my radio.'

Mrs G was very sweet and very nosy. She wouldn't be listening to the radio. She would be listening to me. I picked up the phone with the tips of my fingers.

'Hello,' I said.

'Hi, Julia, hi.' Sasha was one of the only people in the world who knew who I really was. She pretended not to hate me, but it didn't work – I could hear it in her voice, under the topcoat of brightness. Hatred. 'How are you?' she asked.

'Fine,' I said.

'Good. Good. So. I had a call from the hospital,' she said. I felt it as a fishing hook lowered down my throat, snagging on my tonsils and trying to turn me inside out. 'How's Molly? Getting used to the cast?'

Molly was offensively proud of her cast. She'd only had to wear the sling for the weekend, and I had been glad to slide both her arms into her coat on Monday morning. When she had worn her coat with the sling the empty sleeve had flapped ghoulishly. On Monday I eased it down over the cast, so only the white edge peeped out, and she hoiked it back up, determined that the plaster should be the first thing anyone noticed about her. She walked into school with it held aloft, like a trophy, and came back with felt-tip drawings from elbow to palm. She spent a long time pointing at different pictures and telling me who had drawn them, and when we got back to the flat she asked me to add my own. I didn't.

'She's fine,' I said.

'Good,' said Sasha. 'That's good. Well, I just thought it might be a good idea if you popped in to see me. Just for a quick meeting. I was wondering about tomorrow morning. Would that work?'

'Tomorrow?' I said.

'The morning. Ten? Would ten work for you?'

'But Molly's fine.'

'Shall we just chat tomorrow?'

I didn't want to chat tomorrow. I wanted to tell Sasha that her saying 'just' so many times didn't make the things she was talking about any less threatening, and I wanted to ask who had snitched on me. My guess was the slit-eyed doctor who thought I had hurt Molly on purpose. Mrs G had started humming along to the music on the radio, and the clock on the wall told me I needed to leave to collect Molly from school, and my throat felt narrowed to a thin rubber tube.

'Tomorrow. Fine. Bye,' I said. I put down the phone. It hurt to swallow. It hurt to breathe. I tried to push away the blockage between my collarbones, but it stuck.

If Mrs G hadn't been clacking her knitting needles behind me, I would have asked Sasha whether the point of the meeting was to tell me they were taking Molly away, and she would have made high-pitched objection noises and changed the subject. I was glad that that pantomime hadn't been played out. They had wanted to take Molly for years but hadn't been able to find a reason, and now it was here, big and clumsy and covered in felt-tip scribbles. I thought of the peeling-can voice I had heard on the phone. *Chrissie.* Whoever it was had tracked me down somehow. They must have spoken to someone who knew me, someone who hated me. Sasha knew me. She hated me.

The pain was a tight band across my shoulders, spreading through the base of my skull. I arched my back against it. It was the same pain I felt every year, sprouting with spring and waning with summer. Sometimes, when I felt it spread from my shoulders to my head, I imagined it as blood in water. Dark red hands reaching into clear fluid.

I rubbed the bumps of spine that rippled the back of my neck.

'You have a stiff neck?' Mrs G asked.

'It's fine,' I said, but she was already behind me, a head shorter and twice as wide. She moved my hands away and I felt her thick fingers on me. The skin on the pads was hard from years of guiding knitting needles through wool. I smelt spices and sawdust and found, abruptly, that I wanted to cry. The brush of her skin on mine made me feel young and bare. I clenched my teeth. I never cried.

'You have a very stiff neck, dear,' she said. She moved her thumbs in steady circles at my hairline. 'Very stiff neck and shoulders. Is all this hunching over the fryer that Arun is making you do. I will have words with him. You should lie on the floor every day for twenty minutes. Put books under your head and lie flat on the floor. Very still. Yes?'

I nodded but didn't speak. I took off my apron, pulled on my coat, and walked into the cold afternoon.

It had all been for nothing. The months of sickness and stretching, the years of washing and working and worrying. I had bought Molly trainers with lights in the heels and taken her to church on Christmas Eve and taught her to look both ways before crossing the road, and I might as well have thrown her baby body in a corner and waited for her to cry herself to death. Both versions ended the same way: with me alone again.

The week before she fell off the wall she had stopped chewing in the middle of tea and stared at me, bug-eyed, fingers on her mouth.

'My tooth, my tooth,' she had squeaked.

'Does it hurt?'

'It feels funny.'

'Funny sore?'

'It feels funny.'

That was the worst thing – the fact that Sasha was cruel to take her, and wicked to take her, and right to take her. Because any kid who stayed with me would grow up a jigsaw of rotted, crumbling parts. If Molly stayed with me, she would grow up to be Chrissie.

Halfway down the high street I ducked into an alley and leant against the wall. I undid the zip on my coat and flapped it open, letting the wind chill the sweat under my arms. I imagined it turning to drifts of frost that crunched when I moved. In my chest, my heart felt small and tinny, like a bell on a cat's collar. The smell of pee was strong, and it got worse when I crouched on the ground. Worse when I wobbled onto my knees. Worse when I put my forehead on the concrete. Worst when I opened my mouth to scream.

CHRISSIE

Mam was standing at my wardrobe when I woke up the next morning.

'You're not going to school today,' she said.

I felt around my chin. 'Have I got mumps?' I asked. Lots of people had been off school with mumps.

'No,' she said. She took my church dress out of the wardrobe and sniffed it under the arms, then squirted it with flowery perfume from a pretty glass bottle. I didn't know why she was getting out my church dress on a Friday. I picked the crust from the corner of my eye.

'Are we going to church?' I asked.

'No,' she said. 'Course not. It's Friday. Get dressed.'

'Have you filled up the lectric?' I asked.

'Get dressed,' she said.

She left, but I didn't get up straight away. I lay in bed, running my knuckles over the xylophone of ribs that striped me under my nipples.

I didn't really like going to school, because I didn't like Miss White and I didn't like worksheets and I didn't like sitting next to Richard, but I did like being milk monitor. When you were milk monitor you got to go out of the class-room door at break time, pull in the crate of milk bottles from the playground, and put a bottle and straw on every-one's desk. When all the milk had been handed out Miss White came round with the biscuit tin and put one next to everyone's bottle. I had been trying for a long time to get Miss White to let me be biscuit monitor, because that would have been even better than being milk monitor, but she always said no.

'Biscuit monitor has to be a grown-up,' she said.

'Why?' I asked.

'Because it's a grown-up's job,' she said.

'I think it should be a kid,' I said. 'I think it should be me.'

'Chrissie,' she said. 'Having you as biscuit monitor would be what we call a recipe for disaster.'

I had no idea what she was on about.

You could tell whether it was going to be a good milk day or a bad milk day by looking at the bottles in the crate. The best was when they were covered in a thin layer of water droplets, like sweat beads, because that meant the milk inside would be fresh and cold. It wasn't so good when they were frosted, because that meant the milk would be frozen and you would have to thaw it on top of the radiator, and that took a long time. The worst was when the sun had been shining all morning and the white in the bottles had turned butter-coloured. That meant the milk would be warm like bathwater, thickened and cheesy.

The best thing about being milk monitor was that once you had given out the milk bottles you took the crate back to the playground, and then you could drink the spares. There were almost always spares, because there were almost always people away. On a good day it could be five or six little bottles. When I had put the crate on the ground under the windowsill I ducked down and pushed my thumb through the bottle tops. It was funner to poke a straw through the foil – that made a lovely popping sound – but you had to be fast-fast-fast when you were drinking spare milk, and straws were slow-slow-slow. I had been milk monitor for the whole of the spring term, and I had got very fast. Bottle, thumb, gulp, done. I could get a bottle down in one swallow. Really and truly, I didn't like milk very much, but drinking a lot of it made it easier not to mind about getting no food after school. When break was finished I had to sit very still at my desk, because my belly was so swishy I knew I would be sick if I moved too fast. I thought that was probably why Miss White had let me be milk monitor for so long – because it made me quiet after break.

Mam called for me to get a move on, and I pushed back my blanket thinking about how not going to school would mean no milk, and no school dinner either. It was going to be a very empty day, but that was just the way life was sometimes. You had to keep your chin up.

When I got out of bed I looked at my sheets, which were patterned with overlapping yellow stains. They were the same as the circles I had had on my arms when the ring-worms had been eating my insides: dark at the edges and all different sizes. In the middle of the bed the sheets were wet, and I was cold and sticky under my nightie. Mam had left her perfume bottle on the windowsill, and I squirted some onto the worst bed stains. It didn't make the smell much better. It actually made it a bit worse. I covered up the sheets with a blanket and hoped they would be dry by nighttime.

In the kitchen Mam pulled my hair into tight plaits. Her fingers were rough and the pulling made it feel like my head skin was going to split, but I didn't make a fuss because that would have made her pull harder. When she finished she put a hand on my head and whispered, 'Father, protect me. God, keep me safe.' Her hand was cold and we smelt the same: flowers on top and dirt underneath. After the prayer she wiped her palm on her hip, like she was wiping me away.

We left the house and walked down the street together. Her shoes made a *clip-clop-clip-clop* pony sound and her fingers dug dents in my wrist. We walked past a few boys on the corner playing with an old bike tyre, but most people were at school. I was disappointed about that. I wanted them to see me and Mam, walking through the streets in our church clothes, almost holding hands. By the time we were close to town my church shoes were digging into my heels, but when I slowed down Mam yanked my arm to make me go faster. We got to the high street and walked past the greengrocer's and the butcher's and Woolworth's. I asked Mam where we were going but she didn't hear, or pretended she didn't hear, and when we were almost at the end of the street she pulled me through a shop doorway so fast I didn't have time to read the sign above it.

On the inside, the shop wasn't a shop at all. It was a waiting room, the same as the waiting rooms at the doctor's and the dentist's. I had seen those waiting rooms in the videos they showed us at school. One of them was called 'Going to the Doctor' and the other was called 'Going to the Dentist'. Everything in this waiting room was a soft, washed-out colour, and on the walls there were pictures of families with wide white smiles, so I thought perhaps it was a dentist's, and perhaps Mam had brought me there to get my rotten tooth fixed. She pulled me up to a desk where a woman was talking on a telephone. When the woman saw us she put the phone down and smiled the same smile as the people on the walls, except her teeth were like wonky yellow paving stones crunched up against each other. I didn't think people with teeth like that should be allowed to work at the dentist's. I didn't really think people with teeth like that should be allowed to leave their houses.

'This is my daughter,' said Mam. 'Her name's Christine. I need to have her adopted.'

'Um,' said the woman at the desk.

'Adopted,' said Mam.

'Er,' said the woman at the desk.

'I need to have Christine adopted,' said Mam.

'You've said that lots of times now,' I said.

'Shut up,' she said.

I traced a pattern on the carpet with the toe of my church shoe. My face was hot. Mam didn't understand what adopted meant. Adopted was when you got to keep a kid that wasn't yours, like Michelle's mammy adopted her from cruel people in London and got to keep her even though she wasn't her real kid. I was Mam's kid to begin with. She got to keep me without having to make me adopted. I hated when Mam made mistakes like that. It made my face so hot. When I looked up I saw the woman at the desk licking her lips, and I thought she was going to explain about adopted to Mam, but she turned to me instead.

'Hello, pet,' she said. 'Christine's a pretty name. My name's Ann. Would you like to sit down while I have a little chat with your mammy? I can get you some orange squash if you like?'

I sat in one of the scratchy blue chairs by the window and Ann brought me the squash in a plastic cup. It was so weak I thought it must actually be the water she had rinsed out of a plastic cup that used to have real squash in it. I used it to wet my finger and draw shapes on the chair arm. Mam didn't look at me. She stood very straight, with one arm wrapped around her middle and one hand gripping the side of her coat. Her fingers were clawed and white.

Ann went back to the desk and was about to talk to Mam in a voice she didn't want me to hear when a door opened down the corridor and we all heard somebody crying. They were muffled, snuffly cries, like someone was holding a handkerchief over their mouth, and after a while a woman came down the corridor holding a hand-kerchief over her mouth. I thought it was probably her who had been doing the crying. The handkerchief was white turned grey and too wet to let in any more tears, but the woman kept on pushing them out. When she got to the end of the corridor and saw Mam and me in the waiting room she stopped walking and wobbled on her feet. She folded the handkerchief in half and blew her nose, then folded it again and wiped under her eyes. She blinked lots of times in a row.

She was beautiful. Her face was blotchy from crying and her make-up had smudged around her eyes, but she was still beautiful. She had yellow hair and powder on her cheeks. I looked at her legs, which were wrapped in skin-coloured stockings, making her as smooth as a doll. Mam's legs were covered in nicks and scaly patches of dry skin, same as mine. Mam was ugly, same as me. This woman wasn't ugly. She was like an angel.

When she had managed to stop crying she went to the desk and said to Ann, 'It's fallen through. They're letting his mother keep him. After all that. It's not right. They can't do this to people.'

Ann wrinkled her forehead and started to say, 'Oh, I'm so—' but Mam interrupted. 'You wanting to adopt a kid?' she asked. The beautiful woman nodded tightly while she took clean tissues from the box on Ann's desk. Mam walked over very fast and pulled me up by the elbow so hard I spilt watery orange squash all over myself. She pushed me in front of her, towards the beautiful woman, and said, 'This is Chrissie. She's mine. But she's being adopted. You can have her.'

Ann said 'but' and 'wait' and 'no' and the beautiful woman said 'but' and 'I' and 'oh'. Mam put her hand on my back and took it away again, like she was touching something very hot, or very sharp, or very horrible. Like she was putting her hand on someone made of broken glass. Then she walked out. The waiting room was quiet. I heard Mam in my ears, saying, 'She's mine.' She hadn't ever said that about me before.

I looked down at my church dress, wet with squash and coming down at the hem. I wondered whether the beautiful woman would buy me a beautiful new dress when she took me to her house. Michelle was just a fat little baby when her mammy adopted her from the cruel people in London, but she still got bought dresses and toys and pretty soft-soled shoes. I hoped that was what the beautiful woman was planning for me.

'I'd like a new dress,' I told her, in case she was feeling too shy to offer. 'We can get it on the way back to your house.'

Her tongue licked at her bottom lip in a lizardy way, and she turned and pressed herself up against the desk to speak to Ann. I heard 'go after her' and 'clearly not well' and 'afraid I can't help' and 'wanted a baby' and 'far too old, yes *far* too old'. By the time she turned back around I had sat back down. She walked towards me, stopped, flicked her eyes and licked her lips. She said, 'I . . .' then did a silly little giggle and a sillier little wave, and rushed through the door in a cloud of powder and yellow hair.

Ann put on her coat and gathered up her bag and chattered in the gabbling way grown-ups chatter when they think they can keep you from crying by blocking your ears with noise. I wanted to tell her she didn't need to do that because I never cried, but I had a funny bubbling feeling in the back of my nose and throat that made it hard to talk. I thought perhaps I was getting a cold. Ann tried to take my hand but I shoved it into my coat pocket so hard it went right through the lining. I hung behind her as we walked down the street, scuffing the toes of my church shoes on the pavement. It was raining, and people were walking with their bodies bent in half. Ann kept stopping and nagging me to keep up, but that just made me walk even slower. An old woman was hobbling beside me, and the fourth time Ann stopped and nagged she said, 'You want to keep up with your mammy. Enough of this silly dawdling, eh?' I stuck my tongue out at her. 'Well that's not very nice, is it, young lady?' she said.

'*I'm* not very nice,' I said. 'And I'm *not* a lady.'

'Humph. Well. No. Quite,' she said.

Once we were away from town I had to lead the way back to the streets, because Ann didn't know where I lived. It was stupid that she was there at all, bobbing half a stupid step behind me with her stupid wonky teeth. We walked past the alleys and she looked at the blue house and I knew what she was thinking.

'I was there when he died, you know,' I said.

Her eyebrows went up into her stupid fringe. 'There when he died?' she said.

'Well. I was there when they found him, which is almost as good,' I said. 'I saw the man find him in the house and carry him down to his mammy. He was covered in blood. It was coming out of his mouth and ears and everywhere. His mammy was crying like this.' I howled and heaved like a dying fox to show her how Steven's mammy had sounded. Her face went a bit grey.

'It must be very scary for you to think about what happened to that little boy,' she said in her stupid icing-sugar voice. 'It's a terrible thing to have happened to a kid. But you know you're safe, don't you? The police will catch whoever hurt him, and they won't be able to hurt any more kids.'

The sherbet feeling started inside me. 'They might,' I said.

'What?' she said.

'They might hurt more kids. The one who killed Steven. They might hurt more.'

'No they won't,' she said. She tried to pat my shoulder but I jerked away, so she patted the space where I wasn't. 'No more kids are going to get hurt. I promise.'

People were always promising things, like *promise* was anything more than a stupid word.

'You can't promise that,' I said. 'You can't stop it happening. No one can.'

She loosened the collar of her stupid coat around her stupid neck. Pinpricks of sweat had started bubbling out of the skin on her nose, even though it was cold. 'Well,' she said. 'I think the police will keep all the kids safe. So that's the important thing. The important thing is that you're safe.'

'I never said I wasn't,' I said. I wanted to tell her that since I had killed Steven I had felt safer than ever before, because I was the one people needed to watch out for, and being the one people needed to watch out for was the safest way to be. I decided she wasn't the right person to tell. She was too stupid.

When we got to the house she started coming up the path behind me. I turned round and stood still, blocking the door.

'I'm just going to pop in and have a word with your mammy, Christine,' she said.

'No you're not,' I said.

'There's nothing for you to worry about,' she said. She tried to get past me. 'I just want to have a very quick chat with your mammy. Just to make sure everything's OK with both of you.'

'Everything *is* OK with both of us,' I said. 'But you can't speak to her. She's busy. She's working.'

'In the house?'

'Yeah.'

'What work is it your mammy does?'

An upstairs window was cracked open, and the sound of Mam crying came through it. Ann looked up at the window, then down at me, then up at the window again.

'She's a painter,' I said. Mam cried out a big, loud wail. Ann raised her eyebrows. 'Sometimes her paintings don't go how she wants them to go,' I said.

I thought Ann would leave me alone then, but she barged forward and pressed her stupid finger against the doorbell. She had to press it three times before Mam came to the door, wearing a dressing gown that showed too much of her legs. I didn't want to hear any more of Ann's stupid talking or Mam's stupid crying, so I pushed past them both, up the stairs, along the landing, into my room. It still stank of pee and perfume. I pulled the sheets off the bed and stuffed them in the wardrobe. The mattress underneath was just as stained and rotten, but I stretched the blanket over it and pretended it was clean. After a few minutes I heard the front door close, heard Mam come back up the stairs and go back into her bedroom. She didn't start crying again. We both sat in our rooms, listening to each other listening to each other.

When I realised Mam wasn't going to come and see me, not even to shout, I went to the window and watched the fists of rain beating down outside. It had only just gone dinnertime, but I couldn't knock for anyone because they were all at school. Mam's perfume bottle was still in my room, sitting on the windowsill, and I took out the stopper, opened the window, and poured it into the rain. When the bottle was empty I dropped it. I wanted it to shatter into a million glittering pieces that would cut up Mam's feet next time she went out barefoot, but it hit the path with a dull crack and bounced into the grass.

Hunger had started to sluice through me, but the kitchen cupboards had nothing inside except sugar and moths. I opened and closed them, thinking about the milk bottles clustered in the crate at school. It was cold that day, and it was Friday, and that meant the milk would have been fresh and the school dinner would have been fish and chips. That was my favourite. I kicked the metal base of the cooker hard, and a packet of Angel Delight slipped out from behind it. The powder made a thick paste on my tongue. Upstairs, Mam started crying again: a mewing, kittenish kind of cry. I tried not to listen, but it stuffed itself into my head, snaked around inside me like ivy growing round the bars of a gate.

When I went back up the stairs I kept my eyes down, staring at the hair and ash and caked-in dirt on the floor, but outside Mam's room I looked up without meaning to. The door was open. It hadn't been open when I had gone to the kitchen, which meant Mam had heard me go down the stairs, scuttled to the door, opened it, scuttled back. She was sitting on her bed with her back against the headboard, moaning. I looked for the tears to go with the noise but there weren't any. Her cheeks were dry. She was forcing out the sound in a long ribbon, and every few seconds she flicked her eyes to the side to make sure I was watching.

'What you crying for?' I asked. 'Is it because I came back?'

She didn't answer. I pulled the door shut, because it seemed like I was making things worse, not better. There was a shriek, then the sound of something hard and heavy thrown against the wall.

'You don't understand,' she shrieked. 'You don't even care. You don't even *care*, Chrissie.'

She stopped crying quite quickly after that, probably because I couldn't see her and she realised I wasn't coming in to tell her I did care. If she wasn't going to get me to do anything by crying, she wasn't going to get much from crying at all, except sore eyes and a scratchy throat. I squeezed the muscles in my belly, bent over, and sicked Angel Delight onto the floor. It dripped through the cracks between the boards. Mam could clear it up. I wiped my mouth with the back of my hand, stepped over the cream-coloured puddle, and went into my bedroom. Shut the door behind me. Jumped onto the bed, front first. Told myself the next morning I would hurt someone, anyone, as many-one as I liked. Took a lump of pillow in my mouth and roared.

JULIA

In the six months Molly had been at school, I had never been late to collect her. The closest I had come was the day she had broken up for Christmas, when I had been stuck in a queue in the toy shop. I had paid, run back to the flat, and hidden the marble run in my wardrobe, next to a box of stocking toys I had been squirrelling since August. I had slipped through the school gates at three thirty, just as Miss King had led out the crocodile of four- and-five-year-olds. Molly had scampered over with holly painted on her cheeks and a chocolate Father Christmas in her fist.

'We had a party and there was missing-toe, you kiss people under it, me and Abigail didn't kiss, we just rubbed our noses together, can I eat this now?'

I had been so blind and so lucky back then. I hadn't even been properly late. This time the gates were swung wide and the tide of other-mothers and other-kids was working against me. I stood still, waiting for them to pass. I felt I was an outline with nothing inside. Being bumped by the crowd would have made me crumple.

Molly was standing by the water fountains with Miss King, who saw me and launched her my way.

'You were late,' Molly said when she reached me.

'I was on the phone,' I said.

We got to the seafront and she pointed to the skeleton of the funfair, which was open but empty, with frozen rides and men smoking roll-ups in control booths.

'Can we go there?' she asked.

'No,' I said.

'Why not?' she asked.

'Because it's just a normal day. The fair isn't for normal days.'

'What days is it for?'

'Special days.'

'Like the first day of spring?'

'No. Not like that at all.'

I tried pressing the skin around my eyes again, but I couldn't squash the pain cloyed in the sockets. Molly kicked a pebble onto the grass and made a noise that was halfway between a groan and a whine. 'You never let me do anything fun,' she said.

'Sorry,' I said.

A woman and little girl joined the path in front of us. The girl was wearing a flouncy dress and slip-on shoes that gapped from her heels when she walked. Before I could stop it, the tally machine in my head whirred to life.

It's cold. She should be wearing tights. Molly is wearing tights. Molly's legs aren't cold. One point.

Those shoes are too big, and they don't have any support. Her feet won't grow properly. Molly's shoes are the right ones for growing feet. The woman in the shoe shop told me. Two points.

That's not a sensible dress. She won't be able to run around in it. She'll have to worry about getting it dirty. Her mam shouldn't use her like a doll. Molly's clothes are made for living, not for show. Three points.

The woman bent and lifted the girl onto her hip. The girl wrapped her legs around her waist and dropped her head onto her shoulder.

She has a proper mother. Molly doesn't. Soon, Molly won't have a mother at all. Minus points. Minus all the points you ever earned.

I looked at Molly hopping over cracks in the path. The wind had whipped colour into her cheeks, and it made her prettier, because it made her less like me. That was where the best bits of Molly lived – in the gaps between her and Chrissie, in her soft mouth and clear eyes. I sometimes felt there was a template kid, a pale, dark-haired little girl, and Molly and Chrissie were there to show what happened when she was fed or starved, clean or grimy. Since I had been in the real world I had washed every day and eaten away the sharpest of my edges, and it gave me a warm thrill to know how much Molly looked like me. It stopped me having to think about the genes that weren't mine.

The man who had given me Molly had been less a man than a boy, and less a boy than a gangling mesh of limbs and bravado. He was called Nathan; it said so on his badge. My badge said Lucy, because that was the first new name they gave me when they let me out, the first new life I slipped into. Nathan and Lucy stacked shelves at the hardware store where probation officer Jan had found me a job. Jan always talked about how good it was that I was out in the real world, because life in the real world was so much better than life in prison. At the hardware store interview they laid out a selection of screws and bolts and doorknobs and asked us to choose the item we were most like, ready to 'present' to the group. People clamoured at the table until the only thing left was a packet of iron nails. I pressed one into the pad of my finger as I waited for my turn to say how strong and sharp I was, and I thought of Haverleigh. It had been a kind of prison. It hadn't been nearly as bad as this.

Nathan liked to tell me which pub he had been to at the weekend, who he had been with, and which football match they had watched. He stammered, but only on words beginning with *T*. His local pub was the Tavern, his football team was Tottenham, and all his friends seemed to be called either Tom or Tony. One of the checkout girls told me he liked me, and I laughed, because nobody liked me. I didn't laugh when he asked me out for a drink. I said, 'OK.'

We went to the pub by the train station. I didn't know what I would tell him if he asked about my life before the hardware store. Luckily he didn't. He didn't seem interested in any part of my life, but he still asked if I wanted to go back to his flat. I said, 'OK.'

I was wearing my work polo shirt: blue, with the Penton Supplies logo on the chest. He pulled it over my head without undoing the buttons, left my ears ringing. He wore a crucifix on a silver chain around his neck, and while it was happening I counted how many times the pendant bumped against my face. When I lost track I turned my head to the side and read the titles of the videos stacked next to his telly. I felt I was being pushed against very hard, as if he was trying to break through a solid wall inside me. I thought how frightening it was to be crushed underneath someone bigger and stronger than you, their body blocking the light, squeezing out your air. It was horrid, feeling frightened. I wished it hurt more.

'Are you OK?' he asked from above me, again and again.

'OK,' I said from below him, again and again. I was flat on the floor, his weight drilling into me, my body cracking and seeping like a stretched scab. I was a lot of things. 'OK' wasn't one of them.

'Oh,' I said when the pain changed from an ache to a stab. He made a grunting noise at the back of his throat. 'Oh,' I said again. He grunted again. It was a happy sort of grunt. It made me think he liked me. I wondered how anyone ever knew this thing was over, whether it would go on indefinitely, whether he would know when to stop, whether he would tell me it had finished. After a long time he went still, gasped, and slid out, and I was relieved that the ending, at least, was clear: a stinging emptiness. We rolled away from each other. I pulled up my jeans and curled my knees into my chest. I felt open and sticky, like a wound.

'Right,' I thought. 'So that's that.'

We did it five more times over the next three weeks. It didn't hurt after the first time, just felt like stretching, like being a glove full of hot oil. He liked it, and I liked the feeling of him liking it. It felt almost the same as him liking me. I wasn't sure if I liked it or not – the act itself, the smells and sounds and heavy closeness – but there was a peace to it, an occupied feeling, and I liked that. I didn't feel much about him, and he gave me no reason to think he felt much about me. We never talked about what we were doing. We looked in opposite directions while it happened. I sometimes felt it was a secret we were trying to keep from each other.

A month after the first time, I was putting paint tins on shelves when the checkout girl tapped my back.

'Can you cover my till for five minutes?' she asked. 'I've got to run to the chemist.'

'OK,' I said.

'Thanks,' she said, and leant in. 'Morning-after pill.'

'OK,' I said, suddenly feeling a lot less than OK, suddenly hot and sick. I bought a test instead of dinner, and sat in the fourth-floor toilet that no one used because the window didn't close and the cold tap was broken. There was a poster advertising halogen lightbulbs on the back of the door, and I read it from start to finish while I waited, trousers and underpants wrinkled at my ankles. I learnt a lot. The two lines came up like swearing fingers.

'Right,' I thought. 'So that's that.'

I held Molly's sleeve as we crossed the road in front of the shop. Inside, Arun was filling the pickled egg jar. Eyeball globes in murky brown vinegar. I could smell them from the pavement, and I felt the sickness as a spider, inching hairy legs onto the back of my tongue. As I looked for the key to the flat, Molly dawdled in the strip-lit doorway, looking for attention.

'Hi, Arun,' she called when he didn't immediately oblige.

'Hello, Miss Molly,' he said, wiping his hands on his apron and drinking from a can of Coke. 'How are you this afternoon? How is the poor arm?'

'OK,' she said. 'How many chips have you cooked today?'

'Oh, today is slow day,' he said. 'We only cook fifteen thousand today.'

'Yesterday it was twenty.'

'I know. And the day before it is twenty-five. What can I do?'

'Don't know.'

'Today we do not even sell all the chips we cook. Is nightmare. So many left over. I am thinking – do I know any hungry little girls? But then I am thinking, no, I can't think of anyone . . . not anyone at all. . . .'

'She's not hungry,' I muttered. I found the key and crunched it into the lock, but Molly was already in the shop. I heard the scrape of metal on tile as she pushed past the stools by the mirror.

'You know *me*, Arun,' she said.

'Molly, can you come inside please?' I called. When she didn't appear I leant round to look through the shop doorway. She was at the counter, her face pressed to the heated display, watching Arun rustle chips onto a sheet of white paper.

'No, Arun, really,' I said. 'We've got food. She doesn't need those.'

'Is nothing, is nothing, Julie,' he said. He wrapped the chips in a parcel that he handed to Molly, which she clutched like a newborn. Upstairs, she deposited it on the table and peeled away the layers of paper. I breathed through my mouth. In the shop the smell of oil bounced off the tiles, but the flat was made of carpet and curtains, made to suck up the stink of grease. I opened the window.

Watching Molly eat, I felt a dull, itchy panic. It was four o'clock. Four wasn't teatime. Four was snack time, ready for four thirty reading time, ready for five o'clock *Blue Peter* time. If Molly had tea at four we would have an empty slot at five thirty – half an hour of blank time I wouldn't know how to fill – and then she might be hungry again by bedtime, and I wouldn't know whether or not to feed her, what to feed her, whether to brush her teeth again, how long she should wait between eating and sleeping.

The phone began to ring, and I pushed my head out of the window. The air was cool and slightly sweet, and I sipped it through clenched teeth. Outside, a man was trying to get into the house next to the souvenir shop. He banged on the door with the flat of his hand, forced it with his shoulder. It was like watching a lump of unproved bread dough thrown against a wall: bluntly, yeastily ineffective. He slithered down to the ground, tried to drink from a glass bottle, missed his mouth. Started to cry. The trill of the phone seemed to grow with each ring – louder, more insistent – and I imagined the journalist on the other end of the line. I felt her perfume, the *tip-tap* of her nails on the typewriter.

'Why have you got the window open?' Molly called. 'It's cold.'

'Just getting some air,' I said. The phone stopped ringing, and I ducked back in to lean against the glass. The explanation had solidified in my mind on the walk back from school: the doctor had called Sasha, and Sasha had called the papers. I rummaged around inside myself for panic or betrayal, but it wasn't there. Sasha would have been paid a lot of money for my phone number, more money than she'd earn in a year of work. It was horrid to be poor. I felt numb.

'I really need a party dress, you know,' Molly said.

'What?' I said.

'I need a party dress. For Alice's party.'

I touched my forehead: chilled, spongy, like the skin on a dead person. I went to the bathroom and spread the mat on the floor. Molly maintained a stream of vague dress-based grumbling, which blended with the grumble of water into the tub. It occurred to me that it didn't matter whether I kept her clean any more, because keeping her clean was part of keeping her, and I wasn't getting to keep her. It occurred to me that if I didn't give her a bath, there would be more unstructured time to fill before she went to sleep. The taps stayed on. I tried not to picture her trussed in puff sleeves and a sash. I knelt next to the tub, rested my head on the side, and watched the water rise.

When Molly had been growing inside me, I had spent most of my life looking at bathrooms side-on. I was sick in a way I had never been sick before, in a way I thought, surely, no one had ever been sick before. At night I would wake with bladed fingers squeezing my stomach, and crawl to press my cheek to the cold lip of the tub. My sweat was so salty it felt like granules pushing out of my skin, milled crystals running down my neck. My belly would cramp and then it would come, a retch that sent me choking into the toilet bowl, so violent I expected to throw up the baby in a swish of bile.

Since they had let me out, I had been doing my best to disappear, but Molly made me neon. Strange women beamed at me, asked if it was a boy or a girl, asked when it was due, asked if I was tired, tried to give me their seat on the bus. I felt like a con artist. If they had known who I was, they would have kicked me under the bus's wheels. As I got bigger – comically big, unnecessarily big, surely the biggest anyone had ever been – I left the flat less and less. I looked down at the foreign mass stuck to the front of my body and thought, 'Please get out, please get out, please, somebody, get it out of me.' And then night would come, and I would be back on the bathroom floor. I would hold my hands to my belly, feeling the knobs of knee and elbow through my skin. She didn't feel foreign. She felt like a friend. I had been so lonely before.

At Haverleigh we had planted sunflower seeds, and I had told the keepers mine would grow shrivelled, because I was the bad seed and any seed I planted was bad too. My flower grew yellow and strong. You wouldn't have known it had come from a seed at all. That was what I thought of as I knelt on the bathroom floor at night: the bright, soft petals. Babies grew from seeds. Matron had said so. I clenched my teeth in prayer. 'Please stay inside. Please stay inside. Please, whoever you are, stay inside me.'

CHRISSIE

When Steven had been dead for a while most mammies stopped keeping their kids at home with them after school, because it got warmer and they got sick of having their kids at home with them after school. Mam was still sick of me, but she didn't try to give me away again. She was usually out when I got back from school or from playing, or else she was in her room with the door closed and the light off. We still went to church every Sunday. Mam always liked God, even when she didn't like me. We had to get there late and leave early because Mam didn't like other people, and if we got there late and left early other people barely noticed we were there. Church was the only time Mam was really happy – when she was singing 'Lord of the Dance' and 'Morning Has Broken' and 'Bread of Heaven' with her eyes closed and her face tilted towards the sky. Her singing didn't fit with the rest of her. It was high and pretty. I quite liked church, because sometimes I could steal some coins off the collection plates at the back, and I liked the vicar touching my head when I went to the front to get blessed.

When we got back to the house Mam usually slithered into a lump on the doormat. I tried to make her come into the lounge but she wouldn't move, and she was too heavy to lift. In the end I usually lay down beside her in the hallway, took a piece of her hair in my fingers and ran it around my mouth. It felt like a feather. I didn't know why she got so sad after church, but I thought it was probably because she knew she wasn't going to get to sing any more hymns for a whole week.

The only person who still didn't come out to play was Susan. She didn't even come to school. I only saw her in the evenings, when she stood at her bedroom window with her hands pressed against the glass. I never knew if she saw me. When she hadn't been at school for two whole weeks I went up to one of the Class Six girls at playtime and asked where she was.

'Susan?' she said. 'You mean the one with the dead brother?'

'Yeah,' I said.

'Don't know,' she said. 'At home, probably.' Then she ran off, because Class Six girls weren't meant to talk to Class Four girls. I turned it over in my head – 'Susan, the one with the dead brother.' Before it had always been 'Susan, the one with the long hair.'

Betty wasn't at school either, but she had mumps, not a dead brother. Miss White said we had to tell her straight away if we thought we might have mumps too. I told her every day, lots of times, but she just said, 'Stop being silly and get on with your worksheet, Chrissie.' At afternoon play I snuck back into the classroom and broke all the colouring pencils in the colouring pencil tray. Snap-snap-snap-snap. I-hate-Miss-White.

On Tuesday I went bottle collecting with Linda after school. Lots of people threw their glass bottles in the bin like they weren't worth anything, but we fished them out and swapped them for sweets. Sometimes the bottles had dark drops of Coca-Cola at the bottom, and I shook them onto my tongue. Linda said that was gross. The bad Coca-Cola drops were gross, tasted rotten, but the good ones were like sugar syrup. It was worth the risk. On Monday we took Linda's cousins with us, but they didn't really help with the bottle collecting. They were just silly little boys. It wasn't a good bottle day, because the bins had just been emptied and no one had had time to drink any Coca-Cola. I always asked Miss White if I could have the crates of empty milk bottles from school but she always said no, which was typical Miss White. If I'd had the milk bottles I would probably have been a millionaire by the time I was nine. I found two cream soda bottles in the gutter but one of them was smashed in half. I took it anyway. Linda just found one and the boys just made fire engine noises.

'This is rubbish,' said Linda as we walked to the shop. 'We never get this little of bottles.'

'Well it's not my fault,' I said.

'Whose fault is it?' she asked.

'I don't know,' I said. 'Probably Prime Minister's.'

'Why's it his fault?' she asked.

'Linda,' I said. 'Everything is his fault.' Sometimes it was tiring having a best friend who was thick.

When we got to the shop Mrs Bunty said she would only give us a quarter pound of sweets, which wasn't nearly as much as we deserved, but that was typical Mrs Bunty. She was mean, mean, mean. Whenever she weighed out sweets she dropped them into the silver bowl of the scales one by one, until the needle was just brushing the right number, then screwed the lid of the jar on tight. When Mrs Bunty's bad knee was too bad, Mrs Harold worked in the shop, and you could tell she wasn't mean because she poured the sweets into the scales until the needle was way over the right number, and then she said, 'Ah well, a few extra sweeties can't hurt a kiddie.' Mrs Bunty never did that. Mean, mean, mean, mean.

Me and Linda couldn't agree on what sweets we wanted for a long time. In the end we got licorice allsorts because that was what I wanted and I was the one who had found two bottles (including the smashed one, even though Mrs Bunty wouldn't take it). Also we basically always did what I wanted in the end. Mrs Bunty weighed them out and poured them into a white paper bag.

'That's barely *any*,' I said. She twisted the bag shut at the top.

'You can be grateful or you can go without, Chrissie Banks,' she said. 'Honestly. You kids don't know you're born, do you? Things weren't always easy like this, you know. Not when I was a kid. There was a war on.'

'Ugh,' I said. 'Why does no one ever talk about anything except the stupid old *war*?'

We went to the playground after the shop. Me and Linda sat on the roundabout and the boys ran around. Every few minutes they came to me with their hands held out for sweets and I bit one in half and split it between them. They were only little, so they only needed a little bit of sweet.

I was lying on my back when Linda whispered, 'Look,' and hit me on the arm. She pointed at the gate. I sat up and saw Steven's mammy pushing it open. At first I thought she looked all right, because she was wearing a normal dress and cardigan, but then I saw that her feet were bare. She didn't look at us, but she did look at the boys. They had stopped running and were trying to climb the swing poles. She smiled a sleepy sort of smile and went towards them. When she got close she knelt down and put her arms out.

'Come here, Stevie,' we heard her say. 'I knew I'd find you.'

The boys ran away crying, and we ran too, out of the playground and up the street. Before we went round the corner I looked over my shoulder. Steven's mammy was sitting on the ground under the swing poles. She was making that sound like a fox with a thorn, the same sound she had made when the man had carried Steven out of the blue house. I tried to find my inside-fizzing but it wasn't there. Remembering was a blunt, twisty ache, like someone was doing a Chinese burn on my guts.

'She's crazy,' said Linda when I caught her up. She kept looking back to see if Steven's mammy was following us, but I knew she wouldn't be. 'Who do you think killed Steven?' she asked.

'Don't know,' I said. 'Doesn't even matter anyway. He'll be back soon. Like my da.'

'Your da hasn't been back for ages,' she said.

'Not that ages,' I said.

'I don't think Steven will come back,' she said. 'My grandda never did.'

I didn't feel like explaining to Linda about people dying and coming back, so I stuffed the rest of the licorice allsorts into my mouth to make my teeth too gummed up to talk. She shoved me.

'Oi! Pig,' she said. Brown dribble oozed down my chin. When Linda went into her house I spat the sweets into the gutter. I ran my tongue around my mouth to see if I had spat the rotten tooth out too, but it was still there, creaking in the gum.

On Wednesday I forgot about trying to get sent home sick with mumps because the police came back to school, and this time they talked to all the classes, not just the babies. I saw them through the glass in the door, all polished shoes and shiny buttons. I got a feeling in my belly like an elastic band pulled to nearly snapping or a handful of sherbet dropped in a cup of Coca-Cola. Miss White let them in and said we all had to listen very carefully, so I turned round to face the front. Richard kicked me and I smacked his bare leg. Miss White told us to calm down and stop being silly, and one of the policemen looked at me and smiled with half his mouth. The elastic band snapped. The sherbet foamed up. I felt like God again.

The policemen said all the same things Mr Michaels had said right after Steven died: that we might have heard a very sad thing happened to a little boy who lived in the streets and we mustn't go playing in the alleys any more and some of us might have known the little boy and if any of us had seen him the day he died we had to go and talk to them. I put my hand up as soon as they finished speaking, and Miss White said, 'Chrissie, the policemen are very busy and they need to speak to Class Five and Class Six too; we don't have time for silliness.'

'I saw him,' I said. I looked her straight in the eye.

'Did you?' she said. She looked me straight back.

'Yes,' I said.

'You saw him that day?' asked one of the policemen.

'Yes,' I said.

'Right,' he said. 'Would you like to come over here with us for a moment, lass?'

I stood up and walked to the front. I could feel everyone's eyes on my back, and I bubbled with the power of it. The policeman put his hand on my shoulder and we went and sat on the chairs in the library corner. In the background I could hear whispering and Miss White telling everyone to finish their worksheets, but more than that I could hear fizzing and popping and whooshing. When Steven's mammy had come to the playground I had been scared my fizzing might be gone for good, because I had felt so cold and quiet inside, but now it was back and better than ever. No one was really finishing their worksheets. They were watching me.

'What's your name, lass?' asked one of the policemen when we had sat down. They were too big for the little chairs in the library corner. They spilt over the sides.

'Chrissie Banks,' I said. The other policeman wrote it down in a notebook.

'Hiya, Chrissie. My name's PC Scott and this is PC Woods,' he said. 'So, you think you saw Steven the day he passed away?'

'What does PC stand for?' I asked. 'Is it police copper?'

'Close. Police constable,' he said. 'You think you saw Steven, do you?'

'I know I did,' I said. I realised my head was completely empty, with nothing in it that I could say next.

The policemen were looking at me hard, and I could tell they wanted me to carry on, but I just looked at them hard back.

'Could you tell us a bit more about that?' asked PC Scott.

'I saw him in the morning,' I said.

'All right,' he said, and PC Woods wrote something else in his notebook. I thought it was probably 'She saw him in the morning.'

'Whereabouts did you see him?' asked PC Scott.

'At the shop,' I said.

'The shop at the end of Madeley Street?' he asked. 'The newsagent's?'

'I don't know if it sells any news,' I said. 'We just go there for sweets.'

He turned his mouth in at the corners the way people do when they are trying not to laugh. 'Right,' he said. 'And was he with anyone?'

They waited for me to carry on again, but I didn't again, because I didn't know what I was going to say next again.

'Who was he with?' he asked.

'His da,' I said. The way they looked at each other and raised their eyebrows made me think that was a very clever thing to have said.

'What time was this?' asked PC Scott.

'Don't know,' I said.

'What sort of time? Early morning, late morning . . .'

'Afternoon,' I said.

'Afternoon?' he said. 'Are you sure? You said it was morning.'

'No, I don't think it was, actually,' I said. 'I think it was afternoon. Nearly teatime.'

They looked at each other again, and PC Woods scribbled something in the corner of his notebook and showed it to PC Scott. They looked so clumsy, stuffed into the little library corner chairs. I felt like they were my very own person-sized dolls.

'Chrissie, what day was it you saw Steven?' asked PC Scott.

'The day he died,' I said.

'Yes, but what day was that? Do you remember?'

'Sunday,' I said.

'Ah,' he said. 'You're sure it was Sunday?'

'Yes,' I said. 'I wasn't at school, and there was church in the morning.'

'Ah,' he said again. The air went out of him like a flattened football. I knew why. Steven had died on Saturday, not Sunday. No one had seen him on Sunday, because by Sunday he was buried in the ground. I had got the policemen sniffing and slobbering over nothing, and all without telling them the biggest secret of all. The biggest secret of all was that *I* was the biggest secret of all. I felt even more like God than ever.

'Well, thanks very much for your help, lass,' said PC Scott.

'You're very welcome,' I said. He stood up and PC Woods copied. I wasn't sure PC Woods was a real policeman at all. He seemed more like a secretary. 'Are you going to catch the person who killed him?' I asked. PC Scott coughed and looked around at the other kids, who were all staring at him.

'We're going to find out exactly what happened,' he said loudly. 'Don't you worry.'

'I'm not worried,' I said. I went back to my place. Richard jabbed my arm with his pencil.

'What did you talk about?' he whispered. I watched the policemen speak to Miss White. I couldn't hear what they were saying, but I saw PC Woods throw the page of notes he had been writing into the bin by her desk.

'Shhh,' I said. Richard was balanced on the two side legs of his chair, with his arm pressed against mine and our cheeks almost touching. He sniffed three times in a row.

'You smell of pee,' he said. I scooted my chair back from the table so he toppled into my lap, and before he could sit up I slammed my fist down hard on his ear, like my fist was a hammer and his head was the top of a nail. I was holding my pencil. The point went into his ear hole. He wailed. Miss White said good-bye to the policemen looking flustered, and the policemen said good-bye to Miss White looking like they were very glad they were men, not women, because that meant they could be policemen, not teachers. When Miss White came over, Richard was crying too hard to tell her what had happened.

'He just toppled over, miss,' I said. 'I think maybe his chair broke. Maybe because he's quite fat.'

'Christine Banks,' she said. 'We don't make personal remarks.'

'It's not personal,' I said. 'It's just true.'

When Richard stopped wailing Miss White said we could do colouring until break time, because everyone was overexcited and no one was finishing their worksheets, but then she said actually we couldn't do colouring after all because someone had broken all the colouring pencils in the colouring pencil tray. She asked if anyone wanted to own up to that. I knew she knew it was me and she knew I knew it was me, and we both knew no one could prove it was me. What an excellent day it was turning out to be.

When we went out to play everyone gathered in a huddle to say what they thought had happened to Steven. Roddy thought there had been baddies in the alleys who had been shooting at each other and one of their bullets had hit Steven by accident. Eve thought he had had a heart attack that made him fall over dead without anyone knowing he was even ill. Some people had such good ideas, I thought they must be right. The thing was, I didn't always remember I had killed him. It slipped soapily out of my head, and when I went to look for it, there was nothing there. It always slipped back in eventually, and the slipping back in felt different every time. It could be a firework exploding or a block of lead falling or a splash of icy water. It could be a toothache twinge, like when I was watching Steven's mammy in the playground, or a butter-in-a-pan sizzle, like the night I walked to church in my nightie. But most of the time it just wasn't there. I liked it that way. It meant I got to be a killer, but I also got days off from being a killer, because a killer was quite a tiring thing to be.

We lined up to go back into the classroom and I saw the policemen through the railings. They were walking to their car and talking to each other. I got a bang of sadness so hard it made me bend over. As they moved away the bubbly power I had felt when I was walking to the library corner got smaller and smaller. I wanted to claw it back. It was the same power I had felt with my hands on Steven's neck, hearing the spittly wheezing sound, watching the popping eyes. The feeling of my body being made of lectric.

'I need it back,' I thought. 'I need it again. I need to do it more, more, more.'

The line ahead of me started filing into the classroom and Catherine pushed me to make me follow, so I pushed her back and she fell over and that meant everyone in the line behind her fell over too. Toppled like dominoes. She cried and Miss White told me off, but I couldn't hear her over the pulse of my inside clock.

Tick. Tick. Tick. Tick. Tick. Tick.

*

I wanted to see the policemen again after school, but their car wasn't parked where it was normally parked and I didn't know where else to look. I hung around outside Steven's house for a long time and the policemen didn't come, so I started walking to the playground. I was nearly there when I saw Donna coming towards me, pulling a little girl by the hand. She didn't look like any other little girl I had ever seen in real life. She was wearing a puffy blue dress with matching blue shoes, and there was even a blue bow in her hair. It was long hair, and orange coloured, like tiger fur. She didn't have any mud on her knees. She didn't even have any mud on her socks. She didn't look like she came from the streets at all.

The thing about the streets was that everyone living there was poor. Some people were a bit less poor, and you could always tell who those people were because they called things 'common'. Betty wasn't that poor, and the things her mammy called common were pink clothes, tinsel, knee socks, saying 'what' instead of 'pardon', tinned fruit, shorts, salad cream, not taking your shoes off inside the house, tulips, saying 'toilet' instead of 'loo', felt-tip pens, toothpaste with a stripe in it, loud music, cartoons, and icing. Also, on the table in the hallway of Betty's house there was a big glass jar where her mammy and da put their pennies so they wouldn't weigh down their pockets. That was another way you could tell someone wasn't that poor – they didn't think pennies were real money; they thought they were just the same as stones or bottle tops. I once asked Betty what they did with all the pennies when the jar was filled up to the top.

'I think Mammy takes them to church for the donation bucket,' she said. 'But it hasn't been full up in ages. Not since before you started coming to my house.'

'I think we should talk about something else now,' I said.

So I knew Betty was richer than me, and I knew I was richer than the kids in the alleys, but we were all still basically poor. That was why the little girl looked so different, and that was why I stared. She didn't look poor at all.

'Hi,' said Donna. She put her hands on the little girl's shoulders the way mammies do when they want to show off their kids. 'This is Ruthie. I'm looking after her.'

'Why's she wearing them clothes?' I asked.

'Her mammy dresses her nicely. She showed me all the clothes in her wardrobe. They're all like this.'

'Is she rich?'

'Nah. They live in a flat. It's tiny. They're waiting to move into a house.'

'How comes she looks like that, then?'

'Her mammy spends all her money on her. Every single bit of money she has. She just only ever spends it on Ruthie.'

'It looks like a doll dress.'

'Yeah. My dress is nice too, isn't it? It's new. My nana made it for me.' She held out the skirt of her dress, which was made of a curtainy sort of material with little tassels on the edge. 'I think this dress is just as nice as Ruthie's. Don't you?'

'No,' I said. 'You look like a lamp. Where's her flat?'

'Near the high street. But her mammy still let me take her here even though it's far. She said I seemed like a dispensable girl.'

'What does that mean?'

'Grown-up and good. Do I really look like a lamp?'

'Yup.'

Ruthie was getting bored. She wriggled out from under Donna's fingers. Donna leant forward so their faces were almost touching and spoke in a syrupy voice. 'Do you want to go into the playground with Donna, Ruthie? Do you want Donna to push you on the swings?'

Ruthie stepped backwards and screwed up her nose as if Donna's breath smelt bad. That made me like her a little bit more. When we got inside the playground she ran to the only baby swing left on the poles and tried to climb in by herself, but it was too high and she kept slipping. She shoved Donna away the first three times she tried to lift her, so Donna came and stood by the roundabout with me. The fifth time Ruthie pulled herself up and fell back down she yelled at us to lift her. It took both of us to get her into the seat. When I tried to push her she screamed and slapped my hand, so I slapped her back. It was a hard slap – it left a pink mark on her soft arm – but she didn't cry. She looked half-cross and half-impressed. Donna tried to push her and

she screamed even louder, so we went and sat on the roundabout and let her flap around by herself.

'She's got so many toys at home,' said Donna.

'How many?' I asked.

'More than you've ever seen before in your whole wide
life. Her mammy gets her everything she wants.'

'Why?'

'Just does. But my mammy says it's bad for kids to have
everything they want.'

I didn't think it would be bad for me to have everything
I wanted. I watched Ruthie thrashing in the swing, crum-
pling up her dress. I didn't think Ruthie was a very good
person. If I had had a dress as pretty as that I would have
sat still all day to make sure it didn't get creased or dirty.
I didn't properly know Ruthie, and I hadn't ever seen her
flat or her toys or her mammy, but even without seeing
them I knew she didn't deserve them. She didn't deserve
any of it.

When Ruthie got bored of the swings Donna said she
was going to take her home, because I wasn't a dispensable
girl and Ruthie's mammy only wanted her to play with dispensable girls. I called Ruthie a lump and Donna a lamp, but
Donna just took Ruthie's hand and said, 'Come on, Ruthie,
let's go home to your mammy.' I said I would go with them,
because I wanted to look at all Ruthie's toys, but when we
got to the end of the road I saw two policemen walking
towards the church. I wanted to speak to the policemen

more than I wanted to see the toys, so I ran after them. They were quite a long way ahead of me, and before I could reach them they got in their car and drove off. I kicked the kerb and felt my toenail break. I didn't care. I wished Ruthie had still been there. I wanted to slam her against the kerb. I wanted to see what colour her blue dress would turn when it had her brains smashed all over it.

JULIA

'Guess what,' Molly called. I turned off the taps and went back to the kitchen. 'It's assembly next week,' she said. Her voice was muffled.

'Don't talk with your mouth full,' I said.

She leant over, opened her mouth and gently released a clod of chewed potato onto the chip paper. 'It's assembly next week,' she said.

'Why did you do that?' I asked.

'You told me to,' she said.

It was four thirty. I took her reading book out of her book bag and sat down at the table opposite her.

'Come on. Reading,' I said.

She knelt up on her chair and stretched until a sliver of skin appeared under her polo shirt. 'I think I'm going to be a cat,' she said.

'What?' I said.

'I'm going to be a cat. That means I only talk in "meow" and I do things like this.' She curled her hand over, licked the back, and rubbed it behind her ear. 'I play it with Abigail. It's a really fun game.'

'You can be a cat later,' I said. 'Now you're going to read your book.'

'Cats can't read,' she said.

'I think this one can,' I said.

'Meow,' she said.

After fifteen minutes, I agreed that I would stop trying to make her read if she stopped meowing. She trotted into the bathroom looking mildly victorious, and stood on the mat, waiting for me to undress her.

'Do you know what I'm being in assembly?' she asked as I peeled off her vest.

'What?'

'Narrator Four,' she said. She was bare now, ribs cording the skin above her belly, which stuck out like a mixing bowl. Her knees were patch-worked with bruises, pushed to the surface of the skin in a pearly mauve-brown sheen. I lifted her into the tub and propped her plastered arm on a stool.

'*Narrator Four*,' she said.

'Wow,' I said.

'It's the most important one in the whole assembly,' she said.

'How many narrators are there?' I asked.

'Four,' she said. 'Miss King said Narrator Four is the most important.'

The First Day of Spring

According to Molly, Miss King spent most of her working life telling Molly she was better than all the other kids in the class. I wasn't sure it was ever an honour to be the last in a procession of narrators. Linda had been Narrator Five (of five) three years in a row, because she couldn't read and she cried whenever she had to speak in front of people. The first year it happened I was next to her on the stage. I knew her lines as well as mine, because I knew everyone's lines, and when I realised she wasn't going to say them I stood up and said them for her. I was surprised there was room in my head for the memory – I felt stuffed to the sides of my skull with echoes of Sasha's voice and visions of Molly's new mother – but it slipped fluidly into the cracks. Linda's pale face. The silence before I rescued her. The feel of her hand, cold and sweaty, curled around my wrist.

I filled a plastic cup with water, tipped Molly's head back, and poured it over her hair. It turned it to a thin black snake, and the heat turned her skin slick and spongy. Sometimes I felt I was closest to Molly when she was in the bath, because in water she was back to the creature I remembered: a thing made of naked tissue, like a girl-shaped graze. That was how she was when she tore out of me, washed through in a wave of pain that made me want to collar someone and say, 'This can't be real, this must be a joke, you can't seriously expect me to cope with this,' because nothing that was natural could hurt so much. She came out screaming, as if I was the one who had hurt her, and I wanted to say, 'This isn't fair. It isn't fair of you to act this way. You're the one who hurt me.'

The pain crested and dissolved, and a nurse held her up like an offering.

'Skin-to-skin, skin-to-skin!' she said.

'I don't want it on my skin,' I thought. 'It hurt me.'

'Time for a cuddle!' she said.

'I don't want to cuddle it,' I thought. 'It's too loud.'

'Lovely healthy girl!' she said.

'A girl,' I thought. 'A girl like me.'

Then she was there, hot and slimy on my chest. Her face looked made of folds of skin, and it struck me that perhaps this was my punishment. Not the years behind locked doors or the lifetime of probation. My punishment was to have given birth to a baby with no face, only fold upon fold of skin. I heaved, and the nurse shoved a kidney-shaped bowl under my chin, and I vomited into it. Molly stopped screaming, lulled by the hacking she had heard every night for nine months. She was still covered in a fine layer of my insides, and it struck me that she was like an organ, that I felt about her the way I would have felt if someone had scooped out my heart and put it on top of me.

'Well done, Mum!' said the nurse.

'That's not my name,' I thought.

'Looks like she's hungry!' she said.

'What if I'm hungry?' I thought.

She took hold of Molly's head and clamped her firmly onto my nipple.

'There! You're a natural!' she said, but that wasn't what I heard. I heard what I was used to hearing: 'You're unnatural.' *'Eight years old and killed a kid? That's not normal. She's unnatural.'* I looked at the nurse, wondering how she had found out who I was. She touched the back of Molly's head and nodded. 'A natural,' she said. I heard it properly that time. I took hold of it like I had taken hold of 'Well done', stored the compliments in my cheeks like a rodent hoarding food. My gown had fallen down when the nurse had shoved her onto me, so I was bare to my belly button. It was suddenly horrible to be so bare in front of a loud woman I didn't know. I wanted to cry. I looked at Molly, lying across me. She made me less naked, and I felt she was doing it on purpose. I felt she was feeding not for her but for me, so I could use her body as a blanket over my chest. When she stopped sucking the nurse reached over, hooked a finger between her lips, and unstuck my nipple from her gums.

'I'll put her here so you can get some rest,' she said, lifting her into the plastic box next to the bed. I felt untethered without her weight, as if I would float up to the ceiling. When she was put in the box she squawked. 'You want to go back to Mum, eh, madam?' said the nurse. She returned her and watched as I curled my hand around the back of her head. I thought I was probably doing it wrong. 'Has she got a name?' she asked.

'Molly,' I whispered. It was the only name I had picked out, which made me wonder whether I had somehow felt her girlness inside me. I hadn't known a Molly in any of my lives; it was fresh and untainted. I liked the softness of the letters in my mouth, the way saying it felt like chewing on silk.

'Lovely,' said the nurse, and bustled away.

'Do you like me, then?' I whispered to Molly. She moved her head around as she fell asleep. It was sort of like a nod.

I lifted Molly out of the bath at five fifteen and dried her with a large blue towel. She wasn't usually allowed more than an hour of telly each day, because too much telly would turn her brain to soup, but once she was in her pyjamas I turned it on, knowing I wouldn't turn it off until the kids' programmes finished at seven. I sat at the kitchen table, feeding leftover chips into my mouth one after another.

At some point between the start and end of *Chuckle-Vision* it came to me that I wouldn't be going to see Sasha in the morning. It wasn't a decision I had to make; it arrived in my head fully formed. I wouldn't be at the Children's Services building at ten, because to walk into that building would be to hand Molly over, and I would walk into the sea before I gave her away. The prospect of the meeting had been a vice around my chest, and without it my lungs had room to swell. Molly and I were ruled by can'ts, musts, the juddering arc of the hands on the clock, because that was the way I steered our rickety carriage. The wheels had come off now; we had careened away from the tracks and were falling through the air. The crash was inevitable – they would find us, they would take her – but until we hit the ground we were free. I didn't know how long we had before the vultures came pounding at the door, and I didn't want Molly's last memory of me to be my face turning white as an angry mob wrestled me to the floor. So we wouldn't stay. We would run. There were things I had sworn I would never do, places I had sworn I would never go, because they couldn't be allowed to leach into Molly's bubble. That didn't matter any more. I was losing her. Nothing mattered.

At seven I turned off the telly and started brushing her hair.

'I think we might go away tomorrow,' I said, running a finger down her parting.

'Where?' she asked.

'Just away,' I said.

'Somewhere I know?' she asked.

'No,' I said. Molly only knew the seaside. She was too small to remember the first new life, the Lucy/Nathan/hardware store life. In that life I had existed in the three square rooms of a ground-floor flat, subsisted on metal-tasting food from cans. When I found out I was pregnant I stopped going to work. Like the decision about the meeting, it wasn't one I had to make; it came to me as fact. Nathan couldn't find out

I was pregnant. I couldn't go to work without him finding out I was pregnant. I couldn't go to work. Jan registered me for benefits, and I spent the next eight months sleeping all day and being sick all night.

They tracked us down when Molly was a small, soft bundle, wrapped in a blanket and draped over my shoulder. They gathered outside with cameras that clicked like an army of crickets. We had to run down the garden path covered in bedsheets, and her head bumped against my chin hard enough to close my teeth around my tongue, and by the time we were in the police car my mouth was full of blood. It tasted of salt and grease. I spat it into my hands. Molly stared up at me, and I was glad she wouldn't remember this, wouldn't remember running to the car dressed as a ghost or seeing me spit blood into my hands.

After Lucy I was Julia, and they promised me no one would ever find out that Julia had once been Chrissie. But they had promised me no one would ever find out that Lucy had once been Chrissie. *Promise* was just a word and a name was just a name and I wasn't Chrissie, not inside, not any more, but the vultures didn't care about that. Jan found me the flat above Arun's shop, which came with a job frying fish and mopping floors.

'Not for now,' she said. 'Just for when you're ready. Maybe not until she starts school. Your benefit money will cover the rent until then, and once you start work they'll do a reduced rate. They're kind.'

The First Day of Spring

Nobody asked me if I wanted to fry fish and mop floors. When you used to be Chrissie you didn't get to choose. Jan thought it was the perfect arrangement, because Arun and Mrs G were the sort of people who chose not to see things they thought you didn't want them to see, who twisted facts as much as they needed in order to believe what they had always believed: that people are all, in essence, good.

Jan drove us to the new town and helped carry our boxes up to the flat. It didn't take long; we didn't have much. Mrs G had left a film-wrapped cake on the kitchen table. It was dark with seeds, and next to it there was a note: 'Welcome, Julie'. When the car was empty we stood on the pavement outside the shop. Molly had been crying and I had strapped her to my chest in a sling. I liked having her there, holding my pieces together.

'Right, then,' said Jan. 'I'll say my good-byes.'

It turned out that when the vultures had tracked us down they had taken away more than my flat and my name, the hours of sleep I had started to piece together at night. They had taken away Jan. I was under a new probation officer now, attached to the police force in the new town. I had just been starting to like Jan.

She stepped forward and put her hand on Molly's back through the fabric of the sling. 'Bye, Molly,' she said. She moved her hand to my elbow and squeezed it tight. 'Bye, Lucy.'

I stood on the pavement as she got into her car. I watched her drive down the high street and disappear round the corner. 'Bye, Lucy,' I said.

'How long are we going away for?' Molly asked.

'Not sure. A bit.'

'Will we be back on Friday? It's show-and-tell. I have to be back for that.'

'Mmm.'

I let my eyes tip shut. My brain felt tender in my skull, like a bruised peach, juice seeping through cracks in the skin. Molly followed me to her bedroom and climbed into bed when I turned back the duvet.

'Can I get something for show-and-tell from the place we're going to?' she asked.

'Good night,' I said, and sat down on the mattress next to her bed.

When she had been a baby, I had sat by her cot until she was asleep every night. Sometimes she had glared at me through the bars and roared, and I had tensed at the indignant fury of it, but the book I had stolen from the library said I shouldn't pick her up every time she cried. I closed my eyes against the screwed, pink segments of her face, whispered, 'Please don't be sad, please don't be sad, please don't be sad.'

By the time she was three months old she never cried at night, and the silence scared me more than the screaming.

I counted down the minutes until I was allowed to pick her up and hold her on my chest to feed. I did it sitting on the floor, my shoulder blades digging into the wall behind me. I was allowed to hold her to feed, because that was for her. I wasn't allowed to hold her for me, for the comfort of feeling her warm weight in my arms. That was the rule I had made when she was born: I would give her everything, and ask nothing in return.

Reading the book chapter on weaning made my throat thicken with cotton-wool dread. There were chirpy pictures of babies gumming plastic spoons and paragraphs headed 'Moving On from Milk!' I felt I might as well be reading about putting Molly in a cardboard box outside the front door, waving and trilling, 'Time to move on, Molly! Time to move on from me!' Feeding her straight from my body – knowing that even if we had no money and no home and nothing but each other, she still wouldn't be hungry – had given me a warm nugget of power, held in my rib cage. I bought vegetables that I mashed with a fork and pushed through a sieve, that Molly massaged into her hair and pasted up her nostrils. She eyed the bottle of formula with disgust, and when I put it to her mouth she curled away, pawing at my top. I put her in the cot. I slipped out of the room, shut the door, sat on the floor with my arms crossed over my swollen chest.

'She won't cry for long,' I thought.

'She'll go to sleep soon,' I thought.

'She can't be that hungry,' I thought.

'The book says this is right,' I thought.

I watched the clock on the wall. I listened to Molly cry. Twin wet circles soaked through my clothes, and I smelt rotten-sweet, like rancid melon. I took off my jumper before I opened the door, peeled off my T-shirt as I went to the cot, unhooked my bra and let it fall to the floor, and picked her up. Her eyelashes were spiked into small black triangles and her fat starfish hand clenched on my breast as she gulped. I unsnapped her from her babygro, so she was bare and our skins were pressed together. Sweat made it slippy between us. She drank until she was asleep (undesirable) and I laid her down on the mattress beside me (unthinkable) and curled myself in a bracket around her like a crescent moon (unforgivable).

I breastfed until she was two. Steven had been two when he died. I didn't know whether his mammy had still been breastfeeding, whether she had swelled and leaked and ached without him. It hurt to see Molly drink from a beaker and feel myself desiccate from the inside out, and that was good. I deserved hurt.

I didn't stop sitting by her bed when she stopped waking at night. At Haverleigh they had closed and locked my door at bedtime, but a keeper had still sat outside the room, flicking open the shutter every ten minutes to peer at me. If I needed the toilet I knocked on the door and they unlocked it, followed me into the bathroom, stood in the corner as I peed. When we got back to my bedroom they locked me back in and wrote in my notes that I had been to the toilet. They wrote in my notes when I turned over in my sleep. They wrote in my notes when I snored. Molly didn't have notes, but she had me by her side at night, on the mattress I had pulled off my bed. It was how you looked after a kid. It was what Haverleigh had taught me.

That night I waited until she was asleep, then climbed into bed behind her. We didn't touch, but she was like a tiny radiator, and her warmth made me feel we were fused. I ran my hand across my belly. I missed being curved and hard with her – the unmatchable closeness, the knowledge that no one could take her away. When she had moved in, my body had been like an alley house – dank and grimy and rotten at the edges – but she had still wanted to live there. She had clung on, determined, refusing to evacuate in a shock of blood on porcelain. I didn't understand why she wanted me – but then, I didn't understand why I still wanted Mam.

After Haverleigh, I ached for Mam with a hungry in-tensity. I saw it as the part of me that was animal – soft, hot, made of flesh and fur. Each time I was knocked I found myself scuttling to her, like a badger retreating into a burrow. Each time I left I felt caked in a layer of grime so thick I had to stand under a hot shower and scrub my skin until it smarted, and I told myself I would not see her again. Months passed. Another knock. I scuttled back. The need was always there, like a pickled lemon, yellow flesh perfectly preserved under the rind. I came to think I didn't want her, not really, not the way she was. I crawled back because I hoped one day I might find her changed to the way she wasn't.

I had last seen her three weeks before Molly was born, when I was grey with sickness and tired to the cord of marrow inside my bones. She opened the door and licked me up and down with her eyes.

'Fucking hell,' she said. 'You got fat.'

'I'm pregnant,' I said. 'You know that.'

'There's big and there's big,' she said. 'I was never fat with you.'

She would have liked to pretend she hadn't carried me in her body at all, to claim I had grown in a tank on her bedside table. I stayed for two sour, push-and-pull hours, and when I got up to leave she pressed a piece of paper into my hand. It had become ritual.

'Off again?' I said.

'Yeah,' she said. 'This place doesn't suit me. Neighbours are shits. Council found me somewhere better. New flats. They're in a block.'

'Right,' I said. I opened the folded slip and read the address. I recognized the postcode: back in the streets.

'Why are you going back?' I asked.

Her eyes flicked from side to side, as though she was hoping she might find the answer in a corner of the space around her. She shrugged. 'Home, isn't it?' she said.

I didn't stop wanting her when Molly was born; if anything, I wanted her more. Molly was my second heart for nine months, but when the nurses ripped her out I didn't think of my body, robbed of its pendulum. I thought, 'Twenty years ago, Molly was me. Twenty years ago, I was Mam,' and I felt closer to her than I had ever felt when we had lived in the same house, breathed the same air. When Molly cried I wanted to turn up on Mam's doorstep with my throbbing head, sore chest, and bundle of baby. 'Is this how you felt?' I wanted to ask. 'Did you feel this mad? This tired? Did you feel like other people had a secret book you'd never been given? Is this why you were the way you were? Will she turn out like me?'

Beside me in bed, Molly snuffled and started in her sleep. I lifted a piece of her hair off the pillow and ran it around my mouth. It felt like a feather.

'I made this,' I thought. 'I made this hair, this skin, the blood in these spiderweb veins. I made it all. It came from me.' I wanted to hear her say it – hear her tell me, 'Yes, look at you, look at her, you did it. You did that, Chrissie. You did something good.' It had to be her voice: scratchy, like wire wool. When I closed my eyes I saw her face seared onto the lids.

Mam.

CHRISSIE

The day after I spoke to the police I came back from school and found a tin on the kitchen table. It was blue with a swirly gold pattern on the top, and when I peeled it open I saw chocolates stacked in neat columns. I took it into the lounge, sat on the couch, and ate them. I had to eat them all up, because Mam had bought them for me, and when Mam bought me things I had to eat them all up. If I didn't she cried and said, 'I got that for you special, Christine. What's wrong with you? Don't you care?'

When Mam cooked me things it was extra important that I ate them all up, because if I didn't she would think I extra-didn't care. She didn't cook much. The last time was Christmas when I was seven, when she'd been given a turkey by Mr Godwin the butcher. I didn't know why he had given it to her. It sat in the kitchen for lots of days before Christmas, big and ugly and covered in pimpled white skin. On Christmas Day Mam put it in a saucepan with lots of water and boiled and boiled and boiled. The whole house smelt of meat, and the kitchen windows steamed up, and all the spoons and surfaces got coated in a layer of slippy grease. I sat on the floor in the hallway wearing the scarf I'd got as my present from the Sunday school Christmas party over my nose and mouth. I had not had a fun time at the Sunday school Christmas party. It had happened straight after the Sunday school Nativity play, which had also been unfun because Mrs Idiot Samuels hadn't given me the right part. I badly wanted to be the baby Jesus but she said it had to be a doll, and then I badly wanted to be Herod but she said it had to be a boy, and then I badly wanted to be a shepherd but she said it had to be someone who had brought a tea towel to wear on their head. The angel of the Lord had to be someone pretty and Mary had to be someone whose mammy had given Mrs Samuels a nice bottle of wine. I had to be a goat. That was not my idea of a fun time at all, and I showed her I was not having fun by making a very loud bleating noise whenever anyone else tried to say their lines. I didn't care about ruining the stupid play. My da hadn't even come to watch.

As the turkey cooked I made a paper chain and Mam drank whisky, which put her in a happy mood. She was so happy, she went upstairs and got the radio from her bedroom. It hissed out a fuzzy sound when she first turned it on, and I had to put my hands over my ears, because the fuzzy sound made me think someone was trapped in the radio and I really didn't like that idea, but she fiddled with the buttons then pulled me up by my wrists and spun me around the kitchen, singing, 'I saw three ships, I saw three ships, I saw three ships,' because she didn't know the rest of the words. I felt so good, I didn't care about not having Da there or any proper presents. The radio started playing 'O Little Town of Bethlehem' and I put my arms around Mam's middle and pressed my face into her belly. A lot of turkey water had splattered on her, so she was damp and smelt of bones, but I didn't care. She didn't push me away. She let me hug her. She put her hands on my back and rubbed up and down. It was probably the best happy mood she had ever been in, probably even happier than the happy mood that Mary must have got in when the baby Jesus was born.

It was dark by the time Mam turned off the cooker. She told me to come to the table, and she put a bowl and a cracker in front of me and said, 'Isn't this a treat? Turkey for Christmas.' She sat opposite. She didn't have any turkey, just the end of the bottle of whisky. The stuff in the bowl didn't look much like a treat. It was grey, with foamy scum gathered at the edges. I blew on it for as long as I could, and then I spent a lot of time picking up spoonfuls and letting them pour back into the bowl.

'Stop playing and eat,' said Mam.

'Will you do my cracker with me?' I asked.

'Eat your food,' she said.

In the first mouthful I bit down on something that wasn't quite bone and wasn't quite meat, a gristly lump that crunched when it went between my teeth. The taste was wax and skin and toilets. I spat it back into the bowl. I didn't look at Mam. I looked at the oily circles collected on top of the grey, growing and shrinking like screaming mouths.

'I think the turkey wasn't right, Mam,' I said. 'I think it was in the bag for too long. I think it went mouldy. It doesn't taste right.'

I didn't have to look at her to know she had got out of the happy mood. I could feel it. The happy-sad switch was like opening a window to cold air.

'I've spent all day cooking that, Christine,' she said. 'You sit here and you eat it.'

'But I think it went mouldy, Mam,' I said. 'I think it's not right.'

'You sit here. And you eat it,' she said.

'Can you do my cracker with me?' I asked again.

Her chair made a screeching sound when she pushed it back from the table. 'Will you ever stop wanting things, Christine?' she shouted. 'It's fucking Christmas. I'm trying to make things nice. Cooked you that turkey, got you them crackers. I even topped up the lectric for us to watch telly later. Thought we could watch something nice together. Why is nothing ever enough for you? Why can't you just be good?'

She walked out of the room, down the hallway, stepping on my paper chain and leaving it flat. I felt like it was my head she had stepped on, like she had put her foot on my cheek and trodden down until she felt the bones splinter into shards. I pulled my cracker with my two hands. The right hand won: a blue paper hat and a baby set of cards. The joke fluttered under the table. When Mam's bedroom door closed I took my bowl out of the kitchen, opened the front door, went down the garden path, and put it outside the front gate. I hoped a dog might come and eat the horrid grey soup. I stood on the garden path for a long time, leaning on the gate. I could see the coloured lights on Betty's Christmas tree, winking through the net curtains in her lounge window. Then I went inside and watched telly until the lectric ran out.

The things Mam got me to eat were usually much better than the rotten turkey, because she usually didn't cook them, usually just bought them, so it usually wasn't too hard to eat them all up. When I had eaten all the chocolates, I left the empty tin on the kitchen table and went back to lie on the couch. After that, there was no food for a week. I tried to stay at other people's houses long enough that they gave me tea, or I ate what I could find in the kitchen cupboards. Tins of sardines with fingernail bones that clawed my throat, spoonfuls of milk powder from the big red tub. One day I got sent to Mr Michaels for taking Donna's biscuit at break time, but I didn't care because by then I had already eaten it, so he couldn't make me give it back.

I started to think Mam must have moved away, because I hadn't seen her for days and days, not even on

Sunday for church. I wandered through the rooms of the house, running my fingers along the walls, wondering if I was an orphan. I had only ever read about orphans. I didn't know if they were real like God or pretend like witches.

I had just got used to the idea of being an orphan, a real live orphan, when I went downstairs on Saturday and found Mam at the kitchen table.

'Did you like the chocolates?' she asked.

'Yeah,' I said.

'Did you eat them all?' she asked.

'Yeah,' I said.

'Good. I got you them special,' she said.

'Thank you,' I said.

I didn't really know what to do. I pushed my feet into my shoes and did the laces in tight knots, pulling until all the blood was squeezed out of my feet.

'I'm going out now,' I said.

'That's right,' said Mam. 'Go off and leave me. Go off and leave me right after I got you them chocolates, right after I spent my own money getting you them chocolates. Leave me all by myself.'

'Do you want me to stay?' I asked.

'Get lost, Chrissie,' she said. 'I want you to get lost and never get found. That's what I want.'

'OK,' I said. I left the front door open behind me. I'd preferred being an orphan.

I knocked for Linda and we walked up the hill on only the front-garden walls. I was brilliant at wall walking. William timed me once, before his wristwatch got stolen: all the way from Mr Jenks' to the haunted house in four minutes and thirty-three seconds. I wanted him to time me again so I could get faster and faster, and he said he would if I helped him find out who had stolen his wristwatch. Unfortunately it was me who had stolen his wristwatch, so I had to say I actually didn't want to be timed again, but four minutes and thirty-three seconds was still faster than any other kid in the whole of the streets.

When we got to Steven's house I saw that the front room curtains were closed. It was the only house in the street with its curtains closed, and that made the inside of the hidden room so much more exciting than it ever could have been with the curtains open. Steven's tricycle was in the front garden. The yellow paint on the seat was peeling. I jumped down from the wall.

'Let's knock,' I said.

'We can't,' said Linda. 'My mammy says she has to be left.'

'Why?'

'Don't know. But Donna's mammy was going to take her flowers and she asked if my mammy wanted to go too and my mammy said no. She doesn't think it's right that so many mammies are taking her so many things all the time.'

She wiped a scrape on her leg with her cardigan sleeve before blood wormed into her white sock.

'My mammy said it's brutal,' she said. 'She said, "It's brutal, what that woman's going through. You wouldn't wish it on your worst enemy." That's what she said.'

I thought Steven's mammy probably would wish someone else's kid had died, especially if it could have been someone else's kid instead of Steven. She probably wished it could have been any other kid in the whole wide world, even her best friend's kid. Usually when people said you wouldn't wish something on your worst enemy it meant you probably would wish it on your worst enemy, and in fact you'd find it quite fun to watch it happen to them. There wasn't much I wouldn't wish on Donna.

Linda was still talking without really saying anything new, which was unfortunately something that she did a lot.

'She says it's worse because he was the apple of their eye,' she said. 'I asked her what that means and she said it's that he was the one they all loved the most. I said we knew that already. You and me did know that, didn't we? We did, didn't we, Chrissie? We knew they made a big huge fuss of him, didn't we? We was always saying that, wasn't we?'

'Linda,' I said. 'You need to stop talking now. You are giving me a headache in my ears.'

'Oh no. Sorry,' she said.

I went up Steven's garden path and knocked on the door with three hard taps. No one answered for a long time. I thought Steven's mammy must have got so sad she had just

119

lain down and died too. I would have given up on her ever coming at all, but then Linda would have been right and I couldn't stand for Linda to be right, so I knocked again and didn't stop knocking until the door opened.

Steven's mammy looked a lot worse than she had looked at the playground. Her face was the colour of the layer of grey skin on the inside of fish batter and her cheeks were hanging all loose from their bones, slack and swinging under milky pink eyes.

'What you want?' she asked in a grey-sounding voice. I didn't really know what to say. I hadn't expected her to look so bad. I couldn't really remember why I had wanted to knock in the first place.

'Hello,' I said.

'What do you want?' she asked again.

'The police have been at your house a lot,' I said. 'Why have they?'

'Go away,' she said. 'Stop meddling in things you oughtn't to be meddling in.'

I was about to tell her that Steven being killed and the police looking for who had done the killing were things I *did* ought to be meddling in, because it was actually *me* who had done the killing, but I swallowed it down. I thought it probably wasn't what she wanted to hear right then. She started to close the door but I pushed it back open.

'Is he still dead?' I asked. That wasn't just talking to fill the time – I wanted to know the answer. It had been so many days since Steven had died that I had lost count, and I thought he must be going to come back soon. He was only little, and I was sure that should mean he came back alive quicker than a grown-up. Steven's mammy's face flopped in on itself like a burst balloon, like all the bones had disappeared or turned to water.

'Do you know what you are, Chrissie Banks?' she said.

'What?' I asked.

'You're a bad seed,' she said.

Bad seed. I liked that.

'Have they found out who killed him yet?' I asked.

'Go away,' she said again. I thought of Steven's baby-bird body, carried out of the blue house by the great big man. Smooth and still, might have been asleep, in a pair of arms so bubbled with muscle they could have crushed him. Behind Steven's mammy the lounge door opened and his da came out. I could smell his body from where I was standing. It smelt very strongly of a body, of skin and sweat and stale air. He stopped in the hallway and looked at me over Steven's mammy's shoulder.

'Is Susan here?' I asked.

'Susan?' said Steven's mammy, as if she didn't know who that was.

'Is she here?' I asked.

Without moving or even breathing in, Steven's da shouted, 'SUSAN!' so loudly I jumped. There was no answer.

'She's out,' he said.

'Do you know where she is?' I asked.

'She'll be somewhere,' said Steven's mammy.

'Well everyone's somewhere,' I said. Steven's da went down the hallway and into the kitchen. He pushed the door closed behind him but a sicky smell still slipped out. Steven's mammy looked like she was going to try to shut the front door again, so I said, 'It was a man who killed him, wasn't it?'

'What?' she said.

'It was a man who killed Steven. The man I saw.' It dribbled out easily. It was just another version of the story I had told the policemen at school.

'What man you saw?'

I could feel her creeping into my palm, so I shrugged and said, 'Oh. Nothing. It doesn't matter.'

'What man you saw?'

'I saw a man walking away from the alleys that day. The day Steven got killed.'

'That day? Saturday? Are you sure?'

I shrugged again. Since she had opened the door I had been feeling sort of cold, sort of dead, but as her face changed from ghost to person I felt myself come alive again too. 'Sort of sure,' I said.

'Did you tell the police? They went to your school, didn't they? Did you tell them?'

'Maybe. Can't really remember.'

The First Day of Spring

She stepped forward and stood so close I had to turn my face away. 'You've got to tell them,' she said. 'You've got to tell them anything you saw. Specially anything you saw that day. Are you listening, Chrissie?'

'I thought I wasn't to meddle,' I said. At the end of the hallway Steven's da came back out of the kitchen, and the smell came out after him, strong enough to make me dizzy. I imagined the kitchen humming and dark with flies. I thought of them buzzing around flowers mounded on the table, and buzzing around apples shrivelled in the fruit bowl, but most of all buzzing around the stews and hams the mammies had brought, oozing in the glare of the sun.

I ran down the garden path, through the gate, and up the street. Linda ran after me. Steven's mammy called our names but we didn't stop running, and when I looked round she wasn't following, just standing on the pavement. We didn't slow down until we were at the top of the hill. Linda panted and I dragged my knuckles along the front-garden walls, pressing hard enough to make beads of blood swell up from the skin. I brought my fist to my mouth. The taste was iron and dust. When we got to the handstand wall we dropped down to sit with our backs against it.

'Did you really see a man?' Linda asked once she had her breath back.

'Maybe,' I said.

'Are you going to tell the police?' she asked.

'Maybe,' I said, and then I had to do a handstand so she would stop asking questions. She did one too because she always did whatever I did. While I was upside down I thought about Steven's mammy, sitting with his dead-looking da in a house with a yellow tricycle in the front garden. I thought another day I might go back and ask her if I could have the tricycle, seeing as she didn't need it any more. It was small but so was I, and there was no point wasting a perfectly good tricycle, no matter who was dead.

When we had handstood so much our faces were pink, we played telly. It wasn't much fun playing telly with Linda. She kept asking me what to say next, and when she said it she didn't sound anything like anyone on the real telly. The only person who was even nearly as good as me at playing telly was Donna, which was annoying because people who look like potatoes are never actually on telly.

'If you could be anyone famous, who would you be?' I asked Linda.

'Probably just you,' she said.

'I'm not famous,' I said.

'But you're the best at nearly everything,' she said.

'Yeah,' I said. 'I know. I'll probably be famous one day.'

We couldn't think of anything else to play outside, so we went back to Linda's house. When her mammy had finished huffing and puffing about me being there for tea she gave us soup with bread and margarine. I ate the soup while it was still too hot, and it burnt the inside of my mouth to sandpaper. I didn't talk much. I had Steven's mammy's grey face in front of my eyes and it wouldn't go away, even when I shook my head.

I stayed at Linda's until her mammy took her upstairs for a bath. Then I stayed a bit longer, sitting on my own in the lounge. I looked at the pictures on the mantelpiece, the ones of Christmas and holidays and Linda's first Holy Communion. Upstairs, I heard Linda's mammy hissing at Linda's da. I heard 'still here' and 'get her to go' and 'how long's it been' and 'you'd know if you came out of your precious shed once in a blue moon'. Linda's da came down the stairs and into the lounge and said, 'Hiya, our Chrissie. Want me to walk you home?' I didn't want him to walk me so I had to say I would go by myself, though actually what I really wanted was to stay.

I wasn't surprised that the front door of the house was locked. Mam always locked it after she shouted at me. I had to go round the back and climb through the kitchen window, which was broken and never closed properly. It was a squeeze to get through, and as I was squeezing I thought maybe that was why Mam didn't give me much food, because she knew if I got too fat I wouldn't be able to squeeze through the kitchen window when I needed to. It was just her way of looking out for me, really, I thought, as I stood with my feet in the sink. It just showed how much she cared.

*

I went out before school on Monday, when the streets were full of milk-bottle clinks. The milkman saw me and did a little salute, but he didn't put any bottles on our doorstep because we didn't get milk delivered. Mrs Walter did. She lived next door. She kept birds in cages and was so old she had started to grow backwards, shrinking down so she was barely taller than me. The milkman put two bottles of milk on her door-step, got back in his little cart, and drove away. I didn't take a bottle until he was round the corner. Mrs Walter once told me off for screaming too loudly in the back garden, and she was also unnecessarily old. She didn't need that much milk. I took big swigs as I walked, the creamy top clagging in my throat.

When I got to the handstand wall I saw Susan, sitting on the ground with her back against the bricks. Her hair was knotty. I sat down, and she looked at me with her nothing-coloured eyes.

'Why has your hair gone so horrible?' I asked. I pressed the milk bottle against my knee. She looked at the rat's tail of hair hanging over her shoulder.

'Just has,' she said.

'It's really knotty,' I said.

'Yeah,' she said.

'Has your mammy lost the comb?' I asked.

'Don't know,' she said. She had *The Secret Garden* open in her lap, and she looked down at the page, but I didn't think she was really reading. Whenever I had seen Susan recently she had had *The Secret Garden* with her, and it was always open at about the same place. Before Steven had died she had had a different book every week.

'Why aren't you at home?' I asked.

'Why aren't you?' she said. I moved the bottle around my knee to find the coldest bit of glass. Susan looked back at her book, but she never turned any pages. She was wearing a cardigan with sleeves that drooped over her hands, and the sleeves were chewed to strings. As I watched, she took some of the strings in her mouth and chewed them some more. I wasn't sure she knew she was doing it.

'Your mammy came to the playground the other day,' I said.

'I know,' she said.

'How do you know?' I asked.

'Vicky's mammy brought her home. She told my da what happened.'

'Was she crying?'

Susan moved her head forwards and backwards in a strange, robot nod, and took more of her cardigan sleeve into her mouth.

'Does she do anything else except cry?'

'Sleeps.'

'Did she ever do anything except look after Steven when he was alive? Or was being his mammy her only job?'

'*Susan* and Steven,' she said. There was something sharp in her voice, like a razor blade in the middle of a cotton-wool ball. I didn't know what she meant.

'What?'

'*Susan* and Steven. She was *both* of ours mammy. Her job was to look after *both* of us.'

'Whatever.'

'Well, she doesn't do it any more anyway.'

'Do you want some milk?' I asked. She took the bottle and swallowed the rest in noisy gulps. When it was all gone she wiped her mouth with the back of her hand and rolled the bottle into the gutter. I didn't tell her about Mrs Bunty giving you sweets if you took your bottles back to the shop. I was already wishing I hadn't told Donna.

'Do the police still come to your house a lot?' I asked.

'Yeah.'

'What do they do when they come?'

'Ask questions to my mammy and da.'

'What kind of questions?'

'About Steven.'

'Do they not ask questions to you?'

'No.'

'How do you know what they ask, then?'

'Listen through the lounge door.'

'Do they know who killed him yet?'

'No.'

The remembering was warm this time; a tiny fire lit in my belly. 'Do you think they're going to find out?'

'Don't know.'

'I don't think they will.'

She just shrugged. She was like a piece of wet lettuce. No fun at all. I raked my fingernails along the insides of my arms and brought away a cloud of white dust, and I thought about the tub of cream that sat on the shelf in the corner of the medical room at school. When my eczema bled at school Miss White sent me to the medical room and Mrs Bradley smeared cream on my arms in a layer so thick I could write my name in it. Sometimes I scratched myself raw under the desk when Miss White wasn't looking, just so I could go and sit in medical with my arms wrapped in creamy white sleeves. While Susan pretended to read *The Secret Garden* I dragged my nails over my skin in a sandpaper scritch-scratch. I imagined jumping into a whole bathtub full of cream, cool on my blistered creases.

'What's the time?' I asked.

'Don't know,' said Susan without looking at her watch.

'Give it,' I said, and pulled her wrist towards me.

'Doesn't work. It's stopped,' she said.

'You should get your mammy to take you to Woolworths. They put batteries in watches. She could probably get a new comb too,' I said.

She moved her head forwards and backwards in the same robot nod, and as she nodded she started to cry. She didn't make any noise. The tears just came out of her eyeballs. She let them run down her face and fall off her chin. I had never seen anyone cry that way before. I watched and watched. It was such an odd way to cry.

'That's a really boring book, isn't it?' I said, pointing to *The Secret Garden*. She sniffed and dragged her sleeve across her face.

'Have you read it?' she asked.

'Miss White reads us some if we finish our worksheets early. I hate it. It's really boring,' I said.

'I like it,' she said. 'It's got a nice garden in.'

'It's got loads of miserable people in too. You're never going to stop being miserable if you read books like that. You should read a joke book. That would make you laugh.'

'Not allowed,' she said.

'You are,' I said. 'You can read anything you want. If it's not rude. And joke books aren't rude. They've got one in the library at school.'

'I mean I'm not allowed to laugh,' she said.

'Why?' I asked.

'Because my little brother died,' she said.

'Oh,' I said. I watched her wipe some more tears off her cheeks and some snot off her lip with her sleeve. 'You really talk about having a dead brother a lot, you know,' I said.

Being with Susan was the same amount of fun as being with a mouldy cauliflower, and I knew I had to go and be somewhere else before I got bored to death. I thought I might go round to Donna's and pretend I had just fallen over in the street outside, because then her mammy might give me a plaster and some breakfast. Donna was definitely my worst enemy, but at her house there was always lots of food and lots of lectric. I reckoned if I picked the top off one of the sugary scabs on my knee I could get quite a lot of blood out, and her mammy couldn't tell me to go away if I had blood all over me. I'd do that just as I arrived at their door.

'Bye, then,' I said.

'Bye,' said Susan.

When I got to Donna's her mammy let me sit on the couch with Donna and her brothers and watch the cartoons on the telly. She gave me a wet cloth to press on my knee and a bowl of Frosties to eat. The flakes swam in thick, cream-globbed milk, and when I ate them I felt my belly burble, 'Please, please, not *more* milk.' I ignored it. I ate until the bowl was empty: chewed and swallowed and clanked my teeth on the cold spoon.

JULIA

The café at the train station was called Choo-Choo's. I could see that before it had been called Choo-Choo's it had been called Chew-Chew's – the spikes of the Ws showed through the new paint. I wasn't sure I would have bothered to change from the first ridiculous name to the second. When I bought Molly's hot chocolate and package of three custard creams I noticed 'Happy Birthday' bunting strung across the counter, and I asked the old woman at the till whose birthday it was. I was surprised to be asking. I couldn't remember the last time I had talked to a stranger. The old woman looked surprised to be asked.

'No one's,' she said.

'Why does it say it on that?' I asked.

'Oh, that's been up since last summer,' she said. 'It was the café's birthday. We'd been open ten years. Then we never got round to taking it down. And every day's someone's birthday, isn't it?'

I counted out the money with my hands in my bag. I didn't want her to see my purse, bulging with everything

I owned. She gave me my change and gestured to Molly, sitting at a table by the window.

'Your little one's been in the wars, eh?' she said. 'How did that happen?'

I looked round and saw that Molly had wriggled out of her coat. She had her cast on the table and was stroking the drawings. I picked up the biscuits and the polystyrene cup.

'Just did,' I said.

When Molly had drunk her hot chocolate and eaten two and a half custard creams, and I had checked the street outside for police and eaten half a custard cream, we looked through the case of secondhand books in the corner of the café. I missed books like this, with tea-coloured pages softened to the texture of petals. When Molly was younger I had given her a pound to spend at the charity shop each Saturday, and while she had inspected ornaments and board games I had slid paperbacks off the shelves, put them to my nose, and breathed almonds and dust. One week I had seen Steven's face, smooth and snub-nosed, beaming out from a front cover. *My Brother Steven: An Angel Taken by the Devil.* Susan's book, the one that had thrust me back into the spotlight just as I had been uncoiling in the dark, started the hunt that had finished in Molly and me running to the police car under bedsheets. It had ended my life as Lucy, and I thought perhaps that was what Susan had wanted – to take a part of me like I had taken a part of her. We stopped going to charity shops after that, because the thought of stumbling across the book again was too frightening. I missed the warmth, the smell of damp carpets, and Molly missed the battered trinkets she had treated as treasures. She asked why we couldn't go any more, and I wanted to say, 'Don't ask me. Ask Chrissie. She's the one who worms in and takes things from you. She's the one who's famous. It's all her fault.' I told her it was because we were too busy.

I was looking at a vegetarian cookery book when an other-mother and two other-kids came into the café. The boy and girl sat at a table and wriggled out of their puffer jackets while the woman bought them drinks and bacon rolls. She was older than me, a proper grown-up. When she had settled the kids with their breakfast she took a hardback book from her handbag and opened it to a marked page. I watched them while pretending not to watch them.

'Now, where were we . . . ? Ah, yes. We'd just had the chapter about the dragon, hadn't we? Do you remember?'

The girl nodded and moved her chair so she could lean into the woman's side. Every so often she pointed to a picture, and the woman angled the book to show the boy. I saw Molly peer round the edge of the bookshelf so she could see the pictures too.

Look at her, reading to her kids. Look at the way her daughter leans against her. You haven't brought anything to keep Molly entertained. Your body isn't a pillow to Molly. You have too many sharp corners, hard edges. Minus one point. Minus two points. Minus three.

'Molly,' I said, louder than I meant to. The girl looked round, eyed us, and snuggled back into the other-mother. 'Do you want to choose a book?'

'From here?'

'Yes. Choose one with pictures. And chapters. A long one.'

'Why?'

'I want to read it to you.'

She gave the other-mother and other-kids a long look, stepped towards me, and lowered her voice. 'Why are you copying?' she asked. Heat spread across my cheeks.

'Get your coat,' I said. 'We'll miss the train.'

Molly spent the first hour of the train ride sulking, and I spent it trying to hold myself together. I listed what I saw around me and went to the toilet to run cold water on my wrists and concentrated on my breathing so hard I felt I wasn't a person at all any more, just a long-limbed iron lung.

Ten o'clock came when we had been on the train for an hour and a half, and a restless thrum set up in my head. My time with Molly didn't stretch into the distance like a spool of ribbon any more; it had a hard end, the ground swoop-ing up to meet our de-wheeled carriage. Miles away, in the Children's Services building, Sasha would be walking into reception. She would be looking around. She would be waiting for me. In half an hour she might realise I wasn't coming, and in an hour she might call the police. The beat in my ears was a countdown.

Molly breathed a cloud onto the window and drew a sad face in it. 'That's how I felt when you said I couldn't get a book. Even though first you said I could get one. By the way.'

'Thanks for letting me know,' I said.

'Where are we going?' she asked.

'To where I used to live,' I said.

She tipped her head to one side. 'The school?'

'No,' I said. 'Not there. That place doesn't exist any more. It's gone.'

I had lost Haverleigh in fast slashes. The first came the Christmas I was eighteen. I was lying under the tree in the lounge, slitting my eyes until the lights blended into a rainbow. *The Wizard of Oz* was playing on the telly. When it finished I sat up and saw Mr Hayworth standing in the doorway. He flapped his hand for me to come. Coloured lights still danced in front of my eyes. He took me into the meeting room, where I sat at the big oval table and listened to the grown-ups explain what was going to happen to me.

'We're all confident this is the right decision – to let you out, I mean,' said the warden. 'We're all completely sure of that. But we can't guarantee that others will feel the same. Some people believe children who commit crimes should be kept in custody just as long as adults, and those people won't be pleased that you've been let out. If your identity wasn't changed, there would be a lot of people who would make it their mission to find out where you were living, and . . .'

'We'd be sending you off to be killed, love,' said Matron.

'So I have to pretend I'm not me?' I said.

'It's a new identity,' said the warden. 'We'll give you all the documents you need for claiming benefits, applying for jobs. All of it. We'll help you find somewhere to live, get you set up with a probation officer you can check in with regularly. And then – yes. Effectively, you'll be living as a new person. Fresh start.'

'But when people say the new name I won't know they're talking to me,' I said. 'I won't turn around. I'll think they mean someone else.'

'It'll take a bit of getting used to,' he said, 'but I think you might be surprised by how quickly it starts to feel normal.'

'When am I going?' I asked.

'Wednesday,' said Mr Hayworth.

'What if I wanted to be here for Christmas?' I asked.

'Wednesday,' he said.

'What if I wanted to stay Chrissie?' I asked. No one answered. They started shuffling papers and standing up, and I stayed hunched over in my chair, feeling like a person-shaped secret.

When Molly was born my body was with her, feeding and changing and putting down and picking up, but my mind was wandering Haverleigh's rooms. Remembering Haverleigh warmed the space Molly had left in my belly when she had moved out. I held on to it like the key to an escape hatch, told myself that if things got bad, really bad, we could turn up on the doorstep and ask the keepers to take us in. 'I can work,' I imagined myself saying. 'I can do anything. Cooking. Cleaning. Molly can go to the school here, and you can look after her, but I can still see her.' It would be best for both of us, I thought: the keepers would look after her the way she ought to be looked after, and I would still get to sit by her bed at night. 'We only need one room,' I imagined myself saying. 'We're used to sharing.'

When Molly was a few months old, I sat in Jan's office at the police station and listened to her say, 'The secure centre's closing. The one you were at. Haverleigh.' I felt the words hit my gut, the whomp and wheeze as my lungs flattened and refilled.

'I'm sorry,' she said. 'It was a good place for you, wasn't it? You felt safe there.'

'Not that good of a place,' I said.

Stay with us, Chrissie. What can you see?

Desk. Carpet. Cabinet. Police file.

'I don't think you wanted to leave,' said Jan.

'*They* didn't want me to leave,' I said. 'They made me a cake with pink icing on it and the icing spelled out "Goodbye Chrissie", and when I cut it they all sang "For She's a Jolly Good Fellow" and everyone cheered. And when we were driving away in the car you could still hear them from all the way inside. They were all still cheering and shouting good-bye, and some of them were crying.'

'That's quite a send-off,' she said.

'I'm not lying,' I said.

'I didn't say you were,' she said. 'It sounds as though you did well there. It must be tough to know it's going.'

'I really don't care,' I said. 'Can I go now? I need to get to the shops.'

When she let me go I wheeled Molly into the lift, through the foyer, out onto the pavement. She was starting to arch her back and rub her fists across her face. I tried not to think of baby Steven, squirming in his pram in the playground, but the door was open to the fragments I usually kept locked away. Steven toddling in the street. Susan's face, pale behind her window. The smell of the Haverleigh corridors – play dough and polish and damp winter coats – the way I had breathed in grateful lungs of it whenever we had got back from a trip out.

The day I had left Haverleigh we had eaten sausages and potatoes for dinner, and afterwards the cook had brought out a Swiss roll cake cut into thick chunks. It was the sort you got at a corner shop: sponge that tasted drily of cocoa, grains of sugar on the outside. She put it in the middle of the table and said, 'Right, everyone, now this is Chrissie's cake so she's to be the first to choose a slice. Got it?' Everyone groaned and watched me, hawk-eyed, as I slid a piece onto my plate. I didn't check it was the biggest piece. It tasted like leather.

After dinner I took my suitcase out onto the drive, and Mr Hayworth lifted it into the car. He put one of his big hands on my shoulder. 'See you, kid,' he said. The others were having a snowball fight in the garden. They didn't stop to say good-bye.

The air outside the train station was different to the air by the sea – denser, dirtier – and muggy enough that the atmosphere felt paused in the moment before a thunderclap. Everything was grey. We were used to the grey of the waves, of the clouds above them and the stones beside them, but our grey was a hundred different shades and shapes, changing with every swipe of the wind. The grey outside the station was the colour of dead things and never-alive things.

It was noon. By now, Sasha would have worked out that I wasn't just late. She would have called the shop and heard I wasn't at work, called the school and heard Molly wasn't sitting on the carpet listening to Miss King tell her she was the best in the class. The police would be looking for us. An itch began at the back of my jaw and spread to my teeth, my gums, my lips. My tongue was suddenly slick and swollen, like a slug or a slice of uncooked fish. I bent and retched under a Pay and Display machine. It made my eyes stream. When I straightened I saw pinpricks of light dancing in arcs, and I felt light and fragile, as if I had become old on the train, the insides of my bones wasted to honeycomb. Molly stood with her back against the wall, watching.

'Are you ill?' she asked.

'No,' I said.

'Are you train sick?' she asked.

'No,' I said.

'Me either,' she said. 'I'm hungry.'

There was a café on the high street, the kind full of sticky plastic tables and lonely old men. I steered Molly inside and ordered a full English breakfast. The plate that arrived was heaving, with grease collected around the sausages and over the phlegmy yolks of the eggs. She tackled it with quiet determination. As soon as she finished eating, I paid the boy behind the counter and bundled her into her coat. I knew I should make the most of this time, when she was content and we were together, but I wanted it all to be over.

As our bus wound its way towards the streets, the names of the stops played a singsong lilt in my head. Donna and Linda had learnt the bus route one summer, and they had sung it to the tune of 'Ring a Ring o' Roses' – *Morley Park and Morley Shops, Conway Road and Hepton Street, CLOVEdale Way, COPley Close and Sel-ton Green.* When the church came into view my mouth filled with thin, penny-tasting saliva, and I pressed the bell on the pole. I pushed Molly through the folding doors and spat at the base of the angel statue.

'You shouldn't spit there,' she said. 'That's an angel. And that's a church. This is a Godish place. You can't spit in Godish places.'

'I don't believe in God,' I said.

'Miss King does,' she said.

'I'm not Miss King,' I said.

'I know,' she sighed. She walked past me, up the path that cut through the graveyard, and threw herself onto the bench at the end. I followed slowly. I couldn't tell whether the cold on my insides was freezing cold or boiling cold, the kind of cold that made your fingers fall off or the kind you didn't realise was heat until you saw the blisters bubbling. I only knew it was hurting cold. Splints of pain jolted up my legs as I went to the bench, and I felt a long way away from the ground, as if I were on stilts, as if my feet weren't really touching the path. There were clusters of daisies growing in the grass. When I sat down I picked two, threaded them together, and held them out to Molly. She looked away. I dropped them onto the ground and crushed them with my toe.

'You know who lives here?' I said. 'Not in the church. But in this place. Around here.'

'Who?'

'My mam. Your grandma.'

'You never told me that before.'

'Do you want to meet her?'

She bent down, picked two daisies, and tried to thread them together. She made the split in the stalk too big, and when she realised she couldn't repair it she started shredding them. I watched her tear the petals from the yellow centres and scatter them across her lap.

'Does she live where you used to live?' she asked.

'No,' I said. 'Not any more.'

Mam had had to move out of the house when I had gone to Haverleigh. People had started spray-painting the walls and pelting the windows with rotten food when I was arrested, and during the trial it had got worse. One night somebody put a petrol bomb through the letter box. She told me about it when she came to visit, all glinting eyes and look-what-you-have-done. I didn't know whether anyone had bought the house since then. It was hard to imagine anyone wanting to. The papers had called it the Satan Pit, and though the estate agents probably hadn't, they couldn't change what people knew. Reputation cloaked it in sticky filth.

When Mam came to Haverleigh for the last time, she passed me the first in a procession of slips of white paper.

'That's my address,' she said. 'And my phone number. Just in case. You ought to have them.'

I folded the scrap in half and put it in my pocket. 'I don't think I'll need it,' I said.

'No,' she said. 'I didn't think you would. Didn't really want to give it to you. But the people here said I should.'

It was the same game we had been playing for eighteen years: seeing how much we could push away while still holding on with our fingernails.

'Coming out, then,' she said. 'Coming to live in the real world. Like the rest of us.'

'Mmm,' I said.

'Well, bloody cheer up,' she said. 'It's what you wanted. It's freedom.'

'Mmm,' I said.

On the first night of the first new life, I lay on my bed with my hands between my legs, listening for sounds that weren't there. There were no footsteps on the floor outside, no rattle of keys as doors were locked and unlocked. No one shouting. No one crying. No keepers keeping me safe. I was used to nights filled with clinks and clanks, screams and sobs, so I couldn't understand why the flat seemed too noisy for me to sleep. It was deafening: the hum of the fridge in the kitchen, the purr of the cars in the street outside. I felt as though I had been living in a house for a decade and someone had suddenly taken all the walls away. Cold air and danger whistled around me. I stretched my eyes wide open and said Mam's address and phone number over and over in my head, like a lullaby, like a string between who I was and who I had been. The words blurred to nonsense and new ones rose up in their place. *Why is everything so big? Why is everything so loud? What do I do now?* I tried counting, breathing, listing the things I saw around me. In the end I went to the bathroom and sat on the toilet with my head in my hands. That made me feel better. There was a lock on the bathroom door. At Haverleigh everyone had known me and there had been nothing to hide. My insides cramped as I thought of the cage of high fences within which I had walked without stooping, stood without hunching, because freedom wasn't the same as feeling free.

Molly threw her daisy heads onto the grass and brushed the petals off her hands. 'Is there a telly at Grandma's house?' she asked.

'Expect so,' I said.

'OK, then,' she said. 'Let's go there.'

CHRISSIE

Steven had been dead for so long, I had lost count of all the days, but the number of policemen in the streets was getting bigger, not smaller. I had started sitting on the flat roof of the church hall, which you could get to by sneaking up the fire escape at the back of the building. The policemen always parked their cars outside the church hall, and they came back to their cars to talk and drink flasks of tea, and when I was sitting on the roof I could see and hear them but they couldn't see or hear me. That was how I felt all the time, really: like a ghost.

I was sitting on the roof one afternoon when I saw my da come round the corner and up the street with a big grey bag slung over his shoulder. Mam had told me I wasn't to call him Da, told me if anyone asked he was my uncle Jim, her brother who sometimes stayed with us.

'But he's not my uncle,' I had said.

'No. But if they think you've not got a da then I get money for looking after you by myself,' she had said.

'But you don't look after me,' I had said.

'Fuck off, Chrissie,' she had said.

When I saw him coming up the street I climbed down the fire escape, ran onto the pavement, and shouted, 'Da!' He turned, and for a second he looked confused, almost like he didn't know who I was, but then he remembered I was me, remembered how much he loved me, and he smiled. He would have done a bigger smile if he could have. Sometimes when you smile too big it hurts your cheeks, so he just smiled in a little way, just so it didn't hurt him. If it hadn't been for the cheek thing he would have smiled big enough to break his face in half, because he loved me big enough to burst. He held out his arms. He looked very different to how Mam looked when she held out her arms to me, which she sometimes did if there were people watching and she needed to make them think she liked me. Her hands stuck out in front like scissor points, and she stiffened herself like someone reaching into fire. Da's arms were soft, his hands strong in my armpits, and he lifted me up so easily I felt made of feathers. I pressed my face into his neck, where the skin was cold and damp. I wanted to sink my teeth in.

When he put me down he pushed the hair away from my face and held my chin in his hand. He was so tall his head was halfway to the sky. 'What you doing all the way out here?' he asked, because the church hall was right on the edge of the streets. I wrapped my arms around his middle so I didn't have to answer. He unhooked my hands and we walked side by side with our fingers knotted together.

'Did you get alive again?' I asked. That was one of the special things about my da: he died and came alive again. The first time it happened I was in Miss Ingham's class. Da had been living with us for a while, doing normal da things like picking me up from school. He didn't wait in the playground at the end of the day like the mammies, and he wasn't always there, but sometimes when Miss Ingham let us out of the classroom he was walking past the railings and I saw him and shouted, 'Da! Da!' He pretended to be surprised to see me but that was just his joke. He was really there to pick me up. And even if he didn't pick me up from school, I always saw him in the evening. Almost every evening. He came through the door and flopped onto the couch and I leant against his side. He smelt of sweat and something else, something sweet and bready. If there was lectric we watched telly, but if there wasn't we just sat together. I didn't really care about telly when Da was there. When he went to sleep I lifted his arm and put it around me. He would have put his arm round me himself if he hadn't been so tired. I was just helping him.

One day I came back from school and he wasn't there. I sat on my windowsill looking down at the pavement and every time I saw a man at the top of the street my chest did a little jump, but none of them were Da. It got dark and my eyes got heavy and he didn't come. The streetlights came on and lit the ground in yellowed pools and he didn't come.

My head tipped forward and I jolted awake just before I fell onto the floor. He didn't come.

In the end I got off the windowsill and climbed into bed. I was nearly asleep when I heard the front door slam, but I woke up quickly and went out onto the landing. I knew it was Da. There were heavy Da-footsteps downstairs. I was going to go down and jump into his arms, but then him and Mam started shouting. I lay down flat on my belly and watched through the bannisters, my cheek pressed against the dirty floorboards. Da pulled Mam into the hallway by the front of her top and threw her against the wall like a sack of potatoes, then crashed out of the house. Mam lay very still, looking at where he wasn't, and I lay very still, looking at where she was. She didn't move the whole time I looked. In the end I tiptoed downstairs. I stood in front of her, watching her tears make a puddle on the floor.

'Are you dead?' I whispered. She didn't answer, just sniffed. 'You can't sniff if you're dead, so you must not be dead,' I said, and went back upstairs. I lay on my bed, thinking I would hear her moving around soon, but the house stayed quiet. I tried to go to sleep. I closed my eyes and thought my going-to-sleep thoughts, the imagining ones I saved for bedtime. I imagined winning *New Faces*. I imagined the Queen visiting Class Three and telling Miss Ingham I was the best kid in the class so she had better stop telling me off so much. I imagined Mam and Da coming to pick me up from school together, the way Betty's mammy and da always came to pick her up together, walking down the street with my hands in their hands the way she did. I imagined getting all the right numbers on the lottery and being so rich I could build towers of money notes that stretched from the floor to the ceiling.

When I had thought all my going-to-sleep thoughts and still hadn't gone to sleep, I listened for Mam again. She still wasn't making any noise. I went back downstairs and got a blanket from the cupboard. She had closed her eyes, and she didn't move when I put the blanket over her, so she could have been dead, but I didn't think so. She wasn't the sort to die.

In the morning I checked the couch, but Da wasn't there. Mam was in the kitchen, shuffling around with her head so far down I couldn't see all of her face. On the table there was a glass of yellow-brown stuff that looked like apple juice. I had only ever had apple juice once before, at Betty's birthday party, and I still remembered the taste – syrupy, like melted sweets – so I went to drink it. Mam moved so fast I barely saw her. She snatched the glass.

'Leave it,' she said. I saw her face properly. Half of it was purple-blue and puffy, like the split skin of a rotten plum. I reached up to touch it but she slapped my hand away. 'Go to school,' she said.

'Where's Da?' I asked.

'Not here,' she said.

'When's he coming back?' I asked.

'He's not,' she said.

'Not until when?'

'Not ever.'

I felt a creeping hotness starting in my neck, crawling up to my ears. I touched my face, but it didn't feel hot; it felt like cold clay. So cold it got pins and needles. So cold I had to sit down on the floor.

'Is he dead?' I asked. Mam made a snorting sound at the back of her throat and drank all the apple juice in one gulp.

'Yeah,' she said. 'He's dead.'

All day I had the same words in my ears. *Da is dead, Da is dead, Da is dead.* I didn't cry because I never cried, but at school I was even badder than usual.

'What has got *into* you today, Chrissie Banks?' said Miss Ingham.

'Nothing's got *into* me. Something's got *out* of me,' I said.

'Stop talking nonsense,' she said.

'It's not nonsense,' I said.

'Don't argue, Chrissie,' she said.

'Don't arg *me*, Miss Ingham,' I said.

She went to her desk and took a headache pill.

After school I went out to play with Stacey and Shannon. Shannon said she didn't want to play *Stars in Their Eyes*, so I kicked her in the stomach. Stacey said she was going to tell their mammy, so I kicked her too. Hard. She fell over. I left them in a crying heap. I didn't care if they told on me.

You had to hurt people when they annoyed you, to teach them a lesson. There wouldn't be anyone to teach Mam her lessons now that Da was dead. That was a very serious problem indeed.

Da was dead for lots of weeks, but then I got back from school one day and he was in the kitchen, drinking a can of beer. He waved when I came through the door.

'All right, Chris?' he said.

'Da?' I said.

'How are you doing?'

'You came back.'

'Yep.'

'You came back from being dead.'

He laughed and took a big gulp of beer. 'Yep,' he said. 'That's right.'

'How?' I asked.

He reached into his pocket and took out a marble the size of a gobstopper. 'Here – got you this,' he said. He put it in my hand. There was a tongue of light coming through the kitchen window, and when it licked the marble I saw it had all the colours in the world inside. Threads of pink and blue and yellow and green and bright, sparkly white, all pressing their faces up to the surface. I curled my fingers around it one by one, and squeezed so tight I could feel my bones bending. It was the best thing anyone had ever given me.

Da died a lot more times after that, but I didn't mind as much because I had my marble to remind me it wasn't forever. I squeezed it tight in my fist, or rolled it between my palms, or put it in my mouth so it stretched out the skin of my cheek. I never, ever let anyone else play with it or even touch it. Da always came back alive again in the end, and as soon as he was alive again he always came to find me, before he did anything else. That was how much he loved me. Sometimes when he found me he looked me all the way up and all the way down and rubbed his hand backwards and forwards across his chin. It made the same sound Mam's nails made when she rubbed them on the emery board – *scratch-scratch-scrib-scrub*. He looked around the house – at the empty cupboards in the kitchen and the ripped-down curtains in the lounge – and rubbed, rubbed, rubbed.

'I've just got to get myself sorted, you know, Chris?' he said. 'I've just got to get myself together, and then I'll get you out of here. We'll go somewhere new. Just the two of us. I've just got to get myself sorted.'

'Where will we go?' I asked.

'Wherever you want,' he said.

'Seaside?'

'If you want.'

'What will our house be like?'

I always tried to get him to talk more about what it would be like when he took me away from the streets, but he never wanted to. He just said, 'Yeah, yeah, when I get myself together, as soon as I get myself sorted, Chris.' Then he

153

went to the pub. Usually when he was at the pub Mam came downstairs with her hair brushed and make-up on her face.

'Was your da here?' she asked. 'I thought I heard your da.'

'He was here,' I said. 'He's gone to the pub now.'

When I said that, Mam's face slipped away. The make-up was still there, locked in a pretty mask, but there was no one underneath it. Her mouth went straight and her eyes went unsparkly, like plastic pretending to be glass. Then she went back upstairs.

Anyway, that was how I knew being dead wasn't forever. Not always. People who talked about dying as if it was forever were either lying or stupid, because I knew two people who definitely, *definitely* came back from being dead. One was Da and the other was Jesus.

There weren't many kids playing out as Da and I walked through the streets. I wished there were more, because I wanted everyone to see us together. He stopped to buy me a paper bag of dolly mixtures from the shop, so at least Mrs Bunty got to see us together. I hugged his arm as he paid and looked her straight in the eye, which made her screw her mouth into an ugly little wrinkle. She dropped Da's change into his hand without touching him and said, 'Forty pence back, *sir*,' in a voice that told me she didn't think he was a sir at all, she thought he was just a him.

Inside the Bull's Head the smell was of smoke and beer, and everything was sticky, and solid men sat in corners talking in grizzled voices. Da lifted me onto a stool and bought me a can of cream soda.

'What you been up to, then?' he asked when he had swallowed half his pint and burped over his shoulder.

'Lots of things. Lots of worksheets,' I said. 'Mrs Bunty's not giving us enough sweets for the bottles and Donna bit me. And there's this little boy that's got dead.'

'What?' said Da.

'Mam says I have to call you Uncle Jim,' I said, because I was having a day off from being the one who had killed Steven and I really wasn't in the mood to turn it into a day on. Da snorted and drank the rest of his pint in one gulp. I wondered how much more he would drink, and hoped it wouldn't be so much he started shouting. I had odd ends of memory from the last time he had been alive, and all the odd ends smelt of beer and sounded of shouting. I was just thinking about what other exciting things I could tell him when one of his friends came and clapped a hand on his shoulder, and he turned his back on me to talk to him. They talked for a lot of time and Da drank a lot more beer. I lined my dolly mixtures up in a row on the high strip of table in front of my stool.

After a long time Da wobbled away from his friends, past the tables, and out of the door, and I jumped down to follow him. It was almost like he had forgotten I was there, except obviously he hadn't. I was the whole point of him coming back alive again. When I caught up with him he held on to my arm, and as we walked he kept stumbling and yanking it so hard I thought it was going to come out of its socket. I didn't care. If he had torn my arm away from my body and kept it for himself, I wouldn't have minded. I would have said, 'You can have the rest of me, too. The other arm, and both my legs, and my belly and face and heart. It's all there for you, if you want it.'

Mam wasn't at the house when we got back. We hadn't been there for long when the door knocked and Da told me to go to my room. I climbed the stairs and lay down on my front on the landing. I heard the man at the door say 'Steven' and my stomach whirled. I pushed myself forward as slowly and quietly as I could, until I was lying in the special spot where I could see the person at the door but they couldn't see me, the same as the special spot on the church hall roof. It was easier to understand what people were saying when I could see their mouths. The man on the doorstep was a policeman.

'I was hoping to talk to . . . Christine? Christine Banks. Is that your daughter, Mr Banks?'

'No.'

'Oh.'

'I'm her uncle.'

'Oh, I see. I'm sorry, I—'

'What you want with Chrissie? She's eight.'

'We're speaking to all the kids in the area. It's part of our investigation into the death of Steven Mitchell.'

'Waste of time, speaking to kids.'

'Is Christine at home, Mr Banks? I've just got a few questions for her. It won't take long.'

'No.'

'It's very important that—'

'She's not here.'

'Oh. Where is she?'

'Her mam's taken her away.'

'Taken her away? Is this permanent?'

'Don't know. Could be a week, could be a year. You never know with Chrissie's mam.'

'Oh.'

The policeman took his notebook out of his pocket and wrote something down. I thought it was probably 'Chrissie is not here.'

'Do you know whether Christine was here on the twentieth of March, Mr Banks? Around that time?'

'Don't know. I was inside.'

'Oh.'

'I shouldn't think she was. Chrissie and her mam don't spend much time here. Was it a school holiday?'

'No, but it was a weekend. A Saturday.'

'Won't have been here, then. They'll have been with her sister.'

'Is that your other sister?'

'Her mam's other sister. She's my brother's kid.'

'I see. Could I take the name of your sister-in-law?'

157

A very noisy car went down the street just then, so I didn't hear what Da said. I thought it could have been 'Alison' or 'Abigail' or 'Annabel' or 'Angela'. One of those names.

'And where does she live?' asked the policeman.

'Don't know. Never asked.'

'Is it local?'

'Don't think so. Think it's on the coast. By the sea somewhere.'

'And you think Christine was staying with her aunt on the twentieth of March?'

'Don't think nothing. But she could have been.'

'Right. I see. Well, thanks for your help. I'll come back another day. Try to catch her.'

The policeman went down the garden path and out of the gate. Da stuck his middle finger up as soon as his back was turned. By the time I got downstairs, he was already outside, leaning against the garden wall. Smoke bloomed around him in a cloud.

'Why did you tell that policeman I wasn't here?' I asked, hoisting myself onto the wall next to him.

'They're pigs, they are, Chris. The lot of them. Fucking pigs. It's all our fucking jobs to keep them from getting what they want.'

'Did you mean you were inside heaven?' I asked.

'Eh?'

'When they asked if I was here when Steven died. You said you were inside. Did you mean inside heaven?'

He cleared his throat and spat onto the ground. His spit was made of tiny white bubbles. 'Yep,' he said. 'That's what I meant. Did you know that little lad what died, then?'

'Yeah. He lived on Marner Street,' I said.

'Did you play with him?'

'Sometimes.'

I felt see-through then, like anyone could look past my clothes and skin and see my heart ticking and my lungs puffing. The policeman had turned my day off to a day on, and remembering was a narrow blade slid into my neck. I was sure Da could see I had killed Steven, and I wondered whether that was why he had told the policeman those lies. A part of me hoped he did know, hoped he'd told the lies to stop the policeman finding me out. You have to care about things to want to keep them safe.

'Sick old world, eh?' said Da, and blew out a thin grey stream.

'Yeah,' I said. 'Sick old world.'

CHRISSIE

In the Easter holidays time lost its size and shape. Da stayed for a couple of weeks. He sat at the bar in the Bull's Head most days, came back most evenings to shout at Mam and sleep. The shouting kept me awake. I heard it through the walls and floor – not the words, just an underwater burble of grown-up hate. It usually finished with a slam, of Mam or the door. Once, after the slam, there were creaks on the stairs and she slid into bed behind me. I pretended to be asleep, but she started crying, so I had to turn around and wipe her tears away. I licked them off my fingers. In the morning she was gone and my pillow was dry. My mouth still tasted thinly of salt.

The holidays finished and I went back to school, which meant school dinners as well as worksheets, so it was good as well as bad. Nothing very interesting happened at school, and I wouldn't have known that time was even passing at all if the classroom hadn't got hotter and the milk hadn't got lumpier. The police didn't come back. I still saw them in the streets sometimes, and Linda said one day they had knocked on her door to speak to her. She said they had asked the same questions they'd asked at school, about whether she ever played with Steven and whether she had been playing with him the day he died. I wished Da hadn't made them think I didn't live in the streets any more. I really wanted to talk to them again. I decided that if they did come and talk to me, I would tell them I saw Steven going towards the alleys with Donna the day he died. That would get her back properly for biting my arm.

Linda's birthday came on a Sunday, which was bad luck because it meant she had to go to church in the morning. I went round to her house after church and gave her a *Beano* comic as a present. It was actually her *Beano* comic that I had taken from her room when I had been there on Thursday, hidden between my vest and jersey. I'd finishing reading it, so I didn't need it any more. When she opened it she frowned.

'Haven't I already got this one?' she said.

'No,' I said. 'Don't be stupid.'

'Oh,' she said. 'Sorry. Thank you.'

After tea we sat in the lounge with all her new toys and I asked her if her mammy and da had fights when she was in bed at night.

'Don't know,' she said. She was trying to get her new doll out of its plastic box, but it was held inside with wire twists.

'But do they, though?' I asked.

'Yeah. Maybe sometimes,' she said. She tried to bite through the wire. I could hear it scrape her teeth.

'What kind of things do they fight about?' I asked.

'Just me and Pete,' she said.

'How?' I asked.

'Mammy gets cross with Da for spending so much time in the shed and not picking me up from school. And they fight about my reading. Because Da says don't worry about it and Mammy says do worry. And sometimes they fight about Pete's wonky foot. That kind of stuff.'

'Oh,' I said.

'Do yours?' she asked.

'Sometimes,' I said.

'What about?'

'Just about me,' I said. 'Like about which one of them gets to pick me up from school. They really both want to do it. So they fight.'

'But no one ever picks you up from school,' she said.

'Sometimes you're so stupid it makes me think I'm dying,' I said.

'Oh. Sorry,' she said.

Linda's mammy brought in her birthday cake on a china plate, and her da came in with Pete on his hip, and we all sang 'Happy Birthday'. I watched the candles until I had yellow flickers in my eyes when I blinked. Me and Linda took our cake into the garden and sat on the bricks by the shed.

'What did you wish for?' I asked.

'Can't tell you,' she said.

'It still comes true if you only tell one person,' I said.

'Are you sure?' she asked. I wasn't sure, but I did want to know, so I nodded.

'I wished for another brother or sister,' she said. She licked some icing off her finger.

'Why would you wish for that?' I asked. 'They cry all the time. And they smell.'

'Pete doesn't smell,' she said. 'I like babies. Pete's big now. I want a new baby.'

I was glad Linda had told me her birthday wish, because that meant it wouldn't come true, and it was a silly waste of a wish. I didn't know why anyone would want even one brother or sister, let alone two. As soon as you had a brother or sister your mammy and da could only care about you half as much, because the other half had to be for the baby. If Mam had another kid the bit of care she had left for me would be so small you'd have to have a magnifying glass to see it. Luckily she really hated kids, so it was really not likely she would ever try to get another one.

'If you could only have one out of Pete or me, who would you have?' I asked Linda.

She frowned. 'Pete's my brother.'

'You can only have one.'

'Pete, then.'

I didn't think she had properly understood the question. That was another thing that unfortunately happened a lot with Linda: she didn't understand perfectly easy questions.

'I mean if you could only have one of us. Me or Pete. You could have me, and I'd still be your best friend and the best at almost everything, or you could have Pete, who's just a stupid old baby who can't do handstands or walk on walls or stop people being mean to you at school.'

'I said. Pete.'

'But I'm your best friend.'

'He's my brother.'

Something cold slithered down inside me, like winter water running down the inside of a drainpipe. I quite wanted to go home, but I knew if I left there was no chance I would get another piece of birthday cake. It wasn't a risk worth taking. Sunday meant no school, and that meant no school dinner.

'I think you should probably try to love Pete a bit less,' I said.

'Why?' asked Linda.

'Make it easier for you when he's not here any more,' I said.

'Why's he not going to be here any more?' she asked.

'Might get lost or dead.'

'That won't happen. We take too much care of him.'

'Yeah. Exactly. You do. Going to make it really sad for you when he dies.'

'What'll you wish for on your birthday?' she asked, scratching a bug bite on her leg.

'Mine's not for ages,' I said. I wiped my finger around my plate to pick up the last cake crumbs. If my birthday had been right then, right that second, I would have wished that Linda would give me the rest of her piece of cake.

'But what'll you wish for when it is?' she asked.

'Don't know,' I said, poking my toe through the hole where the sole was coming away from the top of my shoe. 'Probably just to be able to fly or have an ice cream van. Something like that.'

'Yeah,' she said. 'Those are good wishes.'

It wasn't true. I would wish Mam and Da fought about me when I was in bed at night.

A few weeks after Linda's birthday it was half term, and she went to the seaside to visit her nana. The day she came back I sat on her doorstep from very early in the morning, and when I saw her car coming down the road I stood up and waved. She opened the car door, shouted, 'Chrissie!' and ran up the path to stand next to me. She smelt different to usual, less like laundry and more like an old woman's house, but that did make sense, because her nana was an old woman and she had been staying in her house. I didn't mind the different smell. It had felt funny her being away, like a bit of me had been missing. Not a big bit. Just like a finger or thumb. I had still missed it.

'Chrissie,' said Linda's mammy, coming up the path. 'Would have been nice to have had a bit of time to unpack and get settled before we had any visitors.' She unlocked the door and carried Pete inside.

'Too bad I'm already here, then,' I said, following her.

When me and Linda had had a biscuit and some squash, we went upstairs and lay on her bedroom floor with her sea glass collection spread all around us. Whenever Linda went to her nana's she came home with clatters of fresh sea glass, and we sorted it by colour into jars under her bed. I always snuck some for myself while we were sorting, as much as I could stuff in my pockets without making clinking sounds when I walked. I didn't have much of a place to put sea glass that day, because it was stickily hot and I was wearing a summer dress that flared in a circle when I spun but that didn't have any pockets. I preferred wearing clothes with pockets because then I could keep Da's marble with me, and I liked to have Da's marble with me all the time, but sometimes it was just too hot for pockets. I put some sea glass into my underpants when Linda went to the toilet. Cool against my secret skin.

We had just finished filling up the green jar when Linda's mammy came in. Her face was red and sweaty and the front of her dress was covered in flour. I thought she had probably been making scones. She was always making scones.

'Oh. Chrissie,' she said when she saw me on the floor. 'You're still here.'

'Yes. I am,' I said. Linda sat up and looked like she'd been doing something bad, but I stayed flat on my belly. My dress had ridden all the way up my back, but I didn't pull it down. Linda's mammy looked at my bare legs and greying underpants with the elastic worn out, and her face went slicker and redder and crosser. I would have stayed on the floor and let her boil until she exploded, but I thought she might be able to see the sea glass outlined on top of my bottom, so I sat up. I sat with my legs spread wide. She looked away.

'Linda, can you take Pete out?' she asked. 'I'm getting a headache.'

'Yeah,' said Linda, and started putting her shoes on. I smiled her mammy a syrupy smile.

'I'll help with Pete too,' I said. She put her fingers to her forehead, as if I had made her headache a lot worse, and went back downstairs.

'She hates me,' I said to Linda.

'Yeah,' she said. 'I know.'

'Why?' I asked, though I knew it was because of the grey hair thing.

'She doesn't like your mammy,' said Linda. My face felt splashed with hot water. I only had one shoe on, and I used that foot to kick her leg, leaving a red mark in the shape of my heel. She yelped and her eyes glassed with tears. I was glad.

'She doesn't even know Mam,' I said. 'She shouldn't be talking about her. No one should.'

'All right, all right,' said Linda. She went back to her laces, breathing hard out of one side of her mouth. 'That's not even the only reason my mammy doesn't like you,' she said. 'There's another thing too.'

'What?' I asked, getting ready to kick her again.

'You gave me nits,' she said.

I didn't kick. I smiled. 'Yeah,' I said. 'I did.'

I liked remembering about the nits. They had lived in my hair when I was seven, biting and sucking and making me itch so much I wanted to peel the skin off my head, itching even worse than my eczema. I scratched until my nails were catching on big, oozy scabs, and they were still there, black speckles I had to dust off my pillow every morning. One playtime Linda was getting on my nerves, so I clamped my hands on either side of her eyes, pulled her head against mine, and rubbed. She kicked my legs and tried to twist her face to bite my wrists but I held tight. By the next day she was scratching. By the end of the week she was off school, sitting in a cold tub while her mammy pulled a comb through her hair and gagged when dead nit bodies fell into the water. That never happened to me. Mam cut my hair off instead.

Linda was crouched over her shoe, breathing like she had just run up the hill that went to the alleys. The bows she was tying in her laces were so big and floppy that by the time one was finished the other had worked itself free again.

I walked forward on my knees. 'I'll do it,' I said. I tied them in my special knots, the ones that never came undone, no matter how much you ran around. I usually ended up doing Linda's laces for her, just like I usually ended up saying her lines in assembly and doing her worksheet if she got stuck. I finished the knots and patted her foot.

'There you go,' I said. 'They'll never come undone.'

'You're so clever, Chrissie,' she said.

'I know,' I said.

As soon as we got outside a soupy wave of heat glopped over us, sticking my dress to my back with sweat. It was the sort of day where, if we had been at school, the milk would have been sour and cheesy by playtime. Lots of mammies were sitting outside their houses with their skirts hoicked up to their thighs, and some of them had babies with them, bare except for nappies and dribble. Pete was wearing a sun hat that used to be Linda's. He looked like a fat mushroom. I thought it was ridiculous, but I knew some grown-ups might think it was sweet, so we took him to the shop in case Mrs Bunty was one of those grown-ups. Turned out she wasn't. When I lifted Pete up she said, 'Nope. I know your tricks, Chrissie. They won't wash today.'

'I haven't got any tricks,' I said. (Wasn't true. I was champion of tricks.) 'We're looking after Pete. His mammy's got a headache. He wants some licorice allsorts.'

'Likely story. Off with you now,' she said.

Pete started to grizzle as Linda carried him out of the shop, and I gave Mrs Bunty a glare that said, 'See what you have done. Everybody is sad now and it is all your fault.' She didn't look nearly as guilty as she should have looked.

'Shoo, Chrissie,' she said. 'And don't try swiping anything today. I'm watching you, and so's him up there.'

I put my hands over my ears. 'I *wish* people would stop going *on* and *on* about boring old *God*,' I shouted, and ran out of the shop.

The day felt very long with nothing to do and no sweets to eat. We went to the playground because we couldn't think of anything better. Donna and Betty were there, doing clapping games under the tree.

'Where's that little girl you had that time?' I asked Donna.

'Ruthie?'

'Yeah.'

'Her mammy doesn't like her playing out a lot,' she said. 'She thinks it's not safe.'

I wished Ruthie was there. I remembered slapping her arm. I'd enjoyed that. Linda joined in the clapping games but I didn't because clapping games were for babies. I climbed the tree instead, crouched in the branches, and looked across at the alleys. I could just see the edge of the blue house, and looking at it made my belly fizz. I hung down from a high branch by my hands.

'Look! Look at me!' I shouted. Donna barely even stopped clapping.

'Anyone can do that,' she said. 'You're not special.'

'Well I *know* something special, lamp girl,' I said. My arms were starting to come loose in their sockets but I didn't drop down.

'What?' asked Betty.

'I know who killed Steven,' I said. I didn't need to remember; it was already there, at the front of my brain. Saying it felt like a delicious firework that would never stop exploding.

'Oh, shut up, Chrissie,' said Donna. 'Stop showing off. Steven died ages ago. No one even cares any more.'

My fingers slipped and I fell. Donna laughed. Rage ballooned inside me, a sharp lasso. I kicked her in the back, and Betty squawked and slapped my ankle. I kicked her too. They both cried, so I called them crybabies, and Linda fussed over them so I called her a sick-brain. The crying was very boring to watch. When it had been going on for maybe seven hours I told Linda to come and have a hanging-upside-down-on-the-swing-poles competition with me.

'No,' she said. 'I've got to look after Pete.'

'Betty?' I asked.

'No,' she said. 'My back hurts.'

'Lamp girl?' I asked.

'No,' said Donna. 'I don't like you. And that's not my name.'

'WHY DOES NOBODY LIKE ME?' I roared. Nobody said what they were supposed to say – that they did like me really – so I sat under the tree in a cross heap, pulling up handfuls of grass.

'People do too still care who killed Steven,' I said when everyone had stopped snivelling.

'Who did, then?' asked Betty. Donna elbowed her to show that that wasn't the right thing to have said at all.

'Not telling,' I said. I wasn't going to waste it on them.

'See,' said Donna. 'You don't know.'

'I do too know,' I said. 'But I'm not telling. Linda, come on. Let's go somewhere else.'

She had rolled onto her back and put her legs in the air, and she was helping Pete balance on the soles of her feet. He squealed and gripped her hands.

'I want to stay here,' she said.

'Well I don't,' I said.

'You go if you want to,' she said. 'I'm staying. Pete's having fun. I'm staying with him.'

The ticking got louder. Each tick sounded like a door slamming. I looked at Pete's chubby arms and legs, his head tipped towards Linda's chest.

'You look so stupid, Linda,' I said. 'Everyone can see your underpants.' She put Pete down and pulled at her dress. 'Let's play hide-and-seek,' I said.

Pete clapped his hands. 'Hidey seek! Hidey seek!'

Ticking. Louder. Fizzing. Thrumming.

'Come on,' I said. 'Linda, you can count.'

She looked surprised, because usually when we played hide-and-seek I was the first one to count, and then sometimes I was the second and third and fourth and only one to count if that was what I wanted.

'OK,' she said. 'Pete, come on, you be on my team.'

'No,' I said. I took his wrist. 'He's on my team.'

He whined and reached for Linda, but I bent down next to him. 'If you come with me I'll give you jelly babies,' I said in his ear. He stopped whining and clapped his hands. I didn't have any jelly babies. He didn't know that.

'Are you sure you want to go with Chrissie?' Linda asked him.

He nodded. 'Hidey seek!' he chirruped.

'You can't make him hide anywhere dangerous,' she said.

'I know,' I said.

'All right,' she said. 'Shall I do thirty or forty?'

'A hundred,' I said.

'What? We never do a hundred. That's too long.'

'No it's not. We'll be able to get into better hiding places if you do a hundred. Go on. Just do it.'

She looked at Donna and Betty, but Betty was busy trying to repair one of her daisy chains and Donna was busy looking like a lamp and a potato at the same time. She turned towards the tree.

'One . . . two . . . three . . .'

Donna and Betty ran off together, into the bushes at the back of the playground. I pulled Pete in the other direction. Towards the gate. Out of the playground. Up the street and round the corner. The ticking in my ears was so loud I was sure the rest of the world must be able to hear it. Pete was already having to trot to keep up, but I needed him to go faster. Once we turned the corner we couldn't see the playground any more, and I couldn't hear Linda at the tree. I tried to keep count in my head, giving each tick a number. I thought she must be on about thirty. I had seventy more ticks until she started looking.

By the end of Copley Street, Pete's wonky foot was dragging on the ground. I could see the alleys, but we weren't close enough. If Linda started looking now she would find us before we got there. Pete pulled his wrist out of my hand and stopped in the middle of the pavement.

'Come on,' I said. 'Walk.'

'Babies?' he said, reaching up.

'You can have one when we get there,' I said. I pointed to the blue house. 'There, see? That's where we need to get to. That's the hiding place.' I lifted him up and walked a few steps with him on my hip, but he was heavy and kept slipping down.

'Come *on. Walk*,' I said again when he landed on the ground for the third time. He shook his head, and his chin dimpled, and he put his fists over his eyes.

'Linda,' he said.

'She's coming,' I said. 'She's going to meet us there. Come on.'

We were nearly at the end of the street. All that was left between us and the blue house was the stretch of scrubby land leading up to the alleys, but as we passed the church hall a policeman got out of his car and stood in the middle of the pavement, blocking our way.

'Everything all right?' he asked, in a voice that meant, 'Everything is clearly not all right.'

'Yes,' I said. 'We're fine.'

'Where are you off to?' he asked. I had to think very quickly. We were right at the end of the road, and the only places the road led to were the alleys and church.

'Church,' I said.

'You're on the wrong side of the road,' he said.

'I know,' I said. 'We were just going to cross. You disturbed us.'

'Funny time for church,' he said. 'Not Sunday.'

'Our mammy's there,' I said. 'She's helping the vicar get ready for Sunday school. She told us to come when we finished playing in the playground.'

He nodded the way people nod when they are wondering whether to believe you. 'You weren't thinking of going up there, by any chance?' he said, pointing to the alleys.

'No,' I said. 'We're not allowed. It's not safe.'

'That's right,' he said. 'Not safe at all.'

'No. Not at all,' I said. My belly clenched, and I wondered whether we could still get to the blue house before Linda finished counting. I wouldn't need long. It didn't take long. The policeman bent down to look at Pete. He had stopped crying and was staring.

'You all right, son?' he said. 'What the tears for, eh?'

'That's my brother,' I said. 'He always cries. And he smells.'

The policeman laughed. 'Your brother, is he? What did you say your name was?'

'Linda,' I said. 'Linda Moore. This is Pete.'

He looked from me to Pete and pushed out his lips in a kissing shape. 'You don't look much the same, do you?'

I stepped towards him and cupped my hands around my mouth. He bent down slowly, so my hands could make a tunnel between us.

'He's not my real brother,' I whispered. 'My mammy and da adopted him. That's why they love me more than him. But he's not supposed to know.'

I stepped back and the policeman straightened. He nodded in a 'Your secret is safe with me' sort of way, and smiled at Pete.

'All right, kids,' he said. 'Well, I'll take you across to your mammy now. Make sure you get there safe and sound.'

'What's the time, sir?' I asked. I didn't like having to call him sir, because I didn't like him, but I thought it would help. He looked at his wristwatch.

'Just gone quarter past twelve,' he said.

'Mammy won't be at church any more,' I said.

'Oh?' he said. 'Thought you said that's where you were heading.'

'Yes. We were. But you've held us up,' I said. 'She said if we didn't finish in the playground before twelve we should go home. I just didn't know the time. She'll have our dinner waiting. We'd better hurry.'

I began to pull Pete back down the street, but the policeman took my shoulder. 'Where is it you live?' he asked.

'Selton Street,' I said. 'Number a hundred and fifty-six. Right at the end.'

I could see him thinking about how long the streets were, and how if he came with us it would be uphill all the way back to his car. He was quite a tubby policeman. 'All right,' he said. 'Well, you go straight home now. But best not to be playing round here. Especially with a little one.'

'Yes,' I said. 'I'll tell Mammy. Good-bye.'

I took Pete's arm and we walked back towards the playground.

'Baby?' he said, holding out his hand.

'I haven't got any,' I said.

We could hear Linda crying before we turned the corner. She was standing next to the roundabout with her hands over her eyes, looking the same as Pete had looked when he had cried in the street. Donna and Betty were running through the bushes, calling, 'Pete! Pete!' When we got to the gate Betty saw us, shouted, 'Linda, there!' and Linda took her hands away from her face. She didn't move. She looked like she was going to be sick. Pete pushed open the gate and ran towards her, and she picked him up and started crying all over again. Only someone really thick would do that. Thick to cry when you were pleased about something.

Donna thumped me on the arm. 'Where did you take him?' she asked. 'Linda was so worried she nearly died.'

'You don't die from being worried,' I said.

'Well you do because Linda just nearly did,' she said. 'Where did you go?'

'To find a good hiding place,' I said.

'But you went out of the playground,' said Betty. 'That's against the rules.'

'No it's not,' I said. 'I'm in charge of rules. I never made that a rule.'

'You're in charge of *everything*,' said Donna.

'Yes. Obviously,' I said.

Linda had slithered down onto the ground with her face buried in Pete's shoulder. She was sniffing and gulping and saying, 'Pete, Pete, Pete.' She didn't once look up to make sure I was safe too. She didn't once say, 'Chrissie, Chrissie, Chrissie.' I went over and stood right in front of her, and I was about to give her a little kick, just to remind her I was there, when she said, 'Why – did – you – take – him?' Her voice sounded like that, like each word was a different sentence, because the crying meant she only had enough breath to say one word at a time. She sounded so stupid.

'We were doing hide-and-seek,' I said. 'I was taking him to hide.'

'But – you – took – him – out – of – the—'

'We were just going to find a really good hiding place. That's why I told you to count to a hundred. So we could find really good places.'

'But – we're – not – meant – to – go – out – of – the – play – ground – in – hide – and—'

'You didn't even want him any more,' I said. She looked up at me properly then, and she stopped making the silly gulping sounds. Pete wriggled off her lap and toddled to the roundabout. Betty went to push him but Donna stayed watching us because she was nosy.

'What?' said Linda.

'You said. On your birthday. You said.'

'Said what?'

'You wanted another baby. You said Pete was big and you didn't want him any more.'

'I never said I didn't want him.'

'You said you wanted a new baby. That's the same as not wanting the old one.'

'No it's not. It's not even nearly the same,' said Donna.

'Shut your mouth, potato face,' I said.

'I love Pete. He's my brother,' said Linda. 'You know you shouldn't have taken him.'

'I can do whatever I want,' I said. 'I'm the bad seed.'

'You're what?' said Linda.

'I'm fed up of this,' I said. I went out of the playground, clanged the gate shut behind me, and walked down the street. I knew Linda and Donna were watching me. I didn't feel special. I felt like I was getting a rash.

I wandered around the streets being cross for a long time. I didn't want to go back to the house because I was still pretending to be lost forever, to teach Mam a lesson, but I didn't have anywhere else to go because no one liked me any more. When it started to go dark I went to the hand-stand wall. I didn't see Susan until I was nearly on top of her. She had a scrubby square of muslin wrapped around her hand, which she was stroking against her face. Her hair was cut to her chin.

'What happened to your hair?' I asked.

'Cut it off,' she said.

'Did the hairdresser?' I asked.

'No,' she said. 'Me.'

'You never,' I said.

'I did,' she said.

'Did you have nits?' I asked. She shook her head. 'Why did you, then?' I asked. She shrugged. The ends of her hair came all at different places, wonky and uneven. I thought of her snipping it away with kitchen scissors. I didn't under-stand. She must have known it was the best thing about her.

'Did you get in loads of trouble?' I asked.

'Who from?'

'Your mammy.'

'She didn't really notice.'

'But she's always fussing with your hair.'

'Always used to.'

'What did you do with it?' I asked. I was wondering if I could have it.

'Just chucked it away,' she said.

I kicked the wall next to her back. 'Stupid waste,' I said.

'Don't really care,' she said. She flattened out the muslin and held it to her cheek with her palm.

'What's that?' I asked, sitting down next to her.

'Steven's.' She took a corner in her mouth and sucked. Up close I could see it was the kind of grey that white things go when they've been dropped and sucked and cried on a lot, the washed-out grey of grimy water.

'It's gross,' I said.

'No it's not,' she said. 'I like it. Smells nice.'

The air was cooler now the sun had gone in. The sweat that had stuck my dress to my back had dried, making my skin tight and itchy, as if I was crusted in a layer of salt. I scratched myself against the wall.

'Do you miss him?' I asked.

'I miss my mammy.'

'Has she died too?'

'Nah. She's just in bed all the time.'

'Still?'

'Yeah.'

'Oh. Well, she'll probably get up soon. It's been ages.'

'I did ask her. I asked her when she was going to go back to normal. She just rolled over. And then I said I was fed

up of her crying all the time and being in bed all the time
and not being a proper mammy any more. She told me to
go away.'

'Bit mean.'

'She's quite mean now.'

'Maybe she deserved for Steven to get dead.'

'Don't really think so.'

The dark had come quickly, like a black glove clamped
over our heads. I couldn't see much of Susan or the muslin
any more, even though I was sitting close to both of them.
I only knew she was still there because I could still hear
her sucking. I had a hard feeling in my belly, like my guts
weren't guts at all any more, just one big lump of cold,
rough stone. Since I had killed Steven I had had lots of
time to think about doing it again, and most of the time I
felt like I wanted to do it lots and lots more. I wanted the
fizzing in my hands and the ticking in my head, the feeling
of being a little piece of God. Listening to Susan sniffing
and sucking, I didn't want to do it so much any more. Not
so many more times. Maybe just three times, or two times,
or even one time more might be enough. If I did it one more
time everything would probably be better. I'd probably feel
good enough if I just did it one more time.

'Why are you always out?' Susan asked.

'Because I want to be,' I said.

'Does your mammy not make you go home?'

'No.'

'Does she not care?'

'Do you sometimes think your mammy must have loved Steven more than you?' I said. 'Because that's what I would think. I would think, "She's so sad all the time now, and she's still got me, she just hasn't got Steven. So she must have only loved Steven, not me at all." Don't you think that if she loved you a bit more she wouldn't be so sad all the time? Don't you think?'

I said it all in a rush, like throwing up. The words tasted like throw-up too – sour and pink.

Susan stood. 'I'm going home,' she said. 'Mammy will want me back.'

'She won't,' I said. 'She doesn't care. She only cares about Steven. He's the only one she wants back.'

I thought she would turn around and yell at me, or at least run off crying, but she just walked away.

'She doesn't care about you,' I shouted. I didn't know if she heard me or not.

When I had been walking to the alleys with Pete my fizzing had rumbled and roared, but now it was gone and I couldn't get it back. I thought of what Donna had said. *Steven died ages ago. No one even cares any more.* I thought of Linda holding Pete's little body with both her arms, as if I wasn't even there. I moved my bottom away from the wall, wrapped my dress around my legs, and lay down on my side. The night felt loose and vast around me. My spine rubbed against the bricks. I closed my eyes.

'Mam will probably come looking for me soon,' I thought. 'I'll probably hear her going up and down all the streets and calling for me. Probably any minute now. Probably.'

JULIA

When we came out of the graveyard I turned towards town. I knew Mam lived in a block of flats, and there weren't any flats in the streets, just matchbox houses. I couldn't risk telling Molly I didn't know exactly where we were going. I was already on thin ice.

'Does Grandma live in a house or a flat?' she asked.

'Flat.'

'Like ours?'

'It's not above a shop. I think it's in a block. It'll be a tall building. It's called Parkhill. Keep an eye out.'

'I thought you knew where it was.'

'I do. But just keep an eye out anyway.'

We started up the steep bit of hill that branched at the end, to town in one direction and the alleys in the other.

'Is she nice?' Molly asked.

'Mam?'

'Grandma.'

'I haven't seen her for a long time.'

'Was she nice when you did see her?'

I thought of Mam, sitting in the Haverleigh visiting room. She had liked me better as a killer. None of the psychologists or psychiatrists or psychotherapists had told me that. I had worked it out for myself. Before I was a killer, I was good and she was bad, because I was her kid and she should have liked me but she didn't. When I killed, the balance shifted. I was a kid no one should like, and she was the person who'd known it all along. I made her into a psychic, and she repaid me by visiting in messy gluts. Sometimes she was at Haverleigh every day, sitting in the foyer on the dot of six o'clock visiting hour. She would keep it up for a week or two, then I wouldn't see her for months. In another phase she arrived each day at six forty-five and made a scene when they asked her to leave after fifteen minutes. Sometimes she only visited on weekdays, sometimes only on Saturdays, sometimes only when it was sunny.

When she was there, she spent most of our time together telling me all the things that were wrong in her life. The new flat had damp in the bathroom. Her throat hurt. She had an ulcer on her lip. A neighbour had spray-painted a pitchfork on her garden wall. If I did or said something she didn't like she stormed out, shouting, 'I'm never coming to visit you again,' and stayed away for so long I believed her. But it was never forever. She always came back. We were bonded by something thicker than water, thicker than blood: a tar-dark soup of hate-want-need.

'*Was* she nice?' Molly asked.

'She was just like other people,' I said. 'Nice sometimes and not-nice other times.'

'Will she be nice to me?' she asked.

'I expect so,' I said. 'And if she's not we'll leave.'

At the top of the hill I learnt two things: that they had made the land that used to be the alleys into the Parkhill development, and that Mam was living on the land that used to be the alleys. Walking onto the estate, I could almost forget that the same path used to take me to the blue house. The flats were split into two tower blocks, and the ground between them had been made into a basketball court. Three skinny boys were riding bikes around the edge, demonstrably not at school. They looked at us with hooded, wary eyes.

The lift was out of order, and when I opened the door to the stairwell the smell of dirt and pee was like a plastic bag clamped over my head. Molly pressed her fingers to her nose.

'Ewwww,' she said. 'It stinks.'

'Breathe through your mouth,' I said.

'I don't want to go in there. It really smells,' she said.

'I know. But we have to,' I said.

'Why can't we go in the lift?' she asked.

'It's broken.'

'Isn't there another lift?'

'No, that's the only one. Come on.'

'Can't we go and see if there's another lift?'

'There won't be. And even if there was one it would probably smell just as bad as this.'

'But I don't want to—'

'*Molly!*'

It wasn't a loud shout, but I was standing in the stairwell, surrounded by hard surfaces. A hundred half-formed echoes of Molly's name came back to meet us. I walked past her, all the way up to the sixth floor, without stopping to catch my breath. By the time I reached the balcony I was dizzy. Molly was still only halfway up the steps, taking the time to ensure each stomp conveyed sufficient rage.

'Come on,' I said, holding open the door at the top. 'Hurry up.' I felt my voice fit the words like a foot slipped into a second-day sock, and wondered how many times I had said them before. 'Hurry up, we'll be late for school', 'Hurry up, it's nearly bedtime', 'Hurry up, this is taking too long'. It seemed suddenly, explosively cruel that I had spent so much time rushing Molly away.

'It's number sixty-six,' I said as she emerged from the stairwell. She looked at the numbers on the doors beside us.

'That'll be further down,' she said.

'I know,' I said. I sounded petty, as if I was becoming younger as I drew closer to Mam.

Molly ran ahead, counting off the numbers aloud: 'Sixty-two, sixty-three, sixty-four, sixty-five – this one, it's this one, sixty-six. Can I knock?'

'Wait,' I said. I knelt down in front of her, licked my thumb, and rubbed away the food marks around her mouth. A porthole in my middle had opened, and thinking of Mam on the other side of the wall made it stretch.

'Can I *knock*?' Molly asked again, spinning around on one toe.

'Go on, then,' I said.

She thumped on the door and we waited for five breaths. I counted. There was no answer, and she looked up at me.

'Try again,' I said. She knocked harder, eight loud raps. We waited again. No one came. It hadn't occurred to me that Mam might not be there. I had no plan for what we would do if she didn't answer, and the thought of her absence was liquid lead poured into the cups of my lungs. Molly raised her fist to knock again, but I put a hand on her shoulder.

'Wait,' I said. We heard footsteps inside, the click of the door being unlocked, and a slow swish as it opened. The lead in my lungs set hard.

Mam had clearly been asleep. She was wearing a dressing gown and her face was puffy. When she had visited me at Haverleigh her hair had been dyed yellow, but badly, so the roots had splayed out from her parting in dark fingers. Now the colour was grown out, and she was as much grey as black. There was no powder caking her face. I could see the freckles and pock marks. She seemed to have aged more than five years in the time since I had last seen her, but that made sense – I sometimes felt I was twenty years older than I had been when Molly was born. I couldn't tell if that was what Mam was thinking as she looked at me. I couldn't tell if she knew who I was.

'Oh,' she said.

'Hello,' I said.

'It's you.'

'Yes.'

'Huh.' She looked at Molly, her mouth screwed like the grey star at the bottom of an apple. 'She's got a broken arm.'

'Wrist.' My mouth was horribly dry. Speaking felt like chewing on dead leaves. 'It took us a long time to get here. Can we come in?'

Her eyes were still on Molly. She sucked her teeth. 'Jesus. She's just like you,' she said.

Something in me flared. I put my arm around Molly's shoulders, and she scrabbled at my hand. It was a long time since the skin on our hands had touched. She was warmer than I remembered.

'Are we coming in?' I asked.

Mam stepped to the side and gestured into the hallway. 'Not giving me much choice, are you?' she said.

The flat was clean, but it had a strange smell: yeasty, like a fold of unwashed skin. It reminded me of when Molly had

had tonsillitis and her throat had been webbed with yellow-white strings – the sweet-sour smell of infection. The couch and coffee table in the lounge had the look of objects sinking into the sea, because the blue carpet was inches thick. It was so thick that walking on it felt like treading on sponge. Mam was in front, but when we got into the room she trotted behind us and raked over the dents our feet had left with her heel. She tried to smooth over her own steps too, but she kept making more. I wondered how long she spent doing this when she was by herself: walking in circles, trying to hide her own trail.

Next to the telly cabinet was a mantelpiece crowded with frames. Up close, I saw that most of them weren't filled with photos, but pictures cut out from magazines. There was a strong baby-animal theme: kittens and puppies and next to them a small painting of Jesus. I imagined Mam sitting at the coffee table, cutting around the pictures, sliding the crinkling squares into the frames. There was only one proper photo in the row – a black-and-white print of a woman and baby. I picked it up.

'Is this you and me?' I asked.

'No,' she said.

'Who is it?'

'Me and my mam.'

I checked for frames tucked at the back. 'Why don't you have any of me?'

'Just don't.'

'But why not?'

'I just don't.'

I looked along the row of animals and Jesus. If we had been alone in the room I would have swiped my hand across the mantelpiece and swept the pictures to the floor. I couldn't do it with Molly there. It would frighten her. She already seemed frightened, looking from me to Mam, her hand holding tight to the pocket of my jacket.

'Why does it smell so bad in here?' I asked.

'It's damp,' said Mam. 'They're all damp. All the flats on this level. We're trying to get them to do something about it.'

'It's disgusting.'

'It's not that bad.'

'The furniture's probably mouldy.'

I could feel myself goading, trying to make her lash out and fit into the space I had carved for her. She seemed too heavy to rise to it.

'Don't know what you want to do,' she said. She picked up a cereal bowl from the arm of the couch. 'There's some magazines there. There's telly. I'll go and wash this up.'

She left before I could ask why she was presenting her lounge like a waiting room. The magazines she had gestured to were on the shelf of the coffee table. Most of them seemed to be about horses. I flicked through the telly channels until I found a high-pitched kids' programme. Before I let Molly sit down on the couch I spread my jacket across the seat. I didn't particularly want to do it, but I wanted Mam to see that I had done it.

'I need you to stay here,' I said.

'Where will you be?' Molly asked.

'Just in the kitchen. I'm just going to talk to Grandma.'

'She's cross.'

'Yeah. Don't come in. Shout if you need me. OK?'

'Yeah.'

She had put her good hand under her cast, and was cradling it to her front.

'Is your wrist OK?' I asked.

'Yeah,' she said. She looked down at the plaster and rubbed her finger across an illegible message. 'That's what Rosie wrote. It says "Get Well Soon, Molly".'

'That was a stupid thing to write. You are well.'

'My wrist's not well.'

'Don't come into the kitchen, OK? If you need me, call. I'll hear you.'

'OK.'

I put my hand on her parting, over the bright white line. I thought of Mam doing it: her palm on my head, the whispered prayer. 'Father, protect me. God, keep me safe.' It was what she had said before she had tried to have me adopted, and again whenever she had tried to get rid of me after that. I hadn't taken much notice of the words. They were prayer words, Jesus words, thrown in a corner with the vicar's droning and Mrs Bunty's nagging. I thought about them as Molly's scalp heated my hand. Mam had asked God to protect her. She could have asked him to protect me, or both of us, in the same number of words. She never had.

CHRISSIE

The police came back to my door the next day. They rang the bell early in the morning, when I was still in my nightie. I had got back late the night before, because I had spent so long lying by the handstand wall waiting for Mam to come and find me. She hadn't come, but she had wedged the front door open so I wouldn't have to climb through the kitchen window, which was actually almost better, if you thought about it.

The policeman was the same one who had spoken to Da, but this time he had a friend with him, a shorter one with shinier shoes. My belly danced when I opened the door and saw their silver buttons. I felt like I had been standing in the middle of a dark stage and someone had just turned on the spotlight. They asked whether Mam was home and I told them she was asleep upstairs, which might have been true or not true. They asked if I could wake her and I said I couldn't because she was sick, which was definitely not true. The taller policeman sighed and started to leave. I wanted them to stay. I wanted the same sherbet feeling I had had in the library corner. My days were hanging long and loose, and I had nothing better to do.

'You're looking for who killed Steven, aren't you?' I said, leaning against the doorframe. The taller policeman turned back around. 'I saw him,' I said. 'The day he died. I just remembered. I saw him with Donna. They were going towards the alleys.'

The policemen looked at each other and the shorter one got out his notebook, flicked through, and showed the taller one something written on a page. I thought it might be the notes PC Woods had made when they had talked to me at school, but then I remembered that those notes had gone in the bin. These policemen didn't know anyone had ever spoken to me before. People kept forgetting me. It wasn't good enough.

'Donna Nevison?' the tall one asked.

'Yes. She's in my class,' I said. 'She lives on Conway Road. She's got a green front door.'

'Where did you see them?' he asked.

'Walking up Steven's road,' I said. 'They were near the end. Where it goes to the alleys.'

'You're sure it was her?' he asked.

'I think it was. It was a girl with yellow hair.' I thought if I said that, they might go after Betty when they found out it wasn't Donna, because she had yellow hair too and I didn't much like her either. I wondered whether they might find out that it really *was* Donna who had killed Steven, and whether they would take her straight to prison, and then I remembered. This time it was a balloon end, pulled taut and then punctured, so the air hissed out in a sigh. For the first time ever I sort of wished it was Donna who had killed him and not me at all. It was getting harder and harder to have days off from it; whenever I tried, the remembering snuck across me, like drizzle or a shadow. It was really tiring without days off.

The policemen were looking at each other and seemed to be speaking with their eyes. I didn't know what they were saying. The tall one went down the path and out of the gate, but the short one stayed on the front step, tucking his notebook into his inside pocket.

'Do you go to stay with your aunt a lot, Christine?' he asked.

'Yes,' I said.

'Where does she live?' he asked.

'Don't know,' I said.

'Is it close?'

'No,' I said. 'It's by the sea somewhere.'

'Do you sometimes miss school when you're staying with her?' he asked.

'Yes,' I said.

'Were you at school when some of our officers visited?' he asked.

'What's officers?' I asked. I sort of knew the answer, but I wanted to keep him there for as long as possible.

He smiled. 'Officers are policemen. Like us,' he said.

'Oh,' I said. 'No. I don't think I was there.'

He nodded and went down the path. As he got to the gate a third policeman came round the corner, shaking his head and tapping his hand with his notebook. I remembered him from school – PC Woods. The tall policeman asked the short policeman something, and the short policeman said, 'No, she wasn't there at the school visits. Must have been with the aunt.' PC Woods looked at me and said, 'Yes she was. We spoke to her.' Then they all looked at me. I was surprised they couldn't hear me fizzing from all the way down the path.

When they had muttered for a bit the tall policeman and PC Woods came back up the path. 'So, Christine, PC Woods thinks—' the tall one started to say.

'Oh yeah,' I said. 'I was there. I remember now. I just got confused before. That's all.'

'You were a bit confused when you spoke to us at school, weren't you?' said PC Woods. 'I seem to remember you thought you'd seen Steven the day . . . on that day, but then it turned out to have been a different day? A Sunday? Sunday of the week before? Something like that?'

'Yeah. But I realised actually it was that day. The day he got killed.'

'The Saturday?'

'Yeah. I saw him on Saturday. In the morning.'

'With his father?' said PC Woods.

'His father?' said the tall one.

'No. Not his da. It was actually a girl. I got it wrong. It was Donna.'

The policemen did a lot of talking with their eyes but I couldn't get what they were saying. Eventually PC Woods took out his notebook, scribbled something on the page, and showed it to the tall one. I leant forward to see but he snapped it shut. I hoped it said, 'Let's stop all this talking with our eyes and talk out loud so Chrissie can hear us.'

'Christine,' said the tall one in a stern voice. 'You do understand, don't you, that this is serious. It's not a game. We're working hard to find out what happened to Steven. We need to find out what happened to him because we want to keep you and all the other kids in the streets safe. We can't do that if anyone's telling lies. Do you understand that?'

'I am safe,' I said. He looked like that wasn't what he'd expected me to say.

'Well, we'll make sure you're all safe,' he said.

'I *am* safe,' I said again. 'And I'm *not* telling lies.'

'Right. Good. Well, Christine, I think we're going to come back and have another word with you when your mammy's better,' he said.

'Better from what?' I asked.

'I thought you said she was ill,' he said.

'Oh,' I said. 'Yeah. She is *very* ill. She's actually probably dead by now.'

'What?' said PC Woods.

'Has something happened to your mammy, Christine?'
asked the tall one.

'Well. No. Obviously. She's just got gout,' I said. I didn't
know exactly what gout was, but I knew it was a very bad
illness because it was what Mrs Bunty's husband had and
she never stopped talking about how bad it was, except for
when she talked about the war or God.

'Are you going to speak to Donna?' I asked.

'We'll speak to everyone we need to speak to,' said PC
Woods. 'Don't you worry yourself.'

I sighed loud enough to be sure they would definitely
hear it, because I was getting sick of people thinking I was
worrying myself when myself had actually never been less
worried. '*You* should worry yourselves,' I said. '*You* should
worry yourselves about *Donna*.'

'All right, Christine,' said PC Woods, and he went back
down the path to where the short one was waiting by the
gate. The two of them started to walk away, but the tall one
stayed on the doorstep. He had his notebook in his hand and
was flipping through the pages. I tried again to see what
was written in it, but he hugged it close to his chest. I wasn't
surprised. I had learnt lots of things since Steven had died,
and one of them was that what policemen loved more than
anything else in the whole world was notebooks.

'Just one more thing, Christine,' he said. 'This aunt you go and stay with. What's her name?'

My tongue grew a bit bigger in my mouth. The tall policeman was watching me, and I tried and tried to remember the name I had heard Da say when the police had asked him about the made-up aunt.

'Um. Abigail,' I said. He looked back down at his notebook, but in a way that made me think he was looking because he wanted me to see him looking, not because he needed to read what was written on the page.

'Hmm,' he said. 'Funny that. Your da seemed to think it was Angela.'

'Oh. Yeah. That's right. Angela,' I said. 'It's Angela. Auntie Angela. I just got—'

'Confused?'

'Yeah. I got confused.'

He snapped his notebook shut and put it back in his pocket.

'All right, Christine,' he said. 'See you soon.' Before he went to join the other policemen on the street he said something in eye-talk that even I could hear. He said, 'I'm watching you.'

Talking to the policemen left me twitchy, and when they were out of sight I put on some clothes and went to call for Linda. We walked to the shop and I made her distract Mrs Bunty by asking her to take down the jar of rosy

apples, then the jar of jelly beans, then the jar of raspberry bonbons, each time saying, 'No, no, I didn't mean
that one, I meant *that* one'. When I had taken the bag
of toffees and tucked it up my dress I made Linda say,
'Actually I don't want any sweets today. It's too compli-
cated to choose.'

'Bye, Mrs Bunty,' I said, waving as I pulled open the
door. 'Thanks for the sweets.' She looked confused, then
cross enough to explode. We ran out of the shop, round the
corner, up the hill, towards the alleys.

The blue house had the same mouldy smell it had had the
last time we were there, with Donna and William, and the
downstairs rooms were still carpeted with broken window
glass. It sounded like tiny bones breaking under my feet.
When we got to the upstairs room we both looked at the
patch of floor under the hole in the roof, which was bubbled
with damp. Rain had soaked into the wood and sun had
heated up the rain and the boards had turned mushy as wet
paper. I went towards it slowly, feeling my steps go from
stamp to scud, wood to mush. When I got to the place where
the floor was darkest, Linda said, 'Be careful. You might
fall through.' I ignored her. I pushed a toe into the middle
of the patch, lifted away a layer of wood, and watched egg-
backed woodlice seethe onto my shoe. When I shook them
off they scattered, wiggling to the corners of the room, but
one got stuck in a dip in the floor. I hooked it out with my
heel, trod down and rubbed back and forth. When I took

my foot away there was no more woodlouse, just a silvery smear.

I had a pencil in my pocket, and while Linda ate the toffees I used it to scribble on the white-painted walls. Scribbling on walls was one of my favourite things to do, because it was never, ever allowed and it always, always made someone cross. I wasn't sure who would get cross with me for scribbling on the walls of the blue house, but I knew someone would, in the end. I started out with lines, then pictures, then words. I wrote them as big as I could, swooping my arm like an eagle wing. I wrote until the pencil was completely flat at the end, then stood back and looked at the wall. Read the words. Fizzed.

'You shouldn't say that,' said Linda from behind me.

'What?'

'That.' She got up and pointed.

'Why not?'

'It's really rude.'

'That's not rude. *This* one's rude.' I went to the other end of the wall and pointed to a shorter word, scrawled sideways in letters that got bigger as it went on. She tipped her head to see, her plaits falling in straight lines towards the floor.

'Oh yeah. That's really rude,' she said. She couldn't read it.

The fizzing made me feel like a can of paint, like my insides were squeezed into a tight metal case. I knew if someone had pressed down on my head my guts would have sprayed out and coated the walls in words and shapes. I jumped up and down and then I yelled, a bird squawk shaped by a grinning mouth. It bounced around the room and came back as an answer. I was beating with energy, pulsing in places I didn't know I could pulse, hunger and excitement and red-hot fury, lava in my belly, straining against my skin. I ran to the end of the room, pushed myself off the wall with my hands and feet, ran to the other end, pushed myself off, back and forth and forth and back, and every time I got to a wall I thought, 'I can run up this wall, run onto the ceiling, run right round the room with my feet on the walls.' Da's marble banged against my leg through the fabric of my pocket. My breath was coming in gasps and my feet were getting lazy, throbbing from bouncing me off the walls, so I wound to a stop in the middle of the room like a wind-up car all out of wind. My legs quivered and my chest ached and still I seethed in my belly. I pulled up my dress, squatted, and peed. The seething hissed out of me and trickled towards the rotten patch in the middle of the floor. It smelt stale and secret.

When I finished peeing I stood up with my legs apart like a toddler. I hadn't pulled down my underpants. They were soaked. I felt softer. Warmer. Linda's face was whiter than the walls underneath my scribbles. I went out of the room, and she followed without speaking. We crunched through the glass on the downstairs floor and out onto the scrubby patch of earth where Steven had been handed to his mammy. I turned back to look at the upstairs room. I couldn't see my wall writing from outside, but I knew it was there.

I am here, I am here, I am here. You will not forget me.

There was a rumbling noise coming from the streets that got louder as we got closer, the noise of shoes on pavement and voices chanting. At the top of Marner Street we saw them, a crowd of mammies and das and kids, walking with signs held high above their heads. The signs said things like MAKE THE STREETS SAFE AGAIN, SAVE OUR TOWN AND SAVE OUR BAIRNS. They were painted in big letters on bedsheets and folded-out cereal boxes. When the crowd got really close I saw Steven's mammy at the front. She had her arm linked through Betty's mammy's arm and was holding a picture of Steven against her chest. I could tell Betty's mammy was pleased she was the one standing at the front with Steven's mammy. She was crying the sort of tears you only cry because there are people watching and you want them to see you crying. Steven's mammy wasn't crying. She did have shoes on. I wondered whether there was still meat rotting in her kitchen.

The crowd reached the top of the street and me and Linda were swallowed into its middle. They were chanting, 'Find the killer, lock him up, make him pay for Steven's blood.' I joined in. I shouted until my throat hurt. The man beside me gave me his sign, written in big letters on an opened-out cornflakes box, and lifted me onto his shoulders. I held the sign high above my head and screamed into the wind. *Find the killer, lock him up, make him pay for Steven's blood.* My sign said, AN EYE FOR AN EYE AND A TOOTH FOR A TOOTH'.

When we got to Vicky's house everyone went inside. Me and Linda had got to the back of the crowd, and we didn't catch up quick enough to get swept inside with the others. By the time we were at the garden gate the front door had closed. I went up the path to knock it but Linda pulled me back.

'What are you doing?' she asked.

'Knocking,' I said.

'Why?' she asked.

'Because I want to go in,' I said.

'You can't. We haven't been invited.'

'Don't care.'

'You can't go in places you've not been invited.'

'Who says?'

'Mammy.'

I rolled my eyes right back into my head. 'Honestly, Linda,' I said. 'Your mammy's not God, you know.'

I went the rest of the way up the path and knocked the door very loudly. Vicky's mammy opened it with a jug of squash in her hand and a flustery look on her face.

'What is it?' she asked.

'You left us behind,' I said.

'What?' she said.

'We were doing the marching as well. Everyone else came in here but we got left behind. On an accident,' I said.

'I don't think that's really what happened,' she said.

'Well don't worry,' I said. 'We're here now.' I stepped forward so she had to let me past, and Linda scuttled in after me, staring at the floor. Everyone was in the lounge, the mammies on couches and chairs and the kids in a clump by the window. The mammies all looked round when we came in. Donna's mammy said, 'Oh, hello, you two,' and Vicky's mammy said, 'They just turned up,' and Mrs Harold said, 'Nice to see you girls, come on in and get something to eat,' and Vicky's mammy looked like she was going to scream.

It had definitely been a good idea to come in. Vicky's mammy had laid out cakes and sausage rolls and corned beef sandwiches and lemonade on a table in the corner. It was one of the best party teas I had ever seen, like the ones Steven's mammy used to do for Susan's and Steven's birthday parties. I suddenly thought that if Steven's mammy never stopped being sad about Steven she might never do a party tea for Susan ever again. I hadn't thought of that before. It made me feel very cross about everything. I filled my plate so full that Vicky's mammy tapped me on the shoulder and told me off for being greedy, and then me and Linda sat on the floor with the other kids, eating the food and drinking the lemonade. Steven's mammy was sitting on the couch with Vicky's mammy on one side and Donna's mammy on the other. As I watched, Vicky's mammy rubbed her arm and said, 'How are you doing, love? You're being ever so brave.'

'Yes,' said Donna's mammy, putting her tea down so fast the cup nearly tipped over and curling her whole arm around Steven's mammy. 'You poor, poor dear. Such a hard day for you.'

Steven's mammy nodded and said, 'Mmm,' and looked as if she wanted to hit them. I knew how she felt. When bad things happened to you, people always said things like 'Poor you' and 'You're so brave', and it was meant to make you feel better but usually it just made you feel worse, because you didn't want to be brave and poor, you just wanted the bad thing not to be happening. It was like when I was the only one in Class Four who didn't have their mammy or da come to watch the assembly, and Miss White said, 'Mammy and Da not here, Chrissie? Poor old you,' and I kicked her shin so hard she got a hole in her tights. She wanted to stop me being in the assembly after that, but she couldn't because then there would have been no one to say my lines. Or Linda's.

The mammies were just doing their normal gossiping when Steven's mammy made a splutterish crying noise and suddenly everyone was flapping. I leant around Donna to see.

'What's the matter, Mary?' asked Mrs Harold.

'It's not him,' she said.

'What's not?' asked Vicky's mammy.

'It's not him,' she said.

'What do you mean?' asked Donna's mammy.

Steven's mammy lurched forward and pulled a newspaper from the shelf under the coffee table. I stood up on my knees to see, but the stupid mammies were crowded around in a thick clump that blocked my view, so I had to go and stand on the other side of the table and look over. The newspaper had a picture of a little boy on the front, and above him it said, MONTHS AND NO ARREST: BABY STRANGLER STILL AT LARGE. Steven's mammy was batting the page but she had her head twisted away, her chin digging into her shoulder. A vein in her neck stuck out like a purple worm.

'It's not him,' she said.

'Oh God, it's Robert,' said Robert's mammy. She put her hand on her chest and panted. 'That's my Robbie.'

'How the hell did they manage that?' said Vicky's mammy.

'They were in the photo together,' said Robert's mammy. 'It was at the school fete. There. You can see Steven's arm. People said they looked like twins.'

'So they cut it in half and used the wrong boy?' said Donna's mammy.

'Lazy sods,' said Vicky's mammy. 'How long would it have taken them to check?'

'They were probably rushed,' said Mrs Harold.

'That's my Robbie,' said Robert's mammy.

Steven's mammy was making a wheezing noise. She had let go of the paper but her hands were clawed like she was still holding it, and tears were coming down her cheeks in sheets. I went to the tea table, picked up a fairy cake and a napkin, went back to the space in front of the mammies, and held the napkin out to her. The mammies stopped twittering. Steven's mammy looked at me, took the napkin, and pressed it against her face.

'Thank you,' she said.

'That was nice of you, Chrissie,' said Mrs Harold. Everyone seemed quite surprised that I had done something nice. I put the whole fairy cake into my mouth and tried to swallow but it wouldn't go down. Vicky's mammy had to come and slap me on the back. It came unstuck from my throat and I spat it into my hand, mushed up and gluey. I held it out to her.

'I don't really want this any more,' I said.

'Oh, Chrissie,' she said, screwing up her nose. 'That's horrid. Go and throw it in the bin.' She pushed me into the kitchen. I didn't like her calling me horrid. I stepped around the bin and pasted the chewed-up fairy cake sponge into the gap between the fridge and the oven, just to teach her a lesson. I could hear her in the other room, picking up teacups with a *clink-clink* sound.

'Honestly,' I heard her say. 'She wants a good slap, that kid.' I knew she was talking about me, and I went back into the lounge.

'No I don't,' I said.

'Don't what, pet?' asked Mrs Harold.

'I don't want a good slap,' I said.

'Oh,' said Mrs Harold. 'I don't think—'

'That's not something I want at all,' I said.

'I think perhaps—' said Mrs Harold.

'No one wants a slap,' I said.

'Of course you—' said Mrs Harold.

'Slaps aren't good, anyway,' I said.

Steven's mammy stood up in a slow, heaving way, like her body was a mountain of wet sand she was having to mush into a castle. All the other mammies flapped and twittered, and I decided I didn't care enough to carry on nagging about the good slap. I didn't think Vicky's mammy would really slap me, even if she thought that was what I wanted. She was too scared of me. Most people were scared of me, at least a little bit. Just how I liked it.

Someone said Steven's mammy shouldn't go home by herself, and everyone looked at Betty's mammy because she had been making sure everyone knew she was the one looking after Steven's mammy when we were marching. She got flustered, probably because she knew if she took Steven's mammy home she wouldn't be there for the gossip that would start as soon as Steven's mammy was out of the door. I could see her searching for a reason not to go, but she couldn't find one in time, so she left looking fed up. I thought she would probably dump Steven's mammy at her gate and run all the way back.

'Poor lamb,' said Donna's mammy as soon as they were out of the door. 'What a thing to happen.'

'Of everyone, they mixed him up with my Robbie,' said Robert's mammy.

'Makes you mad, doesn't it?' said Vicky's mammy. 'When they catch him, whoever it is that did this, you can bet they'll get *his* picture right. Won't be mixing him up with any other murdering bastard.'

'She's so thin,' said Mrs Harold.

'She is,' said Vicky's mammy. 'I took round a stew but she probably never touched it.'

'Yes,' said Donna's mammy. 'I took round a shepherd's pie and a chicken casserole and a coffee cake and some soup for the freezer.'

'Oh,' said Vicky's mammy. 'Well. That was nice of you.'

'I've not taken any food yet, but Robbie drew a lovely picture for her. I took that,' said Robert's mammy.

'Did you?' said Vicky's mammy.

'Yes,' said Robert's mammy. 'You know, I think it was just what she needed.'

I sort of thought if your kid was dead then a picture drawn by a kid that wasn't dead might not really be what you needed at all. But then I didn't really have any kids, so I didn't really know.

'Awful smell when I was there,' said Mrs Harold. 'Really putrid. I said to her, "Mary, would you let me clean the place?" but she wouldn't. She wouldn't even let me into the kitchen to make a brew.'

'Been speaking to the kids, haven't they?' said Vicky's mammy in a secrety voice. She jerked her head at us in case the other mammies had forgotten what kids were. Vicky and Linda were blowing bubbles in their lemonade and laughing, and I pretended to be doing that too, so the mammies wouldn't know I was listening. 'Came asking for Harry the other day. Harry! "You do know he's five?" I said!'

'And Donna,' said Donna's mammy. 'They came this morning wanting Donna. Seemed to think she must have seen him that morning but wouldn't say why. Sent them away with a bit of a flea in their ear, I did. "We were at my mam's all weekend," I told them. "She couldn't have seen nothing."'

Then the other mammies all had to take turns saying the police had been to speak to their kids too. Bad temper grumbled in my guts. I wished Donna hadn't been at her nana's that weekend. That meant she definitely wouldn't be going to prison.

'Seeing Robbie's little face in that picture . . .' said Robert's mammy. 'That's made me upset enough to die, that has. That's just made me upset enough to be sick. Really.'

'Jennifer,' said Donna's mammy sharply. 'Die *or* be sick. It's very much one or the other.'

'Well, that's all very well for you to say,' said Robert's mammy. 'You've not had the shock I've had. His little face looking out at me . . . It makes you think, doesn't it? The worst thing about this isn't Steven dying. It's not about burying a little boy. It's about burying an era. All those times we let the kids play out and thought they were safe, didn't think a thing like this could happen in the streets. That's what we've really lost. Our innocence. What happened to Steven – that's just the way we lost it.'

She stopped talking just as I had started to think she was going to carry on forever, droning and droning like the vicar on Sundays. The other mammies looked at each other with faces that said, 'What was that all about?' and 'Why did she say all that?' and 'Do you think she's actually gone mad?' and then Vicky's mammy said, 'I think it might be best if you didn't say that sort of thing in front of Mary, Jennifer.'

It started to get dark outside and Vicky's mammy started clearing away the food in the way people clear away food when they have decided it's time for other people to leave their house. Robert's mammy was looking at the paper again. I thought she was probably going to slip it into her handbag, so she could show some other people the picture of Robert-not-Steven and tell them how much it made her want to die and be sick. She seemed quite a lot more interested in the picture of Robert than she did in actual Robert the kid, who was licking one of the plug sockets on the wall.

'Shall we go handstand wall?' I asked Linda when we got outside. It wasn't really properly night yet, and the dark coming down was the summery kind, pale and baggy.

'Can't,' she said. 'It's nearly dark. Mammy will be waiting for me at home.'

I put my finger and thumb around a pouch of skin on her arm and pinched. '"Mammy will be waiting for me,"' I said in a making-fun voice.

She carried on walking, rubbing her arm. 'You're sometimes not a very nice best friend, Chrissie,' she said.

I watched the corners of her mouth drag down in sad little pleats. 'I *am* your best friend, though,' I said. She scrubbed her fist across her eyes and looked like she wasn't very sure. My heart did a little trip. 'You're my best friend,' I said. 'You're always my best friend. And I'm a good best friend, really. Way better than anyone else. I'm always making sure other people aren't mean to you. And no one else wants to be your best friend anyway. So I am still your best friend, aren't I?'

'Yeah,' she said. She sounded a bit tired.

When I got back to the house I called for Da. I had hoped he might be on the couch, drinking beer. He wasn't. I thought he was probably dead again. Missing him was a smoke burn in my middle: a small round hole, black at the edges.

In the bathroom I ran water into the tub. It came out in a hot sputter, brown from the rust inside the taps. Steam rose up and wetted my face, and I peeled off my dress but kept my underpants on. When I climbed in, the heat made my skin sting. I rubbed the sliver of soap across my arms and legs, and the hairs curled like pinworms in milk. I took my underpants off in the water, smeared them with soap, rinsed them and put them over the side of the tub to dry. My hair was getting matted at the ends, so I wetted it and tried to pick apart the worst clumps.

After I had washed my body I sat with my arms wrapped round my legs, pressing my mouth against my knee, harder and harder until I felt my teeth press my lips like plasticine. Just when I thought my teeth were going to come through my lips and clatter my knee bone, I heard a creak on the floorboards outside. I climbed out of the tub and cracked open the bathroom door. Mam was standing on the landing, just outside her bedroom. I opened the door wider, and stood with my feet apart. Her eyes went across the whole of me.

'Where's Da?' I asked.

'Not here,' she said.

'Where is he?'

'Don't know.'

'When's he coming back?'

'Why do you want him?'

I picked up a towel and wrapped it around my shoulders. Sometimes Mam said things just to trick me, just to give her an excuse to shout. I looked at her face to see if that was what she was doing this time. I didn't think so. When she was tricking her lip curled up on one side, making a dark wrinkle at the top of one of her nose holes. She wasn't doing that. Her lips were tight and there was a crease between her eyebrows.

'I just want him,' I said.

'But you've got me,' she said.

That didn't really make any sense. It was like saying I didn't need a toothbrush because I had a twig, or I didn't need a blanket because I had a sheet of tinfoil. The two things weren't the same: the one I wanted was what I needed, and the one I had was much, much worse.

'I don't want you,' I said. 'I want him.'

She swallowed, and the skin between her neck and shoulders went very tight, and for a second I thought she was going to scream.

'Chrissie,' she said. 'That little boy.'

My heartbeat thrummed in my throat. It wasn't ticking. Too fast for ticking. Flap-flap-flap, a moth-wing flutter. My muscles felt like icy poles.

'Yeah,' I said.

'You,' she said. I thought she would carry on – 'You knew him' or 'You played with him' or even 'You killed him' – but she didn't. She just looked at me. Her teeth clenched and something twitched in her jaw, like an insect trapped under the skin. Then she backed into her bedroom and shut the door.

JULIA

Mam was standing by the sink in the kitchen. It was a narrow room, with a small table and two chairs in the space at the end. I opened one of the cupboards above the worktop, expecting empty shelves. Packets of biscuits were stacked as deep as my arm. Three cartons of eggs stood on top of each other.

'So you buy food now,' I said. 'Now that it's just you.'

'Do you want a drink?' she asked. She took a tumbler from a shelf and poured an inch of amber into it.

'I don't drink.'

She drained the glass in one swallow. 'Why not?'

'I've got Molly.'

She frowned as though that wasn't relevant, and took her second drink to the table, where she sat with her back to me. I opened the rest of the cupboards one by one. I didn't particularly care what was in them, barely looked, barely saw, but I wanted her to hear me opening them. I wanted her to feel I was groping my hands around her insides.

When I sat down opposite her she didn't look up. She was hunched and small inside the dressing gown.

'Is this where you were moving last time I saw you?' I asked.

'Yeah,' she said. 'Been here five years.'

'Why did you come back?'

'Just wanted to. The other places never felt like home. At least here I know what's what.'

'Does it feel like home here?'

She shrugged and took a juddery breath. It struck me that she might be going to cry, which I found repulsive. I cast around for how I could take her from sadness to rage.

'Do you get any bother?' I asked.

When Mam had visited me at Haverleigh she had loved to tell me about the bother she was having. She brought in the notes that had come through the letter box, scrawled and screaming. MURDERER MAMMY OUT. HELL FOR SATAN-MAKER.

She sipped her drink. 'Nothing major. Touch wood.' She tapped the table, which was clearly plastic. Neither of us spoke for a while. When I had imagined being with her I hadn't imagined this: the tight words moored by gaping white silence. I had imagined shouting, tears, thrusting Molly forward. 'Look. Look what I did, Mam. I made her. I did something good.' Mam dropping to her knees on the floor, pushing the hair away from Molly's face. 'Yeah. You did. Well done. She's beautiful, Chrissie. She's beautiful.'

I hated myself for having believed it might happen, and more for still wanting it to happen.

'Have you got a job now?' I asked.

'Cleaning,' she said. 'The offices in town.'

'OK.'

'It's early in the morning. Get there at four, five. Come back midday to sleep. That's why I was asleep. When you arrived. I don't normally just – you know. I only sleep in the day if I've worked the morning.'

'OK.'

A tic nibbled at the corner of her eye. She dipped her finger into her drink and pressed the wet tip to where she was twitching. It didn't stop. She ran the droplet around the rim of her glass. I remembered Da doing it – the fine hum that had throbbed the air.

'Do you know where Da is?' I asked.

'Lost touch. Could be anywhere,' she said.

'Oh,' I said.

'Good riddance,' she said, coming alive at the edges. 'He was a bastard.'

Da hadn't been to visit me at Haverleigh until I was sixteen. He had turned up three days after my birthday, lumbered into the visiting room with a bag of wrapped sweets the keepers had had to open and check for drugs or razor blades. When he got to the table he dropped them in front of me. Most of them spilt onto the floor. Neither of us picked them up.

'Happy birthday,' he said.

'Thanks,' I said.

'Grown up now,' he said.

'Yep,' I said.

'Bigger,' he said.

I didn't say anything.

'All all right here?' he asked, waving his hand at the window. Outside you could see the ten-foot perimeter fence.

'Great,' I said. He flicked his thumbnail against his teeth and we watched the telly mounted in the corner of the room. Inside, I felt warmed by a small, defiant flame. He had come. He had come to see me. He had come to see me and bring me sweets. He had come to see me and bring me sweets for my birthday. He looked and sounded the same as I remembered, and I wanted to lunge across the table and put my face in the crook of his neck, in the place where the skin was cool and clammy.

When the telly programme finished Da cleared his throat. 'Suppose I'll head off, then,' he said.

'But you only just got here,' I said.

'Been half an hour almost,' he said.

'No it hasn't.'

'I've got things to be getting on with.'

'But I want you to stay.'

He sat down, picked up a sweet, unwrapped it, and put it in his mouth. I heard it rattle against his teeth. We watched another telly programme. When it finished he laid his palms flat on the table.

'See you soon, then,' he said.

'Are you going to come back?'

'Yeah. Expect so.'

'I've only got two more years here. I have to leave after that. Will you come back before I leave?'

'Sure I will. Sure.'

'Thanks,' I said, and I knew he wouldn't, but I still felt grateful for the almost-hour with a grown-up who hadn't been paid to be with me. He pushed his chair back and I walked round the table and pressed myself against him. When I had hugged him as a kid my face had pushed into the soft dome of his belly, but now the bone of my nose braced the bones of his chest. I turned my head so my cheek was flush with his shirt. He patted my back, then pushed me away by the shoulders, but not like he wanted me to fall backwards, like he just needed there to be space between us. Sometimes you have to have space between you and someone else, even when you really like them, even when you love them, like because you're too hot or because you need to breathe. That wasn't why Da pushed me back: he did it because he didn't want my body pressed against his. Because I had grown and strained and sprouted, but I was still the bad seed.

'He came to see me a few times,' I said to Mam. 'He wasn't that bad.'

'He was,' said Mam.

'He was better than you,' I said.

223

'When? When was he better? He was never there.'

'He was. Sometimes he was.'

'Once in a blue moon.'

'Well it wasn't his fault. He had other stuff on. It was your job to look after me, not his.'

'Why?'

'Because you were the mam.' She didn't retort, and the silence left me space to hear myself in my head – deluded, whingeing – which made me angrier than anything she could have said. 'He didn't need to be there to be better than you. At least when I saw him he was nice to me.'

She made a snorting sound at the back of her throat. 'Yeah,' she said. 'Nice to *you*.'

Another memory, greyly translucent, like a photo negative. Seven years old, seeing Da from my bedroom window, running out of the door and into his arms. Mam at the door, Mam on the path, calling as we walked down the street hand in hand. 'Da, she wants you.' 'Keep walking.' Mam in the house when we got back that night, sitting on the stairs, leaning against the wall. 'Go to bed, Chrissie.' 'I'm not sleepy.' 'Go to your fucking bed.' Standing in my room, listening to the shouting. 'So you're just going to leave?' 'I've seen the kid, done my bit.' 'But what about me?' 'Don't embarrass yourself.' 'What about *me*?' 'You sound like a kid, Eleanor.' Gate creaking, warm breath on the cold window, Da walking away, Mam barefoot outside, 'Come back, come back, please, come *back*.' Voice breaking, jagged edges. Footsteps on the stairs. Mam in my bedroom, Mam hitting my face, a thunderclap pain and a whipcrack sound. 'This is *all* because of *you.*' Palm on my cheek, hot, tender like meat. 'Yes. All because of me. All *for* me. He came back for me. Not for you. Didn't you hear him?'

My chair screeched as I got up from the table. 'I'm going to check on Molly,' I said. She was where I had left her: on the couch, her face lit by a history programme.

'Are you all right?' I asked. She didn't look over when I sat down on the couch arm.

'Why does she say Chrissie?' she asked.

'That's what I was called when I was little,' I said.

'But not any more?' she said.

'No,' I said.

'Why not?'

'Just got changed.'

'Will I get changed from Molly?'

'No,' I said, though it occurred to me that I didn't know what would happen to her name when she moved to the new parents'. A part of me hoped they might change it. I hated the idea of her soft syllables in their mouths. I wondered whether, when I was in prison, I would find I still needed to say her name a certain number of times a day in order to feel whole. I imagined myself chanting it, alone, hunched on my bunk.

On the way back to the kitchen I stopped to look into the room next to the lounge. It was messier than the rest of the flat, the bed covered in knotted tights and blouses. There was a person-shaped indentation in the middle, and I pictured Mam curled within it, like a mouse burrowed into a nest.

She was still at the kitchen table, her head resting on one hand. As I walked past the worktop I ran my fingers along the boxes of cereal stacked against the wall.

'You buy food now,' I said as I sat down.

'Why do you keep saying that?' she asked.

'Because you didn't bother when I lived with you.'

'Didn't I?'

'No. I never had enough to eat. I was starving. I stuffed my bedsheets in my mouth at night just so I had something to chew.'

'But I remember buying you things. Sweets and things. I remember it.'

'That was – what – once a month? The rest of the time there was nothing.'

'Well I didn't know that. I don't remember being hungry.'

'You weren't.'

It was true: even when the cupboards had been bare, Mam had had enough to eat. Sometimes when she had come back at night I had waited until she was quiet in her room, then gone downstairs and pawed through the handbag she had dropped in the hallway. There had always been something coiled at the bottom, a crisp packet or rustle of chip paper. I had always hoped it was chip paper. When it had been chip paper I had sucked off the ketchup. We had been like a gone-wrong bird family, me and Mam: her out scavenging, me in the nest. She had only sometimes hacked up half-chewed worm parts for me, and whatever scraps she had given me I had swallowed down. I thought of it now and felt coldly degraded.

'I was hungry,' I said.

'OK,' she said. 'I get it. But, come on. It was only food.'

The snag of anger caught me in the soft place where my jaw met my neck. I couldn't think how to articulate that food stopped being food when you didn't have it, that it swelled and bloated as you shrank. It became the way you ticked off the hours, how you judged a good day from a bad one, something you stored when you had it and mourned when you didn't. I couldn't think how to explain the hunger, and I wasn't sure there was any point in trying. You couldn't understand hunger like that unless you had felt it. I wanted to tell her how it had shaped me, made me, because it had been huge and I had been tiny and it had always been there, a gnawing, nagging constant. It would have been mad to say I had killed because I was hungry, but the hunger had been a form of madness. It had driven so much of what I had done back then. Sometimes I wondered if the hunger could have stopped my brain growing the way normal brains grew, because I had never had any sustenance to make into new cells.

At Haverleigh we had all eaten together, sitting on long benches either side of the dining table. The table was wide enough that we couldn't kick the people opposite us when we were sitting down, so we had to kick the people next to us instead. They tried to sit us next to people we liked so we wouldn't kick them, but no one liked me and I kicked everyone. I always stopped kicking when the food arrived. The keepers put plates of sandwiches in the middle and I grabbed as many as I could fit in my hands, piled them onto my plate, grabbed more, piled them higher, made a shield with my arm as I pushed them into my mouth. I didn't taste food at Haverleigh; tasting wasn't the point. Eating wasn't the point. The point was having, and keeping, and filling. Sometimes, when we were doing cooking with the keepers in the kitchen, I snuck away to the larder. My feet made soft slapping sounds on the lino floor, and I peeled open the door with a quiet sigh. It wasn't about being caught or not – I was always caught – it was about how much I could swallow before the ugly strip light snapped on above my head. Different foods moved down my throat in different ways: cornflakes scratched, jam oozed, butter slid. When the keepers found me they sighed loudly, much louder than the larder door. They pulled me to the bathroom and washed the sticky gloves off my hands. I screamed.

'Be *quiet*, Chrissie.'

'But it *hurts*.'

'What hurts?'

'My *belly* hurts. My *belly* hurts.'

'Of course it hurts. You're too full. You shouldn't have stuffed yourself like that.'

'But it *hurts*. It *hurts*. I *hurt*.'

They sighed even louder, and I screamed even louder, because they didn't understand. My belly hurt in a sicky, low-down ache, like an iron fist squeezing my guts, and then I hurt in other places, secret places, in my throat and head and chest. I hurt because I missed Da and Linda and the handstand wall and my marble. I screamed so much I was sick, and then I was quiet. I felt better when I had been sick. The keepers usually didn't, because I had usually been sick on them.

After a while they put a lock on the larder door, so I started stealing things from the breakfast table. I squir-relled them in my cupboard and ate them under the covers at night.

'Why is there raspberry jam on your sheets, Chrissie?' a keeper asked one Sunday, peering over my shoulder as I stripped my bed.

'What raspberry jam?' I asked.

'That raspberry jam,' he said.

'That's not raspberry jam,' I said. 'That's blood. I had a nosebleed.'

'Hmm,' he said, taking the sheets from me. 'A nosebleed with seeds in it. Interesting.'

'Well I am the bad seed,' I said.

By the time I left Haverleigh I had learnt to fear the strength and size of my appetite, because what I had eaten there had strapped itself to my body. Each time I splashed my face with water my hands brushed over bulges at my cheeks and chin. When I left I barely ate, and my bones rose back to the surface like curds separating from whey. The hunger was always there, beating fists against the tight seal I had fastened around it, but I pushed it down. It hurt too much to be big. Too big to fit in the clothes that smelt of Linda and the streets. Too big to hide. Too big to love.

'Is there a reason you've come here?' Mam asked.

I put my elbows on the table and pressed my fingers into my eye sockets. The ache in my head was so strong I saw rings of pink and blue light each time I blinked. I could picture every cell inside my skull, red and raw and angry with pain. I didn't want to tell her that I needed her. She didn't deserve it.

'It's not like I've never been to see you,' I said. 'I used to come all the time.'

'Not for ages, though,' she said. 'Not for years.'

'You'd never met Molly,' I said. I willed her to bite. *Of course, of course, your daughter, your little girl. She's amazing, Chrissie. I'm going to go into the lounge right now and just look at her.*

She put her hand up her sleeve. The sound of her scratching her arm was like a knife scraping fish scales. 'Why now, though?' she asked.

'Sometimes it just feels like the right time for something,' I said. 'Like when you thought it was the right time to have me adopted.'

It worked just as I had wanted: no more scratching, no more noise. She drew her hand out slowly, and I saw the fine powder of skin cells collected under her nails.

'I didn't know you remembered that,' she said.

'It's not like I was a baby. I was eight.'

'Well, what do you want me to say? I didn't know how to look after you. How was I supposed to know? No one ever told me. My mam never looked after me. You don't just know things if no one ever tells you.'

'It's not that hard,' I said.

'You weren't an easy kid to look after.'

'You weren't an easy mam to be looked after by.'

'Leave it, Chrissie. Why can't you just leave it?'

I could feel her closing up. I clawed for the list of questions I had assembled on the train. 'Did you know?' I asked.

'What?' she said.

'That it was me that did it. With Steven. Before everyone else knew.'

She sat back in her chair and looked to the side. I could tell she was trying to lift away the layers of what-I-know-now to get to the kernel of what-I-knew-then.

'Yeah,' she said. 'I think so.'

'How?'

'Well, I didn't know for sure. But I remember being at church and them – you know – them busybody women. They were whispering to each other, and one of them was saying, "They're speaking to all the kids, aren't they?" and the other one was saying, "Yeah, they're thinking something really bad's gone on." Or something like that. You could tell what they meant – that everyone was starting to say it was a kid that done it. And I just remember thinking, "Oh. So it was her."'

'Is that it?'

'That's all I remember.'

'You must have felt something.'

'Just felt like I'd known all along.'

'Why didn't you tell anyone? If you knew for that long, why didn't you tell the police?'

'Don't really know.'

'You could have been rid of me sooner. That's what you wanted, isn't it?' I knew I was digging, mining her for affection. *I didn't want rid of you. I wanted to keep you with me. I care about you. You're my Chrissie.* She pulled the sleeves of her dressing gown over her hands and slid them under her thighs.

'I don't really know what I wanted,' she said. 'I don't remember it that clearly. If I'd dobbed you in it would have been a faff – a big to-do. I think I just couldn't be bothered.

Felt a bit like – well. He's dead now. What does it really matter?'

'Oh,' I said. There was something humiliating about mattering so little.

'I can't believe you just did nothing,' I said.

'I didn't do nothing,' she said. 'I tried to do something.'

'What?'

'You know what I mean.'

I heard the lounge door open and went to where Molly stood in the hallway. 'What's the matter?' I asked.

'Telly's gone weird,' she said, pointing to the screen. It was striped with grey bars. I crouched behind the set and looked at the knots of cables until I found which one to push in.

'Better?' I asked.

'Yeah,' she said.

I moved to stand up, but stopped when I saw a square metal tin in the space behind the telly table. I eased off the lid and found a thick sheaf of birthday cards inside, splashed with sickly pictures. Teddy bears, love hearts, cakes with yellow candles. My bag was next to the table; I tucked the tin into it, making sure Molly didn't see. My knees clicked when I straightened.

'We'll go soon,' I said.

'OK,' said Molly. She had sunk back into the corner of the couch and refastened her gaze to the screen. Under the bluish light, her cheeks and lips looked smooth, like china-doll features. Reflected pictures danced in her eyes. It was suddenly infuriating to me that she was so perfect – so far removed from the hundreds of thousands of ordinary kids in the world. I was always going to lose her. That was always going to be the end of this story. It seemed vividly unfair for her to be so special.

Mam didn't look up when I came back.

'She's fine,' I said. 'Just something with the telly. I fixed it.'

'Oh. Yeah. It's old,' she said.

'You're not really interested in her, are you?'

'She's not my kid.'

'No. But I am. And she's my kid. So you should care.'

She blew air through her teeth, making her lips puff out, and loosened the belt on her dressing gown. 'You're not a kid,' she said. 'You've not been a kid in years.'

'I meant I'm *your* kid,' I said. 'Not *a* kid. I'm *your* kid.'

I remembered this in Mam – the pull and push, cling and reject. She had been the same when we had lived together: crying until I stayed, screaming until I left. It took so little to tip her from one to the other that I rarely knew what I had done to cause the switch. As she had visited me at Haverleigh I had got better at putting my finger on the nothings she turned into everythings. I couldn't be certain this time, because I was out of practice, but I thought she was probably hurt that I had gone to check on Molly rather than stay with her.

'Did you just come here to show me you're a better mam than me?' she asked.

'What?' I said. 'I never said I was a good mam.'

'Don't have to say it. You're fussing over her all the time. It's to show me, isn't it?'

'I'm just looking after her. She's a kid. Kids need looking after.'

'Not as much as everyone thinks.'

'Yes. Just as much as everyone thinks. Probably more,' I said. 'I didn't come to show you anything. I just wanted you to meet her. She's what I've been doing all this time. Probably the only good thing I've ever done.'

'Well. That must be nice for you,' she said. 'Nice not to have had a kid who made the world worse.'

She had sanded away my top layer with her show of helplessness, leaving me with as much armour as a peeled grape. The jab slid through to my jellied inner tissue. It burnt.

'Why did you even have me?' I asked. 'You didn't want a kid. You could have got rid of me. You didn't want me.'

She made a hopeless noise – a kind of 'eh' – as though it was a question she couldn't be expected to answer. 'I don't know,' she said. 'I wanted something. Maybe it was your da. Maybe I thought, "I'll have a kid, he'll stick around." And even if he didn't, maybe I thought, "Well. I'll still have a kid. It'll love me." And then I had you. And you didn't.'

'Because you never did anything for me. Kids aren't born loving you. Needing you, maybe. But not loving you. You have to put the work in for love.'

'But I told you. No one ever told me what the work was. I didn't know what to do.'

'No one told me either. No one ever told me any of it. But if you want to, you figure it out. And then you figure it out a bit better the next day. And you carry on doing that for all the days. Most of the time it's really hard and boring, but it's not impossible. You just have to really want to do it.'

'Right,' she said, and it seemed that all the air went out of her. She sank back into the folds of her dressing gown. I noticed an embroidered teddy bear on the pocket. 'So you're saying I didn't want to. Not enough.'

'What is it you do want?' I asked. 'Now, I mean. What is it you want?'

'Oh, you know,' she said. 'Lots of things.'

'What are they, though?'

She began biting the dry skin on her lips. I watched a clear graft come away and disappear on her tongue. She lifted it with a finger and wiped it on the table.

'Well. It'd be nice not to be scared of people spitting at me in the street, for starters. And to have a home that felt like home. I suppose I want to be younger. Think every-one wants that. I'd like to be twenty-five, like you. Have everything in front of me. I suppose I just want to start again.'

The First Day of Spring

It was probably the most honest she had ever been with me, and it felt too big to take inside. I stood up, but there still wasn't room. It all felt too big – Mam's words, the dingy flat, the land that pulsed with blue-house memories. My face felt like a balloon full of boiling water, and I went to the fridge, opened the door, and crouched down in front to soak up the cool air. One shelf was stacked with Coke cans. I imagined the swish of cold down my throat, the chalky grind of sugared teeth. At Haverleigh they had only let us drink Coke at Christmas, so when I got out it was all I drank, and for a few weeks I felt it was always Christmas. I was recklessly, extravagantly unhealthy when I got out. I coated my food in so much salt it scratched my gums, and woke in the night itching with thirst, and reached for the two-litre bottle of Coke I kept by my bed. When I swilled it against my teeth I felt enamel peel away in papery layers. Sometimes it felt like an experiment: seeing how much of a pummelling my insides could take before they stopped working. The day I found out I was pregnant I drank four litres of Coke, then none for nine months. I forced down water, gagging on the eerie nothing-taste. My stomach emptied of carbon and filled with Molly, and each day I felt her join more of my rotted pieces together.

Perhaps that was what felt biggest of all – having found Mam unrotted. She was smaller and quieter and better than before. She was clean. She was stable. She was earning money and stocking her cupboards. It was what had happened for me when I had found out I was pregnant with Molly, except it had happened in reverse. I had built myself up because Molly had arrived. Mam had done it because I had left.

Crouching was making my legs prickle, so I closed the fridge door, sat down, leant forward, and rested my forehead against the cool plastic. I was full to the ends of my fingers with echoes of what she had said. *So it was her. What does it matter? I'd like to be twenty-five, like you. I didn't do nothing. I tried to do something.* I could work out what she meant, and the horror was strong, but other things were stronger – like the tremor of anger that ran through me when I thought of people spitting at her in the street, and the burr of warmth that came from knowing she remembered how old I was.

CHRISSIE

When I saw Mam on Saturday I thought she must be ill. I was sitting on the doormat in the hallway, tying my shoe-laces in the knots that never came undone, and she walked out of the lounge. I hadn't known she was there. Her cheeks were very pink and her eyes were very shiny, and she was twisting her mouth in a very odd shape. I stood up.

'Hello,' she said. She came and stood next to me. I thought perhaps she wanted to hug me but couldn't make herself do it. She patted my shoulder instead. Up close, she smelt darkly of women, of blood and meat and toilets. I breathed through my mouth so it didn't get inside me.

'Are you ill?' I asked.

'No,' she said.

'You don't have gout?' I asked.

'Why would I have gout?'

'Don't know. Mrs Bunty's husband has it.'

'I'm fine. Are you going out to play?' I nodded, still with my nose blocked. 'Who'll you play with?'

'Linda,' I said.

Nancy Tucker

'Ah. Yes. Linda. Lovely,' she said. She didn't even really know who Linda was. She took a tube of Smarties out from behind her back. 'I got these for you. For you to eat. While you play.'

I reached out. She let me take the tube. It was smooth in my hand.

'All right,' I said. I went to open the door but she grabbed my arm and pulled me back, holding so tight I felt finger-print bruises rise on my skin.

'I bought them sweeties for you, all right? Had to use my own money to buy them, and I only bought them for you. So don't you go sharing them with any other kids. All right?'

I shook my head to say I wouldn't, and I was telling the truth, because I hadn't even thought about sharing them with any other kids. She bent down and kissed my cheek, quick and rough. Her lips were like tree bark against my skin.

'You eat them all yourself. Eat them all up,' she said.

'I will,' I said. She put her hand on my head, closed her eyes, and muttered, 'Father, protect me. God, keep me safe.' I wanted to look at her properly, to check she was really Mam and not a different woman dressed up as Mam, but as soon as she finished praying she went into the kitchen and shut the door. I left with my fingers on my cheek in the place she had kissed.

I knocked for Linda and we walked up the hill to the playground, the Smarties rattling against my leg.

The First Day of Spring

'What's that noise?' asked Linda.

'Not telling,' I said. I turned the sugar shell of the secret over on my tongue.

William and Richard and Paula were already at the play-ground. William and Richard were throwing stones at a tree and Paula was eating grass.

'Look what Mam gave me this morning,' I said, showing them the cardboard tube. Richard made a tsk-ing noise.

'That's not special. My mammy gives me them all the time. Gives me loads of sweets.' I knew that was true because he was fat, but I still kicked his ankle. He laughed and wobbled off to the roundabout, which made a scream-ing sound when he jumped on.

'Give us one,' said William. He held out his hand and Paula copied.

'Do you want one?' I asked Linda. She nodded and held her hand out too. I looked at the little line of hands, two big, one small, and at the three excited faces. 'Well, you're not getting any,' I said. I ran off to sit by the railings. I knew they would follow.

'That's not fair!' said William when he caught me up. He kicked the gate. 'I share my things with you.'

'You never.'

'I do too. I gave you some of that pie I had, didn't I?'

'Only because I let you put your hand in my underpants,' I said. His ears turned the colour of ham.

'You let him *what*?' said Linda.

'You heard,' I said.

William kicked the gate again, so hard I thought I heard his toes crunch. Paula smiled and reached for the Smarties.

'No, you're not having any,' I said. I sat down and opened the tube. William tried to drag Paula away but she squealed and pointed. He picked her up and carried her to the roundabout. Linda sat down next to me.

'Just let me have one. I'm your best friend.'

'Go away. Mam gave them to me just for me. She told me not to share them with anyone else.'

'Liar. She never told you that. Mammies never say not to share.'

'Well mine did. They're only for me.'

'If you don't let me have one I won't let you come to my party.'

'Didn't want to come anyway. Your parties are rubbish.'

She pinched me. I slapped her. She ran off shouting, 'You're not my best friend any more, Chrissie Banks!' over her shoulder. I didn't care. Linda's parties *were* rubbish, because her mammy said musical statues was too silly and musical bumps was too noisy and musical chairs was too dangerous. The only thing Linda's mammy really thought was a good idea was colouring-in, and colouring-in wasn't even a little bit partyish. So it was true that Linda's parties were rubbish, and it was a good idea for her to know that. And anyway, it would take a lot more than Smarties to stop her being best friends with me.

The First Day of Spring

While the others played on the roundabout I shook a clatter of sweets into my hand. They looked different to the pictures on the tube – smaller, and all the same greyish colour. The coating on their outsides was powdery. When I put one in my mouth and pressed it between my teeth it crumbled, and chalky glue spread across my tongue. I thought perhaps Mam had bought them ages ago and forgotten to give them to me, kept them in a drawer for so long the chocolate inside the shells had gone to dust. Linda was watching me from the roundabout with her jaw set hard, so I crunched two more. My belly heaved.

I ate half the Smarties in the tube. It was easier to get them down if I tipped my head to the sky and swallowed them whole, but sometimes they stuck in my throat. I tried to cough quietly, so Linda and William and Richard didn't notice (Paula didn't notice anything because she was too busy eating dandelions). If they hadn't been watching I would have thrown the sweets in the bin, but they watched and watched and that meant I had to eat and eat. When I had no more spit left to swallow with I put the tube in my pocket and ran over to the roundabout. Linda turned her back to me, but the others had forgotten they were supposed to be cross. Paula pressed her face into my leg and left a trail of snot on my dress. Richard pushed us round, and I closed my eyes and tried not to think about the squirming in my belly or the bitter taste in my mouth. I decided next time I got sweets I wouldn't choose Smarties. I wouldn't choose Smarties ever again.

Richard got tired of pushing the roundabout quite quickly, and no one else wanted to do it instead, so we went to the swing poles. Me and Linda sat on the ground and William and Richard had a hanging-upside-down competition. I wanted to join in, because I was the best at hanging upside down, but when I stood up the world spun in front of my eyes. I pressed my face against one of the poles. The metal was cool on my cheek.

'Are you all right?' asked Linda. 'You look funny. Your face is the wrong colour.'

'What do you mean?' I wanted to say. It didn't come out right. I tried again – 'What do you mean?' – but my tongue was too big in my mouth. I felt a trickle of dribble go down my chin and a trickle of sweat go down my forehead. I leant over and a whoosh of sick shot down to the ground. William and Richard let go of the swing pole, and Richard lifted Paula away just before she put her hands in the sick. She probably would have eaten that too.

'Has she got mumps?' William asked.

'No,' said Richard. 'She's not fat round her chin.'

'*You're* fat round your chin,' said William, and Richard shoved him. I could hear what they were saying, see what they were doing, but it was like I was listening and watching through three feet of water. I was horribly thirsty, and I tried to ask for a drink, but I just sicked up some more. It covered my clothes, pooled at my feet. I heard feet running away, and I thought perhaps everyone was leaving me because I hadn't shared my Smarties, and even before I hadn't shared my Smarties I hadn't been nice, so no one had really liked me in the first place, but then I felt warm fingers wind around my arm. Linda lifted the hair off the back of my neck and blew on the sweat-wet skin.

'Don't worry, Chrissie,' she said. 'You'll be OK. You're just a bit ill. Richard's gone to get his mammy. You're still my best friend, really. You can come to my party. We won't do colouring-in.'

After a while I saw a short pink jelly of a person coming towards us, and behind her a taller, darker streak of a person. The jelly flapped her hands and made high-pitched noises and the streak put one arm under my shoulders and the other under my knees, lifted me up, and held me tight. Someone said, 'Eaten anything funny?' and someone else reached into my pocket, took out the Smarties tube, 'Only these', the rattle of Smarties into someone's hand, 'Not sweets, look at them, they're not sweets.' And then I was in a car, or a truck, or a milk van, and then a big room where everything was white and everyone was worried. And then there was sleep, or something close to sleep. It came like a thrown blanket, soft and sudden.

I knew I wasn't at the house before I opened my eyes, because the bed underneath me was dry. The bed was never dry when I woke up at the house. I moved my legs around under the sheets and listened to the noises wrinkling the air – clanks and rattles and women's voices. The smell of cleaning was sharp in my nose. When I opened my eyes a woman in a white cap and apron was looming over me. Her head was right below a bright white light in the ceiling, and the glow around her face made a halo.

'Hello, Christine,' she said. Her teeth were as white as her apron. 'How are you feeling, pet?'

I tried to sit up, but pain twanged in my head like a snapped elastic band. My mouth tasted of dead things.

'Thirsty,' I whispered.

'Yes, pet. I'm sure. Let's sit you up and I'll fetch you some water. And some breakfast, too? Does that sound good?'

I wasn't hungry. It felt so odd to be not-hungry that I wondered if I had been magicked into someone else while I was asleep. The woman told me her name was Nurse Howard, and she put her hands under my arms and lifted me up to a sitting position. I saw I was in a room full of metal beds with white sheets over small bodies. There were other nurses walking around in click-clack shoes, talking in voices too quiet for me to hear. In the bed opposite mine a little boy was chasing cornflakes round a bowl with a spoon, one arm wrapped in plaster.

When Nurse Howard had sat me up she tidied my sheets and click-clacked out of the white room. I looked down at myself. My belly stuck out in a pregnant dome, and the dome was full of sickness. Green and swirling. It didn't feel part of me. My skin was so tight I thought it must be close to splitting. I wondered what would happen if it split – whether I would spill out all over the bed, all my guts and sickness and secrets.

Nurse Howard click-clacked back with a tray, which she put down on my lap. There was a cup of water and a bowl of porridge gritted with sugar.

'I'm not very hungry,' I said.

'I think you should have a go at eating something, pet,' she said. 'You haven't had anything to eat since yesterday. It'll be good for your sore throat and your poor belly.'

I thought about shouting and swearing and throwing the bowl on the floor, but I was too tired to be bad. Nurse Howard click-clacked off to another girl and I scooped up a gob of porridge. It was jellied, holding its shape on the spoon, but I put it in my mouth and it tasted less sicky than it looked. When I swallowed it my throat was coated in a gluey layer of thickened milk, and it didn't hurt my rotten tooth because it didn't need chewing. Nurse Howard came back as I was picking up the last sparkles of sugar with my finger.

'Hungry after all, were we, pet?' she said.

'Why am I here?' I asked.

'You know you're in hospital, don't you?' she said. I nodded. I hadn't really known that before she had said it but I didn't want to look thick. She put my breakfast tray on the floor and sat down on the edge of the bed. 'You're in hospital because yesterday you swallowed something you shouldn't have. Some tablets. Do you remember that? They were in a sweetie packet. You might have thought they were sweeties. Do you remember?'

'They were Smarties,' I said.

She nodded. 'Well, actually, they weren't Smarties, pet. They were tablets. Some grown-ups use them to help them go to sleep. They're not for kids at all. So when you swallowed them they made you sick.'

'Oh,' I said.

She licked her lips. 'Did someone give you those Smarties?' she asked. She touched my hand. I looked at her nails, short and rounded. My nails were different lengths, some of them snapped off low down, others so long they nearly curled over, all of them caked with dirt. I bent my fingers to hide them.

'I don't remember how I got them,' I said. 'Must have found them somewhere. Maybe on the ground somewhere. I don't remember.' Nurse Howard looked disappointed. She picked up the tray and stood, leaving a dent in the bedsheets.

'Well,' she said. 'Maybe you can have a think about it. Hmm?'

'Was I dead?' I asked. 'Before I came to the hospital. When I swallowed the tablets. Was I dead?'

She laughed. 'Of course not. If you were dead you wouldn't be talking to me now, would you?' She was obviously another one who didn't understand about the different kinds of dying. Thinking about people coming back alive again gave me a grasping feeling in my throat, and I looked on either side of my bed.

'What's the matter?' she asked.

'Where are my clothes?'

'The clothes you were wearing when you came in? We'll have kept them somewhere. Don't worry. They won't be lost.'

'I need them now,' I said. My voice sounded full and wet, and I hated sounding that way, but I had to carry on talking. 'It's important.'

'Why?' she asked.

'There was important stuff in my pockets,' I said.

'Was there? Well, I expect it's still—'

'I need them *now*,' I shouted. Nurse Howard made her eyes very wide, then she click-clacked off. She disappeared through the door at the end of the white room and I was going to run after her but she came back again quickly, carrying my clothes in a folded pile.

'Here you are,' she said, dropping them onto my bed. 'Better now?'

I didn't answer. I was too busy digging my hands into the pockets of my skirt. My fingers closed around the marble and I nodded. 'Yeah,' I said. 'Better.'

Now that I knew my marble was safe I didn't really want the clothes any more, so I pushed them onto the floor and pushed myself back up to the head of the bed. The boy with the broken arm had had his breakfast tray taken away and was turning the pages of a picture book with his good hand. On the floor next to him was a shopping bag bulging with toys and books and packets of sweets. I held my marble on my palm, so if he looked over he would think someone had come to bring me toys too.

It was boring sitting in bed with no one to talk to and nothing to do, so I was glad when a white-coated man and his click-clack nurses swept in. He had a stethoscope around his neck, which I knew was called a stethoscope because there was a stethoscope in the doctor's set Donna's nana had given her last Christmas and she never let anyone else have a turn with it. The white-coat doctor didn't speak to me, just to the nurses, who nodded and twittered and scribbled things on pieces of paper. He had dark hair and thin fingers, and I thought he probably didn't ever let anyone else have a go with his stethoscope either.

'Flat on the bed, please,' he said, snapping on a pair of stretchy plastic gloves. Two nurses came forward, stripped the sheets away from my body, and made me as flat and straight as I would be in a coffin. The doctor pulled up my smock and pressed on my swollen belly with his thin fingers. I didn't have anything on under the smock, not even any underpants. My body felt bare and my face felt hot. He took out a pencil-shaped stick that lit up with a click and shone it straight onto my eyeballs. The blob of light floated in front of me for a long time after he took it away. When he had listened to my chest from the front and back with his stethoscope, he snapped off his white gloves and gave them to one of the nurses. She took them with her fingertips and threw them in the bin at the end of the bed, like touching me had made them dirty.

'Now,' said the doctor, 'you've been very lucky, young lady. If you hadn't been brought to the hospital so fast, you wouldn't be here now.'

'No. Obviously,' I said. 'I'd still be in the playground.'

He lifted up one dark eyebrow and one corner of his thin pink top lip. 'You won't be so silly again, will you?' he said. I knew he wanted me to shake my head, but I didn't. I stared him straight in the eye and squeezed my marble under the sheets until he swept away in a flourish of creases and nurses.

Once he was gone time curdled again, lumpy like my porridge. I looked out of the window at the end of the white room, but all I could see were rooftops and rain. I told a nurse I needed the toilet and she brought me a cold metal pan. She pulled up my smock and helped me to sit on it, there in the white room with everyone watching. When the pee trickled out of me it felt like pushing out razor blades. I didn't cry. I never cried.

After years of curdled time the doors of the white room opened again and Mam was there.

'Chrissie! My *Chrissie*! My *precious girl*! My *poor* little *lamb*!'

She was at the bed, throwing herself forward, wrapping me in her arms. I had been eating rice pudding and jam from a china bowl, and it fell off my lap. I watched it splatter across the floor in gummy pink clots. I hoped someone would bring me some more. Mam smelt of perfume pasted over dirt, and at the edges the other smell, the woman smell that made me heave. My smock got wet from the rain on her clothes. Over her shoulder I saw Nurse Howard coming towards us.

'Hello,' she said when Mam let go of me. 'You must be Mrs Banks.'

'Yes. Yes. I am,' said Mam.

'It's nice to meet you, Mrs Banks. We're taking good care of Christine.'

Mam nodded and stroked my cheek with one finger. 'Thank you, nurse. I've been so worried. I came here as soon as I heard. I've been away working, and my sister only called to tell me this morning. I came straight here. My poor, brave Chrissie . . .'

Mam didn't have a sister. Not one we went to stay with at the seaside and not one who had told her I was in hospital. She was a big fat smelly liar. Nurse Howard smiled, because she didn't know about the big fat smelly lying. Mam moved up the bed and snaked an arm around my back. Her hand rested just above my elbow, where my smock sleeve ended.

'Christine has been ever so brave,' said Nurse Howard. 'As your sister may have told you, she was very poorly when she came in. She'd somehow managed to get her hands on some tablets – sleeping tablets – and she'd taken quite a few of them. We think she may have thought they were sweets.'

Mam's arm tensed behind my back. 'That would be just like my Chrissie,' she said too loudly. 'She's a greedy girl. And careless. She'll put anything in her mouth, anything she finds, things from the medicine cupboard.'

'They were in a sweet packet,' said Nurse Howard. Her voice was much quieter than Mam's, but it still made Mam stop talking. 'Christine's had her stomach pumped, and she seems much better this morning. Obviously we want to find out how she came by the tablets – if someone gave them to her intentionally, it will be a matter for the police.' She looked from Mam to me, and made her voice softer. 'I did want to ask you again, love – have you thought any more about how you came to have those sweets? Where you found them?'

Mam's fingers closed hard on a fold of skin above my elbow. I clenched my teeth. 'I can't remember,' I said. 'I think I just found them. I really can't remember.' Mam patted my knee.

'Well, nurse, like I said. She'll put anything in her mouth. There are some nasty types round where we live, nurse. I'm sure you heard about the business with the little boy. I try my best to keep Chrissie safe, but sometimes I have to work away from home, and her da's not around as much as I'd like. There's always someone watching her, but you never know how careful they're going to be, do you? I told my sister, "Look after her proper, she's very precious." I can't do more than that, can I? Not my fault if she doesn't take good care of her, not when I'm away working.'

I could see that Nurse Howard wasn't listening to much of what Mam was saying. She was looking at her all over, from the knots in her hair to the rips in her stockings. I didn't know if she could tell she was saying lies, lies, lies. I didn't know if I wanted her to be able to tell. When Mam ran out of words Nurse Howard smiled a tight smile and click-clacked off. Mam turned to me and tucked the hair behind my ears. She didn't look at my eyes. She spoke in a high, humming voice.

'Oh, my poor little Chrissie. Poor, unlucky Chrissie. Terrible luck for a kid, to have a packet of sweeties turn out to be tablets. Terrible bad luck for a kid. Such a shame she can't remember where she found them.' She grabbed my face in her hand and squeezed my cheeks so my mouth popped open. 'But she *can't* remember. *Can* she?' I shook my head.

'Good,' she said. She let go of my face, but I could still feel her fingers there, pressing my cheeks into my teeth. 'Good. Because if Chrissie ever remembered how she came by them tablets, she might find that other things started getting remembered. Things she doesn't want anyone to know.'

She put her mouth by my ear. I could smell her stronger than ever. Stale. Bloody. 'About Steven,' she whispered.

When she sat back she did look at my eyes. We stared at each other until the air between us had a heartbeat. Her hands were on the bed, and I broke out of the staring match to look down at them. I turned one over, so it was palm up, and lifted it back to my face. She let me lift her, made her arm loose like a puppet's. I put her hand on my cheek and pressed both my hands over it, then tipped myself forward until the top of my head was on her chest. She knew what I had done. She was the only other person in the world who knew what I had done. I wanted to crawl back inside her belly, because that was how close I felt we were, both of us together, knotted inside the secret.

She let me sit with my head against her chest for a while, rising and falling as she breathed in and out. Then she stood. I kept my head down. I didn't watch her gather her bag and walk down the aisle between the beds. I only knew she was gone because I heard the door at the end of the room open and close.

The little girl in the bed next to mine was sitting up and crying, and I lay down with my back to her, curled in the shape of a question mark. There was a small warmth at the bottom of my belly, like the glow of a blown-out candle. Mam knew what had happened with Steven. She knew and she hadn't told anyone. She hadn't told anyone because she didn't want me to go to prison, wanted to keep me with her, wanted to keep me safe. You have to care about things to want to keep them safe.

JULIA

By the time I went back to the lounge, Molly had lost inter-
est in the telly. She was headstanding on the couch. I wasn't
sure headstands were the best thing for a broken wrist, but I
felt too heavy to care. Mam leant against the wall, watching
me thread Molly's cast through the sleeve of her coat. Our
last visit had ended in shouting – 'Get *out of my house*!'
'I'm *never coming back*!' – and it had been safe, because it
had happened on the surface. We had been able to scream at
each other and still hold on to the nub of feeling underneath,
the nub that said, 'I'll be back. I need you and you need
me.' There were no fireworks this time. There was nothing
to shout. We both knew I wouldn't be back. She followed
us to the door, and I stepped through it feeling like a blister:
thin-skinned, tight with oozings. I walked along the balcony
without looking back.

'Are we going home now?' Molly asked when we got to
the stairwell.

'Yeah,' I said.

'Promise?' she said.

'Promise,' I said. Like *promise* was anything more than a stupid word.

We had to go back through the streets to get to the bus stop. When we passed the playground Molly trailed her fingers along the railings. 'Looks like a good playground,' she said, to no one but also to me. I looked over the fence. The concrete had been covered in the same springy surface that covered the ground under Molly's school climbing frame, and the new equipment was so bright and sturdy it was hard to remember the stark metal poles I had hung on with Linda and Donna and William.

'Go on, then,' I said.

'What?' said Molly.

'You can play for a bit.'

'Really?'

'Yeah. Just for a bit.'

She pushed open the gate, ran to the roundabout, and began working up speed with her foot, jumped on when it was spinning, off again without waiting for it to slow. The words welled up in my throat – 'Mind your wrist, bend your knees, not so fast' – but I swallowed them. When I pushed her on the swing she shouted, 'Higher! Higher!' and I thrust my hands against her back, flinging her towards the sky. It wouldn't matter if she flew out of the seat and arced through the air. I would just be exchanging one kind of crash for another.

When she got bored of the swing I sat on the bench, pulled my bag onto my lap, and took out the tin I had found behind Mam's telly. The cards looked even more garish in the sunlight. I opened the one on top.

Dearest Mammy,

Wishing you a brilliant birthday. I hope you have all the happiness you deserve.

Mammy, I miss you so much while I am here. I think and think of you, all the time wishing you could come and take me home. I know it is my fault that we are apart. I wish I could make it up to you. I am so sorry for all I have done.

All my love to you, mammy.

Chrissie

I opened the rest in a slow procession, piling them next to me on the bench when I finished reading.

Love you with all my heart, mammy.

You didn't do anything to deserve such a bad daughter.

I cry every day for the pain I have caused you.

You are the best mammy anyone could wish for.

They had all been written in black ink, with letters that grew and shrank and moved up and down across the page, and not one of them had been written by me. It was Mam's writing. They were Mam's words.

At the bottom of the tin was a folded photograph of Mam and me. We were standing on the step outside the house, her in a dressing gown, me in a green-checked dress. Linda's dress. Her mammy had washed and ironed and sent it home with me, and she had sent a clean vest and clean underpants and clean socks too.

'Why you giving me these?' I had asked when she had handed me the carrier bag. I was standing outside their front door, trying not to leave.

'First day of school tomorrow,' she said. 'Got to be clean and smart. I've done the same for Linda.'

'Why?' I asked.

'Everyone needs clean clothes for the first day of school,' she said.

'But you don't like me,' I said.

She looked at me oddly. I couldn't tell if she was going to shout or sigh or shoo me away and go back into the kitchen to make some more scones. Just when I was about to give up waiting to find out she lowered herself onto her knees and pulled me against her pillowy chest. I couldn't put my arms round her because she was holding them to my sides, and I wasn't sure I would have put my arms round her even if I could have, because she was mostly quite mean and grumpy to me and I mostly didn't like her. But I let my head droop onto her shoulder. It felt nice. She smelt of hot milk and Sunday afternoons.

'Oh, Chrissie,' I heard her say. 'What'll we do with you?'

When I put on the clean clothes the next morning they felt funny on my skin: stiff and soft at the same time. I went into the street to wait for Linda and her mammy to walk past. They came up the hill holding hands, and Linda's da was there too, so she was swung between them. They were all in their church clothes. I was going down the path when I heard Mam behind me, putting a bag of rubbish in the bin.

'Morning, Chrissie!' called Linda's da from outside the gate.

'Why are you wearing your church clothes?' I asked.

'Big day, isn't it?' he said. 'You only start school once. Anyone taken your photo yet?'

'No,' I said. Mam tried to go back inside the house but Linda's da said, 'Wait a minute, Eleanor, let's get a quick snap of the two of you.' She turned slowly, like she was hoping if she took long enough he might change his mind and not want her to be in the picture after all. He just waited. When she was facing him she stood like she was frozen, and I stood that way too, as he raised the camera to his face and click-snap-clicked.

In the photo we were standing side by side on the front step, staring, not touching. There was clear space between us with nothing breaking it. Not an arm. Not a hand. Linda's dress hung on me like a clean, ironed sack, and Mam's nightie hung low on her chest. We looked like two ghosts.

The First Day of Spring

I picked up the first card again. She hadn't tried to disguise her writing – the spikes and slants of the letters matched the address slips she had given me each time she had moved. I still had them, crouched in a wad in my purse. It was, I realised, the same as the writing on the hate mail she had brought to Haverleigh to show me, the vicious notes she said had been posted through her door. I wondered whether Mam ever felt stooped under the weight of her strange, sad charade. It wouldn't have made sense to anyone else, but it did to me. 'I am here, I am here, I am here,' she was saying, scrawling threats to herself from herself. 'You will not forget me.'

I put everything back in the tin, the first-day-of-school photograph on top. I still remembered that day: Miss Woodley's grey hair, the milk and school dinner. Most of all I remembered the swing of Linda's dress around my knees, and the way we had pretended to be sisters, because our clothes had smelt of the same washing powder.

Molly groaned theatrically when I told her it was time to leave the playground, but I said that the first person to spot five red cars would be the winner, and she relented. As we walked down the street I looked at the front doors and thought of who had lived behind them when I was Chrissie. *Donna and William. Betty. Mrs Harold. Vicky and Harry.* I knew most of them would have moved on, but it felt good to imagine they were all still contained within those walls, as if life in the streets had paused when I had left.

It took me a moment to recognise the house, because the door had been painted and the front wall rebuilt. We went up the path and rang the bell and she appeared, a toddler on her hip, 'Hello!' on her lips. It died when she saw me.

'Linda,' I said. The toddler burrowed his face into her neck.

'It's OK,' she said to him.

'Mammy,' he said.

'I know. We thought it was your mammy, didn't we? Never mind. She'll be here in a minute.'

'Who dat?' he asked, stabbing a finger at me. She pulled his arm down.

'We don't point, do we?' she said. 'That's another lady. Someone Linda knows.'

She wasn't looking at me. She was swaying on the spot, and I didn't know whether it was to soothe the toddler or herself. Molly started tugging the back of my jacket.

'What is it?' I hissed.

'I need the toilet,' she hissed.

'Can't you wait?' I hissed.

'I'm bursting,' she hissed.

'You can come in,' said Linda, breaking up our snake talk.

'It's fine. We don't have to.'

'Yeah you do. She needs the toilet. Come on, sweetie.'

She backed into the hallway and Molly stepped inside. I shut the door behind us. The house was the same as I remembered, but fresher, cream painted, and teeming with a small zoo of kids. They seemed to spill out of every cupboard and from behind every door, most of them in a cheerful state of half undress. There were drawings taped to the walls, toys stacked in the corners, and a warm smell of cooked potato.

'It's the door you can see from here,' Linda said to Molly. 'The one at the top of the stairs. It hasn't got a lock, but don't worry, no one will come in.'

'That's my daughter,' I said when Molly went upstairs, as if, up to this point, her identity had been a mystery. I wasn't sure I had ever called her my daughter before – it was a starchy word, hard-edged in my mouth. Linda would know about her already. They had put it in the papers when they had found us, debated it on the radio. Men whose voices had sounded fat and balding had asked, 'Can we *really* trust a *child killer* to raise her *own* child?' It was playing in the corner shop where I was counting change for a box of sanitary towels. When I heard it I wrestled the pram out onto the street. I didn't work up the courage to go into another shop until I felt blood soak through my underpants and trickle down my leg in a sticky trail.

'Yeah,' Linda said. 'It's Molly, isn't it? Molly Linda.'

'Oh,' I said. 'You got them.'

In all my different lives, I had always written to Linda. From each of my Haverleigh bedrooms, from when I was Lucy. I had told her the things no one was supposed to know – my address, my phone number, each new name they had given me. Black ink filling up white rectangles. The writing was hungriest when I was little. *Have you got a new best friend yet? Is it Donna? Has your mammy had another baby? Will you come and visit me?* I gave the letters to Matron, asked her if she knew Linda's address, asked her if she *definitely* knew her address, heard her say yes, yes, she'll get it, don't worry, Christine. She never wrote back. I carried on writing and she carried on not writing back. Sometimes I imagined my letters straining against an elastic band on a shelf in Matron's office because she hadn't really known the address but hadn't wanted to say so. That made me feel better. It wasn't that Linda didn't care. It was just that she had never got to know how much I did. I had last written when Molly was a baby, when I had just been made into Julia. *You're probably not even getting these letters. You probably don't even live at this address any more. I just wanted to tell you that I've had a baby girl. I've called her Molly Linda.*

As Molly came down the stairs the bell rang again, and Linda touched my arm. 'Look,' she said. 'It's going to be chaos here for the next half hour or so. All the childminding kids get picked up at this time.'

'We'll go,' I said.

'You don't have to,' she said. 'I mean, not if you don't want to. If you don't mind giving me half an hour to get everyone sorted, things will be calmer. Molly can play with the others. They're – you know –' She gestured vaguely, and I wondered what she meant. 'They're running wild'? 'They're mostly naked'? 'They're multiplying as we speak'? 'But you don't have to stay. Not if you don't want to. Whatever you want. I've got to get this.'

Linda greeted the woman at the door and deposited the toddler in her arms. He started crying immediately. Molly came to stand beside me.

'Would you like to stay here for a bit?' I asked Molly. She looked through to the garden, where assorted kids were playing with balls and hula-hoops in the dying light.

'Yeah,' she said, and led me deeper into the house.

CHRISSIE

They sent me away from hospital after two more days. I didn't want to go. I pretend-coughed and pretend-sneezed and said my belly hurt, my head hurt, my everywhere hurt. They still told Mam I was ready to leave. When we were going, Nurse Howard said, 'Take care of yourself, Chrissie.' I wished she'd said, 'Take care of Chrissie, Mam.' Mam didn't speak to me on the bus. She sat straight-backed and smoked two smokes with a trembling mouth. When the bus dropped us outside church she walked off without me. I didn't try to catch up.

Linda was extra nice to me for the next few days because I had been so poorly. Even her mammy was nicer than usual. When I stayed for tea she gave me as much food as she gave Linda (which she normally didn't) and she didn't make Linda wash her hands after she'd been playing with me (which she normally did). Linda told Donna that I had been so poorly I had nearly died, because that was what I had told her. Donna didn't admit it, but she was really impressed, and she let me have a go on her bike the first time I asked. If I had known people would be so nice to me just because I had been in hospital, I would have tried to get myself in hospital much sooner.

I went back to school on Monday but Miss White wasn't particularly nice to me, and she was even more not-nice to Linda. When we were doing maths she asked her to read the time off the clock on the classroom wall, even though she knew Linda was thick at telling the time. Linda stared and stared at the clock without saying anything and Miss White kept saying, 'What's the time, Linda?' and Linda kept not saying anything. I could almost hear her heart banging from across the room. The rest of us went out to play but Miss White wouldn't let Linda come. She said she had to sit on her own in the empty classroom until she said the right time.

When I got into the playground I went to the classroom window and looked through it. I could see Linda's face from the side. Her mouth had turned down at the corners the way it did when she was going to cry, and under the table she was knotting her fingers so tightly the pads were turning red. I couldn't see them from outside but I knew they were turning red, because the pads of her fingers always turned red when she knotted them like that. In the end she got let out to play because Miss White wanted to go to the staff room and have a cup of tea. I told the teacher on duty I needed the toilet. I didn't go to the toilet. I went into the classroom, climbed up on a chair, took the clock off the wall, and threw it on the floor. It didn't smash because it was made of plastic, so I turned it face up and jumped on it until the numbers were hidden under a spiderweb of cracks. I left it on the floor and went back out to play. When Miss White saw it she looked at Linda, but she knew Linda would never have done something like that. There was only one person in the class who was bad enough to have done something like that. She waited until everyone else was doing worksheets, then called me to her desk. She had the clock in front of her.

'Do you know what happened to our clock, Chrissie?' she asked.

'It's smashed,' I said.

'Yes, it is. Do you know how it got smashed?'

'Must have fallen off the wall.'

'And how might that have happened?'

'Probably just got blown off.'

'Blown off?'

'Yeah. By the wind.'

'Wind?'

I pointed to a leaf skimming across the playground outside. 'It's windy today,' I said. 'Just look at the leaves.'

She sighed. I wanted to say, 'You might have blown it off the wall with one of your sighs, Miss White,' but I thought I had better not.

'You are going to get yourself into serious trouble one day, Christine Banks,' she said.

'Because I'm the bad seed?' I asked.

She made a little snorting sound. 'Did someone tell you that?'

'Yeah. I'm the bad seed. I'm not going to get in trouble, though.'

'Oh?' she said. 'Because you're going to start behaving?'

'No,' I said. 'Because no one's ever going to catch me.'

'Go back to your seat,' she said.

'Did you know I was in hospital, miss?' I asked. 'I was. I got given some sweets but they were actually tablets. They poisoned me.'

'Who gave them to you?' she asked.

I thought of Mam pushing the tube into my hand, pushing her mouth against my cheek. Lips like tree bark on my skin, feeling in my belly like a fluttering feather. *Maybe she likes me now. Maybe I've got good.*

'Just someone,' I said. 'I got poisoned by them. I had a bad belly for loads of days. I nearly died.'

Miss White pulled a stack of worksheets towards her and started ticking and crossing. 'Of course you did, Chrissie,' she said. 'Of course you did.'

The next day at break time I went to bring the milk bottles in from the playground, but Miss White said, 'No, Chrissie. Your turn as milk monitor has finished. Caroline, can you go, please?'

Caroline got up slowly, watching me.

'But it's my job,' I said. 'It's my monitor job.'

'It has been your job, and now it's someone else's turn,' said Miss White.

'But I did it yesterday,' I said.

'Yes. You've been a very lucky girl, haven't you? You've been milk monitor for a long time. Which is why we need to give someone else a turn.' She clapped her hands. 'Come on, Caroline. Spit spot,' she said.

Caroline went out of the door and dragged in the milk bottle crate. She huffed and puffed and acted like it was too heavy to pull, so I went to do it for her, but Miss White put her hand on my shoulder. 'Christine. How many times? It's someone else's turn now. You need to sit down at your desk and wait for your milk. Come on, Caroline. This is taking far too long. Spit spot.'

I stayed standing by Miss White as Caroline started giving out the milk bottles. I looked up at her big, ugly face. 'You're just saying "spit spot" to be like Mary Poppins,' I said. 'But you're not anything like Mary Poppins. She's nice. She's not mean like you. You're the meanest ever.'

'I've had enough of this, Christine,' she said. Her face was going red. Mary Poppins' face never went red. 'Go and sit in the corridor. You're missing your playtime today. You can come back when you've decided not to be so bad-tempered.'

'But what about my milk?' I asked.

The First Day of Spring

'I think you've had enough milk to last you a good long time,' she said.

'But what about my *biscuit*?' I asked.

'You can miss that too. It's hardly going to kill you,' she said.

I went to the door, but as I passed the last line of desks I held out my arm and swiped it across, hitting the row of milk bottles hard enough that they flew into the wall. Milk went everywhere. Lots of kids squealed. Miss White shouted. I turned around.

'I'm just going to sit in the corridor like you *asked* me to,' I said. 'I just knocked over some bottles on an accident. It's just milk. It's hardly going to *kill* anyone.'

In the corridor I slid down the wall under the pegs and sat with my knees against my chest. It was hot that day. As I had left the classroom I had smelt the tang of yellowed milk, droplets collected in sour pimples on the carpet. Soon it would be the summer holidays. Six weeks of no school. Six weeks of no break-time milk and biscuit, no school dinner, no sweets on someone's birthday. My belly made a noise like a faraway train.

*

A new family was moving into number 43. On Saturday I sat on the wall opposite and watched the da carrying boxes in from a van. He hefted them up two at a time, one under each arm, and went back and forth until the van was empty and the house was full. I knew they must have a kid, because some of the boxes (lots of the boxes, most of the boxes) were full of toys, and I knew it must be a girl because one of the toys was a baby doll wearing a puffy pink dress. Boys didn't play with babies, especially babies in puffy pink dresses. The da came back out of the house holding two mugs of tea and two slices of cake on two plates, and he passed one of the mugs and one of the plates of cake to the van driver and leant against the van as they talked. I was too far away to hear what they were saying, but after a while the driver gave the empty plate back to the da and the da waved him off. The van went past me with a clanking growl and the da went back into the house.

If I hadn't seen the da giving the van driver a slice of cake on a plate I might not have knocked on the door of number 43, but my belly was seething with acid and empty air and at that moment I didn't want anything in the whole world as much as I wanted a slice of cake on a plate. So I jumped down from the wall and walked across to the green front door. Reached up and knocked it with three clear taps. Listened for the patter of feet inside.

It was the mammy who answered, and when she saw me she smiled a smile that stretched all the way into her cheeks. She had hair that flew in different directions, yellow like Steven's, not knotty and dark like Mam's. Behind her the hallway of the house was full of the boxes the da had carried in from the van, some of them half-unpacked. I thought that was probably why her hair was flying in all different directions.

'Hello, pet,' she said. I didn't say anything, because I was busy realising something, then quickly realising something else. The first thing I realised was that she was the woman who hadn't adopted me; the beautiful woman who had been there when Mam had left me at the adoption agency, who had said I was too old to love. The second thing I realised was that she didn't remember me. She was looking at me with her head tilted to one side, yellow hair falling in a fringe over her forehead, and her eyes weren't clouding the way they do for remembering. They were crinkling the way they do for meeting-for-the-first-time.

'Can I help you, pet?' she asked when I still didn't speak.

'I'm Chrissie,' I said. 'I live down the street. I live at number eighteen.'

'Oh, do you, pet? How lovely. We've just moved in today. As you can see!' She waved her hand at the boxes.

'I know. I saw the van. I just came to see if you wanted any help unpacking your boxes.' That was a lie, because I didn't even slightly want to unpack any boxes, but I did want to be invited into her house and given a slice of cake on a plate. And most of all, now that I knew who she was, I wanted to meet the kid she had chosen instead of me.

'Oh, bless you,' she said. 'What a kind girl. Well, no need for you to help with our unpacking. My Pat has that covered. But come in anyway. There's a fruitcake in the kitchen, and I know my little girl will be excited to meet you.'

My little girl. My little girl. My little girl. At the very least the kid she had chosen could have been a little boy. It could just have been a little boy, and it could just have hurt a little bit less.

In the hallway I had to watch my feet so I didn't tread on any of the things spilling out of the boxes. One was stuffed with flower-patterned plates, another with cloth napkins and tea towels, but all the rest were full of kid things. Hardcover picture books without chewed corners or missing pages. A doctor's set in a square red case, the same as Donna's but newer, shinier, and without the broken clasp. The puffy pink baby doll was in a box with a baby-doll pram and a baby-doll crib and a baby-doll high chair. I leant forward to see better, and the beautiful woman laughed and put her hand on my shoulder.

'Mad really, aren't we? All these toys for one little girl. I'm sure we spoil her. But I expect your mammy's the same with you.' She crossed to open the door at the side of the hallway, so she didn't see me shake my head. She didn't see me reach up to stroke the patch of warm left on my shoulder where she had touched. She picked up the box of baby-doll things and walked into a room I knew would be the lounge, because all the houses on the street had the same rooms in the same places.

'Sweetheart!' she said. 'A special surprise for you! Look – a girl's come to see you! A big girl who lives down the street!'

A big girl. A too-big girl. A girl too big to love.

She beckoned and I picked my way through the boxes to the door. The lounge was bare, but there was a new-looking couch against one wall and a telly on a telly table against the other. The little girl was sitting in the middle of a round white rug on the floor. She had tiger-coloured hair. She was Ruthie.

The beautiful woman knelt down and beckoned me to come closer. I felt like I was being beckoned toward an expensive puppy, and I wanted to tell her I didn't need to be beckoned, because I knew Ruthie already. I knew all about Ruthie and her hundreds of toys and her mammy who dressed her like a doll and bought her everything she wanted. I just hadn't known that that mammy was the beautiful woman who should have been my mammy.

'How old is she?' I asked.

'You're three, aren't you, angel?' said the beautiful woman, leaning over to cup Ruthie's cheek. Her hair had been gathered into bunches either side of her head and tied with ribbons the same pink as her dress. She looked the same as she had when I had seen her in the playground with Donna: neat and smooth as the dolls Linda's mammy kept in cabinets in their lounge. Ruthie looked like she was made of china, and the beautiful woman touched her the same way Linda's mammy touched her dolls, slowly, with her fingers, not her hands. I wanted to ask the beautiful woman whether she had chosen Ruthie and not me because Ruthie was pretty and I was ugly, or whether it was because she was three and I was eight, and at what point between three and eight a kid got too old to love.

Ruthie ignored all the cupping and cuddling. She didn't tell the beautiful woman she had met me before, or that I had slapped her arm and pulled her off the roundabout. She didn't seem very interested in me at all, only in the metal xylophone she was bashing.

'Clever girl, Ruthie!' said the beautiful woman. 'You're showing Chrissie how well you can play your xylophone, aren't you?' Ruthie scowled and did some more bashing. I thought if that was playing the xylophone well, I really didn't want to hear someone play the xylophone badly. It sounded like tin cans being thrown in a dustbin. I knew I was meant to be watching Ruthie, but I watched the beautiful woman watching Ruthie instead. She was drinking her in, letting her flood into her bones, as if Ruthie was a peppermint humbug turned over on her tongue or a can of cream soda made salty by sweaty lips.

'Well, who'd like a slice of cake?' the beautiful woman asked. She rubbed her hands together, and they didn't make the scritch-scratch noise Mam's hands made when they rubbed. The skin was soft and the sound was smooth. I nodded that I did want some cake, and Ruthie nodded too, but as the beautiful woman turned to go to the kitchen Ruthie screamed, 'Mammy, I only want choccy cake, not yucky raisin cake.'

The beautiful woman laughed her tinkle-bell laugh. 'Honestly, Chrissie. I spend a whole afternoon making a lovely fruitcake and as I'm taking it out of the oven Ruthie tells me she doesn't like raisins! But luckily the nice lady in the corner shop found us a choccy cake, didn't she, Ruthie?'

'Was it Mrs Bunty?' I asked.

'The lady in the corner shop?' said the beautiful woman. 'I don't know. Why?'

'Just that if it was Mrs Bunty, she's not nice,' I said. 'She's actually really horrid and mean.'

'Really?' said the beautiful woman. 'Well, this lady certainly seemed very nice. She loved you, didn't she Ruthie?'

Ruthie nodded, and it was like she was saying, 'The thing is, I'm little and pretty and my clothes match, and that means everyone likes me, even mean old women who don't normally like anyone except God.'

'Which would you like, pet?' the beautiful woman asked me. 'Fruit or chocolate?'

'Both,' I said. And then, when I remembered, 'Please.'

She laughed again. 'Now there's a girl who knows what's what, eh? Of course you can have both.'

When she went to get the cake Ruthie took the baby doll out of the box and laid a blanket over it.

'Baby's going to sleep now,' she screamed, not particularly to me, though I was the only one in the room. 'Baby always goes to sleep in the morning. That's her nap. She's only a baby. I don't have a nap any more. I'm not a baby.'

'Stop screaming,' I said.

'When you're a baby you have a nap in the morning,' she screamed. 'I don't have a nap in the morning. My baby's having a nap in the morning. She's a baby.'

'How long have you been living with that woman?' I asked.

'My baby—'

'The woman who was just in here. The woman who made the cake.'

'Mammy?'

'She's not really your mammy, is she? Did you go to the adoption agency? Did she see you there?'

'Come on, baby!' she screamed into its face. 'It's time for breakfast!' She picked it up by its ankle. I thought maybe it needed to be adopted too.

'How long have you been living with that woman?' I asked, nearly shouting. 'How long has she been your mammy?'

I would have shaken her to get her to listen if the beautiful woman hadn't come in with the tea tray. She put it in the middle of the rug because there was no table, and she gave Ruthie the plate with the chocolate cake on it and herself the plate with the fruitcake on it and me the plate with both cakes on it. I remembered to chew on the right side of my mouth, so the cake didn't even hurt me, it just filled me up. Ruthie only played with hers – peeled off the crackly chocolate layer and dug out the icing with her fingers. Brown smears outlined her mouth, and the beautiful woman spat on a cloth napkin and wiped them away. If I had known she was going to do that, I would have tried to make a mess of my face too.

I had just finished my squash when the unpacking man came in with another box of toys. Ruthie saw it, abandoned the baby, and ran to him. He stroked her head. I had never seen two grown-ups kiss and cuddle and stroke a kid so much. You could almost forget what Ruthie's cheeks and top of head looked like, because there was barely a second when they weren't hidden under a grown-up hand. She put up with the kissing and cuddling and stroking the way you put up with bedbug bites: they were annoying but you knew they weren't going to go away, so you just had to try to ignore them.

'Pat, this is Chrissie,' said the beautiful woman to the unpacking man. She put her hand between my shoulder blades and my insides shivered. 'She lives down the street. Did you say it was number eighteen, pet?'

'Yes,' I said.

'She came to meet Ruthie. Ruthie's so excited to have another girl to play with.'

The unpacking man leant down to shake my hand.

'Pleasure to meet you, Chrissie,' he said. He wore glasses with fine gold rims around the edges, and there were two little patches of steam at the bottom of the two lenses. 'I'm Ruthie's da. Lovely for her to have a big girl to play with.'

'Yes,' I said. 'Too-big girl,' I thought.

'How's it looking?' the beautiful woman asked the unpacking man as he sat down on the couch.

'Not too bad,' he said. 'Put most of the boxes in the right rooms. Just need to unpack them now. Chilly up there.'

'Have you put the heater in Ruthie's room? Ought to turn it on for a couple of hours before she goes for her nap.'

'Yep, it's on.' He leant back, steepled his fingers on his chest, and closed his eyes. The beautiful woman gave me a look that said, 'Honestly, my silly husband, going to sleep in the middle of the morning!' and I gave her a look that said, 'Yes, honestly, your silly husband, going to sleep in the middle of the morning!' I felt cosy when we made that look to each other, like we were wrapped in a blanket that was squeezing us together until our noses touched. Then Ruthie's voice came, a shrill squawk, and she was in between us.

'Is my room big, Da?' she screamed.

'Your room is the perfect size for a little girl like you,' he said. 'Why don't you take Chrissie up and show her?'

In the hallway the cold bit my bones. It was sunny outside, but the house was chilled the way houses get chilled when no one lives in them for a long time, the way the alley houses had been chilled since the poorest people had stopped living there. Ruthie led the way up the stairs, her soft-soled shoes stamping on the bare wood. When we got to the landing and I saw the open door at the end I realised her bedroom was a twin with my bedroom, in her house that was a twin with my house, in her life that should have been my life. Inside, I sat on the bed, not listening to Ruthie clattering more toys out of more boxes, and my ticking turned on like a light. It rang in my ears, pumped to the tips of my fingers, so loud I thought I would explode. When it was pulsing in every bit of my body I pulled back the bedclothes, crouched, and peed on the mattress. It sounded different to how it had sounded in the blue house, more muffled, and the pee stood in a round puddle before soaking in. It made the ticking quieter. When I finished I put the covers over the wet patch.

Ruthie had stopped screaming. She was watching me with her big, serious eyes. 'That's for the toilet,' she said.

'*You're* for the toilet,' I said.

She didn't seem to realise what a very clever and mean thing that was to have said, because she didn't gasp or cry. She went back to grabbing toys out of boxes and throwing them on the floor.

I wanted to do a lot of things in that room. I wanted to cut a long slice in my skin, wet my hands with the blood, and drag them over the floor in cherry-coloured trails. I wanted to empty out the boxes of toys, seize them in armfuls, and throw them out of the window. I wanted to run to the shop and steal cans of spray paint, run back and write ugly words all over the walls, the same as the words I had scribbled on the walls of the blue house. I wanted to climb into the wardrobe. I wanted to curl up small enough to lie on the floor of the tall wooden box. I wanted to stay forever in Ruthie's beautiful room, with Ruthie's beautiful mammy. Without Ruthie.

JULIA

Describing the five-to-five-thirty slot at Linda's house as chaotic was like describing a tornado as a slight breeze. It was difficult to count the number of kids present, because they never stopped moving and most of them seemed to be twins, but I thought there must be at least twelve. They ranged from boys and girls in school uniforms to a baby in a bouncer, who glared at us when we came into the kitchen. I sat down at a dining table covered in bowls of congealed shepherd's pie. It had been a long time since I had eaten. If Linda hadn't been swooping in and out I would have clawed up the leftover food with my fingers. Molly went into the garden and started telling a younger girl how to hula-hoop. The doorbell seemed to ring every few seconds, and with each ring Linda scooped up a different kid and returned them to their parent. She smiled at me whenever she came in, and gave me a look that said, 'Isn't this crazy? Isn't this mad? Me, Linda, in charge of all these kids!'

By five forty-five the crowd had thinned. 'Phew,' she said. 'Sorry. It's the busiest time of the day.'

'When are the others getting picked up?' I asked.

'Who?' she asked. I looked into the garden at the kids around Molly: a toddler, twin girls, and an older boy.

'Oh,' she said. 'They're mine.'

'All of them?'

'Yeah.'

'But there's four.'

'There'll be five soon.'

'Really?' I said. I tried not to look at her belly. 'When?'

'Not until October. A while to wait.'

'I don't think I could cope with more than one.'

'No?'

'No.'

It was one of the things I had thought about on the train, during the peace of Molly's sulk. 'Perhaps I could get back here,' I thought. 'I could find someone else to sleep with, and start again with a different baby, and not mess things up. I could be better. I could follow what the book says more carefully. I'm good at starting again. It's the only thing I'm good at.' It had been a cold, deadening thing to think, because I knew it wouldn't work. If Molly was a gift and no-kid was neutrality, then a not-Molly kid was a curse. I could throw away my life and replace it with a new one over and over again, but it wouldn't work with her. She wasn't disposable.

I watched her take off her coat and throw it on the grass. I called for her to bring it to me. She came in scowling. 'That girl's rubbish at hula-hooping,' she said.

'Don't be rude,' I said.

'It's just true,' she said.

She lingered for a minute, looking at the bowls on the table.

'Are you all right, sweetie?' Linda asked.

'No,' she said. 'I'm actually very *very* badly hungry.'

'I'll get you something later,' I said, but Linda was already on her feet.

'You can have some shepherd's pie, Molly. There's loads here. It's still warm.' She looked at me. 'Will you have some too?'

I wanted to refuse, but I also wanted to eat. The urges tussled until Linda took two bowls from a cupboard.

'I'll give you some,' she said. 'You can leave it if you don't want it.'

We ate at the table. I felt like we were two of Linda's kids. The pie was thick, textured with meat and grainy potato. Molly forked it in until her lips were ringed with orange. Linda cleared away the other bowls, pausing to make an appreciative noise about a kid's activity every few minutes. Molly finished and went back into the garden.

'I thought you might not still live here,' I said when Linda sat down.

'Oh, yeah, we do,' she said. 'Didn't make sense to move. We got the house after Mam and Da died. Pete lived with us for a bit, but then he went to Africa.'

'Africa?'

'Yeah. He's a missionary. We're so proud. He's doing such good work.'

'Wow,' I said. I wanted to ask whether he still had a wonky foot, and whether he remembered the afternoon I had tried to take him to the alleys, but I thought those probably wouldn't be helpful things to mention. 'I'm sorry about your mam and da.'

'Yeah. They were quite young. Mam wasn't well for a long time, but it was a shock with Da.'

'I'm sorry.'

'It's OK. You figure it out. So we got the house, me and Kit. That's my husband. It made sense to stay. And he did it up. He's a builder. He put in the French windows and everything. There was a problem with some of the beams. They were weight-bearing or something. So it took ages. But it was really worth it. It's made the kitchen so much brighter. Because it faces the right direction. I can never actually remember which direction, but it's the right one. For the sun.'

'Where did you meet him?'

'Church. You know they always had those helpers at Sunday school? Teenagers? We did that. That's how we met. And then we got married. As soon as we left school.'

'But you were – what – sixteen?'

'We were really ready. We had a lovely wedding. So posh. We had salmon.'

'Yeah?'

'Not even in a tin. In a *fish*.'

'Wow.'

I wished I had something real to say back – 'Salmon in a fish, eh? Good choice. At my wedding we had chicken in a bird' – but our lives felt far apart. To me, sixteen was the fifth Haverleigh bedroom. I shared it with Nina, whose face was decorated with silver-pink knots of scar, because one of the other girls had thrown boiling sugar water in her face the day she'd arrived. I ran in when I heard her screaming. She was writhing on the floor, clutching her cheeks, her skin bubbling and blistering like a vat of jam. Normal boiling water only burnt for a bit, but sugar water stuck like glue. The scalding went on and on. Nina lived in the medical bay for a while after that, and when she came back she never stayed in our bedroom for long. Every couple of weeks she swallowed something that wasn't for swallowing – bleach, batteries, letters from the Scrabble set – and the keepers had to take her to hospital. While Linda was setting up home and churning out kids, I was turning back the blankets on Nina's empty bed, wondering if she would be back or if this time she had managed to swallow herself to death.

'Is Molly's dad . . . ?' Linda said, reaching her hand up her back.

'No,' I said. 'He's not around.'

'Oh. Must be tough. I wouldn't manage without Kit.'

'You've got about five hundred kids, though.'

We watched the five hundred and one kids charge around the garden. Molly was throwing a Frisbee with the oldest boy, and it clipped the toddler on the side of the head. He came into the house howling.

'I'm so sorry,' I said. 'Molly. Come and say sorry.'

'Oh, don't be silly,' said Linda, pushing back her chair and gathering the toddler onto her lap. 'Accident, accident.' She carried him to a cupboard, took a small biscuit from a jar, and slipped it into his fist. His crying stopped like a tap turned off. Outside it was nearly dark, and the kids had a glowing look as they ran around, as though their limbs were lit from inside. The toddler put his head on Linda's shoulder. 'I need to start getting them to bed,' she said.

'Yeah. Of course. Sorry. We'll go,' I said.

'How long will it take you to get home?'

'Few hours. Four, maybe.'

'You can't do that. You wouldn't be home until midnight. Molly's – what – five?'

'We can cope.'

'Why don't you just stay here?'

'It's fine. We'll go.'

'But why don't you stay?'

'We can't. You've already given us loads.'

'Come on. I've just given you some tea. We haven't even talked properly. I want you to stay. Please. Please, just let me be nice to you.'

I spent a lot of the next hour hanging in hallways, feeling spare. Linda was more than capable of executing the bath and bedtime ritual alone, even with an extra kid, even when that kid was Molly, who was drunk and over-confident on the departure from routine. Linda told her she didn't have to have a bath if she didn't want to take her clothes off in a strange house, but she was naked by the time she reached the top of the stairs, jumping into the tub next to the twins, suddenly oblivious to the hunk of plaster around her wrist. I helped her into the Spiderman pyjamas Linda found at the bottom of her son's drawer and squeezed toothpaste onto my finger to rub around her mouth. I was amazed that the process of bathing and changing and tooth brushing took the same amount of time for five kids as for one. When they were all clean and smelling of peppermint Linda gathered them onto her bed for a story, and I felt as though I was in a story, because I hadn't known this kind of anarchic joy existed outside books. I sat with my back against the wardrobe and lis-tened to her read – the way she pointed to the words and sounded out the letters. You would have believed it was for the kids if you hadn't known her as an eight-year-old, hunched over her reading book in the classroom, pink grooves in her knuckles where they pressed against the desk. I thought of what I had said to Mam. *If you want to, you figure it out. Most of the time it's really hard and boring, but it's not impossible. You just have to really want to do it.*

When I settled Molly on the couch downstairs she tucked the blanket under her chin and sighed.

'I like it here,' she said.

'Yeah,' I said.

'It's fun.'

'Yeah.'

'I like that woman.'

'Mmm.'

I stood to leave, but she sat up. 'Where are you going?' she asked.

'Just into the kitchen,' I said.

'Aren't you going to stay?' she asked. It shouldn't have surprised me. In her world, there was no alternative to my sitting by her bed until she went to sleep. I heard the front door open, Linda call, and a man answer. I sat back down.

'Yeah. Course,' I said.

She was asleep within minutes, and when I went into the kitchen Linda and the man were sitting at the table. I felt shy. He was wide-set and stubbly.

'This is Kit,' Linda said. 'I've been telling him about how we used to be friends. At secondary school.'

'So nice to meet you,' he said. 'I don't know many of Linda's friends.'

'Yeah,' I said. 'Well. Thanks for having us. Thanks for letting us stay.'

'Don't be silly,' he said. 'You're brave to accept. It's a madhouse here. We never really know how many we've got for the night anyway.'

Linda fetched plates from the cupboard and served up more shepherd's pie. She gave me some without checking I wanted to eat again. Kit drank a bottle of beer, and when the pie was finished we ate chocolate ice cream from bowls the kids had painted. At nine o'clock Kit stood up and stretched.

'Really sorry, but I'd better turn in. I've got to be on-site at six tomorrow,' he said.

I thought of Mam, sneaking out before the sun came up, head bowed, feet dragging. I pushed her away.

'So nice to meet you, Donna,' he called as he went upstairs. 'Hope I'll see you again soon.'

And then it was just us, Linda and me. It was always us, really.

'I'm so sorry,' she said. 'I hate lying. It's really bad. I just didn't think you'd want me to tell him about you. I thought it was safest to make something up. And I didn't know what you'd want to be called. So I panicked and said you were Donna.'

'Well that's unforgivable,' I said. 'My face looks nothing like a potato.'

She laughed. 'I was going to ask if you remembered that,' she said.

'I was proud of it,' I said. 'It was cutting.'

'It's Julia, isn't it?' she said, taking the ice cream bowls to the sink. 'Your new name, I mean.'

'Yes,' I said. 'I don't really want you to call me that, though. I'd rather you just called me Chrissie.'

Haverleigh was the last place I was really Chrissie. It was the last place I let myself cling to people with her leechlike suction, the last place I stuck out my chin when they told me off. It was the last place I wet the bed. At Haverleigh they understood: our mattresses were rubber, and we had laundry baskets and extra sheets in our rooms, so if you were wet in the morning you could change your sheets between checks without anyone knowing. When I first got there I didn't understand about checks, about the clear fifteen-minute windows between them, and a keeper came into my room while I was taking the wet sheet off my bed. I froze, hunched over, thinking of the damp circle on the back of my nightie. The keeper went to the opposite end of the bed and unhooked the corners of the sheet.

'Why are you in my room?' I asked.

'Just checks,' she said. 'Thought you could use a hand sorting your bed.'

'I don't want your hand. I hate you. You're ugly. I hate the way you look. I don't want you on my checks any more. I want someone else. Anyone who's not you,' I said.

She bundled the sheet into a ball and dropped it into my laundry basket. 'I'm afraid it's me this morning,' she said.

'I spilt some water on my bed,' I said. 'I was having a drink in bed and I spilt it on my sheets.'

We didn't have sinks in our rooms, and we never had drinks in bed, and I couldn't have spilt a drink on the back of my nightie even if I had tried.

'Oh dear,' she said. 'That was bad luck.'

She fetched a clean sheet from the wardrobe and shook it over the mattress. 'You know, a lot of kids here spill their drinks in bed,' she said. 'That's why we have extra sheets in the wardrobes. It's not a problem. Why don't you choose some clothes? Most of the boys aren't up yet. I'll take you for a shower.'

I wet the bed my last night at Haverleigh, then never again. The outside world dried me into a liquidless husk. It was lonely and it was safe. Nothing could hurt me if I had nothing inside. Sometimes I thought what I missed about Haverleigh wasn't Haverleigh at all, but who I had been there. Sometimes I thought what I missed was Chrissie.

'Does Donna still live here?' I asked.

'No,' said Linda. 'She moved into town. Most people our age did. There's not much here. You start to realise that when you're not a kid any more.'

'Where are Steven's family?' I asked.

'They went to the countryside. After that campaign. Did you know about it? The campaign?'

I had seen it on the telly in the Haverleigh lounge. Steven's mammy's face had been big and old-looking on the screen. The hair falling down her back was long and lankly brittle, and her shoulders were dusted with white flecks of dandruff. By then it had been years since Steven had died, but she still looked rotted with grief, like someone who had had their insides pulled out and spread on hot tarmac to fry and stink.

'It's just not right,' she had said to the reporter. 'She's had – what – nine years? Nine years in a glorified boarding school. She's never even seen the inside of a cell. And now they want to let her out? Want to let her start again? How is that justice for my son? Steven doesn't get to start again. I don't. She deserves a life sentence. No – to hell with it. She deserves the death penalty.'

She had had a photograph of Steven clutched against her, the same as the one on the cover of Susan's book. She had pushed it at the reporter. 'Look at him,' she had said. 'Just look at him. Look at him and tell me that monster deserves to be free. He died without his mammy. He died frightened. It's every mammy's worst nightmare: for your kid to be without you and frightened. She's scum.'

That was what happened to kids like Steven: they got frozen in a state of perfection, ever pure, ever wonderful, because they were only ever two years old. Most kids lived long enough to make mistakes and let people down and do bad things, and they weren't perfect, they were just living. Kids like Steven didn't get to carry on living, so they got perfection instead. It was a kind of trade. I didn't much mind the things his mammy had said about me. They were just true. Scum was thin and grimy, and it floated on top of liquid, stretched out, diffuse. That was how I felt: as though I was floating on top of the world, waiting to be skimmed off and thrown away.

Linda pulled out a piece of her hair and started tying it in knots. 'You get it, don't you?' she said. 'Why she couldn't forgive you. I mean. Imagine if it was Molly.'

I wanted to scream. 'Linda, all I do is imagine it was Molly,' I wanted to howl. 'All I've ever done, ever since she was born, is imagine it was Molly. Sometimes I look at Molly and I wonder if I've ever even seen her, ever even seen what she really looks like, because I don't see her face when I look at her. I see a face with the life squeezed out of it. And there are moments where I forget, where Molly's laughing, and I catch myself enjoying her, and then I remember I can't. Because I took that away from other people, and they never get to enjoy their kid laughing, or smiling, or growing. Not ever again. I want them to forgive me, but I know they can't, because I couldn't forgive me if it was Molly. Sometimes I think I didn't need a life sentence, because I got Molly instead. She's my sentence. As long as I have her I won't be able to forget what I did. Not ever. Not *ever*.'

'I should just give up, really, shouldn't I?' I said. My voice sounded thick, as though my nose was blocked, and I made myself laugh to show I wasn't crying.

'What do you mean?' Linda asked.

'I can't ever get the time back. And I can't ever make it right. So it's all pointless. It's all stupid. I should just give up.'

'What "all"? What should you give up?'

'Just all of it. All of the trying.'

'Because people won't forgive you?'

'Yeah.'

'I think that should mean the opposite of giving up.'

'What?'

'I don't think they'll forgive you whatever you do. So you could spend your whole life being as miserable as possible, because you made them as miserable as possible, and they wouldn't forgive you. Or you could just have a normal life, just try, like the rest of us, just try to make things as good as they can be for you and Molly. And they wouldn't forgive you. They don't forgive you in either version. You can't make things better for your kid. But there are two people you can make things better for.'

'One. Molly.'

'Two. Molly and you.'

I didn't say anything. Pointlessness clogged my throat like hardened grease in a drain, and it wasn't the pointlessness of trying to make people forgive me. It was the pointlessness of imagining a future for two people who would soon be wrenched apart.

'They're taking her away,' I said. I hadn't meant it as a retort, but that was how it came out. Clipped and snappy.

'Who? Social?' Linda asked.

'Yeah,' I said.

'Why?'

'Just not much of a mam, I suppose.'

'Not sure anyone feels like much of a mam.'

I laughed. It came out mean. 'Like you're not perfect,' I said.

'Me?' she said. 'What? Have you seen the state of this place? It's a shambles. We've got more kids than we can even nearly afford, and soon there'll be another one. I mean, I love them, I love being their mammy. Of course I do. And I'm better at it than I've been at anything else. But perfect? Not even nearly. Not even close.'

'You seem pretty good to me,' I said.

She looked down, and pink crawled into her cheeks in blotches. It occurred to me that it might be the first time I had ever told her she was good at anything. She couldn't stop the corners of her mouth dragging upwards. It was obvious for me to want to go back in time and undo the big wrongs, but in that moment I would have settled for changing the small ones. I wished we could go back to being eight years old, just so I could be nicer to Linda, just so I could tell her she was good at handstands, a good best friend.

'Why do you think they're going to take Molly?' she asked, scrubbing her face with her sleeve as if she could wipe away the blush.

'Her wrist,' I said.

'Is it broken?'

'Yeah.'

'Poor thing. Lily had a broken wrist last year.'

'Really?'

'Yeah. She liked it at first – the cast and everything – but by the end she was really bored. She wanted to go swimming and stuff. And the year before Jason broke his leg and Charlotte got this awful cut on her head. Any lower and it would have been her eye out. Felt like we lived in A and E that year.'

'Weren't you worried?'

'Well, yeah. But they're sturdy, little ones. They bounce back.'

'They're not sturdy. They can get badly hurt. Really easily. Before you even know what you're doing.'

'This isn't like that. It was an accident.'

'She was on this wall. She wasn't meant to be, but she climbed up. I wasn't looking. I tried to get her down. I pulled her arm. She fell.'

'Exactly. That's an accident. Jason broke his leg because I tripped and knocked into him at the top of the stairs. He fell the whole way down. I felt awful, but you just have to forget about it. You never mean to hurt them.'

We sat without speaking for a while. The dark outside made the French windows into a mirror, so I could see us at the table. Our reflections looked like women, which seemed wrong. In my head we were still two stringy kids, stealing sweets and walking on walls and turning ourselves upside down in handstands.

'Why did you come?' asked Linda.

'Don't really know. I just found out about them taking Molly. Just yesterday. It made me want to come back.'

It was hard to believe Sasha's call had been that recent. The time between then and now had expanded in a bubble-gum stretch, feeling like weeks, not hours. It occurred to me that I should check how long it had been since the meeting. It occurred to me that I wouldn't gain anything from knowing.

'So you didn't come because of the calling? At all?' she said.

'What?'

'I just tried to call you a few times. And then a few weeks ago you picked up. And I thought maybe if you had dialled that number that told you who had been calling, you might have known it was me. And you might have come to see me.' Her voice got quieter as she spoke, until it was only really breath, loosely shaped into words. The effort made it hoarse. Like a can peeling open.

'That was you? You were calling me?'

'Just a few times. I wasn't trying to scare you or any-thing. You gave me your number the last time you wrote.'

'Why were you calling? You didn't before. You never even replied to my letters.'

'I know. I'm sorry. I felt really bad about it. But – you know – I'm still hopeless, Chrissie. I can barely write, even now. I didn't want you to know I was still like that. It was easier to call.'

'But why now?'

'Same as for you, I suppose. Just felt like the right time. I'd just found out I was pregnant. I've always thought of you when I've been pregnant, ever since I knew you had a little girl. I always wondered how you would have coped. This is the last baby we're having. I won't be pregnant again. Just made me want to speak to you.'

For a second, a window into a different world cracked open, a world where Linda and I had been pregnant together and Molly had grown up in step with her twins. It hurt in a hot, bright way, like looking straight at the sun.

'I thought it was the papers calling,' I said. 'I thought our social worker had told them about me.'

'Why would she have done that?'

'Why wouldn't she?'

'Because it's her job to look after you.'

I thought of things to say back – 'No one's ever looked after me' or 'It's no one's job to look after me' or 'It's not her job to look after me'. I dragged my nail in circles on the tabletop.

'I thought you hated me,' I said.

'Well I don't,' said Linda.

'That's just because you're really Christian, though,' I said.

She smiled with half her mouth. 'I am a Christian. But I wouldn't hate you even if I wasn't.'

'Did you miss me?' I asked. It came out unbearable – young and needy – and I had to look at the Linda in the window, not the one next to me, while I waited for her to answer.

'Yeah,' she said.

'I was awful to you.'

'Nah. You just teased. And you looked out for me, didn't you?'

'I was a monster.'

'You were my friend.'

I pulled my legs up onto my chair and pushed my face into my knees, so my lips were pressed flat to my teeth. 'Best friend,' I said into my jeans.

It was what I had said in my cell, on the one day of the trial that had made me upset. I hadn't been upset when Donna's mammy had stood up and called me 'trouble' and 'wicked' and 'evil'. I hadn't been upset when Steven's mammy had stood up and said I deserved to be hung, drawn, and quartered (because I hadn't really known what that meant). I had been upset when it was Linda's mammy's turn.

'How do you know Christine?' asked the man in the white wig.

'She was friends with my daughter, Linda,' said Linda's mammy.

'Close friends?' said White Wig.

'I think Chrissie would have said so,' said Linda's mammy. 'Chrissie would have said they were best friends. My Linda, she's friends with everyone, really. I see lots of little girls at the house – more than I can keep track of, sometimes. Chrissie was just one of them.'

I felt a sharp pain in my middle and put my hand on it. I could feel my pulse under my palm. I wondered if my heart had dropped down to my belly.

'But you saw a lot of Christine,' said White Wig. 'You've told us she spent a good deal of time at your house. More time at your house than at her own.'

Linda's mammy looked to the side, to where Mam was sitting alone on a bench. She turned her body towards White Wig. 'I don't think there was a lot for her to go home to,' she said.

'What do you mean by that?' asked White Wig.

'Chrissie's Mam. Eleanor. She struggled.'

'Struggled in what way?'

'Just struggled. Ever since Chrissie was small. I remember pushing Linda's pram past the house and hearing a baby crying, and it wasn't normal crying, not like they're meant to. Proper howling. Screaming. It happened over and over, and I walked past over and over, because you don't want to pry, do you? Then one day I thought, this isn't right, really, it's not right, and I went to the door and knocked. Took a while but she came in the end – Eleanor – holding Chrissie.

I didn't even get a chance to say anything before she shoved her at me. "She just cries, I can't do it, you take her," she said, and she slammed the door.'

'And what did you do?' asked White Wig.

'What was I supposed to do? She was a scrap. Half Linda's size, and Linda wasn't big. I took her home and gave her a bottle. Three bottles, actually – I kept her a couple of hours, and she was starving. And then I went back and Eleanor opened the door and took her from me like it was a completely normal thing. Like it was completely normal to have given your baby to a stranger for the afternoon.'

'And you didn't think to tell anyone about this? The social services? The police?'

'Of course I thought about it. Didn't think about much else, for a while. But what would I have said? "I know a baby that cries a lot." It would have sounded daft. And sometimes I saw Eleanor at church with the pram, and sometimes the da was there, and I thought, "Well. They're coping. They're fine." I couldn't do it to her. It would have felt like snitching. I couldn't do it to another mam.'

'The relationship between Christine and her mother. From an outside perspective, what was it like as she got older?'

Linda's mammy turned herself further round, so she had her back to Mam. 'Eleanor did what she could to be rid of Chrissie,' she said. 'Like I said, I don't know what it was

– hadn't wanted a kid, couldn't cope with a kid, couldn't cope with *that* kid. Whatever. But you looked at what was going on with them two, and it was hard to believe she cared about Chrissie at all.'

The words burbled up from my chest like sick. 'Shut up,' I said. It was loud enough to make people look at me. 'Shut up, shut up, shut up.'

Linda's mammy didn't look. She stayed facing the judge.

'I always said I'd do my best for Chrissie,' she said. 'I said it to my husband – "We've got to do our best for this little girl, she's not got much." It's what we believe in, what He teaches us. I did do my best for a while. When she was little. I had her round, fed her, gave her some of Linda's clothes. But then she got older. She got tougher. I stopped doing things for her, because I thought if I kept on doing things for her she'd keep on hanging around. I didn't want her playing with Linda all the time. I didn't want people thinking of them as a pair.'

She coughed a wet-sounding cough and wiped something off her cheek. 'She did terrible things. She did. But she's just a kid. She needed people like me to come through for her and I didn't. I failed her. We all did. She's just a little girl.'

She looked at me over her shoulder. It was like she couldn't make her eyes stick. They drooped down to the floor underneath my glass box, and across to the bench where Steven's mammy was sitting.

'I'm sorry,' she said.

I put my hands over my face. I didn't speak. I shouted.

'I hate you, I hate you, I hate you.'

I shouted and panted and stamped my feet on the floor of the box, one and then the other, like I was running or marching. The guards took hold of me under the arms and dragged me down the stairs, into a cell. They held me until I got too tired to kick and scream any more. Then they left.

'We *are* best friends,' I whispered when I was by myself. 'Me and Linda *are* best friends. And I *didn't* need you. And Mam *does* care about me.'

Now, sitting at the table, Linda didn't say anything for long enough that my cheeks boiled and my throat burnt, and then she said, 'Yeah. Best friends,' so quietly I only just heard it. But I did hear it. I swallowed it whole.

'Thanks,' I said.

'You should get some sleep,' she said. 'You must be so tired.'

'Yeah. Probably,' I said. I didn't want to stop talking. Over the years I had spent hours imagining the things I would say to her when we were reunited, and I hadn't voiced even a fraction. It was the way it had been with Mam: these weren't the grand unburdenings I had rehearsed, but surreal run-ins with people very different from the characters who lived in my head. I thought perhaps that was how it would always feel, even if I talked to them for a month, because I couldn't be unburdened from something that was mine to carry.

'Are you going to go home tomorrow?' she asked.

'Maybe. I don't know,' I said.

'Will they be looking for you?'

'Yeah. Molly has this court order. It means I have to do what they say. I can't just take her away if I want to. They treat it like kidnap.'

'OK.' If she was shocked, she managed to keep it out of her voice.

'I don't know if we'll go back tomorrow, though,' I said. 'I was thinking maybe I should wait until they actually track us down. It might be days and days.'

'I think it might be better just to face it,' she said. 'I think they'll feel better about it if you go back and admit you made a mistake.'

'Maybe it would just be better if they took her.'

'Why?'

'Just seems right, doesn't it? For me to lose her. It's what I did to other people, so it's what should happen to me.'

'Like – what – a tooth for a tooth?'

'Kind of.'

'It doesn't work that way though, does it? They gave you a punishment for what you did. You went to prison for a long time. You can't go on being punished and punished forever.'

'I didn't go to prison. I went to a Home.'

'But it wasn't an actual home. It's not like it's somewhere you would have chosen to be. You weren't free.'

The First Day of Spring

I ground my molars together until grit coated my tongue. It was hard to describe the freedoms I had missed when I was at Haverleigh – the scratchy spin of rolling down grass hills, the smell of birthday cake candles – and harder to admit that the losses had been so much smaller than the gains. Underneath the layers of guilt and complication, three things were true: that Haverleigh had given me what I needed; that there had been a price for my being there; and that I hadn't been the one to pay it. It *was* where I would have chosen to be, and if I went back in time I would choose it again, over and over, and if it still existed it was where Molly and I would be at that moment, begging the keepers to take us in.

In court, one of the white wigs had said that the things I had done had lost me my childhood, and that that was punishment enough. He was right and wrong. I had lost something that spring – something light and precious – but without it I could still run around and climb trees and do handstands with my best friend. You couldn't do that if you were dead. Now I was older, and I lived with such a heavy millstone around my neck I sometimes felt my spine would buckle beneath it, but from time to time I became so absorbed in Molly that I forgot who I was, and I shrugged off the weight to rest on the ground. You couldn't do that if your kid was dead.

A high cry jolted me back – 'Mum, Mum, Mum' – but Linda didn't get up.

'You can go,' I said.

'It's Molly, isn't it?' she said.

'Mum, mum, mum.'

'But that's not my name,' I thought as I stood. I went down the hallway and into the lounge. Molly was sitting up straight on the couch, her fists balled against her eyes.

'It's fine,' I said. 'You're fine.'

She gulped and choked. I knelt down next to her. I put one hand on her back. 'It's fine, Molly,' I said. 'You just had a bad dream. You're fine.'

'I – woke – up – and – you – weren't – here –' she said. 'I – thought – you – left – me – here – by – my – self –'

There was space on the seat where her head had been, and I squeezed into it, pulled her backwards onto my lap. I was surprised it felt so much like muscle memory; it wasn't something my muscles had done enough to remember. Her arms went around my shoulders, and I was surprised again, surprised that our bodies fitted together when they had barely had to fit together since she had been inside me. She pressed her face to my neck, making it slick with spit and snot. The wetness made me feel that we were two pools of seawater merging, edgeless and saline. Her tongue touched my skin when she panted. There was a tug at my scalp and I saw a chunk of my hair wrapped around her hand. Haver-leigh came back to me in a wave so heavy I felt it as a blow to my gut.

The First Day of Spring

When the keepers had stopped me stealing food to eat at night I had eaten more at meals. Three times a day, I ate until I was sick. They started putting my food on a plate before I came to the dining room, giving it to me at a desk in the corner while the other kids ate at the trestle table. At night I screamed even louder.

'What's the *matter*, Chrissie?' asked my favourite keeper, coming into my room.

'I'm *hungry*,' I screamed.

'No, you're not, lovey,' she said. 'You had a good tea. You're full up.'

'I *am* hungry. I *am*,' I screamed. She sat down on the floor beside my bed. Most keepers didn't come that close to me, because I was so bad. I stopped screaming. I just whispered.

'I *am* hungry, I *am* hungry, I *am*.'

'You need to get to sleep,' she said. 'Go on. Lie down.'

I put my head on the pillow. She was close enough that I could take a chunk of her hair and grip it in my fist.

'I *am* hungry, I *am* hungry, I *am*.' I whispered it until my eyes were heavy, and just before they closed I whispered, 'Call me lovey again.'

'What, lovey?' she said. And then I was asleep, and when I woke in the morning she was gone. I still had a strand of yellow-brown hair tangled around my fingers, kinked and dead.

I pressed Molly's body closer to mine. She whimpered, and I felt her fist open and close around folds of my jumper. She liked it here. She liked Linda. But she needed me.

'I didn't leave you, lovey,' I said into her shoulder. 'I didn't leave you.'

CHRISSIE

After I got back from hospital I stayed away from the house as much as I could. I knew if I did anything to make Mam cross she could tell the police about Steven, or she could give me more tablet-Smarties, and I wasn't in the mood for either of those things. Sometimes she was cross if I stayed away for too long, because she said it was like I didn't love her. She was more usually cross if I was in the house, because when I was in the house I did annoying things like ask for food. I had decided she had probably given me the tablet-Smarties to try to turn me from a bad kid into a good one, and if she saw me she would realise I was still bad, and she might try something else to get me good. So it was safest to stay away.

'Your mammy will be wondering where you are, Chrissie,' Linda's mammy always said when I was still at her house at teatime. She meant, 'I am wondering why you are still here, Chrissie,' but I pretended not to know that.

'No she won't,' I always said. 'She never wonders where I am.' Linda's mammy liking me because of being in hospital hadn't lasted very long.

There were still policemen around the streets, and they still knocked on doors to talk to kids, and the mammies still twittered about it over their garden walls. Linda's mammy didn't do much twittering. She never really joined in with the other mammies. Probably because she was too old. You could get a heart attack from twittering when you were that old.

On Sunday I stayed after church to help Linda and her mammy put the knee cushions back on the pews, and Robert's mammy helped too. She kept sighing and tutting and saying, 'I don't know, oh, I don't know.' Linda's mammy didn't say anything, so Robert's mammy sighed and tutted and said, 'I don't know, oh, I don't know,' louder and louder until eventually she put her hands on her hips and said, 'I shouldn't tell you, really. I really shouldn't.'

'No need to tell me anything,' said Linda's mammy.

'I really shouldn't say. Not with the kiddies around,' said Robert's mammy.

'No. I'm sure you shouldn't,' said Linda's mammy, and went to the cupboard for the broom. Robert's mammy went too.

'You've heard what they're saying, haven't you?' she said.

'Don't expect I have,' said Linda's mammy. She swept the aisle between the pews and Robert's mammy waited for her to ask what it was that they had been saying. When she realised she wasn't going to, she followed her again.

'About why they've been asking all these questions to the kids? You have heard, haven't you?'

The First Day of Spring

Linda's mammy carried on sweeping. 'It'll just be gossip,' she said. 'Not worth hearing.'

'They're saying it must be a kid that did it,' said Robert's mammy. For a moment, Linda's mammy stopped sweeping and held her brush on the floor. Then she carried on. 'Did you hear me? A kid that did it?' said Robert's mammy.

'I heard,' said Linda's mammy.

'Awful, isn't it?' said Robert's mammy. 'Really chilling. I've felt chilled to my bones since I heard.' She didn't look very chilled to her bones. She looked how kids look when they come to school on their birthday wearing a birthday badge – puffed up and pink. Linda was at the other end of the church, tidying the box of Sunday school things, so she couldn't hear the mammies, but I was right behind them, crouched between two pews. I hunched down low so they wouldn't see me.

'Of course, you've got to wonder . . .' said Robert's mammy.

'Not got to,' said Linda's mammy. She was sweeping over the same patch she'd been sweeping for a while, though it was clean now.

'You've got to wonder,' said Robert's mammy. 'I've been racking my brains, but I don't know the older kids. I don't have an older one like your Linda – and it must have been an older one, mustn't it?'

I had taken off my cardigan before we had started tidying the knee cushions. It was hanging over the back of the pew closest to Linda's mammy. She picked it up, shook it out, and held it in front of her.

'Do you have any ideas?' asked Robert's mammy. Linda's mammy folded my cardigan in half and dropped it back onto the pew. She went to the cupboard to put the broom away.

'Linda,' she called. 'Come on. We're going.' Linda trotted to meet her, and I followed them out of the church and down the road. Linda's mammy was holding on to Linda's wrist and walking fast. When we got to the top of Marner Street she turned around to look at me.

'Go on. Away with you,' she said.

'But I want to play with Linda,' I said.

'Linda's coming home with me.'

'I'll come home too, then.'

'No, Chrissie,' she said. 'You'll not come. It's not your home.'

She pulled Linda down the street. I watched them get smaller and smaller until they went up the path to their house. By that time they were so far away I couldn't see if Linda turned to look at me or not. When I had been crouched between the pews in the church her mammy had swept clouds of dust over me, and I could feel it then, settled on my lungs in a powdery film.

There were lots of hours to fill when I was trying not to be at the house for too much time. When it was light I played out,

with Linda and William and Donna and now with Ruthie.
The others went home at teatime but I stayed out. I stayed
out until it was dark and my eyes were heavy, and then I
snuck into the house, up the stairs, and into bed with the
covers over my head.

On Saturday I was sitting on the grass in the yard of the
Bull's Head by myself, because it was teatime and everyone else had gone home. A man came out to smoke, and I
looked up and saw it was Da.

'Da?' I said. He had to squint his eyes to see me.

'Chris?' he said.

'I thought you were still dead,' I said. His hands were
being lazy and he couldn't get his smoke to light, so I
went and held it still for him. The flame licked the end and
glowed it orange.

'Cheers,' he said. He sucked it for a long time. 'Just
came back, didn't I?'

'When?'

'Just now. Last week, week before maybe.'

'Why didn't you come and see me?'

'You know. Sorting stuff. I was going to come and see
you now. Today. Just popped in for a quick drink.' He sat
down on the step and I sat in front of him. Da always told
me the first thing he did whenever he stopped being dead
was come and see me. He didn't even stop to put his bag
down anywhere, he just came straight to see me. That was
how much he missed me when we weren't together.

315

'Why didn't you come and see me straight away?' I asked.

'Jesus, Chris. Give me a break. I'm seeing you now, aren't I?' I dug my chin hard into my chest. If he had been there sooner I wouldn't have got sick from the Smarties because he would have been there to protect me.

'How're you keeping?' he asked. 'What you been up to?'

I lifted my chin, stuck it out towards him, and looked at his eyes. 'I've been in hospital,' I said.

'What?' he said.

'Mam gave me tablets in a Smarties tube. She told me to eat them all up. I nearly died.'

His hand went to his chin. Rub, rub, rub. Scratch, scratch, scratch. He put his smoke back in his mouth, then he took it out and ground it under his shoe. When both his hands were free he put them in his hair and clenched and unclenched his fingers so the skin on his forehead tightened and sagged.

'I had to be in the hospital for days and days,' I said. 'They had to suck all the stuff out of my belly. If they hadn't done it quick enough I would have died.'

'Don't tell me this, Chris,' he said. He stood up, and his hair stood up too, in sharp spikes. 'Please. Please don't tell me.'

'But you can help me,' I said. 'You're alive now. I can keep you safe so you don't get dead again and you can take me away.'

'No I can't,' he said. His voice sounded like a window with a crack that was letting in rain. 'I can't.'

'But you said you would. You said next time you saw me you would. You *said.*'

'I'm sorry, Chris,' he said. He turned to go back into the pub and I tried to follow him, but he pushed me away. 'Sorry. I'm sorry. I can't,' he said.

'Are you going to die again? Is that why?'

'For fuck's sake,' he said. 'Stop with the fucking dead thing. You're eight years old, Chris. You're too old to believe that. Stop.'

There was a fly crawling up the doorframe. He crushed it with his fist, leaving a smear of blue-black body on the white-painted wood. Normally I loved looking at dead things. When we found dead birds in the playground I poked them with sticks, spreading the gooey insides across the ground while Donna and Linda and the other girls squealed. I only looked at the squashed fly long enough to see that one of its wings had come away from its body and was stuck on its own, like a tiny piece of stained glass. Then I looked away.

'Mam never gives me any food,' I said. 'I'm so hungry. Sometimes I think I'm going to die from being so hungry.'

'Stop telling me,' he nearly shouted. 'I can't be listening to this.'

'You said you would take me away,' I said.

'I can't. I'm sorry. I'm sorry,' he said. He went into the pub. I ran to the wooden fence at the end of the yard and kicked it so hard one of the boards cracked. My cheeks were hot. I wanted to go in, fight my way through the sour-smelling men, and find Da.

'I never believed it,' I wanted to shout. 'Not once. Not ever. I always knew people couldn't come back after they were dead. Even Jesus probably didn't really come back after he was dead, he probably just stayed really quiet in the cave so everyone thought he was dead then jumped out to give them a shock. I never thought you were dead when you went away, and I never thought you came back alive when you came back to see me, and when I killed Steven I knew it would be forever, not just for a day or a week or a month. I knew he would never come back, and that was what I wanted. And the next person I kill is going to be dead forever too, and the person after that and the person after that and the person after that. I'm going to kill so many more people, and they're all going to be dead forever, and *that's* what I *want.'*

It didn't matter that I had believed it about Da being dead, or that I hadn't really realised Steven would never come back. I hated the feeling of other people thinking I was stupid more than almost any other feeling in the whole world. I didn't want Da to think I was stupid. I looked through the back door for a long time, watching dark man shapes wind and twist around one another. I couldn't see

Da. I felt itchy and twitchy, like there were centipedes crawling over my skin, and the centipedes' feet were made of needles. I didn't want to be by myself. I wanted Linda. She knew how rotten it felt to have other people think you were stupid. I went to her house and rang the bell.

'Can Linda come out?' I asked when her mammy opened the door.

'No,' she said.

'Can I come in, then?' I asked.

'No,' she said.

'Why not?' I asked.

'They're about to have their tea,' she said.

'What are they having?' I asked.

'Stew,' she said.

'I like stew,' I said.

'You're not coming in, Chrissie,' she said. 'I don't want you playing with Linda any more. You need to go home. To *your* home.'

She moved her feet on the mat, and for a moment I thought she was going to come down onto her knees and hug me, like she had done before the first day of school. I wouldn't have minded that. I might have quite liked it. She stepped back into the hallway and closed the door. I stood still, thinking of the things I could have said if she hadn't already closed the door.

'You can't stop me and Linda playing together. We're best friends. You can't stop best friends playing together.

That's basically against the law. You can't stop me coming round. I'll wait until you're out, until it's just Linda's da here, and then I'll come back. He'll let me in. You can't make me go home. I don't have a home. I just have a house. You can't make me go there.'

My throat felt stretched and sore with all the words. I rubbed it and squeezed it and then I kept my hands still, resting in the place where my heartbeat scrabbled. Blood skittered under my fingers and words skittered around my head.

I am here. I am here. I am here.
Ticktock. Ticktock. Ticktock.

When I left the house the next morning the world was made of bright white light and I was made of noise. It wasn't fizzing – not like the fizzing I had had before, not sherbet any more. It was a gritty rumble, biting me at the bottom of my belly, gnawing at the place where my body turned into a secret. Like a tiger growling. Like a flame licking. I had sparklers in the ends of my fingers and the tips of my toes and the sparkling made me run the fastest I had ever run, but it wasn't snap-bubble-whizz, it was groan-grumble-roar. I stared at the top of the street as I ran up the hill, and it looked like someone had poured blue paint into the jaggedy hole left by the rooftops jutting into the sky. I had to squint to see clearly, and when I squinted I sparkled even harder.

My body wasn't lectric. It was lava. Step-stamp-stump. Tick-tick-tock.

I got to the shop just as Mrs Bunty was coming out to put the sign on the street. When she saw me her hands went straight to her hips.

'Come on now, Chrissie,' she said. 'Enough of this. You know I'm not going to let you in to pinch things.'

'Not going to pinch anything,' I said. 'I got coins.'

She laughed, which sounded like a turkey gobbling. Her chins wobbled, so she looked like a turkey too. 'And I'm the Queen of Sheba, am I?' she said.

'No. Obviously not. But I have got coins,' I said. I pulled them out of my pocket and held them right up to her face.

'Who'd you nick them off, then?' she asked.

'No one. Got given them,' I said.

'By who?'

I thought of Da, staggering out of the pub as I walked towards the house, taking hold of my elbow with a hot hand. He had reached into his pocket and taken out the clatter of coins, pressed them into my palm, and said, 'Here, take this, it's all I've got, take it and get yourself something to eat.' When he staggered back into the pub I heard him go to the bar and ask Ronnie for another drink. So it wasn't all he had. It was all he had left over after he paid for the things he actually cared about.

'No one,' I said to Mrs Bunty. 'I didn't pinch them, though. They're mine. And I want to buy some sweets.'

She would have liked to tell me I wasn't allowed, but then the vicar came in to buy a newspaper and she had to pretend to be nice so she wouldn't go to hell. I took the big jar of lollipops off the counter and tried to twist off the lid. It was stiff and my hands kept slipping.

'You want some help with that, lass?' asked the vicar, reaching out.

'No,' I said. I gave it one last tug and it moved.

'My,' said the vicar. 'Strong hands you've got there, eh?'

'Yes,' I said. 'I've got very strong hands.'

I bought a lollipop and a bag of jelly babies, even though I didn't like lollipops or jelly babies. Mrs Bunty took my coins as if I had peed on them. I wished I had peed on them.

When I got to Ruthie's house I went up the garden path and rang the bell underneath the door number. No one answered at first, so I rang again and again until the beautiful woman came. She wasn't looking her most beautiful. She was still in her nightie and dressing gown even though it was past breakfast time, and her hair was coming out of its curlers in yellow worms. Her face was the colour of old washing-up water.

'Oh, hello, Chrissie,' she said. Ruthie came out of the lounge and ran into the back of her legs, hitting her so hard she nearly fell on top of me. That was typical Ruthie, I thought. Always making the beautiful woman's life worse. She was dressed in a puff-sleeved cotton dress patterned with red and white checks, and her feet were stuffed into frilly white socks and red leather shoes. Her doctor's case was red too, and she was carrying it by the handle, so she matched from head to toe. There were even red ribbons in her orange hair, making her head look like fire.

'Can I take Ruthie to the playground?' I asked. When Ruthie heard 'playground' she clapped her fat little hands together and pulled on the beautiful woman's arm. Every time the beautiful woman wriggled away Ruthie got hold of her again and pumped her hand up and down.

'Please, Mammy! Playground, Mammy!'

'Get off!' she nearly shouted, wrenching her hand out of reach. Ruthie looked shocked, and I was shocked too. It was the first time I had ever heard the beautiful woman even nearly shout. Pink rose in her cheeks and spread down her neck.

'Sorry, Ruthie,' she said, stroking her hair. 'Sorry, angel. Naughty Mammy getting cross. Naughty, shouty Mammy.'

'Can she come, then?' I asked. The beautiful woman looked out into the street, at the cars whirring along the road and the beer bottle shards glittering in the gutters.

'It's sweet of you to ask, but I'm afraid Ruthie hurt her knee this morning. While she was playing in the garden. It's quite a nasty scratch. I think perhaps she'd better stay inside today.'

The beautiful woman did that quite a lot: made up stories about why Ruthie couldn't come out to play. Ruthie's knees were bare under her dress, and we all stared at them. On the left one there was a pink line the size and shape of a paper cut. Even Ruthie looked at the beautiful woman like she was mad.

'We're only going to the playground,' I said. 'I'll hold her hand. There's no roads to cross.' The beautiful woman peered out of the door again. I thought she was probably wishing for a clap of thunder or a small earthquake – some proper reason to keep Ruthie in. The sky overhead was sea-glass blue and the earth wasn't at all quaky, and as the beautiful woman looked at the beautiful sky she shuddered, bent forward, and made a gagging sound. When she straightened she was even more dishwater-coloured. She pushed Ruthie towards me.

'Yes. Yes. Of course. Do take her. Have a lovely time, Ruthie. Be careful. See you soon.' She ran up the stairs and into the bathroom. We heard her being sick. I thought if I had had to look after Ruthie every day I would probably have been sick too.

When we passed the playground Ruthie pushed the gate, but I pulled her back by the collar of her dress. 'Come on,' I said, taking her wrist in my hand. 'We're not going there.'

'Playground!' she whinged. She tried to wriggle free, but I was too strong for her.

'No. No playground,' I said. She looked like she was revving up to scream loud enough that the beautiful woman would hear it from four streets away, so I stuffed a jelly baby into her mouth like a stopper. She was so surprised she didn't do anything for a minute. Then she chewed and reached out her hand for another.

'More,' she said. I showed her the bag.

'Only if you keep walking and don't make a noise,' I said.

The alley houses looked even more half-there than usual against the perfect sky. When we got to the blue house Ruthie sat down on the scrubby grass outside.

'Tired,' she said. She flopped over so she was lying on the ground. I looked at her orange hair, coiling between blades of grass. Like a tiger. Like a flame.

'Come on,' I said. She didn't move, so I took the lollipop out of my pocket and waved it in her face. 'Do you want this?' She nodded and tried to grab it, but I pulled it out of her reach. 'Only if you follow me.'

Once she was through the door the toes of her shoes scuffed straight away, and dirt crept up the white of her socks. She was very quiet, even though she had finished the jelly baby in her mouth. I pushed her in front of me on the stairs to make sure she got up to the top without falling. The upstairs room was brighter than the rest of the house because of the light coming in through the hole in the roof. The wet patch under the hole had spread. I remembered squatting and peeing there. Ruthie walked in and looked up at the hole. She laughed a high, tinkling giggle. 'Look!' she screamed. 'There's a hole! A hole in the sky!' She sat down on one of the couch cushions next to the wet patch and began unpacking her doctor's case.

'You play doctors with me,' she screamed. 'You be poorly.' She put the stethoscope in her ears and started pressing the end on her arms and hands.

'That's not right, Ruthie,' I said. I walked over and tried to take it from her. 'I'll show you how to do it properly.' She squawked and snatched it back.

'*Mine*,' she screamed. '*My* the doctor.' Her fat little cheeks were pink, and I wanted to kick her, but I kicked over the rest of the doctor's set instead. The ball of bandage that the beautiful woman spent most of her life rerolling unwound, a long white tongue across the floor. I walked round the edge of the room, running my fingers along the walls. My insides were boiling. Lava and lectric.

'Play *doctors*!' Ruthie screamed. She did so much screaming. I had almost never heard her talk without screaming. So much screaming and so many toys and so, so, so much love. She had love spread over her in fat globs. You could see it on her skin. I knew what to look for. I had seen it on Steven.

I leant my back against the far wall and goose bumps rose on my arms, straight-standing hairs making pimples. The sparkler feeling was everywhere – on my face, down my neck, in my belly, bubbling me up until I could barely stand it. I pushed off the wall with one foot and ran to the other end of the room. The space wasn't big enough.

I couldn't build enough speed to run the sparkling out of my legs. I looked up at the sky. The blue burnt my eyes. I wanted to climb through the hole and stand on the roof and roar until my voice ran out.

Ruthie was watching me. 'What you doing?' she asked. I put my hands over my ears. I couldn't get rid of it, her horrid, high-pitched, whiny little voice. It wormed its way inside me.

'Come on,' I said. 'I'll play. I'm being the doctor though. Give me the stethoscope.' She must have been really fed up of playing on her own, because she gave it to me straight away. 'Lie down,' I said.

'Don't want to,' she said. 'Not lie down. Be poorly sitting up.'

I waved the lollipop in her face again. 'Do you want this?' I asked. She nodded. I unwrapped it, and when she was lying down I put it in her mouth. She sucked it like a dummy.

'Good girl,' I said. I put the stethoscope around my neck. 'Now. Is there something wrong with your throat?' I traced my fingers along the crease where her body joined onto her head.

She nodded. 'Coughs,' she said around the lollipop.

'Shall I try to make you better?' I said. The stethoscope hung down, getting in my way. I pulled it off and threw it to the side. I put my hand flat around her neck, fingers curled close to the floor, thumb resting on the place where

327

her heartbeat thrummed. When every part of my hand was pressed to her neck I wrapped the other hand round too. I blinked, and the clockface flashed onto the backs of my eyelids. Its hands were twinned at the top.

'I'm going to give your neck a little rub,' I said. 'It will take the coughs away.' I made my hands hard. She tipped her head back.

'Hurts,' she whined. She wriggled to the side, so she was lying right in the middle of the damp patch of floor. I saw a woodlouse crawl into her hair. I kept hold of her.

'It won't hurt for long,' I said. 'I'm going to make it better. It will be better after this. I've just got to do it one time. One more time. Everything will be better afterwards. I promise.'

I squeezed her neck. I squeezed it with everything I had inside me: all the bubbling and grumbling and grinding. It went down my arms, into my hands, and I used them to squeeze Ruthie's neck. She swiped at my wrists, but it didn't hurt because the beautiful woman kept her nails trimmed to neat pink half-moons. Her hands were weak and mine were strong. In the distance I could hear her whimpering, but she was like a fly buzzing inside a locked cupboard in another room in another house in another country. I swatted her out of my mind. I swatted everything out of my mind except my hands on her neck, my eyes on her eyes, the sound of her feet beating on the floor. She was lying on the patch where I had peed, and I looked for that feeling, the black, delicious thrill. It wasn't there. There wasn't any fizzing this time, there was only hate, hate and hate and the sound of Ruthie's feet beating on the floor, slower and slower until they stopped. Ruthie stopped. Everything stopped.

I kept my hands on her neck for a while after she was dead. The skin was soft. It was soft like a flower petal. It was so soft I wasn't sure where I ended and she began. The lollipop had fallen out of her mouth and left a sticky trail across her cheek. Her eyes were still open, but she had stopped blinking, and the bulging brown circles were marbles in her head.

When I had finished killing Steven I had sat back on my heels and shaken out my seized hands, and I had felt warm and tired and not hungry, for once not hungry, and I had thought, 'This is as good as a person can feel.' I looked at Ruthie and tried to get that feeling back. I tried so hard I thought my insides would be pushed out, because that was what the trying felt like. Straining. Squeezing. I put my hand on her shoulder and gave her a little shake. I tapped her face. 'Come back now,' I whispered. 'Don't be dead. I didn't mean to. Come back.' She stayed quiet. She stayed still. I shook her again, rubbed her cheek, put my face above hers and blew warm breath. I said it right into her ear – 'Come back. Please come back.' She stayed quiet. She stayed still. The sky in the hole above us was hot blue, and the sun was hot on my neck, but my guts were cold. I was tired. My hands were sore. Ruthie was dead. She was never going to come alive again. I tipped my head back and looked up at the hole in the sky. I howled, howled, howled.

JULIA

In Linda's house, the morning mayhem began promptly, with full intensity, at six a.m. I was woken by one of the twins putting her face an inch from mine and shouting, 'GET OFF THE COUCH. WE NEED TO WATCH TELLY.' Linda stuffed small bodies into school uniforms and poured Frosties into bowls and didn't seem to care that no one could hear her over the yammer of cartoons. Molly and I were ready to leave by eight. We had to stand on the doorstep for a while, Linda calling from the kitchen, 'Wait, wait a second, I'm just trying to work out if Mikey's swallowed this or not.'

She came down the hallway with Mikey on her hip. He was grinning proudly.

'What's he swallowed?' I asked.

'It's just a little bit of a toy. But it's only tiny. And I don't think he has. I'm pretty sure he hasn't. And if he has – well – I suppose I'll find out soon.'

I was surprised that any of Linda's kids were still alive.

'We'll get off,' I said.

'Yeah. Things to get back to,' she said.

Mikey coughed and she put him down to pat his back. He leant forward, spluttered, and spat something into her hand. It was a tiny doll head. She wiped it on her T-shirt.

'Well done, poppet,' she said. 'Does that feel a bit better?'

He nodded and barrelled back into the kitchen.

'Phew,' she said. 'One less thing to worry about.'

'You know, earlier, you asked if I came because you called?' I said.

'Oh, I was just being silly. I didn't mean anything by it.'

'I did come to see you,' I said. 'I didn't know it was you calling. But you were the person I really wanted to see.'

It wasn't a lie. It had been Linda I had wanted: not in my brain, in my body. For years I had been hung up on Mam, because your mam was the one who was supposed to fill you up when you felt empty, but she had never done that for me. She had given me dregs and scrapings of warmth, and now that I had seen her again, I believed it was all she had been able to give, but it hadn't been enough. She was never going to give me enough. I knew, because when she had told me what she wanted, she had talked about going back and making things different for her. She hadn't talked about doing things better for me.

Only one person in Chrissie's life had loved her in an ordinary, everyday way, the way you love salt or sunlight. Linda hadn't been able to tie shoelaces or tell the time, but she had been the cleverest at loving, at loyalty, at giving everything and expecting nothing in return. She was the person I had needed to see one more time, before I lost Molly and everything stopped. I knew, because I didn't feel hungry any more. It wasn't just shepherd's pie and chocolate ice cream and Frosties. It was Linda.

'Thanks,' she said. She rolled the doll head between her fingers. 'I didn't know whether to say this or not. I didn't know if it would make you uncomfortable. But I want you to know, we've always prayed for you. Me and Kit, we always have. He does know about you, just doesn't know that's who he met, if that makes sense. After we've prayed for the family and anyone else we know who needs to be lifted up to Him, we've always finished with you.'

'Are we going home now?' Molly asked loudly.

'Yeah, we are,' I said to her, and to Linda, 'Thank you. It doesn't make me uncomfortable. It's really nice of you.'

'I haven't got anything new for show-and-tell,' Molly said.

'It doesn't matter,' I said.

'I *need* something,' she said.

'Show-and-tell, is it, Molly?' said Linda. 'I think I've actually got something you might be able to use. I wanted to give it to your mammy anyway. Well done for reminding me.'

'She doesn't need anything,' I said.

'What is it?' asked Molly. Linda went into the house and up the stairs.

'It's really not that important,' I muttered to Molly.

'It's *show-and-tell*,' she muttered back.

Linda came back sooner than I had expected. I was amazed she could locate anything with speed in a house that was an oozing, seething snake nest of chaos. She put a gobstopper-sized marble on Molly's palm. The sun glanced off its surface. All the colours in the world.

'Would your class like to see that, do you think?' she asked. She didn't look at me. Molly passed it from one hand to the other.

'Is it just a marble?' she asked.

'It's a very special marble,' said Linda.

'Why?'

'Because it used to be your mammy's.'

'Does it do anything special?'

'Well. No. But it's very pretty.'

'Have you got anything else?'

'I didn't think you'd keep that,' I said to Linda.

'Of course I did,' she said. She looked at the marble balanced on Molly's palm, then dropped her gaze to the ground. 'It was my bit of you, wasn't it? It helped. Helped when I was missing you.'

I felt a tug in the tie that had held us together for the past seventeen years. I stepped forward and I hugged her. She was warm and broad, and she held me so tight I felt we would turn into one woman. When she let go I walked down the garden path and through the gate. She stood in the doorway, and Mikey came and hung on her leg, and she looked tall and strong, like a lighthouse. I didn't know why that was what came to me, but it did come, strongly. A lighthouse.

On the train Molly ate a sandwich the length of her arm, then fell asleep with her head on the wrapper. I couldn't see her face, only her dark hair. I felt tired to the gossamer veins at the ends of my fingers, but I couldn't sleep, and travelling backwards made me feel sick, but I didn't move seats. Sitting next to Molly would mean feeling the warmth coming off her body, feeling fused. It would make it more painful to be wrenched apart. By the end of the week, she would be with an infertile couple in a three-bedroom house, earning stars on a chart for eating vegetables and doing homework. I thought I might write a letter to her new parents: tell them about her reading books, what television programmes she liked to watch, how much she wanted a party dress. They could take her to the department store. They could take pictures of her standing on their doorstep, trussed in satin and frills. You could do those things when you didn't have to remember pale, still legs stretching out of a red-and-white-checked skirt.

My future was decided too. I would be arrested for breaching the court order, and if I didn't go to prison I would kill myself. It was another foregone conclusion: without her, there would be no alternative. I would do it before I had time to be scared, before I had time to go back to the flat. Those rooms were impregnated with Molly: her height marks on the doorframe, her smell on the bedsheets. I couldn't walk through them by myself. I would walk into the sea instead.

I rolled the marble in small circles on the train table. My thoughts spooled around, liquid and slippy. When I stopped trying to contain them, they went back to Linda. I imagined her in her matchbox house with her French windows open, kids spilling from drawers and from beneath the floorboards, grubby, semi-naked. I imagined Kit coming home for tea, putting his arms around her from behind, leaning round to kiss her cheek. I thought of her new baby, growing inside. She hadn't seemed embarrassed about the glut of kids she had produced. When I'd had to tell Jan I was pregnant with Molly, my skin had crawled with sicky shame. We had been in her office at the police station, sitting across the desk from one another. She had taken a slow breath through her nose and moved her face around until she stopped looking exasperated.

'Have you thought about what to do?' she asked. She eyed my belly to decide how cross to be, and took another slow nose breath. Very cross.

'Not really,' I said, because I hadn't.

'Well, do you want to keep it?' she asked.

I thought of the clump of new cells anchored inside me, like bubbles or frog spawn, something I had swallowed by accident. Jan knew who I was. She knew what I had done. I felt Steven and Ruthie between us, their small cold bodies laid flat on the desk.

'I can't kill anything else,' I whispered.

'What?' said Jan.

'I'm keeping it,' I said. 'It's mine.'

Jan came to see us while we were in hospital. Molly was clean and dressed in a tiny white babygro. I told Jan she weighed eight pounds, and Jan said that was big, and I almost laughed. Molly was the smallest person I had ever seen. When we had been sitting quietly for a few minutes, Jan straightened in her seat.

'You know I have to ask,' she said.

'Yeah,' I said.

'Your feelings might have changed,' she said. 'There's no shame in that. It would be a lot for anyone to cope with.'

Molly was sucking at me lazily, eyes half-closed. It was a mean trick, I thought, to have slammed her onto my breast the moment she left my body, to have knotted us together with iron rope before I had even agreed to be tied.

Stay with us, Chrissie. What can you see?

Bed. Blankets. Molly.

'She'd be hungry without me,' I said.

'She'd take a bottle,' said Jan.

'She wouldn't like it.'

'She'd get used to it.'

'She'd be hungry before she got used to it.'

'Maybe.'

Molly's mouth came away from my nipple and she started awake. I put my hand on the back of her head and she fastened around me again. One of her hands clutched a fold of my skin.

'She likes me,' I said. 'She really acts like she likes me.'

'Yes,' said Jan. 'You're her world.'

'I want to keep her,' I said.

'OK,' said Jan. 'Well then. That's that.'

Molly lifted her head, squinting. The sandwich wrapper was stuck to her cheek, and when she peeled it away it left creasy marks on her skin. 'My neck hurts,' she said.

I took off my jacket and gave it to her. 'Here. Fold this up and put it against the window. See if you can sleep like that. Your neck's just been in the same position for too long.'

Her eyes didn't close straight away. She looked out of the window, head shuddering when the train went over bumps in the track.

'Was Grandma a nice mum?' she asked.

'Not really,' I said.

'Did she not know how to be a mum?' she asked.

I hadn't thought of it like that before, but as I turned it over in my head I decided to make it true. Mam had been useless; she hadn't been evil. She hadn't wanted me, so she had tried to give me away. She had found out that I had killed Steven, so she had tried to kill me. It could have been to punish me, or protect me, or neither. It could have been because she was tired of trying and failing to love a kid who felt like a stranger. I wouldn't see her again, and

The First Day of Spring

I could choose how to remember her. I chose for her to be
someone who didn't know how to be a mam. I chose for her
to be hopeless and clumsy and carelessly cruel, and to care
about me just enough for it to mean something. Enough to
remember my age. Enough to keep our first-day-of-school
photograph. I chose for her not to be evil.

'No,' I said. 'I suppose not.'

'So were you sad all the time?'

I tipped my head from side to side and felt my neck
creak. I didn't know the right answer. It would have been
easiest to say, 'Yes, I was sad all the time, Molly. I was
horribly, terribly sad, from the moment I woke up to the
moment I went to sleep, every day, every week, every year.
I was so sad, I had to kill people. That was the only reason
I did it, Molly. Because I was so sad.'

It wouldn't have been an out-and-out lie. When I remembered being eight years old I remembered the hunger that
had twisted my brain into sharp shapes, and the shame of
waking between wet sheets, and the feeling of having no
one in the whole world who wanted me. No one in the
whole world who even really liked me. But I also remembered chasing William and Donna down Copley Street and
feeling so light I was sure I would soar into the sky. Stealing sweets behind Mrs Bunty's back and whooping a long,
loud siren as I ran away. Walking along the garden walls
from Mr Jenks' to the haunted house on strong skinny legs.
The tight itch of sunburn and the smell of crayons in the

classroom and the marzipan taste of apple pips. Playing telly with Linda. Learning clapping games with Linda. Doing handstands with Linda.

I remembered the day they took me to the police station, away from the blue house and the hole in the sky. When they finished asking me questions they left me in a bare room. A woman policeman sat on a plastic chair in the corner. She didn't look at me. I swung my legs and drummed my hands and made a loud clicking noise with my tongue against my teeth. She didn't look at me. In the end I gave up trying to make her look at me. I put my cheek on the table and closed my eyes. The room was cold, and when I dragged my mouth across my arm the hairs were spiky on my lips.

'Can I have a blanket?' I asked the woman policeman. She didn't answer. She didn't look at me.

In the police station there was no way of knowing whether it was day or night, because there were no windows and the lights were on all the time. After a while they put me in a cell with a bunk and a toilet and a cheese sandwich on a plate. A bit later they came back, took away the plate, gave me a pillow. I thought that must mean it was bedtime, so I kicked off my shoes and lay down. The bunk was twice as long as me, because the cells weren't meant for kids. If you were younger than ten you didn't usually go to a cell or have a trial, because whatever bad thing you had done, you were just a kid and it wasn't your fault. I was only eight, but

I still got a cell and a trial. Some things were so bad they stopped you being a kid.

My eyes were starting to droop shut when I heard the cell door unlock and swing open. I sat up. Mam was there. She walked in and the guard shut the door.

'I'll just be out here,' he called. 'Knock when you need.'

Mam went and stood with her back against the far wall, so we were opposite each other. We looked at each other for a long time, and then I put my arms out straight in front of me and lifted them up. It was something I had seen little kids do: Steven reaching up to his mammy, Ruthie reaching up to the beautiful woman. I didn't know why I was doing it.

Mam folded her arms across her chest. 'Stop it, Christine,' she said. 'You look like a kid.' Then she went to the door and knocked, and the guard let her out. I kept my arms in the air. I kept them there until all the blood had drained away, until they felt like two lead poles stretching away from my body. Then I lay down and went to sleep.

In the weeks of the trial they kept me in a small white room in the big dark basement of the prison. I didn't know what the outside of the building looked like, because whenever they brought me inside from the van they covered me with a blanket that smelt of sweat and potato peel. The first time they did it I kicked and screamed, and they had to carry me, one policeman on each side. I thought they were taking me to have my head cut off, or to be hung on a cross.

'Don't do it, don't do it, I don't want to be dead,' I screamed.

'No one's going to be dead, Christine,' said the policeman on my right.

'No one *else* is going to be dead,' said the one on my left. He was my least favourite. I bit him and he swore.

When we got to my room I saw there was no cross and no guillotine, so I stopped thrashing. They put me on the bed and I lay limp as a slug, looking at the bare white ceiling. There was nothing in the room except the bed and a telly, up on a shelf in the corner.

'You going to stay calm now?' the right-hand policeman asked. 'What was all that about, eh? Why did you think we was going to kill you?'

I folded my arms and turned towards the wall. The way he talked made it sound like I had been stupid to think they were going to kill me, but that wasn't true at all. You never knew when someone was going to kill you. Just ask Steven and Ruthie.

Every morning they covered me with the potato-peel blanket and put me in a cage in the van to drive me to the courtroom. I leant against the metal mesh and let the rattles bang away my thoughts. I found I felt nothing at all during those journeys, and I knew it was thanks to the rattles. In court I sat in a glass box, looking around the wooden room, and a hundred million pairs of eyes looked back at me. At first I liked it, the feeling of everyone watching me. It made me feel tingly, almost fizzy, almost like God. But the trial went on for days and days, and soon I stopped liking it. People took it in turns to stand up and talk about how bad I was, and I didn't mind them saying that I was bad, but I minded that there were so many of them, and that they all took such a long time to say what they wanted to say. I got tired and fidgety in my box. Sometimes, when the person standing up had been speaking for a long time, I put my head on the ledge in front of me and closed my eyes. A guard always tapped my shoulder, told me to sit up. I always put my head down again. They always tapped me again. It made the time go faster, because it was almost like a game.

When I got into my cage at the end of the day I always felt tired, so tired my eyes itched and my face ached. Back at the prison they put me in my room and brought me my tea on a plastic tray, and I ate it so quickly I got hiccups. Then I lay down on the bed and closed my eyes and disappeared. It didn't feel like going to sleep. It felt like dropping out of the world.

Weekends in prison were the worst, because there was no van and no court and no one looking at me except the guard outside my room. The days passed like treacle moving through a sieve: sticky and slow. In the morning they brought my breakfast under a sweating lid. When it was gone I put the tray on the floor and waited for the next meal. The telly chattered in the corner, but it was on the wrong channel for kids' programmes and the buttons were too high for me to reach. Sometimes I counted how many steps it took me to get from one end of the room to the other: twenty-five if I went heel to toe. Sometimes I did handstands against one of the clean white walls. It wasn't the same as the handstand wall.

The last day of the trial was my ninth birthday. When I got into my box I saw the beautiful woman, sitting next to Steven's mammy on the long wooden bench. She hadn't been there before. She looked pale and fat in the way that meant she was going to have a baby. I spent a long time looking at her belly from behind my glass wall. Then I put my head down on the ledge. There really hadn't been any point in it all. I had killed Ruthie because if I wasn't going to be the beautiful woman's little girl, then no one else was going to be, either. Now she was going to have a baby all her own. I knew it would be another girl. I just knew. I wouldn't be able to kill her because I would be in prison, and that meant she would get to live, get to grow up with the beautiful woman as her mammy, get toys and dresses and kisses. The guard tapped my shoulder to get me to sit up, but I didn't. I was too tired.

I dragged myself up when the judge told me to stand. He looked me in the eye and said I would be going to a Home, and by then I knew *Home* was just another word for *prison*, and I wanted to say, 'But you can't. You can't send me to prison. It's my birthday. It's not fair.' He said words like *wicked* and *reckless* and *evil*, and the guard took my elbow and I realised I would never see the handstand wall again. Never see Linda again. And I wanted to run up to the judge's desk and beat my fists on the wood and roar, 'But I didn't mean it! I didn't mean the killing! I take it back! I take it back! Take me *back*!'

I didn't roar. I didn't even speak. The sound of women wailing exploded around me and, and I looked around just long enough to find Mam, alone on her bench. She wasn't wailing. She wasn't crying. She had her lips pressed together in a thin, dark line. I let the guards lead me out of the room without kicking or biting. Deep down I knew people couldn't go back in time. Deep down I knew people couldn't come back alive again once they were dead. There were lots of things I didn't know about dying – how it felt, how it worked, almost everything, really – but the one thing I had learnt was that it lasted forever. When someone you knew died, you didn't die with them. You carried on, and you went through phases and chapters so different they felt like whole different lives, but in all of those lives the dead person was still dead. Dead whether you were sad or happy, dead whether you thought about them or didn't, dead whether you missed them or not. If it didn't last, it wasn't real dying, it was just someone caring so little they disappeared.

I was quiet as we walked to the cells and quiet as they locked me in. I lay on the bed, put my fingers on my throat, and counted my heartbeats – one, two, three, four, five, six, seven, eight, nine. Sometimes when I turned a new age I used it as my lucky number, so my lucky number was my age number and I could be lucky without even having to try. I decided I wouldn't have nine as my new lucky number.

I dragged my finger along the train window and left a greasy smear. When I thought of the old life I remembered the misery, but also the giddy, euphoric freedom, and that freedom was what I wanted for Molly. Freedom from the flat and from snooty school receptionists and from the routine I strapped around her, like a straitjacket, because it was the only way I could trust myself to keep her safe. I could have told her I had been sad all the time, and it would have made me more comfortable and more of a coward. I had been happy as well as sad, because it had been heaven as well as hell. And I had taken it, chewed it, digested it, and done things that had left two families with no heaven, only hell. That was the truth. Every time, every day. It would always be the truth.

'I was sad a lot. But not all the time,' I said. 'Sometimes I was happy. And sometimes I was angry. Angry enough to hurt people.'

I had laid a path for questions – 'How did you hurt them? Did you push them? Did you hit them? Who were they? Did they hurt you back?' – but they didn't come. Molly had gone back to sleep. Her mouth was open and a clear stream of dribble ran down her chin. I didn't have a tissue. It collected in dark drips on her T-shirt.

The First Day of Spring

I thought of taking Molly to school and struggling for breath in the crowd of other-mothers, watching her disappear into the building and wondering if this would be the day the head teacher phoned to tell me she had attacked another kid, the day I discovered that despite everything I had done, I hadn't stopped her turning into me. I thought of the seize of panic when I looked at the clock and realised we were five minutes late for dinner, tea, bath, bed, the torturous reading-book ritual, the way each missed moment felt like a failing, the way I struggled to hear my thoughts above the jabber of kids' telly. I thought of sitting on my mattress and watching her sleeping face, yellowed by the yolky chink of bulb light coming through the door. Holding her clothes to my nose to see whether they needed washing, breathing in the smell of crayons and school dinners. Carrying her back from the playground the time she grazed her knee, her arms a warm chain around my neck. It had been hell and it had been heaven, and now it was over. She would forget me.

I reached around in my bag for a pen. Molly's bad arm was laid across the table, and I moved it gently, without waking her. There wasn't much white space left, but I found a patch big enough for my name.

Mum.

CHRISSIE

I walked back from the alleys stooped over, like an old person. I knew my insides would fall out if I stood up straight. I had to go the long way round, because I didn't want to pass the beautiful woman's house and have her nag me about where Ruthie was. I really wasn't in the mood to be nagged. The long way round took me past the church and the church clock, and I saw it was getting towards ten o'clock. I had only been with Ruthie for half an hour. It felt like half a year.

When I knocked on Linda's door her da answered, and he smiled in a way her mammy definitely wouldn't have smiled.

'All right, our Chrissie?' he said through a mouthful of toast. Butter and marmalade gathered at the corners of his lips in glistening pockets. 'You'll be wanting Linda.' He wiped his mouth on his sleeve and transferred the oily orange jelly to his shirt in a snail trail. He didn't seem to have been told about the new Linda-not-playing-with-Chrissie rule.

'Look at that sky,' he said, pointing above my head. I looked up. My eyes ached with the blue of it. 'Perfect. Proper spring day.' He looked back at me. 'You all right, Chrissie? You're looking a bit peaky.'

'I'm fine,' I said.

'You sure?'

'Yeah. Can I go up to Linda's room?'

'Course, course. Up you go. I'll be in the shed if you need me.'

Linda had one shoe on and was hopping around, looking for the other. 'Can you see my shoe?' she asked.

I sat down on her bed. 'No.'

'I thought I took it off in here yesterday.'

'Doesn't matter. Don't want to go out.'

She came and sat next to me. 'What do you want to do, then?'

'Can we lie down for a bit?'

'Eh?'

I kicked off my shoes, crawled onto the bed, and lay with my head on the pillow. She leant over and peered at my face. 'Are you poorly?' she asked.

'No. I just want to lie down for a bit.'

'OK.'

She nudged me across and we lay top-to-toe, so our feet were next to each other's heads. I put my cheek against her bare arch. The skin was soft and cool.

'Linda?'

'Yeah.'

'If I went away, what would you do?'

'Don't know.'

'What would you, though?'

'Get a new best friend, I suppose.'

I didn't much like her saying that. She made it sound as if it would be easy. 'Yeah,' I said. 'If you moved away I'd get a new best friend. Might get one anyway. I don't really like you.'

'Is your da taking you away?' she asked. I flexed my foot on the pillow beside her head and one of my toenails tangled in her hair. She squeaked. I pulled away fast, even though I knew it would hurt her.

'Ow!' She pulled herself free. 'That hurt.'

'My da's not taking me away,' I said.

'Why not?' she asked.

'Because I'm the bad seed,' I said.

'Oh,' she said.

'I didn't even want him to take me away in the first place.'

'Why not?'

'Don't like him.'

'But he's nice. He gave you that marble.'

'Shut up.'

Neither of us spoke for a while. Sunlight came through the branches of the tree outside and cast dappled shadows on the carpet. I could feel her hair tickling my toes.

'How comes you're going away?' she asked.

'Just might. Might go away by myself,' I said.

'You can't. You're a kid,' she said.

'I can do whatever I want,' I said.

Pete started grizzling downstairs and Linda's da started singing to him. I knew it was a made-up song, because it had Pete's name in it. Linda's da was always making up songs with Linda's and Pete's names in them, and sometimes when I was there he put my name in too. I loved it when he did that.

'Your new best friend might not be as good as me,' I said.

'Don't know. Might be better,' said Linda.

'Probably not, though.'

'No. Probably not.'

'Will you miss me?'

'Yeah.'

'Will you write to me?'

'I'm rubbish at writing.'

'Yeah. But if I write to you will you read my letters?'

'Probably. If the words aren't too long.'

'I won't make them too long.'

'OK then. I'll read them.'

I still had my cheek pressed against her foot, and I turned my head to the side so my lips touched the round bone at the bottom of her big toe. I kissed it. She giggled.

'What you do that for?'

I sat up. There was no more fizzing left in my belly, not the sherbet kind or the lava kind or the lectric kind, just a hollow space, like someone had reached in and clawed out everything I used to have inside me.

'Come on, Linda,' I said. 'Let's go out.'

From the outside, the blue house looked just the same as it had looked when I had walked up to it with Ruthie. Linda skipped and chattered as we went into the alleys, but I didn't say anything. I kept looking over my shoulder to see if the beautiful woman was coming after me. I knew it wouldn't be long before she started wondering where Ruthie was, and then it wouldn't be long before she realised she wasn't in the playground, and then it wouldn't be long before everyone was searching for her. Thinking about it made me feel tired.

I went first up the crumbling stairs. Ruthie was lying where I had left her, with her dress rucked up around her underpants and her orange hair messed out around her head. When I went closer I saw there were ants gathered around the lollipop that had fallen out of her mouth. One of them was crawling up her cheek, following the trail of sticky dribble that had oozed from the corner of her lips. I crouched down beside her, lifted it away, and squashed it between my finger and thumb.

'Is she asleep?' asked Linda, coming to crouch by her other side.

'No,' I said.

'Is she poorly?'

'No.' I didn't want to have to listen to any more of her guesses, so I said, 'She's dead.'

'How?'

'I did it.'

'You never.'

'I did.'

She stood up and walked backwards until she hit the wall. My legs were starting to go numb from crouching, so I put my bottom down on the floor and rested my chin on my knees. I had a bad pain in my throat that I couldn't remember ever having had before. I thought I must be getting tonsillitis. Linda slid down the wall like a piece of scrambled egg sliding down a plate, and she sat with her knees up to her chest too, so we were mirrors of each other. Ruthie lay between us, smaller than she had been when she was alive.

'Please don't kill me,' said Linda.

'I won't,' I said.

'Did you kill Steven?' she asked. 'Is that why you wrote that?' She looked at the wall behind my head. I didn't need to turn around. The words were stuck to the backs of my eyelids. I saw them every time I blinked.

I am here. I am here. I am here. You will not forget me.

Steven was stuck to the backs of my eyelids too. He was there when I blinked, when I went to sleep, his knee in my belly, my hands on his throat. I was squeezing all the life out of him, until he was lying underneath me like an empty

353

tube of toothpaste, until he was so dead I knew he wouldn't come back alive again for days and days. And then I was leaving his little body in the middle of the floor and running to meet Linda at the handstand wall. I was turning myself upside down beside her. And then Donna's mammy was running past, breasts wobbling, cries ripping, and I was pretending to be just as surprised as anyone else that a little boy was lying dead in the blue house.

'Yeah,' I said. 'I killed him.' I had imagined saying it so many times, and in my head it had always sounded shiny. Out loud it sounded dull. Linda didn't say I wasn't her best friend any more or that I couldn't come to her birthday party. She said the other thing she always said when I did something she didn't like.

'I'm going to tell my mammy.'

She inched herself up the wall with her eyes on me, as if she thought I would leap forward and put my hands on her neck if she moved too quickly. I stayed sitting. I was too tired to do any more killing. I was too tired to do anything at all.

'All right,' I said. She snaked an arm around her back the way she had done when Miss White had been trying to get her to tell the time at school, the way she always did when she was frightened or didn't know the right thing to do. She stood still.

'Why did you?' she asked.

'Why did I what?'

'Kill them.'

Tightness crept into my face. I put my hands on my cheeks so she couldn't see them turning pink.

'It was just an accident,' I whispered.

'You can't kill people by accident,' she said.

'I thought they would come back,' I whispered.

'People don't come back when they're dead,' she said.

'I just wanted to,' I said.

'Why, though?'

'Because it wasn't fair.'

'What wasn't?'

'Just everything,' I said. You couldn't understand about fair and unfair when you had a mammy who made scones and a da who put your name into songs.

'Why did you make me come?' she asked.

'Just did,' I said.

'But I'm going to tell my mammy now. Everyone's going to know it was you,' she said.

'Yeah,' I said.

'Do you want people to know it was you?' she asked.

'I used to,' I said.

'Do you now?' she asked.

'I'm just really tired now,' I said.

It wasn't really true. I felt different to tired, more than tired. I felt the way I had felt the time we had been playing hide-and-seek and I had snuck into the church to hide under the altar. I had curled up small and listened to my heart bamming in my chest, smelt the dusty smell of hymnbooks and old yawns. Donna was doing the seeking. I waited for her to find me. The longer she took the more excited I got, because I was more and more sure that I had won. I waited until my knees went numb. I waited until my back seized up. I waited until the chill of the church got into my bones and made me stiff and sore. It was lonely, being hidden.

In the end I crawled out from under the altar and went back to the streets. I found Linda peering into the bushes at the side of the car park. When she saw me she smiled.

'There you are!' she said.

'Donna's meant to be seeking,' I said.

'She got bored,' she said. 'She went home for dinner. Everyone did.'

'Why didn't you?' I asked.

She looked confused. 'We hadn't found you,' she said.

'You could have just given up,' I said. 'The others did.'

'I didn't want to give up,' she said. 'I wanted to find you.'

'Why?'

'That's the whole point of the game.'

'But you could have given up on the game. You could have played another game without me. Why did you want me?'

'Don't know. You're my best friend. I like you.'

I hugged her. She was taller than me, so my face pressed against her collarbones. I squeezed so tight I felt like we would turn into one girl. Squeezed and squeezed and breathed her in and thought, 'I love you, I love you, I love you.'

That was how I had felt after I had killed Ruthie – not strong and sparkly like after I killed Steven, but cold and numb like when I was crouched under the altar. It had stopped being fun. I didn't want to be hidden any more. I just wanted Linda.

'You're going to go to prison,' she said. She didn't look like she was going to hug me or tell me she liked me this time.

'Yeah,' I said.

'Probably for the whole rest of your life,' she said.

'Yeah,' I said.

'Won't you miss your mammy?' she asked.

'No,' I said.

She took a step to the side, so she was closer to the stairs, but she didn't go down them. She still had her hand behind her, hanging on to the end of one of her plaits. When she pulled it her head tipped back and the skin on her neck stretched taut. I could see the veins under the surface. I could almost see the blood pumping through them.

'I'll have to get a new best friend,' she said.

'Will it be Donna?' I asked.

She shrugged. 'Maybe. Donna or Betty.'

'Donna's got a bike.'

'Donna, then.'

The pain in my throat spread down to my chest. I felt like I was being opened up, like a book being cracked at the spine, and then I was crying, and I knew why I had never felt the pain in my throat before. It was because it was crying pain, and I never cried.

'You're crying,' said Linda. 'You never cry.'

I didn't make any crying sounds. I let the tears fall down my cheeks and plop onto the bib of my dress, where they soaked into penny-sized patches. It was the same way I had seen Susan cry when we had been drinking milk at the handstand wall. Silent and still. I hadn't understood it at all back then; it had seemed such an odd way to cry. I understood it now. It was the way you cried when you were tired to the middle of your bones, when you didn't have enough left inside you to do anything else except cry.

'Are you sad because I'm going to get a new best friend?' asked Linda. That was sort of why, but I didn't want her to know, so I shook my head. When she realised I wasn't going to stop crying she took another step towards the stairs. 'I'm going home now,' she said. 'I'm going to tell my mammy what you did.'

'Wait,' I said. I lifted up the skirt of my dress and used it to wipe my face, then reached into the pocket, took out Da's marble, and pushed it towards her. The sunlight made it glint as it rolled across the floor. All the colours in the world.

'Are you giving it me?' she asked, picking it up.

'Yeah,' I said.

'But it's your marble. Your da gave it you. It's your best thing.'

'I want you to have it.'

'Why?'

I want you to remember me. I want you to remember to be my best friend. I want you to remember that you have to like me, that it's your job to like me, because you're the only one in the whole wide world who does.

'I just do,' I said.

'OK,' she said, and dropped it into her pocket. She walked round the edge of the room, as far away from me as possible, her eyes still stuck to mine. When she got to the top of the stairs she paused and swayed on the spot. She raised her hand and fluttered her fingers in a little wave, and I waved back. Then she picked her way down the stairs and out of sight. I heard her shoes crunch across the glass and grime of the downstairs room, the *slap-slap* sound as she ran towards the streets. When she had been sitting in the corner I had noticed that one of her laces was undone. She wouldn't be able to retie it by herself. I hoped she wouldn't trip.

The upstairs room was quiet with Linda gone and Ruthie dead. All my different types of fizzing had fizzled away: the sherbet type and the lava type and the spooning-out-my-insides type. They were all gone. I felt full of broken glass instead. I thought perhaps that was why if Mam ever had to touch me, she looked like she was being sliced by something sharp. Because she saw what Da and Linda didn't see: that I was broken-glass girl. I hurt other people just by being me. There was a sicky, sour taste in my mouth, and I ran my tongue around my teeth to try to get rid of it. When I got to the rotten one I pushed hard. It came out of its socket with a squelch and a shock of pain. I spat it onto my palm. It was brown and crumbly, and my mouth felt empty without it. I wondered whether the rotten tooth had all my badness in it, whether that was why I had always been bad, whether now it was gone I might be good. I hoped so. I was getting lonely with being so bad. I wiped it on my dress, peeled open Ruthie's hand, and tucked it inside. Her fingers were already starting to go cold.

The light coming into the room was still piercing, the blue still bright enough to make my eyes ache. It bounced off the shiny backs of the woodlice in twinkling sparks. The sun crept into the middle of the hole and beamed straight down onto Ruthie. I looked at her, lying stiff as a baby doll in the middle of the sunlit circle. My hands were tired. My eyes were tired. My heart was tired. Ruthie was never coming back. I shuffled forward on my bottom and lay down next to her, flat and quiet. I wanted my mam. I wanted to put my head on her chest like I had done in the hospital, press her hand to my cheek and feel the lines of her palm on my skin. I didn't know why. I just wanted it. I thought perhaps it was because I felt a bit frightened. It was horrid, feeling frightened. I put my fingers around Ruthie's and my tongue in the gap where there was no more rotten tooth. Waited for the scream of sirens. Waited for the police to come and take me to prison for the rest of my life. Me and Ruthie lay and waited together, under the hole in the sky.

JULIA

There were no blue lights or sirens at the station, no police cars parked outside. There was just an old man sitting at a table in Choo-Choo's, reading a paper and drinking a cup of tea.

We walked onto the street and I looked around. There was no one waiting to pounce. I knew I should be happy – I should seize Molly under the arms, pick her up, swing her round – but I felt coldly frightened. In my mind, the police had been going to bundle me into one car and Molly into another, drive me to prison and her to new parents. I was going to be empty and broken and relieved, because I wasn't going to be in charge any more. Proper grown-ups were going to look after Molly and prison was going to look after me, and giving up the burden of looking after two whole people was going to feel like taking off a bodysuit of lead.

'Come on,' said Molly. She pulled me towards the high street. The sea loomed up in the distance, grey behind the colours of the funfair.

'Do you want to go there?' I asked.

'The fair?' she said.

'Yeah,' I said.

She clapped and bounced on the balls of her feet. 'Yes! I want to go on the helter-skelter!'

The men running the fair seemed flabbergasted to have a customer, and looked at Molly as though she might be a mirage, until she jumped onto the bumper car track hard enough to make the whole structure shake. She galloped to the helter-skelter and flapped at me to come and pay. When I handed over the fifty-pence coin the helter-skelter ruler shook his head.

'She's too little to go on her own,' he said. 'You'll have to go with her. It's a pound for two. You get three rides.'

Molly put her palms flat on my front and patted me lightly. 'You come, you come,' she said. 'You'll like it. It's really fun.'

I gave the man another coin and he handed over another mat. Molly was already disappearing above me, up the snaking curl of steps. They were built from metal mesh, and looking through them made me feel ill. By the time I got to the top the hessian weave of the mat was scratching my ankle where it bounced. Molly was waiting, hopping and twisting as if she was about to wet herself. I let her show me how to lay the mat with the pouch upturned, where to sit, and where to put my feet.

'Now you have to *wait*,' she said sternly. 'You have to *not* push off yet, because I have to get on too. So don't go yet. OK?'

She manoeuvered herself between my legs and pushed back against my chest. She felt very warm, very living, a thing made all of blood and skin and nerves. It didn't fit with what I had seen on her X-ray: the black around her bones.

'In a second. You have to wriggle your bum forward. So we go down,' she said. She was so excited she had to stop in between clumps of words to breathe. 'It will go very fast. But you don't have to be scared. I know how to do this. I can look after you.'

She put her hands next to mine on the rope handles and shouted, *'Go!'* and then we were spiralling towards the ground, bodies flush, salt on our cheeks, and there wasn't space to think or scream or cry.

We went down the helter-skelter nine times, and then the helter-skelter emperor said we could have another three turns for free, 'seeing as she likes it so much'. I had to hold on to the back of Molly's coat to stop her kissing him. I wanted to hit him. The fairground smelt of onions and petrol, and I felt green with sickness.

Twelve helter-skelter rides were enough even for Molly, and when I gave her my last pound coins she spent them on a Prize Every Time stall and a cloud of pink candy floss. We took her Prize Every Time (a blue stuffed animal of inde-terminate species) and candy floss onto the beach, where we sat with wet sand soaking into our bottoms. The damp underneath and the swish of the sea gave me the feeling that everything was liquid.

'I'm going to take this toy for my show-and-tell,' said Molly. She had candy floss spit in a sticky ring around her mouth.

'Are you?' I said.

'Yeah,' she said. 'I didn't really want something from that other place. I actually wanted something from here. I like here way better.'

'OK,' I said. The toy was hideous, but I liked the thought of it lying on her pillow in her new home. It was another way to stretch out the time before she forgot me.

'Are we going to go home now?' she asked.

'No,' I said.

'Where are we going?'

'We have to go and see Sasha.'

She sighed and wiped her mouth on her sleeve, transferring coat fibres to her lips, and I thought that there was probably no other kid in the world as sticky as Molly at that moment, and no other person I felt as indelibly stuck to.

I stood up and reached out a hand, which she looked at for a long time. 'Come on,' I said. I stretched my fingers wider. 'Let's go.'

The Children's Services receptionist had brown hair and brown eyes and was wearing a brown jumper that went all the way up to her chin. She looked like a mud pie. As we approached she lunged for the phone and turned away from the desk in her swivel chair, and I heard her say, 'Yes, yes, just came through the door.' When she turned back to us her cheeks were flushed and her glasses were steamed up at the bottom. I thought this was probably the most exciting thing that had happened to her since she had found a jumper the exact same colour as her hair and eyes.

'We've come to see Sasha,' I said. I tried to keep the wobble out of my voice. The mud pie squeaked something about taking a seat. In the strip-lit foyer, Molly's level of stickiness seemed intolerable, and I took her to the toilets to wash her hands and face.

'I'm hungry,' she said between wipes.

'You just had candy floss,' I said.

'But that's not food,' she said. 'That's just floss.'

'Well I don't have anything for you to eat,' I said. 'You'll have to wait.'

'That's not very good,' she said.

'I know,' I said. 'I'm sorry.'

'OK. I'll forgive you,' she said.

We had just sat down in reception when Sasha came through the swing door, her lanyard tapping the buttons of her cardigan. Her hair was sticking up at odd angles, half in and half out of a ponytail.

'Julia,' she said. 'Really glad you're here.' She touched my arm and crouched down, so she could speak to me without Molly hearing. Molly helpfully came round to stand in front of me, to make sure she absolutely could hear. Sasha looked as though she quite wanted to hit her.

'Julia, I think it might be best if we take Molly into one of the family rooms. Then we can have a chat. Is that OK? I've asked one of my colleagues to sit in there with her.' I nodded. I didn't want to cry, but I felt the tears there, at the top of my throat. Sasha stood and touched Molly's arm. 'Come on, Molly. Edie's waiting for you. Have you met Edie before? I think she's got a jigsaw she needs your help with. And maybe even a biscuit.'

I trailed behind them, feeling spare. Sasha stopped at a door, knocked, and pushed it open. 'Go on in, Molly,' she said. 'I'm just going to have a little chat with your mum in another room. Edie can come and get us if you need anything.'

'Wait,' I said. They both looked at me, and I sympathised with Sasha: wanting to say things that Molly wouldn't hear, when Molly was very present and very keen to hear. 'Will I get to see her again?' I asked.

'Get to see who?' asked Molly.

'No one,' I said.

Sasha touched my arm. I wondered how much time, in total, she spent touching people's arms each day. 'Of course you will,' she said. 'It's not. We just. Let's leave her here with Edie, OK? And we'll go and talk. Of course you'll see her again.' I nodded once. I could tell I wouldn't be able to keep the crying in for much longer, but I didn't want Molly to see it. 'In you go, Molly,' said Sasha. 'Those look like chocolate biscuits to me. We'll see you in a bit.'

She closed the door and carried on down the corridor, up the stairs, and into a large room with a table and chairs in the middle. I sat in one of the chairs and Sasha sat opposite, then changed her mind and moved to the head of the table, so our knees were almost touching. She muttered something about it being cold, got up, and spent some time crouched in front of a portable radiator. It clicked and creaked and began to breathe warm air onto my legs. The room wasn't that cold. She was stalling.

'So,' she said when she sat down again. 'OK. So. The police know you're here. Your probation officer. She's going to come and speak to you. I think she's bringing a colleague.'

'OK.'

'Obviously we had to tell them when you took Molly. Because of Molly's care order. We have to tell them when something like that happens.'

'OK.'

Neither of us spoke for a while, then Sasha jerked back in her seat and flicked her hands out in front of her.

'*Fucking* hell, Julia,' she said. '*Why?*'

I had never heard a social worker swear before. I hadn't thought they were allowed. The tissue in my hand was damp with snot, and I pulled until it broke apart. 'You're going to take her,' I said.

'What?'

'You're going to take her away. The meeting. You're taking her.'

'You mean the meeting we were meant to have yesterday?'

'Yeah.'

'You thought that meeting was to tell you we wanted to take Molly away from you?'

'Yeah.'

'But why? Why would we be doing that?'

'Her wrist. Obviously.'

I could tell Sasha wanted to swear again, but she put her fingers over her mouth, then moved them up to her hair and began raking through it. I thought she had probably been doing that all day, and that was probably why so much of it had come down from the ponytail.

'OK. I see,' she said. She breathed in deliberately. 'Yes, I wanted to have a quick word with you about the accident. We have to follow these things up. That's the whole point of Molly being under a care order. But I mainly just wanted to check you weren't too upset by it. Because we all understand that it was exactly that. An accident.'

'Oh,' I said.

'To be clear, at no point has there been any talk of taking Molly into care. Not ever. Not the whole time we've known you. If a child is under social services, all hospital visits are reported. It's a standard thing. But if we took every child who broke a bone into care there'd be very few families left intact.'

'Other families aren't me,' I said.

'You mean other families don't have your history?'

'Yeah.'

She leant over the desk. With her head bowed, I could see the dark roots of her hair. I didn't know how old she was. I had always thought of her as a proper grown-up, in a different category to me, but hearing her swear and picturing her bleaching her hair over the bathtub made me think she might not be that old at all. I was a grown-up – I had seen it in Linda's French windows. Sasha and I might be the same age. Perhaps she got fed up with being in charge too.

'Where did you go?' she asked, rolling her head onto one hand to look at me. 'Where have you been?'

'We just went away for a bit. We saw a friend. Molly was safe. She wasn't in any danger.'

'OK,' she said. 'Well. That's good.' She sat back in her chair. 'Do you want to know what I was going to say at the meeting yesterday? Once I'd checked Molly's wrist was on the mend? I was going to say how impressed I am with how you've been doing recently. When I visit you Molly always seems happy, she always seems to have everything she needs. It's obvious how much work you put into being her mum, and I think that work is really paying off. I was going to tell you I've been thinking about winding back my involvement quite soon. Because I think you can manage on your own.'

The crying came. Not in noisy cat howls; in a quiet, leaking flow. I felt like a book being cracked at the spine.

The First Day of Spring

Since Molly had been born I had been telling myself a story about scheming social workers crouched in the shadows, waiting to wrench her out of my useless hands. Sasha made it sound as if there was another story, one with goodies as well as baddies, one where you could turn into a goody even after you had been the baddest baddy. I hadn't known that story existed. I had got lost in the terror of having a mewing bundle of a person relying on me for everything in her tiny life, and having to hold her with the same hands that had ended two other tiny lives. I had forgotten that my freedom was a gift, not a sentence, and had put all my energy into building us a new prison.

When I had asked, Mam had said that she wanted to be young, with a whole new life ahead of her. She hadn't said what that really meant: that she wanted to be me. I was the one who had been given the new life. I didn't know if that was right or wrong. I hadn't been the one to decide what would happen to me, so it wasn't my job to know whether it was right or wrong. But even if it was wrong – a travesty, an abomination, the wrongest decision that could have been made – my wasting the new life wouldn't make it right. It wouldn't make things right for Steven and Ruthie. It wouldn't make things right for Molly and me.

I put my head on my arms. Sasha was close beside me, warming my side like the heater warmed my legs. I remembered my conviction that she had called the journalists to rat me out. It seemed garishly unlikely, and faraway, like a fever dream. I screwed my eyes shut so I didn't have to see her kind face.

'I didn't tell you that to upset you,' she said softly. 'I thought you'd want to know how impressed I've been.'

'Am I going to go to prison?' I asked.

'No,' she said. 'Your probation officer's coming, but she just wants to make sure you're OK. Maybe give you a bit of a lecture about not worrying everyone again. Those things I was going to say at the meeting yesterday – they're still true. You shouldn't have run away, but you know that. It doesn't change everything. Not nearly. As far as I can tell, you're still the same mum you were three days ago.'

'Am I good?'

'Good?'

'Do you think I'm a good mum?'

'Yeah. I do. Definitely.'

I sat up and rocked my head from side to side. My neck was stiff. I could feel it click. 'What happens now?' I asked.

'Well, I expect the people from the police will be here soon. You can wait for them here or in the family room with Molly. While you're with them I'll have a chat with my team manager.'

'About what happens to us?'

'Yes.'

'OK. I want to wait with Molly. Can we go down there now?'

'Of course. Is there anything else you want to ask before we go? Or tell me?'

I gathered my tissues into a sticky ball. I was grindingly tired, but the desperation to be freed of responsibility for two people had lifted. I didn't know how. Perhaps it had been helter-skeltered out of me. I was back to the woman who had woken in the flat the morning before and dozed next to Molly, listening to the tick and creak of the pipes in the walls. I had opened my eyes and looked at the radiator under the window. The curtains had fluttered in the rising air. It had been so warm in the room, and had smelt so gently of carpets and boiling water, and at the back of my throat there had been a bubble of something like pride.

'We have enough lectric for the lights and the telly,' I had thought. 'We have cereal in the cupboard and milk in the fridge. We have clothes that haven't had to be cleaned and pressed and passed on in a carrier bag. I have done badly at so many things in my life. But I have done well at being this little girl's mum.' I had wanted so desperately to stay there forever, tucked behind my daughter, watching the radiators breathe heat around us.

If I could have got the words out, I would have told Sasha that I loved Molly. 'I love her because she grew inside me, because she kept me company and saved my life, and because when she came out she liked me straight away,' I would have said. 'She stopped me having to be Chrissie or Lucy or Julia, made me Mum instead. She's my friend and my girl and my funny, stubborn, constant companion. I love her down to the dark space around her bones, and I want to keep her, to have her with me, to smell her on my clothes. I want to tie tinsel in her hair at Christmas and put a new height mark on the door on her sixth birthday and slip into bed beside her before I go to sleep tonight. I want to carry on being her world.'

I couldn't say it. It would have left me too bare.

'Not really,' I said. 'I suppose I just. I just want to carry on being her mum, you know.'

'I do know,' said Sasha. 'I do.'

MOLLY

When Mum had finished talking to the police she took me into the garden. Edie came out with us but she just sat on the bench by the door, so it was like me and Mum were by ourselves. I asked Mum what the police had wanted to speak to her about and she said they just wanted to make sure we were both OK. I didn't believe her, but I didn't say that. Her face was pink, a bit like she had been crying, but she never cried, so I thought perhaps something else was wrong, like maybe she'd got stung by some bees.

The climbing frame in the garden was really for babies but I still went on it. I went down the slide three times and Mum pushed me on the swing.

'This is a bit babyish, isn't it?' Mum said when I had been on the slide and swing and realised there was actually nothing else to do.

'A tiny bit,' I said. 'Can we go to the big playground tomorrow?'

'Mmm,' she said. 'Mmm' was what she said when she wanted me to stop talking about something.

There were daisies growing in the grass around the climbing frame, like the daisies at the church Mum had said wasn't our church. She knelt on the ground and started picking them, so I did too. She was good at threading them together in a long chain. I couldn't do it without splitting the stalk all the way up and spoiling it, so she let me be in charge of picking and I let her be in charge of chaining. We were a good team. She made me a necklace and a crown and two bracelets. I wanted her to have something too, at least a crown or a necklace, but she said she didn't want anything.

My tooth still felt funny. It had been feeling funny for ages, weeks and weeks. I had stopped telling Mum because whenever I talked about it she said, 'Mmm'. I pushed it back and forth with the tip of my tongue, and suddenly it wasn't in my gum any more, just in my mouth. I spat it onto my palm.

'What's that?' Mum asked.

'My tooth,' I said.

'What happened?' she asked.

'Just came out,' I said.

She took my chin and looked at the gap where the tooth used to be, in the front at the bottom. I couldn't see the space but I could feel it. Cold and whistly. Mum took a tissue out of her pocket and pressed it inside my mouth, and when she took it away there was a little red splat of blood.

'Does it hurt?' she asked.

'No,' I said, because it really actually didn't. 'It just came out. Look.'

I put it on her hand. It was white and shaped like a little flipper.

'Why did it come out?' I asked.

'Just time, I think,' she said. 'Just ready.'

'Are they all going to come out?' I asked.

'Yeah. In the end.'

'So I'll have none?'

'You'll get new ones. Bigger ones.'

'When?'

'In a while. Let me see.' She held my chin again and looked at my tooth gap. 'The new one's already coming in there. I can see it. There's a little white bit at the bottom.'

'Can I see?'

'Next time you're in the bathroom you can look in the mirror.'

'Can we go to the bathroom here?'

'Not now.'

I really wanted to see, but I didn't want to make Mum upset. She was looking at my tooth very carefully, turning it over and pressing the tip against her fingers.

'Can I have it?' I asked.

'Yeah. Sorry,' she said. She put it back in my hand, wrapped my fingers around it, and wrapped her hand around my fist. 'It's a good tooth,' she said. 'Well done.'

It was cold outside and Mum saw goose bumps making pimples on my arms, so she gave me her cardigan. The sleeves drooped way down over my hands but we rolled them up. I thought Edie might make us go inside but she had her head tipped back towards the sky and her eyes closed, so actually I didn't think she was going to make us do anything, because actually she was asleep.

'When are we going to go home?' I asked Mum.

'I'm not sure,' she said.

'What am I having for tea?' I asked.

'I'm not sure,' she said. She was sounding a bit cryish, so I didn't ask any more questions. I squeezed my fist until the tip of the tooth nibbled into me.

'Molly?' Mum said.

'Yeah,' I said.

'You know when you're in bed?' she said.

'Yeah,' I said.

'You know, I'm still thinking about you. When you're asleep and I'm awake. If you had a dad I'd talk to him about you. There's just me, but I still think about you. About how to make things good for you.'

'OK,' I said. I thought it was a funny thing to say.

'It won't change,' she said.

'What won't?'

'Me thinking about you.'

'Won't change when?'

'Just won't change. Not ever. No matter what happens.'

'Is something going to happen?'

'Whatever happens. You're my Molly. You always will be.'

I did like Mum saying those things, but they weren't the sorts of things she normally said, so I didn't know what I should say back. She looked like she really wanted me to say something back. In the end I just said, 'You're my mum.'

She pulled me back between her legs and wrapped her arms around my middle. I stretched up and put my arms around her neck, and it hurt because arms aren't meant to bend that way, but I didn't mind. She pressed her chin into my shoulder. She smelt of washing and rain. We stayed like that for a long time. I had to take my arms down after a while because they got too sore, but I put them over Mum's arms instead, so it was like we were both hugging me. She kept her chin on my shoulder and whispered some things very quietly. I couldn't hear them properly, because her head was pressed against one of my ears, and that meant I got to decide for myself what she was saying. I decided she mainly said, 'I love you, Molly.'

When I next looked at the building there was a face in the window above the bench.

'Mum,' I said. 'Sasha.'

Mum looked up. Her body went hard against my back. Sasha came out of the building and touched Edie's shoulder to wake her up. Edie went inside and Sasha came towards us with her jumper sleeves over her hands and her arms crossed over her chest.

'Bit chilly, isn't it?' she said.

'I gave her my jumper,' said Mum. I yawned. Sasha crouched down and patted my leg.

'Been a long day for you, hasn't it?' she said. 'Sorry we've kept you all this time. We're done now.'

I heard a gritty sound above my head. Mum was grinding her teeth together.

'Are you free to pop in again tomorrow?' Sasha asked her. 'When Molly's at school?'

'Why?' she asked.

'A few things to chat about. We've thought of a couple of extra ways to support you. It would be better to talk it through when we're all a bit fresher. Do you think Mr Gupta will be able to spare you for an hour?'

'Are you going to—'

She didn't finish. 'Going to what?' I asked.

'Nothing,' she said.

'No,' said Sasha. 'We're not. Come on, Molly. Time for Mum to take you home, eh?'

I still wanted to know what Mum had been going to say after 'Are you going to', but I was too tired to try to find out. Me and Sasha stood up but Mum stayed sitting on the ground. She didn't move her body at all, so it was still in the same shape it had been in when I had been sitting between her legs, and she looked empty without me there. I held out my hand in case she needed help getting up. She didn't take it. She stared at Sasha.

'We're going back?' she said. 'Both of us?'

'Yes,' said Sasha.

'Really?' she said.

'Yes,' said Sasha.

Mum stood up slowly, without using my hand. She wobbled like she might be going to fall back down and Sasha took hold of both her elbows. They talked to each other with their eyes for a bit, then Sasha went inside. I could just see her, standing in the doorway that went to reception, waiting for us. Mum took my hand and squeezed it tight.

'Come on, Molly,' she said. 'Let's go home.'

ACKNOWLEDGEMENTS

I have always said that my favourite thing about writing books is getting to work with so many talented, interesting people. It is a pleasure and a privilege to have had that experience again.

I would be lost (emotionally, practically, professionally) without my wonderful agent, Hattie Grünewald. Thank you for fielding breakdowns/boy trouble/horrific early drafts with tact and skill; for keeping me sane during the most exciting period of my writing life; for being the better half of the Dream Team. Thank you also to the rest of the team at the Blair Partnership: Georgie Mellor, Mirette El Rafie, Jessica Maslen and Luke Barnard for overseeing foreign rights sales, Ompreet Cheema for keeping everything running like clockwork, and Rory Scarfe for being on hand to offer wisdom and expertise. In the US, thank you Catherine Drayton for embracing me and my work with such enthusiasm, and orchestrating a deal in record time.

In the process of licking this book into shape, I have had the privilege of working with three inspiring editors: Sarah

McGrath, Jocasta Hamilton and Selina Walker. I have spent weeks agonising over how to thank you adequately for all you have done for me – both as a writer and as a young woman. I think it comes down to this: thank you for taking care of me and Chrissie.

Thank you also to the other editors who read and critiqued *The First Day of Spring* along the way: Anna Argenio, Delia Taylor and Alison Fairbrother. I am so grateful that you gave up your time to offer such valuable insights.

Publishing a book takes a village, and I have been lucky to work with a population of wonderful women. Thank you to Rebecca Ikin, Claire Simmonds and Najma Finlay at Hutchinson; Melissa Solis, Caitlin Noonan, Denise Boyd, Amanda Dewey and Anna Jardine at Riverhead.

As well as those who have helped turn this story from something in my head to something I can hold in my hands, there is a whole other contingent of people who scaffold me behind the scenes.

Thank you Arminda, Charlotte, Ellie and the rest of the team at Vincent Square, for tolerating my temperamental moods, relentless texting and compulsion to sing at work.

Thank you Allie, Becci, Carys, Kate, Nimarta, Miranda and Ros, my loyal and generous team of friends, for sharing my joy when things have gone well and helping me pick myself up and dust myself off when they have gone wrong.

Thank you Sarah, for endless WhatsApp counselling/ wise opinions/poppet pictures.

Thank you Mum, Dad, Mattie, Granny, Grandpa and the rest of my family, for helping me, holding me and keeping my feet on the ground through this giddying experience.

Thank you Phil, for making my life better and brighter than I ever imagined it would be; for loving me when I have been objectively unlovable; for being my home.